THE BONDS OF STONE

THE SEVEN ISLES
BOOK FOUR

A.R. KNIGHT

CHAPTER I
CITY LIVING

The Ringed City claimed its name as a gentle snowfall graced the evening. Lit lanterns gave shape to sloping rooftops, to pleasant shadows in quiet alleys. The populace, and there were so many, laughed and sang, bartered and bought their way to the day's end. Wax, after two weeks in the city, no longer jerked his head around at the myriad noises, no longer crinkled his nose at the smells as sewage raced down to the sea. He wore thick Rana linens, buttressed by Whent furs, a new Foti-forged blade on his hip, thicker than a Kance rapier and less likely to get Wax into trouble. Tufted boots and a wool cap added themselves to his new wardrobe, provided by Eujo's largesse.

Kance's Second Queen walked nearby, the two making their way back to her vessel for what its captain, Deux, declared was a special dinner. A recent warm spell, despite it being early winter, had opened a path through the sea ice, or so the rumor said, and they had a chance, now, to make it north to Whent. A celebration tonight, and soon an embarking to that rocky isle.

Neither Eujo nor Wax seemed to find a smile in their slow wandering. Wax couldn't guess at Eujo's reasons for seeming reluctant, but he knew his own lay in the quest itself, in taking up a Renewal's mantle yet again and throwing his family, himself into harm's way. They'd barely survived the last fiend assault, not to mention the traitorous Kance guards, and the nightmares from both had plagued Wax ever since.

How many more would he earn before someone took the new seat on the Wound's throne?

The whispers in his mind flickered at the thought. Three skars, from Vis, Foti, and Rana set their small gemstones into Wax's necklace, one he kept tucked beneath the layers. For all the honors bestowed among the Renewals, he'd learned the isles were often a desperate place, with skars just one more valuable to be stolen or traded. Best to keep them hidden, best to keep his eyes from meeting others.

Such a far cry from Cassignol's casino on Foti's southern coast, when Wax had been feted, paraded about like a celebrity. Now, searching looks seemed to pace his steps, and every sound carried an invisible menace.

"It'll be good to leave," Eujo said, breaking the silence. "A city like this infects you if you stay too long."

"Most things do." Wax fought free of his dour suspicions. Those feelings could take hold when he was alone in his cabin, in the dark. Now, here, he had a standard to uphold. "Think I'll be missing the ale though. Beats our sweet wine any day."

"Really? I love a good mango twist."

Wax's heart twinged a bit at that. Sawi's favorite drink too. Fermented mango juice, spiced with some lemon and a bit of sugar. Like all the best Vis wines, they'd store them deep under the water in airtight barrels, the only place the wine could get cool, get stable enough to keep its flavor. Then, at the right time, the rope and buoy marked with the proper date would get pulled back to the surface, tapped or traded.

"Best find some to take with us then," Wax said as they turned down a narrow, sloping road. The last bit of Noctia's living districts before they hit the port proper. "Can't imagine Whent will have anything like it."

"Oh, they're closer than you think." The Queen adopted a getup much like Wax's own, hiding her royalty beneath standard Noctia garb, dull browns, grays, and furs every-where. "A little ice wine is a delight."

"You know all the best drinks from the isles, then?"

"Do you know what a Queen does, Wax?"

"You're giving me a good idea."

For all the time they'd spent together while Deux had the *Storm's Edge* repaired, Wax and Eujo had avoided getting much into their pasts, their real lives. As if, after the Rana adventures and their near deaths, both needed to adopt a fresh persona. Instead, they'd bandied about the Ringed City trying restaurants, exploring various shops, and seeing how far into the Najahn fortresses they could get before being noticed.

That last had been Torny's idea, a contest from the bandit to, Wax suspected, keep her from simply drinking all the hours away. The four of them—Quik, Wax's brother and a distant presence these days—had set targets, like this Tenet's tower or that school's library, and the first to manage a successful infiltration won, well, more ale.

So it hadn't done much to reduce the drinking, but when you were stuck in port during winter's frosted chill, entertainment was hard to find. Tonight, Wax figured, would be little different.

But at least it would mark an end.

Deux put forth a generous table, overlaid with Kance dishes Wax still hadn't grown used to. The isle, with its avian population and reliance on massive berry groves, crawling ivies, and stiff tubers, had a taste far less sweet than the sugar-filled fruit Wax loved. Even so, tonight, Wax found it hard to keep his mouth from watering as Deux set a personal quiche—cooked with fresh eggs—at every plate. Inlaid with red pepper flakes and asparagus, sprinkling with green onion and steaming, the offering suggested no small award had gone to Noctia's traders that day.

Then again, this was the first meal in more than a week that the whole group had been together. Bliss and Torny, paired off as they often were, held the left side. Their fingers flashed beneath the table at one another, Wax only catching some of the conversation but needing no more to guess at the jokes flying back and forth. Plans, too, for later parties at one of Noctia's endless revels.

Parties Wax would've crashed if it'd been a month or two ago. The jubilation felt wrong now, at odds with what they'd been through, with what was being visited on the isles by the fiends. When Wax had confronted Bliss with the same, she'd delivered a defiant rebuke, signing that if they were going to die, then better have their fun now.

After that, she'd stopped asking Wax to come along.

To Wax's right sat Quik, more distant than ever, but at least no longer reeking with disappointment. He'd been even more a ghost, disappearing for days at a time. Deux muttered that it'd taken multiple messengers to even find Quik and deliver the invitation. As to what his brother had been doing, that marked Wax's post-dinner agenda. Information gathering on his wayward Guardian.

Eujo, at least, filled Wax's schedule with less abrasive opportunity. She used her royal rank and their mutual Renewal status to score dinner and lunch with well-to-do Najahn and city dwellers, all loving the chance to boost their reputations with the Renewals' presence while salving their consciences by helping the pair to a meal, to a gift of some useless trinket, or a promise of future aid should either one become the Aegis.

Wax held back a grin as the meals, the shows, the invitations blurred by. At first he'd been nervous, until Wax realized everyone on Noctia expected him to know nothing of civilized society. They expected a bumbling Vis, lost and confused away from the jungle. Once set, Wax found a devious distraction in playing into and then destroying the idea, leaving the hosts, the other guests in turns offended or delighted.

The latter were the ones that gave the next invite, usually asking Wax to do the same, to prove Noctia's assumptions false. That those people often came from other isles surprised Eujo and Wax not at all.

The Kance Queen, meanwhile, kept her regal mouth shut, playing the diplomat. She praised the wind isle, pushed merchants and artisans to send their business Kance's way, and acted in every way like the ambassador Wax supposed she was.

Until, late at night, they would return to this ship and collapse in their respective cabins, mocking their oblivious hosts the entire way.

"So you're ready, then?" Quik asked, shaking Wax from his quiche and the reverie it brought along. "Back to the Renewal?"

The question came without hooks, honesty his brother's foremost currency.

"She is," Wax said, nodding at Eujo, who frowned. "And she needs Guardians."

"Not what I asked."

The whole table looked at him now. Torny at least spelled the stare with a long visit to her wine glass, the red a delicious Kance blend. Bliss matched Eujo's frown. Deux, at least, offered a supportive nod.

Maybe the captain wouldn't mind holding fast, an excuse to avoid the wintry seas.

"We don't have much choice, do we?" Wax asked Quik. "If the other Renewals fail, then we'd be damning the world by giving up."

News on that score had been hard to determine, but what rumors persisted suggested no Renewal was having an easy time of it. While no isle admitted their Renewal had died, there was no clear leader either. Nobody knocking on Noctia's door claiming a seat on the throne.

"Still not an answer."

Always depend on a brother to press for the truth.

"I signed up for this, didn't I? I'm ready. Are you?"

Quik glanced down at his quiche, as if debating whether he could sneak one more bite in before answering. A quick sigh said otherwise.

"I'm not." Quik nodded after he said it, whatever doubt may have been there fleeing his soul. "I'm staying here. At least for a while."

Now the table truly was silent. Wax, at least, not the focus this time. Bliss recovered first, hands flashing an angry, obvious question.

"Because I need to get better," Quik replied. "The last two isles have been disasters. We've only barely survived, and we all have scars for it. The Renewal isn't supposed to be easy, but we won't live if this keeps up."

'Except now we have a ship,' Bliss countered. 'We can sail right to where the skars are. Easy.'

"So easy," Torny muttered. "Deux, you have another bottle?"

"On it." The captain stood, seeming grateful for the chance to get away.

"Until a fiend attacks again, or someone else lays another trap and we're left alone to lose," Quik said. "We're not ready."

"You heard Wax," Eujo said. "He is. My ship is. We leave in two days. I would like you to come with us."

Quik shook his head. "I've already made another commitment. I'm joining the Najahn."

If quiet wrapped the table before, it never had a chance now. Bliss slapped the table. Torny cursed. Wax and Eujo both asked *why* and *what* and then *how*. Quik had answers to them all, gave them patiently, and took more wine when it came, and still more after that until the voices were exhausted and even Bliss's fingers lay still.

"You gave an oath," Wax said later, on the vessel's bow. Sichi, the pink moon, sparkled above the horizon and made a loving look at the Ringed city. "You're breaking it."

Quik made no move to deny Wax's words. "I'm doing what I think is right, Wax. The only thing that might let us live."

"Sure, until you remember those fiends you just talked about. When one attacks, we won't have you helping us out."

"Then stay here. Let me get stronger. We can get more resources, more Guardians. March with, if not an army, then something close to it." A fire Wax hadn't seen in too long found Quik as his brother spoke. "I'm not just joining the Najahn, I'm going to try and persuade them to join us too. It's not enough to watch the Renewal from the sidelines anymore. They have to help."

"One voice, one Vis voice, isn't going to get their attention."

Quik sniffed. "It's not just any Vis voice. It's me, brother."

"Even you, Quik." Wax, though, saw nothing save determination. He'd seen the same look on Pan's face before the Great Sana. A choice had been made, and Wax wouldn't be changing it. "Then promise me something?"

"What?"

"If I need you, if, somehow, you hear I need your help," Wax said, not quite believing the request as he was making it, but knowing it was necessary all the while, "that you'll come."

"You don't think I would?"

Wax put his hand on his brothers, gripped it hard. "You asked if I was ready in there. Truth is, Quik, the only way I'll be ready is with all of you standing beside me."

"I am. We are. I'll just be away a while, is all. But when you see those purple cloaks, that black armor coming to escort you home, you'll thank me."

If, Wax didn't say, they managed to live that long.

CHAPTER 2

FIRST DAY

A thin satchel, his linens, and his gauntlets. The total accounting of Quik's possessions, all strapped to his person as he climbed Noctia's cobblestones in the early morning frost. Diligent workers kept the streets pebbled over to keep slipping to a minimum, effort Quik's Kance boots, taken from a drowned deckhand who wouldn't need them anymore, appreciated. The footwear felt like a second skin, but lacked Foti weight. Quik felt the same about most things Kance: fancy, sure, but too light and ephemeral to be worth more than decoration.

Except the ships. The ships were as fast, as great as rumored.

The Najahn hit the same mark as Quik reached their portion of the Ringed City. Occupying an entire cliffside, but barring entry to a large gateway halfway up Noctia's crater wall, the Najahn controlled what some called a city within a city. Like the outposts they ran on every isle, safeguarding every skar for the Renewals, the Najahn operated outside the usual bounds.

And not a soul dared challenge them.

The why came as Quik approached the first gate. Standing outside, fresh into their shift, were Najahn guards in their full regalia. Purple tabards ran their chests and back, draping black armor that ran all curves, as if the soldiers were living blades. In one gauntleted hand, the four guards outside the gate each held a voulge. The spears stood almost as tall as the guards themselves, their curling points adding utility to lethality, able to hook or deflect as needed. On their backs, in various colors, rested chakrams, razor metal discs light enough to throw and mean enough to guarantee you only needed one.

Next to the display, Quik felt his own gauntlets bobbing at his waist. On Vis, with their homespun spears, blowguns, and bows, the gauntlets and their hardened wood claws seemed more than strong enough. They could carve a hanoko's hide, sure, but against armor like the Najahn wore, Quik wondered if a single blow wouldn't turn his prized weapons to splinters.

That, though, was why Quik was here. He needed better gear, better training, better everything to deserve his place with Wax. Quik just had to hope his brother would last till Quik could find him again, with all the Najahn and their armory at his back.

Getting through the gate involved showing a letter and the seal inside, one granting Quik entry as a new recruit. The simple paper had been handed to him several days ago not far from these very walls, where the Najahn maintained a civilian office and, with it, a chance for society's lost souls to find a new path. At least, that's what the woman outside had said to the passing people, declaring in her purple-and-black that here was an opportunity to turn fear into ferocity, loss into vengeance, and horror into hope.

The words worked on more than a few.

Quik counted eleven in the room when he entered, all standing in the sparse stone chamber. A single Najahn banner with the Circle's emblem, a gilded black-and-gold chakram in its center, hung on the back wall. The other recruits matched Quik in their shifting nerves, either looking at nothing or everyone, bouncing from foot to foot, or shivering in the cold. Quik, though, lost those affects as he found a spot in the group and took total stock of it, evaluating his competition as any hunter would and finding one, in particular, that didn't belong.

"Sawi?" Quik asked, the name blurting out at the sight, one taking a second to recognize her amid the violet robe Sawi already wore. "What . . . ?"

Sawi didn't seem to share his surprise, offering the same sly smile she shined when she spied some hidden fruit or a swinging path through the jungle. The other recruits, like Quik, had their eyes and ears open, looking around the place like, well, new recruits. Sawi didn't have the same air, scratching a little at her wrist and resting with her back against the wall opposite the door. As if she knew what to expect, as if she'd not been magically transported from Kitaye that very morning.

Nevertheless, Kitaye held that elders should be respected, and Quik had a few good years on Sawi. The old order brushed off the day's confusion and let Quik stomp right past the other recruits, none of whom were Vis, right up to Sawi's side.

"You've a story to tell," Quik said, adopting his older brother tone, the one that used to get answers fast from a rabble eager to avoid punishment or show off their tricks. "So out with it. What are you doing here, wearing that?"

"Nice to see you too, Quik," Sawi replied, letting the grin fade.

She read him. A once over Quik wouldn't have noticed save for the same thing happening every time he, Wax, and Bliss walked into anywhere. The people inside, some savvier than others, would slow their motions and evaluate the trio, decide whether they were risks or not, make a call on where they'd come from and what they wanted.

A skill Quik had used on Vis beasts many a time, that he still lacked when it came to people.

"I'm surprised," Quik said. "That's all."

"So am I. Aren't you supposed to be with Wax?"

"Long story."

The smile sprang back, "Then maybe we'll have to meet up some time and share."

Quik squinted at her. "What's with you?"

Sawi nodded back towards the room, to the other recruits now watching the pair. "When we're not performing for an audience, Quik?"

The Vis hunter's glare at the fresh faces served to turn a good many of them away, but before he could get back to Sawi, their instructor, greeter, commander—Quik wasn't sure what term to use—entered the room. Like the guards outside the gate, the man had on his full uniform, clanking along the hard stone to stand before the purple banner. He rested his voulge on the floor, leaning its haft against his shoulder while he removed a scroll case attached to his waist.

The man began by naming everyone in the room, confirming their presence. When the roll call concluded, two names were left unanswered. The man repeated them louder, and when nobody decided to claim a second title for themselves, the man declared them delinquent. As he did, outside in the hall, loud steps echoed as someone acted on the words.

"They'll soon find themselves brought in to explain their absence," their leader said, showing no pleasure at the situation. "With good reason, they will begin next week. With bad, they'll find themselves sweeping the sewers for a month." He matched eyes with everyone in turn, not shrinking or speeding through any. "Understand this. The Circle, the Najahn, are fair. Just. But we are not lax. We carry the isles, and that is a duty we cannot forsake."

So far, so typical. Quik could admire the Najahn's organization, their lethality without obeying their propaganda. He'd made his oath to Wax, and he'd keep it, marching in at the head of a Najahn host to escort him, and that Kance Queen if need be, all the way to the Wound.

" . . . and you will find yourselves paired through the rotations," the man continued, shaking Quik from his daydream. "A full year may seem like a long time to learn how the Najahn work, how *you* will work, but it is a small drop in the rest of your life serving the Circle. Every Tenet you assist will teach you, and when your year is up, the area most suited to your talents will be your home. Best find one you enjoy, as there are no sadder Najahn than those without a true love."

A true love? Quik glanced at Sawi, hoping to see she thought the same about this drivel as he did. Indeed, she didn't appear to be listening too closely, though not because of mockery, but instead a distinct concentration. Pondering something, her eyes narrowed to match her tight lips.

What was she doing here?

The Najahn speech then turned to matters ordinary, like food and facilities. Libraries open to new recruits, armories to visit for gear fittings, training grounds for exercises. This seemed to capture the others more acutely than the rules for their new lives, something Quik would've found surprising until he reassessed their outfits.

Young, yes, but not wealthy. Slops, rags, and moldy clothes seemed the dominant fashion. Girl and boy alike bore dirt and soot, hands roughed up with days spent earning a hard keep. Vis had its poor and their betters, yes, but the distance between them seemed so much slimmer than what Noctia propagated.

Up till right then, Quik had been faintly disgusted with the whole practice, the beggars and desperate rushing to the streets to find what they could before some Najahn guard hustled them away. Now, though, he understood: the Najahn had jobs that needed doing, that would only be done by those too lost to refuse them.

He fought off the shudder. Vis wasn't all the isles. Things were different here.

"The Oath of Allegiance is sacred. Its words will mark your soul, and bind you forever to our calling," the Najahn man said, his tone changing to the same steel he'd used when calling out the delinquents. "Repeat after me."

Quik found his voice rising with that of the other recruits, their words filling the chamber as they matched the man's own, "I pledge fealty to the Circle, the Najahn, and the Seven Isles. I will face our enemies, protect our people, and put all my will to serving their needs, until Noctia takes me into her warm embrace."

As the last words faded, the Najahn commander gave them all a slow nod before announcing the ceremony's close. They were all to report to their barracks, find their partners, and learn their first rotation.

"I'll see you around, Quik," Sawi said, breezing by him towards the room's exit.

"Wait," Quik tried, but Sawi didn't hesitate a moment,

slipping by recruits picking up their gear and making for the same door. "Sawi, just stop."

She did not, vanishing so fast as to be long gone by the time Quik made it into the hallway, leaving the Vis hunter to be pushed by his peers into his new life.

CHAPTER 3
EXILE'S RETURN

Torny timed it right, dashed out her tongue and snagged the snowflake as it drifted past, the silky chill tweaking the rose warmth offered by her Noctia leathers, overlaid with belts and pouches. Wrist braces offered compartments aplenty, as did similar loops around her thighs. Did the dress up take time? Absolutely.

Did it make her feel like her most perfect self?

'Is that it, then?' Bliss's fingers morphed off to Torny's right as they walked Noctia's port in the late afternoon. 'Finally have all you need?'

The snow drizzled down amongst the ships, bursting and bustling with the warmer spell to get one more journey in before winter put the northern isles in a deep freeze. Porters angled around the two young women, some throwing consternation their way, looks Torny ignored, just as she always had.

"A good Guardian takes the goods," Torny replied. "You might be fine with that stick, but I need accessories."

Bliss, her Foti-bolstered staff lost back on Rana, had found a metal pole cut to her size. She'd been scratching lines into it over their days here, etching Vis and Kitaye sigils and adding a couple razor lines to the end caps. The whole thing was adorable: a personalized smashing stick. Torny didn't have the heart to tell Bliss any bum with a crossbow could still put the girl down without a sweat.

But then, so long as Torny was around, Bliss wouldn't have to worry about that sort of thing.

'And now you have them all?' Bliss signed back.

"Almost," Torny replied. True, she'd collected the knives, found a fresh grapple, replenished a stock of various minor poisons and the darts to deliver them. All well and good, ready to brave the Whent wilds. Save one thing. "There's something I've been saving."

'Saving? Like, a treasure?'

"Sure, why not. Let's call it treasure."

Torny glanced towards the ocean as she replied. Bliss had a way of reading her face, and the fewer questions tossed Torny's way now, the better. Or else she might reconsider.

"It's a bit of a walk," Torny said. "You up for it?"

'You know where I'm from, right?'

Jungle hikes day in and day out. Bliss would have that endurance. Torny coughed into her glove to hide her own annoyance. Not at Bliss's reply, no, but at herself for asking the obvious question. Be better. Don't make mistakes.

Or she might wind up on Foti again, slumming it with lava rocks to earn her dinner.

Bliss kept right on up with Torny as they left the Ringed City's port district behind. The Najahn quarter loomed behind them, a dominating force so far as afternoon shadows were concerned. All those inscrutable towers leering from the cliffs.

If Bliss knew how many times Torny had taken a closer look inside those places . . .

'Where are we now?' Bliss's hand flashed to Torny's right as the pair walked up the rougher street side, smoother cobblestones in the center offering breezy passage to rumbling wagons, porters, and the hissing steam engines puttering them along.

Climbing in the Ringed City meant changing the world around you, a slow morphing from the port district's greasy business to, here, a residential strip's stacked houses and sedate shops. Eateries lacked the coarse curses from dirty sailors, instead targeting families and locals with their specials. An inn or two broke up the parade, packed now with long-term stays as travelers found their winter residences.

Yet Torny didn't linger on any, only pointing things out as Bliss asked. These weren't where her memories lied, and Noctia changed itself over—even now, in the cold, construction and destruction continued—too fast to give nostalgia a hold.

No, Torny only came awake again as their walk curled around Noctia's southwestern end. The Ringed City occupied that part of the smallest isle, enough to allow a dedicated walker to get free from the Najahn spires with an hour's worth of footsteps.

'Okay, this is cool,' Bliss signed, stopping with Torny at Noctia's Knee.

The landmark, denoted by a forlorn stone with the name carved into it, jutted forth towards the sea. A mossy gray wall, less than Torny's height and perfect for sitting, wrapped the cliff, springing up where the last house ended and going till the buildings began again. The stone centered in the space, and Torny walked past it to the absolute point, waiting a moment for several kids to catch her meaning and leave.

"Take a seat," Torny said to Bliss, motioning the Vis to join the bandit on the wall.

Back to the North, from here, the Ringed City fell away along the rocky cliffs, a sprawl that, with the crater's monstrous wall to the east, looked like a view cut in half. Ships crowded in, many at a final anchor in the port's modestly protected surroundings. Pretty, but Torny's heart lay the other way, and she found a smile when Bliss didn't even bother looking back towards the Najahn side.

"Noctia's not only the Najahn," Torny said. "There's beautiful things here too."

The houses ran some ways further along the southern shore, spreading in irregular tranches through easier rock both up and down the cliffs. The density, though, wasn't the same, paving the way for broader cliff side fields. Trees and bushes, skeletal now with winter's onset but entrancing in their own way, crawled along the rock. Jutting terraces, built so many years ago, held plants and animals less able to scale the steep sides, but so essential to the Ringed City's survival. Like scalloped handholds, the outcroppings ran along Noctia's southern edge all the way to the isle's far side beyond the horizon.

"Everything here is real," Torny said. "The real people of Noctia. Not merchants, not sailors, not the Najahn. But us. Me."

'Your family?'

"Sure, they're here somewhere."

Not that Bliss would be meeting them, but that wasn't something Torny needed to discuss now. In fact, reading the sun, there wouldn't be much more for them to discuss tonight.

"Look," Torny said, "I know it's a long walk, but I wanted you to see this before we left. Most people don't like Noctia. They think it's this rocky, ugly place full of dangerous people, but it's like anywhere else, mostly: just families trying to survive."

'You've never talked this way before.'

"Home brings out a weird side of me." Torny put up a frown, glanced in the falling sun's direction. "Speaking of, think I might stop by there."

'Home?'

"Yep. Not sure when we'll be this way again. Figure I ought to say hi. Let them know I'm still alive."

Bliss nodded, waited a second, then nodded again. 'You don't want me to go with you.'

"It's going to be awkward, and long. Maybe next time."

As deliveries went, Torny figured the line went okay. No tremor in the voice, no slip in her eyes. She kept her hands on the stone wall, pressing them against the dirty gray hard enough to ensure no slipping.

'Okay,' Bliss signed. 'Back at the ship, then?'

"I'll be there before Sichi's too high in the sky."

'You better be.'

Bliss, as she so often did, broke the conversation there, slipping off the wall, catching herself lightly on her feet and walking off with a flipping wave. Torny waved back, then tilted her head. Bliss wasn't turning left, heading back home. Instead, she went right, joining the people heading towards the outcroppings, the houses, a life Bliss had no business digging into.

Torny took a lower road. She'd tailed Bliss for a few minutes, keeping careful enough to drag behind towns-people and stay out of sight. The Vis did exactly what she ought to be doing, wandering along and scoping the buildings, the earthworks, the sheep and chickens on offer. Once Torny established Bliss didn't have some ulterior motive, the thief slipped downward at the next break. The thin switchbacks descended alongside cavern crannies, not their official name but what everyone called the narrow homes build into the rock. Supported with heavy beams and not much larger than a small boat, the crannies served as housing for everyone that couldn't afford something better.

And that everyone included more than a few of Torny's former friends.

Thankfully, another not-so-written law of owning a cavern cranny was keeping your door shut. Most opened outward, right into the walkway, so Torny avoided any uncomfortable chance encounters as she wound back and forth several times, always getting closer and closer to the in-and-out waves.

Noctia's southern side bore the goddess's angry whims, the shallows crusted over with jutting rocks and swirling pools. Black sand beaches offered options to those with little else to entertain them, and they were empty now with winter's cold. A summer day would've brought laughing children, tired parents, and couples looking for a little romance. No ships would dock here, no business save some brave food stands, broke in on the fun.

Torny fought away any memory, instead focusing behind the beaches, to caverns and cutaways too old and unstable for any sustained business, for any home. Any, that is, save the one she was going to find. Her boots crunched on the stiff grains as she walked past a few sightseers braving the surf, drawing little and less attention. Like on Foti, everyone here knew to keep to their own affairs.

Catching the wrong eye could ruin so many good things.

The third tidal cave, a sawtooth number whose rock overhangs crusted over with salt, still smelled true to Torny, a faint whiff of pipe smoke and boiled clam brine drifting out. The bandit gave one last look around, found nobody on her tail, and slipped inside. A few steps warmed the air with a fire's comfort, those flickering flames soon drawing up on the dark, pitted walls. Noctia's caves carried with them a bleak history, one written not in the purity of Foti's black lava rock or in the packed sediment of Vis's living caves—something Torny had only heard about. Instead, Noctia offered a lifeless swill, as if someone had taken a stale gruel, thrown in some old black ash, and swirled it together before baking it into bricks. Smooth, dull, and altogether worthless, was Noctia rock.

Less so were the people clustered around the fire and the whole cave, a deceptively large room that looked like a spoon expanding out from Torny's tight entry. The deeper the cavern went, the more the ceiling rose, and Torny could see all the way to the top thanks to the globes strung about the place. The lights gave sight to hammocks and beds carved into the walls, along with lockboxes aplenty. Racks on the floor held both weapons and tools of a certain trade, one practiced by all the faces now realizing who'd arrived.

"You just letting people walk in?" Torny asked by way of introduction, directing her words at the older man crouching near the bonfire, pestering it, as he always seemed to be, with a metal poker. "A new recruitment method?"

"Hardly need to look for new thieves these days," the man replied, matching Torny's look with a single-toothed one of his own. "Especially when missing ones return."

Yarvick delivered a lot with his stare, not least the sledgehammer blow of his own visage, so gnarled by vices unknown that he resembled a fleshy tangle of tree roots all coming in together. One good eye shown out from the mix, with a second replaced by an opal, one actually a Noctia skar for those savvy enough to see, or deep enough in the Nimble Fingers to know. His old hair had long since shriveled away save for a sole thick, black strand he kept tied and coiled about his neck, a dry and shifty snake. The rest of him lay buried beneath a cloak so patchwork any shot at identifying its original color or fabric had long since past.

"What brings you back here, Torny?" Yarvick continued. "Come to offer some payment for your debts, or should I have let my boys skewer you outside?"

"I'm here for a job, Yarvick." Torny didn't hear, didn't see the shifting around the cavern's edges, but she knew it was happening. She'd have a few more sentences to buy her life, and Torny planned to use them. "That debt wasn't getting paid on Foti, so I'm back to do what's right."

Yarvick laughed, full-throated and strong. "What's right? Torny, I don't care about what's right. I care about what's mine." He pulled the poker from the fire, held its orange end up. His opal eye caught the glow, made it seem his face burned. "And what's mine, what has always been mine, is you."

CHAPTER 4
SAND TRAINING

The dive fell short and Sawi hit sand hard, the rocks between the grit gnarling into her hair and teeth. Her arms, reaching for vines that weren't there, lay out wide. A moronic pose. Sawi closed her eyes, suppressed a curse, and waited for the verbal lashing.

"You're using your instinct again," came her teacher's voice, as expected. Ami never missed a chance to criticize. "This isn't Vis. Stop acting like it."

Sawi rolled over, a move harder in these Najahn robes than it needed to be. She'd asked for and been denied a suit of Najahn leathers, Ami declaring Sawi hadn't earned those yet. The Vis would be in a student's robes until she could handle herself, a process that might take a day, a month, or a year.

Right now, if Sawi had to guess, Ami had her bet on the latter.

The flame-haired, golden-faced woman leaned on a thick dark blade as Sawi rose back to her feet, brushing sand off along the way. Why they always trained on the sea-side beach was another question Ami brushed off time and time again: footing, Ami would say during the long walk down the stone steps in the morning, was something you couldn't guarantee. Learn to fight on the terrible dunes and you could dance anywhere.

Sawi wanted to argue that the odds most of her fights would be on sand was a poor proposition, but Ami refused to hear it. As she refused to hear most of what Sawi spoke.

"This time, I want you to attack me," Ami said.

"With what?"

"Your hands."

Sawi blinked, "You've got a sword."

"Thank you for reminding me. I'll use it."

Ami took a single long step back, drew the blade from the dirt and grasped its large, black iron hilt with both hands. The blade itself seemed pitted and in poor form, one of many battered training arms kept down here on the sands. A victim, so Sawi gathered, of sea salt's devastating effect on the metals. Nevertheless, blunted and battered, the blade could still turn Sawi into a sliced sucker.

"What's the point of this, exactly?" Sawi asked. "Is this Gladdring's idea?"

"Gladdring's not your concern. Attack, now. Knock me down."

Sawi sighed, spread her bare feet. The sand tickled with its chilly touch, but the Najahn boots were even worse. Their leather soles told Sawi no stories about where she stood, how much strength she'd need to move. Vis climbing shoes would be better, but Ami kept ordering Sawi to leave all those things behind.

Behind the pair loomed Noctia's craggy rocks, broken up into caverns and tunnels this near the sea. Lapping water occasionally flushed through, leaving the rocks glistening wet and crawling with critters. Gulls and other birds joined in the ocean's song, despite the day growing long. She'd started the morning with the shock of seeing Quik, and now was ending it with a sword angled at her chest.

What a great day.

"Now," Ami said.

Sawi pushed left first, angling towards the waves and putting some sand-spraying distance between her and Ami. The Guardian held her position. A clue to the exercise, then. No active pursuit. Sawi could dawdle, could poke and prod.

"A fiend won't let you run like this," Ami said as Sawi slowed, turned at the brown, wet edge where the waves stopped. A solitary pier ran out behind her, old wood creaking with every wave strike. "They'll follow you as far as you can go and farther still."

"Guess I'll worry about that when I'm facing a fiend."

Sawi bent her knees, reached down and scooped some wet sand. Pressed it into a flimsy ball. Stood back up. Ami, eyes narrowed now, studied her.

Could she guess what Sawi meant to do? Probably.

Ami had seen the world, had fought half of it by the stories the Guardian had told in Sawi's first nights here, before their relationship became so brutal. Before Gladdring changed the game.

Kicking into the sand again, shivering off the sharp gale swiping by, Sawi cut up the beach to the rocky cavern's entry. A slow circle around Ami, forcing the older warrior to turn with the Vis gatherer.

Was she still that, a Vis gatherer? After yesterday, was she not a Najahn recruit?

A question worth answering when Sawi wasn't being tested.

"You're playing," Ami said. "Don't waste my time."

"It's my life on the line. I'll take as much time as I want."

Sawi broke into a loping run, harder and more exhausting on the sand than it should've been, but the sudden speed put Ami on guard. She lurched in her turn, raised the sword as Sawi twisted the angle, putting her route close to Ami's spot. A straight line dash now would bring her right past the Guardian, right on to the sea's southern edge.

As if Sawi would be so stupid.

Two strides away, as Ami angled the sword for what would've been an easy skewer, Sawi dug in her left heel and broke hard right. A turn difficult in the robes, impossible in heavier armor. Sand flew up in a wave, but an angle that would've sent Sawi sprawling on a flat surface held on the sliding grains. Sawi's cutback forced Ami to adjust, a fast turn made harder when Sawi's mud ball smacked Ami right in that golden cheek.

Ami cursed, the blade wavering, slow in its pursuit. Slow enough for Sawi to get inside its reach on Ami's right. She grabbed for Ami's wrist, found it and snared her fingers on the leather gauntlets. Sawi tugged, sending a kick at Ami's shin, hoping together the pulls would send Ami tumbling to the dirt.

The Guardian didn't move. Despite Sawi's pulls, her straining effort, Ami stayed right in the sand, the mud dripping off her face. As Sawi tried one more yank, Ami's eyes met hers, and in them Sawi saw doom.

"A clever tactic undone by idiocy," Ami said an hour later over ales back in the tower. "When you made your move, you should've gone for my eyes, my throat. At worse, pulled the knife from my belt to arm yourself."

The pair sat at a small table in a chaotic room, one lit as much by skars as by the glowing lanterns on the stone walls. A single winding stair circled the space, crawling upwards and out to a hallway that'd lead to some bored, loyal guards before breaching into more open Najahn territory. The skars, the small stones from across the isles, lay in piles small and smaller, each encased in a glass seal far stiffer than it seemed. Sawi knew, because Annalyse, the odd scientist sharing their space—and soon to be returning with dinner—had Sawi test breaking those cages.

She'd tried a staff, a hammer, and even a sword. Nothing.

"A Whent creation," Annalyse had said at the time, almost gleeful. "If Noctia knew what we were doing, they'd all freak out."

Annalyse said things like that all the time, though. Listening to her, Gladdring's tower was a treasure trove of the strange and secret. Then again, that seemed to be why Ami and her skar-sealed golden face plate lived here. Why, according to Gladdring, Sawi would live here too. She'd be a Najahn recruit in name, but in all else, she'd be Gladdring's assistant, or whatever he wanted to call her.

"Eyes and throat?" Sawi asked. "You wanted me to hurt you?"

Ami tapped the golden faceplate, right where a Vis emerald glittered. "You couldn't if you tried. Not unless those tiny hands of yours could snap my neck in a shot."

Sawi glanced at her fingers around the ale mug. Tiny?

"The point is to find your killer instinct, Sawi," Ami said. "You said a fiend nearly killed you, that you're still haunted by how close it came. I'm trying to teach you to take those feelings and turn them around. Use them to find control, to make sure you never feel so helpless again."

Yet she'd felt helpless almost from the second the Najahn boat had sailed off from Vis. Away from friends and family, the adventure Sawi had been expecting never materialized. Instead, Gladdring sucked himself into the intrigue and official nonsense the Najahn required, leaving Sawi to cast about on the vessel alone, watched by curious eyes and ignored by stuffy mouths. That feeling stuck with her when they arrived, with Gladdring casting Sawi off to Ami and Annalyse, promising only that he'd be back when he needed her.

That'd been more than a week ago now, and since then Gladdring's visits had been sparse and more for conversations with Ami and Annalyse than Sawi. Not that Sawi was jealous, no. Not that she spent the later evenings alone in her slim room, looking out the narrow window wondering how she'd made a terrible mistake. No, not that. Never that.

Admitting her error was a step Sawi wouldn't take. Not yet.

"Trying to kill you won't make me feel stronger," Sawi said, then continued on before Ami's opening mouth could lay out more suspect wisdom. "What I want is to know what I'm doing here, Ami. That's what's going to make me more confident, more comfortable. I'm lost."

At that, Ami sat back. Nodded slow. "I've been there. Was lost on this isle for damn near ten years, Sawi."

"That's a long time."

"Goes by quick when you have enough ale and a sword to swing at training dummies." Ami laughed, but it came out hollow. "Joking. It's long as Rana's rivers." She drained her remaining ale in a single swig. "But you're not that lucky. Sawi, it's simple. You're here to help us figure these things out." Ami swung the mug around at the skars. "Learn to talk with'em, how to get them to listen to what we want. Then, we use them to crush the fiends forever."

Too many questions in there to parse. Listen to the skars? Annalyse and Ami hadn't mentioned that before, had barely talked up the gems in the days Sawi had been here. Annalyse only went on about her inventions, had Sawi wear the worst kind of gear while she tested this and that device. Ami kept pushing Sawi to the training ground. No skars, no noble goal.

Only that, under penalty of a swift slice of the head, Sawi wasn't to say a word about what she saw here. Even to Quik, who she'd already ditched tonight.

"That's the same face I made when Gladdring told me," Ami said. "He's probably upset I'm breaking it to you now. But he can go lick lava." Ami glanced at her mug, as if hoping it'd refilled itself in the meantime, but alas. "The man's right. Annalyse is a genius, but she's not a fighter, and it's fighters that will be shoving these magical stones down every fiend's throat if I get my way."

"Why me, though? I don't—"

"You're loyal, or you wouldn't be here." Ami waved off the question. "That's the most important thing, Sawi. Because what's coming, what Gladdring's planning? We can't waver, we can't doubt. When the time comes, the world's going to need us to act. I will, Sawi, and so will you."

Sawi blinked. "And if I don't?"

"Then you'll be dead. I'll kill you myself."

CHAPTER 5

DARK ADVANCE

Like so many in the long line behind and around him, Svarde's body told a story of toil. His beard, grown long and gangly, found kinship with snarled hair pulled into taut braids down his back. Whent armor, stiffer than Foti leathers but molded with the same rock pressing in around him now, creaked along with Svarde's knees, arms, ankles at every step along the cave floor. Aches from a hundred wounds, both real and phantom, haunted his recurring headaches, a prize earned on the beach back to the south. Every breath pushed air past marred teeth, a face only clean thanks to a lucky pool some scout had stumbled upon.

Yet his hands could still hold his axes. His stance still stood tall. His voice bellowed with the best of them, there in the Dark Below.

At his feet, too, clawed his longtime companion, the stone-skinned ferrite Kivi. She vented as they walked now near the long column's head, taking a shift leading the expedition ever onward. Ahead, flashes flickered along the craggy curves, candles blinking or the odd-colored mushrooms lighting up the walls in purples and blues. Those mushrooms would be scraped off as the army passed by, added to the food stores and replaced by pounded lanterns.

As Jochi, the Whent warlord leading this charge put it, this wasn't just a mission, it was a colonization. The rock-biters were tired of ceding territory to the fiends. Instead, they would control it.

The tremors of that control pulsed up through Svarde's soft boots now, the constant hammering behind him as engineers put in those lights, added buttresses to unstable walls, and plotted out places for waystations, inns, whole towns in the largest caverns. Where the people would come from to settle all these places, Svarde wasn't certain, but that problem didn't faze the Whent workers.

Their warriors, too, marched with a conquering army's gusto. Where Svarde and Maena's initial foray into the depths came with quiet urgency, the Whent traveled with songs singing, drums beating, invincible confidence pushing them onward. The change, at first, was so jarring Svarde found himself ranging ahead with Kivi just to feel that solitude, that explorer's edge.

He would've brought Maena with, but the Rana captain seemed increasingly bent inward, tortured with some struggle she refused to discuss. Only during Jochi's regular briefings would Maena light up, as if the logistical challenges inherent in leading thousands through endless caves were life's greatest fascination.

"It's her choice," Svarde said down to Kivi as the ferrite snorted, her orange vents closing in a steamy burst. "I don't like it either."

The fiends, so terrible during the earlier expedition, fell back against Whent power. Crossbows, spears, and bone-crunching rock armor turned the haphazard beasts into so much gruel. More mysterious adversaries either fled or found themselves riddled with bolts from afar. A set of those giant eyes, the mind-warping monsters, found themselves boiled with Whent grenades, lobbed and rolled into their domain with devastating effect.

All in all, Svarde was almost bored.

Which was why he and Kivi were back at the front, with only the scouts between him and fresh fiend meat, or at least an interesting discovery. They'd passed the Aegis's spidery shield two days ago, meaning every step from now on stretched into new territory. A thrill only somewhat cut by the sheer smell of the rumbling, mobile civilization behind him.

"Is this what you had in mind?" Jochi, spoiling Svarde's quieter walk at the column's head, caught up and matched the axe-man's stride. "Your grand mission, now with proper grandeur?"

Svarde had long since decided destroying the fiends had precedence over holding any grudge, but every time he saw Jochi, the Foti Guardian found it hard to dismiss the trials forced at the man's hand. The Pits, the beach battle against those fiends, and the draining wagon trips between both all came at Jochi's direction.

The urge to send the man's head flying with an axe had to be tempered, was tempered by one thing: Catya.

Seeing the Aegis's web gave a warm, distant comfort. She still lived, however much of a shell that life was. A signal, too, that Svarde's mission to ruin the fiends and their origins remained urgent. Both served to keep Svarde's hands steady, to keep his response to Jochi's question congenial.

"If it serves to slaughter the fiends, then it's what I had in mind," Svarde replied.

Jochi laughed. The two body men behind him, hands ever near their own spears, chuckled too. Whether that sort of servitude grated on Jochi—Svarde would've socked any follower acting that way—was a mystery. The warlord seemed unaffected, instead launching into the day's march, or rather the night's walk. Somehow, the Whent scientists following along with them, all stolen from the university city whose sacking Svarde and Maena had prevented, kept track of the time and, in so doing, preserved the army's sanity. Shifts kept the people in line even as daylight fell further and further behind.

For Svarde, walking the nights meant fewer people pressing his steps. A few hours unconscious during the day, rolling in a bedded wagon, was worth the sacrifice. Only the officers received that luxurious treatment, meant to keep them closer to the action even as the army moved and worked at all hours. Others simply had to catch up during their waking moments, a prospect simpler than it would seem, given the grinding pace.

So it went when every few steps demanded a new lantern, a halt for some scientific observation or a fiend execution.

"Yet you don't seem at peace, my friend," Jochi said. "What troubles you? Our inevitable victory?"

"The slow speed that we're going, for one."

Jochi nodded in that sage way leaders had when they pretended to care. "Everything comes with a cost. The more people, the more permanent our conquest, the longer it will take."

"And when the farmers have to return to their fields, what will you have then?"

"The Winter is long in Whent, and our findings here are already making this a profitable journey." Jochi reached out to his right, plucked a purple mushroom off the wall. Glowing bits fell to the damp cavern floor. "Already we're learning how to grow these. Can you imagine, houses filled with both food and light in a single stroke? How much have we lost for fear of the fiends?"

"Too much."

"Indeed. Yet, I must ask if you're willing to lose more."

Jochi's tone slipped with the words, gaining Svarde's focus at the same time.

"What do you need?" the barbarian asked.

"Direction." Jochi waved back at the expedition's long line, though the curling caves put its bulk beyond sight. "My scouts inform me that these tunnels go in every way and for far longer than we can afford. You came down here once before and seemed set in your path. How did you know?"

Svarde pointed at Kivi. "She can hear the stones better than I can. They tell her the warmer roads, the ones leading down and down some more."

"A pity we don't have more ferrites, then," Jochi replied, leaning to pet the lizard only for Kivi to snort and dodge away. Jochi laughed, again matched by his body men, and stood. "She still has the scent, I trust?"

Kivi snorted louder. Vented steam.

"She knows where she's going," Svarde said. "Your scouts have been doing well enough, though."

"A scattered, if valiant, effort. I want you to take the lead with Kivi. My scouts will work with you directly, running the route between you and our force. I to destroy the fiends, Svarde. Spreading our roots throughout the Dark Below can come after. Do you agree?"

"You're offering me a chance to get away from you and all your stinking soldiers? How could I say no?"

This time, at least, Jochi's laugh was genuine. This time, at least, his frowning body men didn't echo it.

The changed assignment took effect immediately, with a scout materializing around the next bend with fresh satchels packed to the brim. The woman, who'd skipped heavier Whent armor for light leathers and belts crowded with tools, asked if Svarde could match a faster pace. When he assented, they shot off through the caverns, with Kivi soon taking the lead and choosing rights, lefts, downs and, on rare occasions, short jaunts up and over to reach viable ways deeper into the dark.

After hours tramping ahead, the Whent army vibrations replaced with a cave's dripping water and hollow wind, Svarde expected to find exhaustion trailing his every step. Instead, his walk came easy, the heavy armor lighter on his shoulders than before.

"It's a sign," the scout said, giving her name as one Olgata, "that you're doing what you're meant to." Her only expressions seemed to be a serious scowl and a slapdash grin, and the latter filled her small lantern's glow in their current rocky home. "We'll take two hours here. Sleep, then move on." She flicked a finger towards the ferrite. "Can that thing keep watch?"

"Her name's Kivi, and she'll keep a better watch asleep than you and I could awake."

"Good enough for me."

Olgata dropped a bedroll on the hard ground, set her satchel as a pillow, and before Svarde could match it, her light snores shuffled through the cavern. Svarde would've smiled at the sound, at the delight in being, again, out in front on his own mission.

Would've, save the other, more distant noises. Growls, scrabbling, a single roar like a forge lighting up for the first time.

The fiends were never far down here.

CHAPTER 6

BATTLE OVER BRUNCH

A last breakfast in the city. They'd be casting off in an hour, but Eujo wanted one more meal outside the ship's confines, nice as they were. The restaurant she chose delivered, with a broad glass window overlooking the port. The place sat above the busy roil, though industry's smells and sounds still filtered in, giving the early meal a gritty edge, one seemingly sought by the place's customers. They numbered among the administrators, the dock masters and supervisors, the Najahn inspectors and captains securing their ships for a long winter in dry dock or, perhaps, for a southern run to Smythe or some city on Kance's coast.

Some few, maybe, would make for Kitaye or Mottilan.

The thought of home struck Wax as he dug the fork—an implement he'd learned to use over the weeks since he'd left home—into an egg-and-bread combo. A lemon slice came with it, one he sucked on after Eujo advised him the fruit was a necessary part of any sea-faring adventure. Particularly one to Whent, where such tropical delights were hard to find.

"Because it's all rocks and dust up there?" Wax asked.

They sat at a small two-person table dominated by rugged plates, earthen mugs filled with brutal coffee that tasted more like acid than the rich cocoa Wax would get back home. Stiff chairs, a floor of stone buttressed here and there by haphazard boards. Mild chatter as people ran through manifests and the day's objectives.

Eujo snapped her eyes back to him. They'd been drifting out to the sea. Her mind, probably, already on the next adventure. Just like his.

"I keep forgetting how little you've seen," Eujo said, then winced. "Sorry, it's reflex. I hadn't seen much either until, well, I made it."

"You never talk about that. Making it. What you mean."

The slightest lip curl. "Someday, when we've had more wine, maybe I'll tell you." She glanced at her coffee mug, her plate as it neared empty. "This was nice. Thank you."

"What, I should thank you. You've paid for everything."

"Oh, you'll earn it back, I'm sure."

Wax laughed. "I'll try. When you're the Aegis, I'll run your errands."

Eujo tilted her head, "You'd stay? If I make it on that throne, you'd stay here? Not go home?"

He'd said a nice thing and dug himself into a tough spot. If there was one thing he knew not to do, though, with a question like that, it was hesitate. Too easy, then, to catch out a lie, to get suspicious.

"Of course. If we both make it that far, figure I'll owe you a lot more than a few meals," Wax shot right back, flashing a sincere grin.

"If you make it that far," said a new man, one belted over tight in Kance leathers wrapping a thin body, a narrowed face spliced over with criss-crossing white lines.

Wax at first thought they were scars, but a closer look, made easy when the man put both hands on their table and grinned at the pair, revealed them instead as tattoos. "An honest question, and one I hope I can put to rest."

Behind the man lurked two others, women both and in stances suggesting something more hostile than innocent breakfast conversation. Like the man, they wore outfits suited for active duty, with rapiers clear on their belts. Where they'd come from, Wax wasn't sure, but they'd drawn the restaurant's full attention, with conversation dwindling and more than a few making for an early exit.

Eujo set the tone quick, launching a furious glare at the man. "What're the Vientas doing here? Aren't you supposed to be protecting our home?"

"That is what we *are* doing, my Queen. Protecting our dear isle from a grievous mistake."

"And what mistake would that be?"

The venom in Eujo's words would've, should've curdled any ordinary man. Wax wanted to grimace on the guy's behalf, but the man's slithery smile dismissed Eujo's tone as easily as if she'd asked him for fresh butter. No authority, no demand would get through his shell.

"Better for our isle if the skars come home and their bearer does not," the man said. "Anything more, you don't need to know."

Wax shoved back his chair, stood. He had no weapon on him, nothing save a breakfast fork in his hand, lingering traumas from the fiend threatening to send fear's lightning through his every nerve, but he'd be damned before letting this slime act on his words. Eujo, though, stayed seated right where she was, only raising a single finger in Wax's direction.

"Even an assassin like you would know better than to

do this here," Eujo said. "There's several Najahn not two tables away. One's already left to fetch guards. You'd be dooming yourselves."

"A small price to save our isle." The man lifted one hand off the table, put it on a small pouch tied to his belt. "A price, however, that you could pay. As every Queen must."

"Yet she won't."

The man removed the pouch. Eujo still had her finger raised. Wax held the fork. Tried to keep eyes on all three, with the two women sliding themselves to block the easiest path to the exits and the cobblestone streets outside.

"Bravery is your domain, I'm afraid," the man said, putting the pouch on the table. "A simple sniff, and all will be well. Please."

Eujo picked up the pouch. Wax tensed, would've done something rash except he'd come to know Eujo a bit better, found the Queen to have a scrappy savvy. One she put to play in the next second, whipping the pouch up into the assassin's face. The bag burst, harmless sand breaking over the man's already-shaking head.

Wax, then, put the fork to good use.

He jammed it down, the rough tines biting into the assassin's left hand, still planted on the breakfast table. Now the man howled a curse, a more appropriate reaction. Eujo shot back her chair, started to stand as the two women reverted from their backup roles to star players. Both grabbed for rapiers while the restaurant's crowd cleared out.

Reaching an exit meant fighting through at least two killers without a weapon. Not even Wax had that level of foolhardy confidence. Instead, he did what he'd learned back on Vis, in the dining room brawl with the Mottilan bruisers: Wax wielded his chair, scooping up the awkward furniture and swiping it across his chest in a broad swing. The forked man responded by ducking the move, reaching with his sand-coated self and drawing out the fork from his own hand, cursing all the while. His back-up hesitated, letting the chair go flying past.

A seeming miss, but Wax hadn't just learned that furniture could be a good defense. He'd picked up, in losing that brawl, that it was better to run than take on an impossible battle. Wax kept his momentum, building it as he spun, and slammed the solid chair into the thin glass pane. The brittle, beautiful window shattered, shards flying.

"Time to go!" Wax shouted, catching Eujo and her own chair-based defense, the back proving adept at snagging a rapier's point and holding its grip.

He took a step onto the crunched glass. Heard Eujo's warning and ducked, the rapier's blow snagging Wax's shoulder and tearing a hole in his nice, Noctia-woven shirt. Red pain flashed, Wax using the fire to dart forward as his skars, resting in a necklace against his chest, burst to life. Their whispers surged, the Vis skar roaring to frenzied chatter as it began addressing the slice.

More distractions to shove aside as Wax plummeted from the restaurant to a battered, sloping roof below. Noctia kept its building caps slanted, gutter linings leading to rain barrels and a chance to secure drinking water on a dry island. Covered now in morning frost, the slates proved a slippery landing spot, Wax falling onto his side and rolling.

Yet he stole a look up, hoping to see Eujo and finding her, flying like some bird in the morning sun, from the restaurant. Her leap outran a rapier's stab, the sword catching light, and the Queen struck the same warehouse Wax had found, joining him in a tumble.

Wax grabbed out for the roof's lip, the gutter making such an arrest possible, but the frost neutered any chance. Wax's fingers, leftover breakfast still on them, found only frozen snow. Off the edge he went, a Vis curse flying free as Wax dropped straight down towards the street. Cobblestones should've been there to greet him, and they were, though Wax's left side found stacked crates instead, his shoulder bouncing off the metal-and-wood boxes to spin him around before he smacked the snow covered ground. The white fluff, piling up and shoveled into alley corners like this one, gave Wax the slightest blanket, so he only found the air leaving his lungs, his shoulder aching, and a dismal freeze coating all parts of him as snow snuck everywhere.

For one moment. In the next, Eujo landed on him, driving Wax deeper into the snowbank and ensuring a sputtering, coughing panic. The Queen, as ever, kept her composure and rolled off, standing on the slick street with natural skill. Her hand found Wax's left arm, yanked it, and him, up to a partial stand.

"You alive?" Eujo asked, continuing to pull.

"I hope," Wax coughed.

Eujo pulled hard again and Wax came free from the snowbank, though his feet weren't ready to take command, and he stumbled right into the Queen, both falling to the alley's other side and the untouched snow waiting there. A sharp clink came from where Eujo had stood, a throwing knife bouncing off down the street.

"Thanks," Eujo said, shoving Wax off. In the same motion, her hand found Wax's and pulled him along the narrow street. "Get moving, Wax. They're killers."

"Figured that out."

With Eujo pulling him, Wax scrambled along, the Vis

skar doing its part to keep him upright. Eujo slanted her way through the port district, dodging around porters, through open stalls, and always breaking towards the sea, towards her ship.

"Who were those three?" Wax asked, finally finding enough air to talk, to manage his own run.

It helped that, as they'd left the warehouses behind, the cleared streets offered better traction.

"The Vientas. A Kance sect," Eujo replied, jumping several ropes as sailors cursed their interference in hauling a ship up to dry dock. Wax followed, uttering apologies along the way. "They work for the Queen, usually."

"Isn't that you?"

"Two Queens, Wax. And they like her more."

"Why's that?"

Eujo's ship lay ahead, sails already getting set to leave. The provisions crates crowding the pier earlier were all gone, loaded and ready. Deux, the captain, must've just been waiting for them.

"Because I'm rough around the edges? How should I know?"

For the first time that morning, Wax read something false in Eujo's snapped reply. The lilt almost threw him, along with an icy spot on the pier, into a sliding dive to the drink. Vis instincts kept Wax stable enough to correct himself, dropping a hand on a rope tie to push himself up. Together they hit the boat ramp, darting up it and calling for Deux to get the vessel going. Deckhands leapt at Eujo's command, untying the ropes and hollering to launch.

Eujo kept moving as she reached the main deck, darting inside to find Deux. Presumably to relay what happened. Wax, though, found a grip on the railing and simply stood, leaning on the Kance wood. He looked back towards the shore, saw three shapes standing out amid the workers, moving with deliberate purpose. The assassin trio stopped as they neared the pier, watching as *Storm's Edge* slid into the sea. Wax met their stares, saw nothing save certainty in their grim looks.

The only satisfaction came from the red-stained bandage around the man's hand. The fork, at least, delivering some justice.

These three, though, marked the second Kance group trying to kill the isle's Queen. And Eujo, Wax suspected, knew exactly why.

CHAPTER 7
THE THIRD HAND

The Tenet's tower sat back against the cliff side, sprawling up along the rock like growing ivy. Blackwood beams supported stacked stone lurching in several directions as it climbed, crossing back and forth every few levels. Windows, scalloped shapes twisting into tinted glass gave no hints as to what happened inside. Neither did the two shapes standing outside the tower's front entry, a slim single door entered not through a rising stair but a descending one, a slow funnel from street level to its sea-blue boards.

"Here for your first tour?" asked one of the shapes as Quik approached, freshly decked in his purple Najahn recruit robes.

The Vis hunter had been given a time, a punctual arrival simply not demanded on Kitaye. Here, though, clocks abounded, their mad ticking driving Quik's every action with a new kind of stress. A shoveled-down breakfast snared from the table stocked for recruits and out he went, joining the rush. Foot traffic, at least, was familiar, though Quik's bulk tended to give him leeway on his jungle home.

Not so here, where deference seemed tied to one's robes and the sashes, medals, or weapons worn.

It'd taken three bumps and earned glares for Quik to learn that lesson.

"I think so?" Quik answered, hating himself for his uncertainty.

One of many pledges to himself that he'd failed to achieve. So far.

The shape turned to the other, a man shrouded in an inverted Najahn robe, one with its purple replaced with the door's light blue colors, the black with white. A golden pin, at least, matched Najahn standards, though Quik hadn't ever seen this one before: a distorted keyhole, as if someone had jabbed at the thing with poor effort and scratched, bent the lock. An odd symbol.

Then again, this being Noctia, someone would tell Quik what it meant soon. Probably with a heaping amount of sighing scorn.

"Is the Tenet ready?" the shape asked.

"Masayo is in her chambers," the other shape, by her voice an older, Tamas woman, replied. "Lead him up."

Following the shape proved more difficult than Quik expected, mostly because, through the door, his sense of his surroundings lost all bearing. The door itself swung open without a sound, hinges greased to immaculate levels. Beyond, where an outside view dictated a circular ground floor with upward, branching stairs, the tower defied logic.

First and foremost, Quik saw no stairs. Instead, he saw refracted light streaming in through the few windows, the beams catching on prisms and bouncing around in a rainbow array that would've been blinding save for its strict lines. By narrowing his eyes, by keeping his stare just off the beams, Quik kept himself from closing off sight completely.

"Take a minute," the shape said. "But only one. In this tower, adaptation must come quickly."

Between the beams lay shadows, but not vacant ones. More shapes moved in those white robes, some followed by more usual Najahn in purple-and-black. Some scurried on Quik's level, but others seemed to rise right up through the air, as if walking on the light itself. Tracking one pair, Quik saw them vanish above to his left, through another door seemingly floating in air. It shut with a very real click. Casual words reached his ears too, conversations underway buttressed by mild thuds as shoes hit stone.

Hanging on the walls around the room were paintings, their contents amorphous, colorful blobs or abstract nonsense. The air inside tickled, a savory spice reminding Quik of cooked eggs and onions.

"You're noticing the breakfast," the shape said, standing just ahead. "That's unimportant. Focus. Your time is nearly up."

Quik shook his head. Stop. Think like a hunter. Use your senses, what you know.

The first clue came from those floating scholars and how they walked. Assured, but with careful steps. Not the carefree climbers Quik had seen in other towers around here, the moves he himself would make on a normal stair. Those steps, too, seemed to dodge the beams, working their way in between the light shafts.

Quik drifted forward, a hand reaching out ahead, through one of the rainbow shafts. On the other side, where not moments ago a robed figure had passed, his fingers found taut rope. Quik glanced back at the shape, said what he'd found.

"Not rope," the shape replied, though his tone marked approval. "A specific cable from Kance. Woven to steer light away. During the day, a skilled eye can make out their pattern and walk upon it. At night, impossible for anyone who hasn't climbed them before."

Now Quik felt stares on him. Others passing through took notice of the recruit, giving him room. To fail, to succeed, Quik didn't know. Couldn't be bothered with.

"Why?" Quik asked. "What's the point?"

He felt more than saw the shape's smile. "That is what you're here to learn. You've found our first secret. Many more wait."

The shape, though, wasn't going to wait himself. He strode to the right, walking around where a prismatic shaft struck the stone floor and stepping onto another cabled stair. Quik followed, suppressed his own tentative urges and walked with what he hoped looked like confidence. Yet, he couldn't keep his eyes from flicking down as he took the first step.

His feet felt the cables, strong and tight with little give from the first go. Even knowing they were there, though, Quik couldn't see their lines. It wasn't so much like he walked on air as he walked on a dim murk, a fogged blur. His boots came in clear enough, but beneath them the stone washed out, the light seeming unable to define the step.

The door, single file like the other entry below—and every door Quik had seen in the tower so far—opened outwards, towards them, when the shape pulled on the handle. The stone wrap around it seemed conventional next to the magical stair.

On the other side, oddities gave way to practicality. To Quik's left, burrowing into the cliff side, waited a broad hallway with closed shock-white doors hinting at rooms. The stair continued on after a few strides, now rendered with normal stacked stone. Tables and chairs lounged around the space, a few occupied with coffee-drinking souls, most with large, leather-bound volumes in their hands.

"A dormitory," the shape said, flowing on towards the next stair. "Should you be so fortunate to join our Tenet, here is where you might live. Unless, of course, Masayo has other needs for you."

"What *is* your Tenet?" Quik asked as they started up the second stair. "They told me to go to this tower. Nothing else."

"Knowledge. Information. Details," the shape said, continuing to walk. "Many names, one purpose. If it happens in the Isles, we know about it. More important, we know *why* it happens." Quik could all but hear the grin as they reached the next door. "Sometimes, we *are* the why."

The description sounded like the Lira, Kitaye's own band of secretive soldiers. An elite society meant to keep Vis safe from various threats, the Lira seemed like they embraced all sorts of odd rituals. Not that Quik knew for sure: they'd never chosen him to join their shadowy sect and Quit had never gone looking for them.

He preferred sleeping to haunting far off treehouses at night.

The third floor offered another dormitory and two off-shoots, no continuing stair. The shape guided Quik to a hard left, wrapping back around the stair's part of the floor to an open archway leading towards the tower's center. At the archway's crest, the shape stopped. Reached to the right and pressed in a stone ever-so-slightly lighter than the ones surrounding it. The little block slid in, a faint ticking noise began, and the shape stepped through.

"Quickly now, it will not wait for you."

Quik did as the shape asked, crossing through the arch before the ticking ceased and the stone returned to its former position.

"What would've happened?" Quik asked.

"Pray you never find out. Every arch in this tower is like that. Make sure you learn where the triggers are."

"Seems needlessly dangerous."

The shape chuckled. "Needlessly? What would be needless is letting our tower grow complacent. Our duty demands constant vigilance, ears and eyes always listening and looking."

A way to keep your people sharp, then. Quik could see the reason for that, though trapping your own home seemed a bit extreme.

Coming back to the tower's central shaft, albeit one without a stairwell, ended their other options. They could've continued straight across to the other outside wing, but the shape instead turned towards the arc cut before them into the cliff side. Another door, single like the rest, waited before them. Its panel alternated the blues and whites. On either side waited chairs, a single table. Nothing bore any decoration except the walls, adorned again with inky paints of storms, swirling seas, or forests so dense they might just be black.

The shape went forward to the door. Knocked once. Quik heard no reply, but the shape pulled the door open anyway. Waved Quik inside. The hunter went on past, crossing the threshold into what looked like a death trap of an office. Shelves abounded, as did tables all done up in glossy dark wood. A bed at the office's back, stuffed in tight beneath the slanting down cliff wall, looked made up with care. A large amber desk sat center, covered with several stacks of scrolls, books, and other random things.

No chairs waited for guests.

Masayo, if she'd been waiting—

Instinct is a hard thing to teach, as is a sense for danger. Quik, though, hadn't grown up in some posh home. He'd burned his years in a dangerous jungle, ears and eyes always open to threats both hidden and clear. The step hitting the wood floor behind him wasn't the same one the shape had been making thus far, but landed quieter, shorter. The air moved too, a rush as someone pushed a robe wide, perfect for a sidelong skewer.

The hunter pivoted. Stuck his left foot and swung himself around, raising his fists to block any attempting strike. Better a knife's gash on his hands than a stuck lung. Instead, Quik found himself looking at the shape, yes, but also not.

The robe now covered not an indistinct man, but a sharp-eyed woman, the one, if Quik had a bet, had been standing outside the tower back when Quik first arrived. In her left hand, the woman held a narrow stiletto. In her right, a Najahn-branded letter.

Seeing Quik take her all in, the woman laughed once. Piercing and short. Then flipped the stiletto over her hands and back into the invisible folds of her robe.

"At least they teach you something on that isle," the woman said. "Leave those fists alone, Quik. I'm not going to kill you now."

Quik took a long, slow breath as the woman went past him towards the desk. She ran a finger along its edge, found her seat on the massive piece's opposite side.

"Can you guess who I am?" the woman asked.

"Is it the obvious answer?"

"Is it, Quik? Or is it some big secret?"

Confidence. That's what she was looking for, and what Quik had, now that he'd pieced the whole dance together.

"Masayo. That's who you are."

"Correct," Masayo nodded. "Now, why would I pull such a mean trick on you?"

"Because you don't like new recruits?"

A real smile, for once . "I don't like hopeless recruits, Quik. Fortunately, for both of us, you appear to be neither." Masayo reached onto her desk, pulled off the top scroll. Offered it to Quik. "This is for you. Your first assignment. Do it well, and there may be a future for you here."

"Wait. That's it? No tour? No explanation?"

Masayo's eyes, cold grey, glittered. "The first rule of success in my tower, Vis, is taking care of yourself. If you want a tour, go out there and take one. Then, I suggest you get started. My patience is thin, but the Circle's is thinner still."

"I'm just a recruit?"

A head shake. "You're a Guardian. An experienced hunter. You'll be used as such, and rewarded if you succeed. Now stop wasting my time, and start using yours."

CHAPTER 8

THIEF'S TRICKS

Torny lay on the sole flat spot on the otherwise sloping roof at the ship's top, covering the captain's cabin like some strange helmet. The flat spot, not much larger than Torny herself and built of sheened Kance wood, existed for accessories. A Kance ship with more military applications might plant a small ballista there, or a firebomb-launching close-range catapult. Eujo had no such desires—more the pity, there—so Torny could use the spot as a place to escape.

A ship underway held a different spirit than one docked. Deckhands swarmed, the sound of the sea battered by calls for this and that. On-the-fly repairs and re-riggings for the sails demanded constant attention. Even Bliss and Wax found themselves pulled into the act, though Wax now, as he always seemed to be, had to take things gingerly while recovering from yet another injury.

What good Guardians they were, letting their Renewal get up close with Kance's claws.

Torny's eyes tracked a gull flapping overhead, chasing their ship while Noctia remained close. "No food for you,"

Torny muttered, then pulled her knife in close and bit off some of the apple sticking from its end. Old and bitter, but setting sail this late in the season meant poor choices for produce. "All this is for me, bird."

The apple might take the edge off a growling stomach, but it did little to dispel the reasons Torny was up here in the first place. Yarvick's grumbles, threats, and growls repeated themselves endlessly, had ever since the Nimble Finger's leader laid out Torny's future in simple, stark terms: complete the request, or find herself a hunted woman across the isles.

Her last failure brought exile. This one would bring death.

And success? What would that provide?

Time was Yarvick's approval would've been enough. Torny, along with too many lost others on Noctia, found themselves under the man's sway. Food, shelter, purpose, and just the right amount of kindness coaxed his targets in. Training followed, sharp words and sharper sticks coming up more and more, pushing her, making her desperate to hear Yarvick's kindness. Be in his favor. Bask in something bigger than herself.

Until stark fate flung her to Foti. Lava and a forge's eternal stink can clear up an awful lot.

So then why had she gone back?

"Torny, you up there?" Deux, the captain. "Have a favor one of your skills might be able to help with."

One of her skills. Everyone hates a thief till they need one.

Three cherry lockboxes, all the same size and all gilded with Kanco royal sigils: glossy silver winding around a blue diamond. Deux had them laid out on the dining room table —the mess for the deckhands lay lower in the ship, complete with a random assortment of tools Deux declared the closest things he had for lockpicks.

"Nice of you to assume I don't have my own," Torny replied, though her hands didn't go near the tools. Not yet. "What're these?"

"The traitors. Their larger trunks weren't sealed so, and we gave away their clothes. These, however, remain locked. The keys must've vanished with them."

"And you want them opened for, what, valuables?"

The bandit and the captain stood alone near the large table and its chairs, set as it always seemed to be for the next meal. Great, slanted windows showcased the gray seas outside, coming together in a broad band across the room's front. In back, two single doors split the ship's core, each leading to halls and the vessel's myriad chambers. Both doors, now, were closed tight.

"How much do you know about Kance royalty?" Deux asked. The captain, as ever, lived and breathed decorum. Full uniform with whites and blues, spotless. A cap that looked to provide zero warmth and utility. A saber on his belt that, at least, seemed real enough.

He stood too straight.

"I know they like to stab each other in the back," Torny replied. "Lotta good gossip about Kance ran around back home."

Deux frowned, but nodded, "Stabbing would be nicer than what often occurs. It's been a long, long time since our two Queens have been friends. Generations."

"Noctia's not much better. The Circle's all a bunch of vipers."

"Indeed. And in that, you might find our reasoning here. Like your Najahn power brokers, the Queens must conduct their treachery in quiet. Common knowledge makes common criminals." Deux pointed at the lockboxes. "If there is any proof, any letters suggesting their actions in there, we might have a way to—"

"What, stop those assassins that nearly killed Wax? Will your other Queen just curl up and die from shame?"

A grim line marked Deux's mouth. "No. Should what we hope be waiting in there, Kance will drag her out and cast her from the tallest cliffs, and we will return to find a new Queen in her place."

Brutal, but then, the Isles were a brutal place. Funny how Wax and Bliss kept forgetting that.

"One better than the old?"

"Who can say? Better, at least, to take the chance." Deux shifted half a stride to the left, watched her.

Torny took another look at the lockboxes, at the frankly useless strips of metal and pliers Deux had laid out on the table. "One thing, captain. Do you have a lockbox of your own?"

"I do?"

"Does it look anything like these?"

"It does?"

"Then how about you leave your key here with me. Promise I won't go pinching. You'll have it back soon." Torny tapped the table once. "The rest of this should be good enough."

Deux reached into his coat, pulled out a ring with several keys on it. Slipped off the shortest, skinniest of the bunch and laid it on the table. "Can I depend on your honor not to hide anything you find?"

"Asking a bandit about her honor?"

"I'm asking a Guardian." A loud whistle outside had Deux wincing. "I'm late for some maneuvering around

Noctia's northern coast. Someone will be back to check on you."

"Check on me?"

Deux, though, only nodded once more, then left the room. Torny heard a click, a very particular click, and followed the captain. Tried the door the man used, found it locked tight. She went to the other, its glimmering silver knob shined spotless. The turn went nowhere. Locked too.

Honor, her ass. So much for trust.

But, so long as she was locked in here, Torny might as well get to working. Yarvick's task meant she'd need to keep everyone here on her good side. That, and Bliss was . . .

Too naive to survive these isles without Torny keeping a watch out for her, that's what.

The lockboxes offered an interesting challenge. Everyone seemed to think lockpicking, the art of the thief, involved some magic talent coupled with a device menagerie worthy of some devious hoarder. In fact, Torny found the small pouch inside a larger one on her waist, always on her waist, holding the simple tools that'd saved her life too many times to leave behind. Untying it, she dumped the contents onto the table. A file and several thin bars of soft metal, unblemished and boring.

Now the bandit worked by feel. She pulled a chair over, sat next to the first lockbox. Read its lines, its hinges, and the keyhole's story. Well-made, but overly ornate. The whole lockbox screamed something given as a gift, rather than crafted to excel at keeping secrets. Could something do both?

Sure, but in Torny's experience, most crafters picked a side. Most good thieves, too, picked a technique. The brutes would simply break the lockbox, but Deux seemed to want them kept intact. Valuable, then. Or perhaps holding something he wouldn't want smashed in the act of entry.

The locks themselves, though, told the story. A simple twist of a key. No tumblers, no dials and combinations like the Najahn had started using—Torny let a smug grin grow at that, the Nimble Fingers having been directly responsible for that change. A good key lock could be unbreakable without force, if you didn't know how such things worked.

Torny reached over, picked up Deux's key. She angled, slipped it into the first lock box. The key went right in, a successful start. She started to turn it, found it blocked. Wiggled it some against the inside, then withdrew it. Measured the marks on Deux's key. Each one gave a clue, one Torny started to use by filing away at one of her soft metal bars.

The work took hours, with Deux coming here and there to check on her progress. Food and drink came and went, Torny for once eschewing wine for an unclouded mind. Bliss visited too, though the Vis struggled to stay fascinated with the carving work and begged off after only a few minutes. Not an issue, not a problem.

Because, while her fingers worked the metal, Torny didn't hear Yarvick's words, didn't find herself pulled back to the past.

The new key, almost like Deux's save for some slight modifications, served to open the lockbox. A few carves after that opened the second, then the third. What lay inside wasn't what Deux and Eujo wanted. Letters, three, mingled with random trinkets. Each one, written out in varying hands, addressed families now left behind. The words asked for forgiveness, professed love, loss, and a desire to see names honored. Lives given meaning by serving their isle in its greatest need.

"Greatest need?" Eujo said, she and Deux joining Torny at the table as night fell. "These are the worst liars. Murderers and traitors, that's all." Eujo dropped the papers. "Toss them into the sea, Deux. Let their names disappear from the world. We'll find another way to prove her evil."

The Queen stood, stomped from the room. Deux reached for the three letters, but Torny grabbed them first.

"I'll handle them," Torny said. "You go do your captain thing."

Deux narrowed his eyes. "The Queen asked me—"

"The Queen's got a lot on her mind. Renewal and all that," Torny snapped back. "So do you. I'd rather not hit an iceberg while you're taking out the trash."

Deux didn't seem moved by the argument. "If those letters aren't destroyed, then you'll find the consequences severe."

"Yeah, well, I've heard that before." Torny shoved the papers into her satchel. Held up the newly fashioned key. "You might want to consider changing the locks on those beauties, or tell your smith to tweak his style. Too easy."

Now Deux just looked confused.

"Too many locks made by the same locksmith. Man's only got so many hours in the day to make the things, so the keys come out nearly the same." Torny stood. "Thanks to you, I bet I can open any Kance lockbox in a few minutes."

"If you try—"

"Severe consequences, got it."

Torny sat near the vessel's aft, on the main deck near a giant spindle with an anchor's rope wrapping 'round. A nearby lantern gave her all the light she needed to read those letters again. So familiar, so like the letters Yarvick would write on behalf of any thief that fell on a mission. A notice dropped under a family's door, telling them a son, a daughter, a father or a mother wouldn't be coming home. A comfort, Yarvick would say, to the family.

Yet every one of those letters gave a place and a person where vengeance might be found. Where Yarvick might earn a new recruit, or a favor to cash in later. That latter bit stayed Torny's hand, had her keep those letters in her satchel.

Wax would be going to Kance eventually. Someone might thank him for delivering closure. Somehow, the idea might keep those voices quiet.

CHAPTER 9

MONSTER WALK

Rare was the morning Sawi didn't wake up with Ami knocking on her door, a fresh weapon inlaid with skars ready to hand over. Sawi would spend breakfast getting acquainted with the whispers those gems spoke in her mind, already able to tease out a Vis's quiet, eager murmurs from a Foti's boisterous hisses. Rana and Kance split the difference, one silky, the other slippery, as if turning away as it spoke. Hearing the whispers, though, was the easiest part. Getting the skars to really respond, to wake up and act, that was something else altogether.

And today, or so Ami said, Sawi wouldn't need to try.

"We're getting out of this tower," Ami said, brandishing a satchel already stocked with food and water. "I'm sick of it, and if you aren't too, you're lying to yourself."

Sawi, tugging on her purple Najahn robes at Ami's request, couldn't deny a sight beyond these dull rock walls would be delightful. Climbing the same tree twice in a week back in Kitaye would be a disappointment, here all Sawi seemed to do was plod up the same steps to and from the low caverns along the beach.

62

"Where are we going?"

"Gladdring and I had a chat," Ami started, hooking Sawi into a different thought before bashing her back home. "No, stop. Focus on me, not the Tenet. He'll see you when you're ready. When I say so. Pay attention."

"I am."

"I was a young girl once too, Sawi, and—"

Sawi's glare came with enough heat to throw Ami off her lecture, the Guardian faltering into a lopsided grin instead.

"Okay, fine. Guess I do have your attention," Ami said. "Which is good, because we're going to the Wound."

Ami did, in fact, also have a weapon for Sawi, though this one bore no skars. A simple spear, nothing more than a haft of blonde wood with a ragged head affixed to the front. Sawi regarded it as they walked through the immense Najahn district, angling towards the mountain trail Ami said would take them all the way up and over the crater. Snowflakes drifted down, though not heavy. Noctia seemed prone to blizzard bursts followed by days upon days of dainty flakes. The snow always seemed to get beneath Sawi's robes, her leathers, and freeze her out from the inside.

"You keep looking at that spear as if it'll change," Ami said as they neared the gravel path. "Let me save you time: it won't."

"It's trash."

"How do you know? Have you fought a fiend with it?"

"Vis has spears everywhere. I know a good—"

Ami turned on her right heel, digging it into one of the last cobblestones. Rather than standing a bit ahead and to Sawi's right, the Guardian now had her ember-red hair and gold-plated face up against Sawi's own.

"For once," Ami said, her voice dropping to a razor whisper, "for once, use your knowledge the right way. Keep quiet, study what's around you, and rather than dismissing it, ask why instead."

Sawi fought to keep her eyes from rolling. "Why, then?"

"Because a novice Najahn, the rank your pin-free, basic robe shows, is forbidden from carrying a real weapon outside training," Ami replied. "You're with me, and that spear is old enough to be a relic, so nobody's made a stink about it. Otherwise, some scholar having a bad day would get you tasked with mess hall chores for a week."

Sawi glanced around, saw the few souls this close to the path not paying them any attention. As ever on Noctia, business was afoot and needed tending to. Wandering eyes and ears would be easier to find near the ports. Still, the thought of scrubbing pots or sweeping the stained stone floors earned a nose wrinkle.

"Then why give it to me at all?"

"Because the Wound's a dangerous place, and I'd rather you have to clear some plates than die under my watch."

Ami's flat end to the conversation killed any further chatting, even when Sawi wanted to ask more about the carvings in the tunnel crossing into Noctia's huge crater. Curiosity would go hungry today, and that was fine. There would be plenty more distractions, starting with the Wound itself, and Ami's curse as they stepped from the cave into the crater.

Legends made manifest struck Sawi with a coarse denial. As if she couldn't quite believe what ran before her. A story, a fable often told as a ritual, laying out the seven gods and their growing faults. Noctia, death's divine arbiter, growing more and more at odds with the life giver, Vis. A breaking of bonds, a traitorous turn—who the traitor was depended on the tale's teller and where their sympathies sat—and a sudden strike. Vis, delivering a mortal stab to his counterpart, creating the crater and, beneath it, the Wound with a Foti-fashioned dagger.

That crater now resembled a living thing, covered with lelune flowers top to bottom, black during the day and a beautiful, astounding pink at night. A thank you, so Sawi's elders said, to Sichi for her helpful light.

Forging through those flowers lay a gravel path much like the one they'd just been walking on, save an important difference: this didn't end in a cave or an outpost, but a fortress. Ami, earlier, had told Sawi to expect tents and guards. Not stone walls, albeit ones supported by standing planks, evidence of haste. Not, too, several barracks erected on the gray dust at the crater's basin. A mess hall and other buildings seemed on the rise, cold weather no impediment to the rapid work.

"It's getting worse," was all Ami said as they took in the development. "It's always getting worse."

"You don't sound surprised?" Sawi asked.

"No . . ." Ami trailed off, her eyes watching the work but no longer seeing it. "It was like this last time. When we arrived to complete the Renewal. The Wound was fortified, the fiends were too frequent, but not like this. Not quite so permanent."

"The Renewals are getting more frequent, right? Maybe it makes sense now to have something here."

Ami flashed a frown, "It means we're running out of time."

The Guardian stomped on before Sawi could throw some corrective in there. True, the Renewals were happening faster—not great!—but years and years would still pass between them. This was hardly like Gladdring's

Mottilan situation, where a single night gone wrong could mean his end. Hardly, too, like Wax's pressure, racing against six others to grab every isle's skar.

But that was Ami. Everything mattered the *most*. Every day was *crucial*. For now, too, Ami controlled most of Sawi's life, so Sawi would try, as much as she could stand, to see things like her teacher.

So Sawi picked up her pace as the pair padded to the crater's bottom.

The Aegis wasn't just surrounded on the outside. Her sparse throne, seeming much too huge for her faded, withered figure and her purple robes, had two Najahn guards in full armor. These two, in contrast to the usual set, gave up their volumes and chakrams for small swords and giant shields. Sawi tried to figure out why till Ami told her: those shields would keep the Aegis safe till other forces brought any fiends down.

And there were other forces aplenty. The Wound, its gash sweeping near the throne and continuing for far too long on either side, had its length patrolled not just by one or two Najahn, but a full squad's worth of archers. Half that many voulges accompanied the crossbow killers, curved spears ready to fend off anything too deadly for a quarrel rain. Chakrams littered the area too, stacked in spaced sets throughout the domed area where any ambitious Najahn could grab and toss within a moment.

Firepower throughout.

After introducing Sawi to the shieldmaiden captain, the Guardian ditched the Vis and made for the Aegis. Sawi, apparently, was supposed to look around, get the feel of the place. Understand what she was working for, who she was protecting.

Hard, though, to feel empathy for so many soldiers

blanketed head to toe in purple and black armor. So unlike her friends and family back home, and so unwilling to give Sawi much more than a glare, a confused glance. As if she were the strange one here in this coarse crater's bed.

None stopped Sawi when she made for the most interesting thing here: the Wound itself. The line through the rock looked like an unnatural fissure, too straight for an earthquake's wild lines, yet so crusted with age and battle to appear marred somehow. A natural wonder despoiled, like a sana with broken petals. Damage had its own fascination, however, and the Wound drew Sawi to its lip. She waited for a gap between the walking archers, their crossbows pointing over the edge, and looked.

Day- and torch-light combined to cast a white-orange hue down the Wound, illuminating sediment lines, some scurrying insects, and claw marks. Bloody splotches, some a far cry from human red, mingled with spent quarrels to show recent battles, recent terrors. Deeper, Sawi tilting her head as if scanning a horizon, brought her to a growing dark. An endless pit, one so black as to render every night sky a balmy bright. The depth pulled at her, seeming to suck the warmth from her body, her breath falling still as her eyes sought something, anything in that dark.

A whistle sounded, sharp and clear, but Sawi pushed the sound away. Another shift change, another Najahn formality. Nothing compared to the void she saw, the Wound demanding her every attention. The distance, the size grew, shoving away the rocky walls, the torch glow until nothing, nothing save that black could be seen.

Only, it wasn't just black. Not now, not anymore. Growing there, just there, if only she could reach it, was a gold pinprick. A glittering gem, the very color of the sun. And Sawi could reach it, she could, she just had to try. Her hand went out, towards that gem, her fingers stretching into the dark.

As she touched it, found that glittering speck, it grew, encouraged by her efforts. Coming, coming to the surface, coming to her. So beautiful, so perfect, and with it, Sawi felt no doubt, only power. Strength to do what Ami wanted, what Kitaye needed, what the world deserved. The gold shined so bright, landing on her finger tip, it's light a . . . a fire.

Sawi's smile flipped, her spirit going cold as the shimmering glory broke into a seething orange, a raging red snarling up her hand, her arm, devouring her. She started to scream, to pull away, only to find her feet slipping, her arm only going deeper into—

"Close your damn eyes," Ami snapped, the Guardian snatching Sawi and throwing her away from the Wound, bouncing the Vis gatherer across the dirt.

The flames vanished, the dark gone, replaced with scrambling guards and crossbows clicking. Something rumbled an angry roar below. Ami paid it no attention, coming to stand before Sawi, her usual glare back on her gilded face.

"Fiends hunt with more than claws," Ami said, not bothering to offer a hand as Sawi, her arm untouched by any flames, found her feet. "They'll rip your mind apart, anything to break you. Don't go tempting them if you're not ready." Ami glanced back towards the Wound, spat towards the gash. "And you, Sawi, are far from ready."

The Vis shivered, rubbed her arm as the crossbows continued to fire, their clicks going on and on until someone whistled the fiend's death. Only then did Ami say they were leaving.

Skipping an offered dinner, skipping any further

lectures and lessons, Sawi retreated back to her skimpy room. The slit window, the thin sheets, the stone walls used to offer little comfort. Now, their certainty gave Sawi everything. She curled up beneath the covers, had her head on the pillow despite the early hour, and would've dropped off to a nightmare sleep right then had not a scratchy sound shot her up. Its source: a letter, pale and clean, sliding in beneath her door. On its front, a particular Tenet's wax seal.

Gladdring.

CHAPTER 10
RUBY ROLL

The deeper they went, the bloodier, the more battle-rended the caves became. Natural walls bore marks not only from claw and fang, but blades and weapons Svarde couldn't identify. Stone chunks, some broken and others clean as if carved off from the perfect ore ceiling lay in their path, easy to avoid as the tunnels grew wide enough for Svarde, Kivi, and the scout Olgata to walk alongside each other.

Forming a line made the fights easier too, the fiends appearing more often as the hours and days crawled by. The monsters came in all shapes, sizes, but matched in a more troubling characteristic: fear. These fiends were fleeing something worse, and while Svarde's trio avoided any massive monsters—Jochi's army would deal with them later—such dodging wouldn't have been possible save for the blind-eyed cowardice in everything they saw. The smaller ones Svarde demanded be cut down, often with a leaping strike from behind or a Kivi ambush from above. Wriggling beetle-like fiends, hapless walking mushrooms, odd mossy horrors, all fell in what became an invigorating cadence: walk, slaughter, camp, and do it all again.

With Kivi's help, the trio would carve out a resting place off the main track, preferably near some pool with drinkable water. Olgata would insist on lighting a small flame, burning some moss, and use that to cook up what they could forage. Boiling, too, the water to ensure any drink came without disease. Stacked stones and Svarde's sheer bulk helped keep the fire's light from traveling, though the fleeing fiends hardly seemed to care.

The flights did, at least, point Svarde in a direction.

"Too many options," Svarde replied early on, when Olgata pondered which branch to take. "We know something's scaring the fiends. Either it's an ally we can use, or it's a worse enemy we need to destroy."

"So long as it's you doing the destroying," Olgata had replied.

Despite her words, the scout was no slouch in combat. She deployed a trick menagerie, using a sling, numerous gadgets fashioned from the rocks and mosses around them, and twin curling stone hammers to annihilate any fiends slipping by Sax. Every time he complimented her on the prowess, though, Olgata would only duck further inside her hood and complain Svarde had forced her hand.

"A scout's job isn't killing," Olgata added just that morning, after they'd crushed a rambling quartet of spindly, spitting spider-like fiends. "Don't like the violence."

"Then you came on the wrong expedition."

"I want to help my isle just the same as you."

Svarde could respect that. He respected, more, Olgata's understanding that principles needed to be set aside when danger demanded it. Where they were going, pacifism wouldn't work.

Nearing midday, they walked out into another pool chamber, this one overflowing with purple and orange fungus. Mushroom caps thin and tall shot up between knotted root tangles. The water beyond bubbled towards the back, some spring making its entry. Only one exit, too, as the cave bent deeper up ahead.

An ideal spot for lunch.

"We break here," Svarde announced, his own stomach already grumbling at the thought. Despite the foraging, despite the fiends they dared eat, soon enough they'd have to find their mark or wait and resupply with Jochi's army. "A long stop."

Olgata defined the two, short and long, as opportunities to grab a bite and take a breath, or clean, prep, and plan. Here, with surprises unlikely and a chance not only to refresh water skins but bathe off the blood from the morning's battle, Svarde figured a few more minutes time might help them push farther into the evening.

Might even get them where they needed to go. The damn world couldn't be too much deeper, could it?

Olgata didn't argue and the pair alternated dips in the water, stepping over the mushrooms into the chilly pool. The cave air always held a loamy stuffiness, always kept a temperature like that of a Foti spring day, minus the occasional hot geyser spewing steam into the stone. While bathing wasn't a big feature of his home isle, where accumulated grit and grime seemed to carry a certain honor, Svarde found his cuts and callouses healed faster when freed from the day's dirt. More so, the baths marked the days better than anything, a sense of progress as Olgata scribed on her growing map the distance between each pool.

Water supplies meant everything to an army on the move.

Jochi's secondary scouts would find her sigils on the cave walls, ones she carved with those stone hammers and pointed chisels. Those would lead the Whent force after them, and—

Kivi's snort turned Svarde around, the pool rippling with his motion. He hadn't gone deep enough to swim, but slick weeds coated the rocks here and even a casual spin sent Svarde off-balance. He flung his arms out in a splash, shook off the water to hear a different noise, a familiar one:

Rana laughter.

Giving Kivi's stone head a pet, mirth bright in her eyes as she stood over Olgata's small fire, was Maena. Svarde's initial elation tempered as fast as it came, the captain's overall appearance proving she wasn't some vanguard, some swift-marching force coming to their relief: Maena's Whent uniform, provided with her rank, bore rips and scuffs everywhere. Her saber belt barely hung on, and Svarde noticed fast she wore only a single shoe.

No satchel in sight, and Maena's face bore the look of someone who'd lived off what her hands could find.

Speaking of finding, Olgata had disappeared. Svarde knew more than to worry, though. The scout likely heard Maena approach and made herself scarce, ready to strike from the shadows if such a thing seemed warranted.

A fiend, after all, could appear as almost anything. And after the mind-taking monster Svarde had seen the last time he'd gone into the depths, he wouldn't disagree with the scout.

"Maena?" Svarde asked, stomping from the pool. His

axes sat near the water's edge. The leathers and other gear remained by the fire. Both hands found hilts, raised the blades. "What are you doing down here?"

"Bored," Maena said, continued to pet Kivi's scales. The lizard snorted again, confused. "They're too slow back there. You were going to get all the glory."

"Glory?"

"You know what I mean."

Svarde had to focus, pick his way through the mushrooms. The tangled fungus tickled his feet, the softness a pleasant shift from dusty rock. That focus, though, meant he couldn't give Maena's words the attention they warranted, because they were strange.

"I do not."

"The end of the fiends, what we're all working for. Why we're down here. I want to be there when it happens." Maena pulled the saber from its sheath, waved it once through the air as Kivi stepped back. "I want to be the one to do it. Destroy the thing that's done so much evil."

Svarde nodded. That, at least, sounded more like the Rana captain. "You and I together."

Maena just grinned back, then looked around the fire as Svarde dressed himself. "Is it just you and Kivi down here?"

Svarde hesitated. Deception wasn't his game, so rather than lying, he chose a different tactic.

"You're looking in bad shape," Svarde said. "Where's your satchel?"

"Lost it. These damn caves, you know?"

"You came alone?"

"Everyone else was too slow. Rasslebeck and Pennifer, they wanted to stay with the army. Where it's safer."

Not the Rasslebeck and Pennifer Svarde knew, but perhaps they'd changed. It'd been days now, and the last dive to the Dark Below had been harrowing. Svarde used his scars to keep charging forward. Others might see them as a reason to slow down.

Svarde waved towards the pool. "Then take the chance to clean up, Maena. We're not in a hurry."

"That, I might do."

Maena unbuckled her sword belt. Svarde reached for a roasted mushroom cap—Olgata had cooked them while Svarde took the first swim—and had the charred, mealy fungus in his mouth when Maena broke into a run, a jump, and then a fully-clothed dive into the pool. The water splashed and Svarde spat out his mushroom, ready to spring to his feet and go after her, when the Rana captain surfaced with a wild laugh. Her voice echoed along the cave walls, bouncing to who knew where.

Kivi snorted. Those echoes would have consequences.

Nonetheless, Maena splashed. She washed herself, her ragged outfight, and Svarde ate. Minutes passed, and Olgata didn't reappear. Something else did.

They came with a steady slither, a slow shake like sand rubbing against stone. Two fiends, their long bodies built not of scales but glittering ruby-like gems. The stones caught the firelight, highlighting opals scattered in amongst the red. Svarde, once again giving up on his lunch, stood and hefted his axes, studied the fiends.

The pair didn't move like snakes, more like liquid, scraping along as a single mass towards Svarde, Kivi, and their fire. They lurched and reformed, almost bobbing along in their motion. No weapons, no claws, no mouths visible.

"What sort of monster are you?" Svarde asked the creatures as they slithered towards him.

"The sort that wants to play!" Maena called from the

pool. "Break them apart, Svarde. Bash them to bits. Or hold on and I'll do it soon."

The captain began splashing her way to shore. Too far to get there in time. Svarde glanced at his axes, tried to figure what'd happen if he tested their Foti-forged metals against a true gemstone. Breaking one down here would put the Guardian in a bad spot.

"Kivi, you're up," Svarde said, taking a step back near the fire and casting his eyes around for another option.

The ferrite took Svarde's invitation and ran with it, literally scurrying to the left and lunging at the nearer ruby rock beast. Kivi led with her mouth, her jaw expanding to reveal gnashing teeth ready to grind stone to delicious dust. The fiend didn't react at all, save to shudder when Kivi bit down on its leading lump. Rather than recoil as Kivi's teeth found purchase, the fiend swept forward, its bulk bunching up and climbing over, around Kivi's head while she chewed.

"Back up!" Svarde called, deciding his axes were worth losing for the ferrite's life.

The Foti warrior brought them both up, made two long strides towards the scrabbling ferrite, now disappearing into the ruby mound. Svarde leapt, flew, and swung both axes down at the creature. The heads bit into the rubies, sparks flying, shudders running up Svarde's arms. The weapon heads held, but they didn't bite in either, Svarde hitting and rolling off the gemstone fiend's back. The monster kept moving forward as Svarde pushed himself to his feet.

Only to see the second one, its stone skin a dark crimson with the fire at its back, bearing down on him without a sound.

CHAPTER II
SWIFT SEA

For someone used to the clean, quiet waters present in Kitaye's tropical inlet, cutting around icebergs and their smaller brethren while waves churned and bitter winds blew made Wax clench the vessel's prow rail with both hands. Leather gloves, fitted and given out by Deux to Bliss, Torny, and Wax as a departure gift proved necessary at blunting the sheer cold. So, too, did the thick cloaks left by the traitorous Kance guards.

'When do we go home again?' Bliss, hunched next to Wax, signed his way. She kept her hands glove free to make it easier, but jammed them into her cloak after every gesture.

Unlike Wax, Bliss seemed solid enough on her feet.

But then, she didn't have the skars rambling in her head. Wax's necklace, carved by the Najahn and placed evermore around his neck, held the three stones. They pressed their warmth against his chest, and with that nearness came a whisper slurry, as if Wax eavesdropped on several conversations at once. In languages he didn't know. Discussing things he couldn't imagine.

Even so, he'd parsed them well enough by now to know them by their whispers. Moreso, by what made them excited. The Vis skar kept itself pretty quiet now, though Wax's lingering aches from the flight out of Noctia kept it muttering. The skar sped the healing along, but it didn't quite work miracles, couldn't turn Wax around in a day.

Then again, if it had, maybe the Rana and Foti skars would be even louder.

The two gemstones seemed to be in a pitched fight, both arguing over the icebergs and the *Storm's Edge*'s deft handling of them. The Rana skar leaped every time Wax laid eyes on the water, as if declaring Wax could swim his way across the ocean with its help. That he'd be far safer among the frigid waves than on the swift boat. And who knew, in warmer waters, maybe the skar really could get him across all that ocean.

The Foti skar pitched opposing advice, howling at Wax to get closer to those floating bergs so it could blast them apart, render the floes little more than the water they floated on. That such a course would freeze Wax as surely as the ice the skar demanded destroyed wasn't a concern. Wax had seen the disregard firsthand when fighting a fiend in Rana's northern marsh: the Foti skar's fire had done in the monster while almost cooking Wax to the core.

"If I win this, I never get to go home," Wax said. "Strange thought, isn't it?"

'Sad, I think.'

"Don't see you having other ideas for how to save the world?"

'Svarde had one.'

The old Foti Guardian? He'd mentioned something about the Dark Below, finding the fiend's source, but Wax hadn't heard anything about the man since leaving Vis.

He'd tried listening around on Noctia, but if Svarde had ever made it to the city, he hadn't been worth noting. Who knew, maybe the man had tried and died just like all the others.

"What, you going to go find some cave and disappear?" Wax asked.

"She wouldn't get far," Torny said, butting into the conversation with several hot tea mugs. "Not without us helping her."

'And how would you help me in a cave?'

Torny's Kance cloak engulfed the smaller bandit, so much so that the steam from her tea mug shrouded her face. Her hands, invisible beneath the cloak's sleeves, left only fingertips on the silver-coated cup. The bandit, though, had been a chipper presence in the several days since leaving Noctia, less bitter and more enthusiastic than before.

A lesson, Wax figured, he could learn.

"Well, I'd point out all the poison mushrooms so you wouldn't gobble them down," Torny said, and when Bliss started signing an objection, Torny kept right on talking. "You'd obviously try to jump in all the wrong pools too, so I'd stop that. Not to mention cooking, which, I've tasted yours, and . . . "

Wax laughed, shook his head. Turned away from the outside while Torny continued poking and prodding Bliss. Raising his tea mug in thanks, the Vis Renewal took a slow walk back into the vessel's upper cabin, squeezing by a deckhand heading out to clear ice from the sails and rigging. A brutal job, that.

Inside, free from the wind, Wax let his hood drop. The skars, too, went quiet as mortal peril left the view, letting him breathe.

"Wax, good timing," Eujo said, walking by on her way to the forward dining room. As usual, the Queen wore a rough regality, with silver-blue Kance robes coupling with a strict stance demanding respect. "Come with me."

Wax looked after her as Eujo kept on walking. No question there, just an order. A habit Eujo hadn't quit, even during their time in Noctia when it seemed like her icy wall was melting, bit by bit. It'd come back on the vessel, though, as if being around her crew and Deux reminded Eujo who she was. Now she prowled the ship intent on action and, finding none, tensed like a hanoko surrounded by hunters.

So Wax had been spending his days mostly outdoors, avoiding Eujo and her biting tongue.

"What do you need?" Wax asked as he followed Eujo into the staid dining room. What'd once seemed so fancy now held scant character, the refined wood and clean walls offering little to love. At least the window gave a good view of the gray sky. "Breakfast?"

"Already had mine." Eujo went to the table's head, beckoned Wax to the foot. "Deux says we're only a day away from Whent's southern coast. The winds are letting us make good time. Which means we have to use what we have left."

"I take it you have an idea. Am I going to like it?"

"You know as well as I do that liking it doesn't matter. If we're going to be successful Renewals, Wax, then we have to use the skars."

"We do? I thought the Aegis just sat there on the throne."

Eujo soured, planted both hands on the table. "Wax, you're not taking this seriously."

"Yeah, well, I'm cold and still hurt. The skars won't stop talking either. Like they're agitated."

"So you hear them."

"Don't you?"

Eujo reached over to her right wrist, where a silver bracer lined her skin with slots for seven skars. Four already lay inside, Kance, Vis, Foti, and Rana. She ran a finger along the gems as she nodded.

"They want to work, Wax. I think we should let them."

Wax laughed, "From what I'm guessing, my Rana skar wants to throw me into the water."

"Exactly." A slight, sly grin.

"Oh, now you want me to drown?"

"I want you to direct it. With me. Use the skar and see what it can do."

The dining room proved nothing more than a preamble, where a deckhand delivered hot tea meant to warm the pair up for the next step. Eujo acquired her cloak, and before Wax could find a real line on what Eujo wanted, they were back outside on the vessel's prow. Again the wind, the whipping waves, the ice sliding left and right as the Kance ship glided past.

"Every time I've used a skar," Wax said, "it's been following the stone's direction. I'm not controlling it. It's an animal."

"That changes today."

"You know how?"

Eujo set her mouth in a line. "Like with anything else, you have to show it who's in charge."

Well, this would be fun. At least Torny and Bliss had retreated inside, so nobody except a couple deckhands working the sails would bear witness to Eujo's bravado.

"Okay, show me how it's done," Wax said, then took a large step right.

"Kance first," Eujo said. "I know it best."

She slid the bracer around so the silver gem shone on top, nearest the back of her hand. Her eyes closed, the fur cloak shuddering with the snapping wind around her. Wax wanted to crack a joke, something to throw off the moment, but nothing came to mind. Not that it mattered: Eujo looked too focused to care.

The reason why made itself known when the ship's sails stretched, a sudden billowing that had the deckhands scrambling to release more tension, keep the canvas from tearing. The vessel shot forward, and someone inside cursed loud enough to overcome the ocean's noise. Ice and water blazed by, Wax grabbing at the railing to steady himself, while Eujo, her left hand clasped over the bracer, appeared utterly unaffected.

Too many minutes went by before the sails relaxed. The ship launched over waves, grazed icebergs in frantic maneuvers. The deckhands scrambled, swapped spots in tumbling exchanges as muscles grew too tired. Through it all, Wax clung to the railing, watching, the cold driving tears down his face. Until, at last, the light dipping into the afternoon, Eujo's eyes opened, her cheeks flushed, and she breathed like she'd just been swinging through the jungle.

"You okay?" Wax asked, letting go his lingering grip.

"Fine," Eujo said, her voice trailing off. "I, I tried to tell it what to do and it didn't listen, Wax. The skar shouted at me." She looked at the bracer, frowned. "I don't understand what it's saying, of course, but it wasn't happy. Not till I relaxed. Until I stopped trying to tell it what to do and let it run wild."

"So it found the sails on its own? Did you see what it did?"

"I felt it." Eujo rubbed the skar, an almost affectionate caress. "It protected me from the wind. Like this cloak, but stronger. Then it came for me."

Wax had felt the same sensations. The Foti skar, after blowing up the Rana fiend, had reached for Wax, snatched at his breath as if to steal it. Even the Vis stone ate at him if the wounds were severe enough.

"So what, then?" Wax asked. "You're saying you can't control it, that it has a mind of its own, that it's not afraid to drink us up if it can. We knew that already."

"I don't think it's that simple. They want things, Wax. They're helping us, and maybe they'll hurt us if we let them. But I don't know why."

Another laugh. "You think the skars have an agenda, Eujo? They're just stones. Awesome stones, but it's not like they're plotting something."

Eujo didn't share the laugh. "Are you sure? The Circle says the skars are pieces of the gods. If that's true, then maybe the gods are still alive in them."

"Getting mystical, Eujo."

"Our world is dying, Wax. It's being invaded, destroyed, torn apart. Reaching for something magical might be our only chance."

The Queen turned to look back over the ocean and Wax followed her gaze. On the horizon, a gray line rose and fell. Whent, almost a full day ahead of schedule. The sight didn't bring the Vis Renewal much comfort.

"Know what I remember from all those legends, Eujo?" Wax muttered.

"What's that?"

"The gods killed each other."

CHAPTER 12
TOWER TRAP

A hunter stalking prey was nothing new. Finding its tracks, learning the creature's preferred foods, its habits, where it slept, Quik had done these things countless times. Masayo, the Third Hand Tenet and Quik's leader for his first Najahn rotation, insisted spying would be much the same.

She had lied.

Quik wiped the spilled tea off the battered mess hall table, the rag already soaking from a dozen other miniature disasters. There'd be another dozen before this pass finished, too. The mess hall, built into a lower Noctia cliff side and benefitting from westward ocean views, a brisk breeze, vaunted its style with sheer size. Several hundred tables mashed into the wood-floored space, buttressed up from the bottom to lunge out into the air. Those tables, bracketed with benches, played host to the Najahn's blubbering masses.

For such an honorable institution, for such well-trained soldiers and scholars, they all descended into slobs once they took their seats.

On Vis, a good meal was something to be valued, savored. Dropping an orange or a mango demanded cleaning off the fruit and, if not eating it yourself, offering it to a pet or delivering it to a composting basket. Here, the plenty invited putrid habits, wanton disregard covering the floors, tables, and chairs.

Yet Quik kept his mouth shut. Followed the shift leader's commands, a man who'd drank too much of his own coffee and seemed on a frenzied quest to keep the mess sparkling clean. An impossible task, but Quik didn't care to tell that frothing face different. Better, as Masayo advised, to keep his eyes open for an opportunity.

If a chance opened for Quik to get near Gladdring's tower, to get inside, he could ditch mess duty forever.

At that thought, just as he had in Masayo's office, Quik scowled. His only audience was another table, another splattered bit of milk and butter. Thievery was Torny's domain. Best it stay that way. His fingers were meant for weapons, not sneaking.

Quik had planned to be subtle with Sawi. Try to meet with her, see if she would help him out, but the gatherer had disappeared. She'd avoided their one planned meeting, a time and place exchanged in a surprise street passing, and while Quik had strived to get to the spot every day since, not once had the Vis kept her word. For now, a lost cause.

Hope, though, came near the shift's end, with the mess moving from breakfast to lunch. A late breakfast order came in, delivered by a harried scholar bearing Gladdring's Trade Tenet pin. The interweaving arrows and satchels didn't gleam much in the winter gray, but as Quik squeezed out his rag into a massive, dirty barrel—dumped, later, into the sea in a spectacular, gross display—he noticed the scholar's own scowl and the man's thin arms.

"You'll need help carrying all that," Quik said as the kitchen's cooks sprang into action, popping eggs into iron pans and pulling onions from sacks about to be set away. "I have the time."

The scholar flicked his eyes up to Quik's face, ran them along the smeared apron protecting Quik's Najahn robes. The scowl flipped up to a curious line, followed by a nod. "I believe you're right on both counts. If you're offering assistance, I'd be glad to have it."

During their long walks on Foti, when Torny would yammer on and on about her bandit life, she'd often come back to confidence and kindness being two great, if often forgotten, tools in a thief's arsenal. Make someone believe you belonged, or that you meant well, and doors would open without needing any key.

Quik deployed that maxim while they waited for the food, pitching questions about the scholar's day, his duties, why he'd wound up in the trade tower. Any defenses the scholar might've put up were disarmed when Quik explained he was a new recruit, just trying to learn how the Najahn worked. When the scholar fell into a far too long, far too detailed diatribe on cross-isle trade negotiations, Quik fought to keep his own smile hidden.

He'd won his way in. And Torny did have a point: it did feel pretty darn satisfying.

In the scholar's defense, the meal would've been impossible for him to carry. Three baskets and a serving tray stuffed with omelettes and sides. Quik nabbed that and looped two baskets over his shoulders, letting the scholar keep a smidge of honor with the third.

The scholar kept up the chattering, taking Quik's single syllable replies as invitations to carry on, all the way to the Trade tower. Quik hesitated as they went inside the normal wood-and-black metal door, expecting some other riddle inside like the Third Hand. Instead, normal hallways, lined with purple carpeting and hanging art, greeted him. The scholar took a sharp left, climbing stairs up one level after another. Quik tried to memorize the details, tried to keep an eye out at every landing for possible things Masayo might find valuable.

All he saw were more scholars, all he heard was muttering about trade deals, questions on lunch or dinner, and the usual complaints about the coming cold.

The scholar directed Quik to what looked like a meeting room, decorated with framed trading contracts and dominated by a single large table. Purple-cushioned chairs lined the dark wood slab, branded with the Trade tower's sigil in the center. Quik set up the food under the scholar's direction, the latter letting his sticky fingers claim some snacks in the process.

"You can find your own way, can't you?" the scholar asked when Quik had finished, the man already sitting near the table's head. "We'll be starting soon and I really don't have time to walk you out."

"I can find it."

The scholar flicked his fingers towards the door, "As you were, then." The man seemed to catch himself as Quik turned to leave. "And welcome to the Najahn. Thank you for the help."

There, see? Not everyone here is so wrapped up in their own minds to be impolite.

Quik shut the door behind him, stepping into a hallway with two options: to his right lay the short path back to the periphery stairs he'd climbed to get here. A straightforward way out, and not the least bit interesting. Instead, Quik took slow steps towards the tower's center. Along the way, he stiffened his spine, tried to shake any curiosity off his face.

He belonged here, in this tower, in this place. He had to, in order to win support for his brother.

Reminding himself of Quik's core purpose played a particular trick, ignited a certain flame. Striding with more purpose, Quik walked past a scholar pair without a question, made it to the tower's center and realized he'd hit the top floor. The only direction lay down.

A curling stair descended through the tower's middle, wide enough for multiple people to travel abreast, and stopping at landings along every level. Quik made the trek with care, padding his feet slow enough to get a good look at the several floors he passed only to find no answers waiting. Najahn bustled about, many on their own work while others escorted merchants or ambassadors from the other isles. Nothing seemed secretive, nothing worth a closer look.

Quik didn't entertain breaking into rooms, testing closed doors. A spy he could pretend to be, but a thief's practical skills lay outside his practice.

Which meant he hit the ground floor and the hall leading to the tower's exit without evidence. Nothing to deliver to Masayo, and therefore nothing to help his brother. The stairs, though, did continue down, and in the first interesting thing he found, Quik realized conversation and clutter's chorus didn't rise from the lower levels.

The dorms, maybe, for people living in the tower. Or something worth his attention.

Put against simply leaving with nothing, choosing to break down the stairs was a simple ask.

Differences made themselves obvious in the first few steps below the tower's main level. The art, first, dwindled.

The stone seemed colder, the steps less worn. The first level down confirmed itself as a dorm, albeit one less crowded than the Third Hand's own. Quik's initial confusion found its answer in the building itself, its purpose. Traders would be moving about, staying on vessels or at the isles striking deals. Not so many needed just at Noctia.

The stairs continued, and so did Quik. At least till he put the next landing in view.

Two chairs, a table. Sitting at it, grubby cards striking the surface between the pair, were guards. Voulges and chakrams. Beyond, a single hallway going off somewhere. No further stairs below.

What would a trader need to protect?

The rush hit and Quik fought the urge to drop into a crouch. This, here, was a chance. A place. But how to get past it? What could he say to the—

A voice carried up. Out from the hallway and up the stairs, coming this way. Sawi. Announcing a meeting with Gladdring that she'd be late for if she didn't get moving. Another voice answered, light and laughing, declaring Sawi was at last getting what she wanted. Quik, halfway down the stairs and yet to draw the guards' attention, turned around.

Only to find a woman as large as himself barring his path. Her face glinted gold, a plate drawing Quik's eye from her folded arms, her scowl. Inset there, twinkling against their host, were three skars. A green Vis, Quik recognized. And a red Foti. But the amber?

"Lose your way?" the woman asked.

Quik tried to find a lie, something that'd make sense. Stumbled out the words, "I was delivering food."

"Nobody down here ordered any food. Try again."

"Upstairs. I got lost."

The woman's eyes narrowed. One hand started to drop towards a dagger on her waist. Below, Quik heard chairs sliding, guards getting to their feet.

"Quik?" Sawi said, making her entrance below. "What are you doing here?"

Quik twisted. His hunter's poise losing itself in a situation he'd never before been in, never been trained for. Masayo, damn her, hadn't told Quik what to do if it all fell apart.

"Oh," the woman mused, "this is getting interesting. Quik, why don't you come with me. When Sawi's done with her little chat, we can decide what to do with you."

When Quik tried to protest, when he repeated his food delivery claim, Sawi could only grimace. Could only say he wouldn't be hurt if he didn't do something stupid. That she was sorry they hadn't met earlier, but she really had to go now.

"You, though, get to stay," the woman said, pushing Quik down the hallway. "And I can guarantee you're going to have a good time."

CHAPTER 13

PARTY TARGET

Whent did not make a good first impression. Eager as she was to get off the zippy Kance vessel, Torny nonetheless slowed her walk towards the ship's side as they drew near the rocky city's port. Lying to the east of a large beach, gliding into the docking meant absorbing a long, clean view of carnage.

Blackened pits marred snowy sands. Broken towers stood in shambles, their bricks and mortar scattered about like a child's playthings. Fire-ravaged buildings beyond left their charred husks open to the winter's bite, with few people working to repair them back to health. The only hope came from the city's academy, its splendor nestled into the cliffside over the port and seemingly untouched by whatever disaster struck its neighbors.

'This is grim,' Bliss signed, joining Torny.

Both had packed satchels beneath their Kance cloaks, walking boots ready. The cloak helped hide Torny's tool menagerie, sparing the bandit any awkward questions. Her twin lives were coming together here, but the longer Torny could put that off, the better. A debt to Yarvick would be better cleansed without the Vis crew ever learning about it.

And if the bandit leader had the right information, the diary he sought would be somewhere in this city. Somewhere nice.

Deux guided the *Storm's Edge* in slow, deckhands scurrying about with their counterparts on the Whent side to tie off the boat. The dock, unlike those in Noctia and, well, everywhere else, was built of stone, with massive, carved gray bricks resting in the sea. When Torny's boots hit the pier, it felt sturdier than some ground she'd walked on. That, coupled with the swaying sensation striking whenever Torny ditched the seas for land, had the thief unsteady for her first few steps.

Bliss, skipping along and utterly unaffected, made no effort to spare her mockery.

"Just wait," Torny countered as the pair made their way to shore, "some day you'll suck at something, and I'll be there ready."

'Not happening.'

A cocky one, that Vis. Also, a trick to leave behind. Torny's excuse had worked on Noctia, but their reason for being the first off here wasn't one of sightseeing but work. Find out where the Whent skars were, then plot the best way to get there. Eujo and Wax would be packing up their materials, making arrangements for Deux and the ship, then coming ashore later to find whatever welcome Whent gave to Renewals.

A welcome Torny needed to enhance.

'So, where do we go now?' Bliss signed as they went into the port proper.

Winter and a smaller size meant the docks were near-deserted, only a couple other Whent caravels rested in the port and neither looked nearing to sail. One lonely tavern had a sign in its frosted window claiming it'd be back in spring. Crates and barrels bore a snowy coat suggesting a long time sitting. Beyond the silent warehouses a gravel street beckoned.

"You want to get to know a place, normally I'd say hit the bars," Torny said as they crunched along towards the first burnt buildings. "But I'm guessing this place is lacking in good cheer." It also seemed empty for its size. Assault or no, the number of clear smokestacks suggested a city half deserted. "Instead, let's use what we've got."

'What's that?'

"Two Renewals, and one of them's a queen."

Torny rode that argument through the town proper—a ramshackle place split between haphazard rebuilding efforts and glazed families trying to cook food—and towards the academy set in the overlooking cliffside. As they neared, though, Torny slanted her direction, making instead for larger homes and a wealthier district set alongside the learning institution.

'You're not talking much,' Bliss signed.

"Thinking. Planning. You know, all those things a thief needs to do."

'A thief? Aren't you a Guardian now?'

"Multiple hats, Bliss."

Torny embodied that ethos in the moment too, trying to run back the details Yarvick gave her. Information, so he said, collected from some hapless former bandit who'd taken on the diary job before Torny came back. That one had narrowed down its location before getting himself caught with grubby hands after a dinner. A quick trip to the Pits and a long, suffering demise followed.

Such was the way of thieves in Whent.

The description Yarvick passed along worked well enough, guiding Torny passed gated, sloping estates pressed up against the rock. Most sprawled out a shrubby yard before the building proper, all wintry beauty as snow clustered on bare tree limbs and spindly bushes. Songbirds, untroubled by their home's near annihilation, hopped about and twittered. The wind seemed to take exception, racing up in unexpected gusts to overpower the chirps with snapping roars. Myriad chimes sounded every time too, shimmering in arched stone windows and entries, as if in answer to the elements.

"That's the one," Torny said aloud, catching herself at Bliss's curious look. "I mean, that's a good place to try."

'To try what?'

"Getting our information."

Torny's target had three levels, all in ascending, contracting layers, like some fabulous cake. After the ground floor, each one began with a wrap-around balcony, white railings that likely bore ivy in the summer providing bare barriers to an open view. Occasional arches and walls jutted out along those levels, splitting the wraparound into private places, some covered and others not. Just like Yarvick's description.

And the place already had a crowd.

Unlike the dockworkers and masons trying to repair the town, the people milling around here looked the type with smooth hands. Even ignoring the two guards at the gate— Torny would have a story ready to spin for them shortly— the people beyond moved with the affected air of the privileged, a floating glide-step around grounds where the snow had been cleared. Someone inside played music, a stringed instrument making its way around a piece with skill too refined for pub nights and chance practices.

"This is definitely what we're looking for," Torny muttered. "Keep quiet, Bliss. I'll do the talking."

'Shouldn't be a problem.'

Torny turned a laugh into a half-smile. Of course Bliss would play along. That's what made her so great. She'd come right into any dumb adventure. The key, though, would be getting Bliss gone when Torny had to do the real thing. Or perhaps gone wasn't the right word.

Was it mean to use your friends? Even if it meant salvaging your life?

The two guards showcased Whent wraps, thick brown overcoats leading to fat picks at their waists, as if they might jump off to start a mine at any moment. One smoked a pipe while the other nursed a steaming mug of something, probably tea. Behind them, a wood gate marked the entry to the estate. Already, Torny felt curious eyes on her from the building. People in a place like this would always be looking for some new drama, some new interest.

Riches only bought boring lives.

"Hey there," Torny opened, drawing blank stares.

"We've already given to the reconstruction efforts," the first guard, the taller and pipe smoker of the two, replied. "You need more help, look for it somewhere else."

Torny nodded, glanced back towards the damaged city. "Yeah, pretty clear your home needs some more help, but that's not what I'm here for." The guard didn't answer, just narrowed his eyes. "See, I'm a Guardian. So's she. Thought your boss might like to know a couple Renewals just landed in your city."

"Renewals from where? It's too cold for sailing."

"Not for a Kance Queen, it isn't. You know they can dodge the ice like it's a stone in a field."

"Then where is she?"

"Dealing with more important things. Tell your lord or lady they can get the two biggest stars on the isle in their place tonight. All it'll cost them is some food, some drink, and a nice fire to warm our hands. Something to take the sea's edge off, you know."

The guard didn't move. Those eyes stayed narrowed. "She comes here, she can say what you did and maybe we'll get to talking."

Torny pressed her lips together. Tried to come up with the next thing to say. Playing the royalty card should've done the trick. At least, that's how it worked in all the stories.

'Is there another place?' Bliss signed at Torny, the guard's curious stare flashing her way. 'If you can't get what you want, try taking it somewhere else. Make them jealous. My mother did that all the time with the traders.'

"Good point," Torny said, turning back to the guard. "My friend and fellow Guardian here senses, like I do, that you're not into playing host. Guess we'll go ask the academy instead. See if they're willing to let the world's saviors come by for a night."

The guard laughed. "The academy? Most of them went off with Jochi. It's as empty as the city. They won't help you."

"Jochi?"

"The reason the city's so deserted. The warlord decided to go on some fool's march into the Dark Below. Took most of our fighting-age people with him. A crusade to save the world, or so he said." The guard shook his head, chuckled. "That's what the Renewal's are for, I said, when he asked me. No way I'm going to *find* more fiends."

Ah, an opening. Always better when a mark gave you the key themselves.

"Then you do think the Renewals are important?" Torny asked.

"Sure, I just . . . " the guard tapered off, glanced over his shoulder back at the house. "Look, you're not lying? Not after something else?"

Bliss shook her head. Torny went straight for the kill, "You don't have to let us in now. We'll be back, Renewals and plenty of proof. You put the word out, and I swear, you and your lord will look like heroes."

"If you're lying, it'll mean my job."

"If I'm telling the truth and you leave us in the streets, that'll be just as bad," Torny countered. Then snapped her fingers, whirled, and pulled off Bliss's hood. "Does she look like a Whent to you? This is a Vis Guardian. Right here, in the flesh."

The two guards had a hard time arguing with the obvious. They gave Torny a few hours head start, told her to come back with the Renewals near the dinner hour—the afternoon, already, was growing long—and the estate would be ready with a proper welcome.

"See?" Torny said as the two loped back towards the docks. "Easy."

'Thanks to me.'

"A hero always needs her sidekick," Torny agreed.

'Not what I meant.'

Torny just laughed, let her mind turn back to the estate, the levels, and where in that massive place a certain diary might be hiding.

CHAPTER 14
CIRCLE SPY

The Tenet faded. Sawi watched Gladdring throughout the long lunch, one where, aside from a few token questions about Vis and how superior she found Noctia, Sawi was ignored. The various scholars and officials there, eight in all, seemed far more interested in getting words in with the Tenet, spewing some random babble his way to earn an approving nod or, the best thing, a remark calling their idea good, their proposal smart, their initiative in the best interests of the Najahn.

Watching Gladdring work outside the desperate and deadly traps in Mottilan took Sawi on a different path than she'd intended. The surprise encounter with Quik, she'd shoved away into the same part of her mind where she stored any lingering feelings for Wax, her family, her culture. A spot to be visited only when the stars came out and Sawi her sole confidant. Instead, Sawi spent the steps turning over questions, offenses, and the general grievance that'd suffused her in the days since coming to this desolate city. She'd been promised adventure, not experiments and thrashings courtesy of Ami and Annalyse. She'd been told to stay loyal, to trust that Gladdring had great things in store for her, and thus far the greatest thing Sawi had seen was the quality of the ale.

Noctia could turn out a good beer, at least.

Gladdring's chosen meeting space worked well to amplify his effect: clustered along walls and floor with various trinkets from across the isles, the place reminded Sawi and everyone else who entered exactly where they were, the Trade Tenet. The setting staged, Gladdring used it to pit his guests against one another, nudging them into greater concessions or onto riskier platforms, where he'd then cut down their plans in public fashion, not quite humiliating but teaching the Najahn attending how to achieve goals at first glance impossible.

"Don't merely secure next season's rice from Rana, but get all their prime wool too," Gladdring suggested once, prompting his target, a sweating man wearing too many robes, to bluster out that such an ask would be too expensive. "Only if you don't find what they value most."

"And how am I supposed to do that? A straight question would get me laughed out of their city."

"Ask the raider captains when they come to our port. Find out what they seek with their cutters, and get it. Buy it all off their targets and hold it ransom." Gladdring kept his hands steepled the entire time, pieces and plays moving behind his eyes. "Then, when they acquiesce, turn around and demand a fee from those same targets for our protection. Everybody, but mostly us, wins."

Nods and mutters of approval smattered around the table, whereupon Gladdring turned to the next received a new problem to eviscerate. Through it all, Sawi ate and listened, waited for her chance, which didn't come until the lunch concluded and the Tenet dismissed all the others from the room. He waved for Sawi to come closer, sit at a nearby chair.

"No reason to shout across the table without all those nattering voices," Gladdring said as Sawi relocated.

"They work for you, don't they?" Sawi asked. "If you don't like them, why keep them?"

"All sorts of reasons, most of them political." Gladdring rubbed his temples. "They're all someone's son, an ambassador's daughter. Favors upon favors." He sighed. "Sawi, I'm sorry to drag you into this game. I can only imagine how much more delightful the trees of Vis must seem right now."

"They are better than the stone box you've put me into."

"A box with a bed and a pillow is far better than some."

Sawi chose to drink her water instead of reply. The cold liquid here always shocked her, so different than the warm rain drops or sweet coconut juice she'd suck down at home. Which was better? She might, grudgingly, give this one to Noctia.

"The Najahn rule Noctia, the Circle rules the Najahn, and Fassle rules the Circle," Gladdring commenced, his voice falling into a teacher's plodding register. "Fassle has two Adepts working beneath him, with the rest of us Tenets a step below. It's a heirarchy, and an immutable one. Anything I do can be forbidden, destroyed, or co-opted by Fassle at his whim."

"If he knows about it, you mean."

Gladdring blinked once, then curled up a lip. "So you're not a novice."

"I've been working with you for a little while now."

"Then yes, yes, you're right. When I had few skars and fewer people working with me, Fassle had little chance of discovery. Little at risk even if he did find I was playing with the gemstones. All Tenets have their own forays." Gladdring reached into his robe, pulled out the amber stone. Ami said that was the source of Gladdring's ability to swing a room, a Tamas skar. "Yet our adventure is growing too large. We're making too much progress. People are noticing.

This leaves us with two options, Sawi. Either I can go to Fassle and ask for his approval, thereby passing over all control to him. What Fassle would do with such control, I'm not sure, though he's so invested in maintaining the old order that I doubt his actions would be helpful. More likely, the skars would be stuffed away, you sent home, and my position replaced with someone more pliable."

"They'd kill you."

Gladdring shrugged, continued twisting the amber stone between his fingers. "It's the right move. I'd represent a threat, especially if I began talking up the skars potential as weapons against the fiends. Fassle hates all threats, particularly those that involve the common people."

"Why?"

"Losing power is any despot's nightmare, Sawi. Fassle believes the only way he'll be removed is if Noctia, all the Najahn, rise up against him."

Sawi shook her head, looked back at her water as if it held some sort of comfort. Nothing Gladdring said seemed a revelation, nothing left her befuddled or in any shock. Instead, it all seemed pointless.

"You're telling me all this why?" Sawi asked.

"Because you're going to help me destroy Fassle in the very way he doesn't expect," Gladdring replied. "With your help, we'll twist those closest to him, tear apart his power, and when the vacuum is exposed, I will fill it. Then, nothing will stop us from using the skars to defend the isles."

"Back on Vis, I used to tell Wax—my friend—all the time that he's getting crazy." Sawi expected the confused glower on Gladdring's face and earned it. "He would go on like you about some grand adventure. But when we pressed him on it, all he had was hunches. Treasure, miracles, something incredible if we could just do all these difficult things. You're the same way."

"Dreamers are truly cursed," Gladdring replied. "Nevertheless, I have something your friend did not: power. Real power. The kind that will ship you back to Vis the moment you refuse my request."

A threat, but probably not the kind Gladdring thought it was. Getting sent back to Vis would mean more sunny days, no more stone cell or strange sessions with Ami. Sawi would have fresh fruits, meals, and friends. Her parents, siblings. A return to a well-lived life.

But she'd lose out on the adventure. How much was that worth, really?

"What's your plan?" Sawi asked.

It couldn't hurt to find out.

The Circle's chamber sat inside the massive central Najahn spire. Visitors, of which Sawi was one, were escorted to an overhead viewing area and reminded, several times, to stay quiet. Any remarks, shouts, or disturbances would prompt immediate banishing, or worse. They searched her, found no daggers, darts, or arrows.

They did not question or take the amber stone from the necklace around her neck.

Sawi began to put together Gladdring's bigger plan while he explained his smaller one, starting with the moment the skar hit her skin. The amber stone spoke differently than the elemental ones she'd tried already, but its whispers weren't so foreign, so surprising. All those sessions with Ami prepared Sawi for the burst in her mind, the soft questions floating through every time she looked at someone.

Right now Sawi leaned on the overlook's edge, lanterns ringing the space sending their orange-gold light down to the circular table in the center. There Fassle sat, decked in gold jewelry over black robes. His Adept pair, masked head to toe in purple cloth, took neighboring chairs. That much clothing couldn't have been comfortable, but the pair didn't shift, didn't make a sound as Fassle droned on through ordinary business.

Gladdring and the other Tenets, at least those on Noctia, filled out the Circle's room. They listened as Fassle described increasing fiend attacks and Najahn countermeasures. As he pitched a new peace brokered between Whent and Rana after the former saved a pursued fleet from fiends. Rumors off Kance, meanwhile, suggested the old Queen had no love for her younger, popular counterpart.

"We cannot have a fracture on that isle, not now," Fassle said, the voice a weaseled rasp. "I look to this group to use what pressures you have to quell their infighting."

The Tamas skar provided more interesting commentary. Sawi focused on Fassle first, sparking the skar into an excited rambling. Sawi couldn't understand the words, but impressions came along with them, much like the Foti skar's aggressive urges or the Kance stone's desire to jump, to fly. Here, the pushes came with moods, Fassle's moods.

Boredom paired with his words, not a worried flicker as he went through the truce, the Kance in-fighting. Nothing here warranted real interest on Fassle's part, real concern.

"Now, the last item this morning," Fassle said, and he dropped the paper, placed his hands palms down on the hard wood table. The Tamas skar buzzed into a different life, setting Sawi's heart running. "Word is a Whent warlord has assembled a large force and sent it into the Dark Below. They are, so our friends on that isle say, attempting to find the fiend's source and stop them." Fassle frowned. "A noble, if foolish goal. Throwing away that many lives with a Renewal in full swing is a terrible disaster. I've asked the ambassador to turn this debacle around. I beseech you all to attempt the same. We must support the Renewal, not these hopeless crusades."

And there it was. The skar giving its smug, unintelligible advice. Fassle was a coward, would do anything to keep his power. As she ran her eyes across the others in the room, Sawi found, thanks to the skar, those feelings were not shared. Other Tenets had the skar revealing disappointment in muttered whispers. Even the guards on station felt deflated at Fassle's announcement.

Gladdring wanted Fassle destroyed. Those in this room seemed willing to see him deposed. But how, how to get these people to act on their feelings? How to turn a miserable silence into an active rebellion?

On that score, at least, Sawi had an idea.

CHAPTER 15

OLD BONES

As a man, Svarde rarely found himself flying. It just wasn't a thing that happened to the barbarian, what with his heavy furs, armors, axes, and demeanor warding away any such contact for fear of losing life and limb. However, when Olgata's swift, slim form slammed into Svarde's side and carried both of them beyond the attacking ruby mass, Svarde forgave the scout immediately and set about standing up, again, on the dusty cave floor.

Olgata's dive sent them into the cavern's swooping wall, opposite the lake and most of the action. While their red quarry didn't so much turn as extend its rippling, shimmering self their way, Kivi's scrabble took on a more interesting twist. The ferrite, freed by Svarde's bellowing charge, used her speed to dance around the creature, darting in and taking bites with random ferocity. Crunched rubies dribbled from Kivi's lips like frozen blood.

More than that, Svarde didn't have time to take in, as he had axes to swing and a fiend to fight. With Olgata dashing off to Svarde's right, up the tunnel, on what seemed to be

105

all fours, Svarde himself took all the fiend's attention. He gave it a worthy curse and slapped his axes at the reaching ruby blob. Near half his size, the fiend rushed right towards Svarde's gut.

Or, at least, it did until meeting Svarde's twin blades. Each axe, honed by Whent stonecraft, bit into the rubies with a sparking crash. Svarde's fingers went numb at the shivering strike, while red flecks caught torchlight to become glittering crimson snow. The fiend halted its outreach, as if surprised to encounter any resistance.

A chance Svarde didn't let go.

He stepped left, circling back down the tunnel with one eye on Olgata, who'd given up her flight and now, instead, had her marking chisel and hammer drawn. The fiend recovered its lapse, turning its bulging mass to follow Svarde, opening up its back—or front? Did this thing really have either?—for Olgata to strike.

Slashing his axes, taking bits and pieces off with every blow, Svarde saw the scout make her move. Saw, too, a different shape following the scout, one taking a moment to recognize at the sheer oddity of her presence: Maena, soaked clothes dripping, stepping into the battle with her saber drawn. She paced Olgata, coming behind the scout. The torchlight from behind cast both in a shadowed black, save for the saber.

The ruby fiend stole Svarde's attention, swiping in low at the man's feet. The attack came in slow, and Svarde chose to leap, a half-jump bringing him up the fiend to land on its shining mass. Gemstone skin proved a slick landing, the leap a poor choice that had Svarde's feet sliding out and dropping him hard onto the fiend's back. Both axes skittered from hands slapped against hard, smooth skin.

"Hurry!" Svarde called, the shout as compressed as his lungs.

The move earned Olgata her time, and the scout bit deep with the chisel, striking it almost in the same motion with her hammer. Chunks flew, and Svarde felt the monster shiver. Wanted to roar in victory, only there, again, was Maena stalking after Olgata. The scout had her hammer raised for a second blow, what would be the last strike as the fiend reversed its swiping appendages, and behind her the Rana captain loomed.

This close, a couple strides apart, Svarde saw a dangerous gleam against Maena's eyes, a reflection off the fiend's scales casting both the scout and her follower in a sunset red. The saber angled towards Olgata's gut, began to drive forward.

"Maena," Svarde growled, only for Olgata to break off her chisel attempt at the last moment. The saber flashed by the scout's right side, struck a ruby outreach Svarde couldn't see, could only hear.

Maena whipped the saber back and forth, swinging with enough force to spark stones across the cavern. Her saber bore the brunt, the blade chipping and breaking until, as Svarde pushed himself off the fiend and fell to the side, all the Rana captain had left was a jagged metal shard. That shard made a questionable weapon against the fiend, its short reach failing as the fiend pressed Maena backward.

One slip, one poor strike, and the captain would be devoured.

"Over here," Olgata said, a dead calm in her voice. "They won't get us in the water."

"How can you know?" Svarde asked, again pushing himself up off the hard ground, making for the pool.

Kivi snorted, her agreement giving Svarde confidence

despite the scout's silence. The ferrite, its own duel apparently ending in a draw, darted past Svarde and jumped into the pool. No light feather, Kivi started to sink, a process stopping only as its rapid paddles and momentum carried it to the rightward wall, whereupon the ferrite scaled the side and took up refuge on the ceiling.

Svarde followed, joining Olgata and soon enough Maena at the pool's edge and beyond. The scout treaded water, urged them all to go deeper. Svarde and Maena obliged, once again embracing the chill. Through it all, while Svarde cursed up a storm, Maena only laughed, waved her saber's ruin about like some hilarious trophy.

"They won't try it," Olgata claimed as Svarde reached her near the pool's center. "Watch."

Indeed, the fiends took Olgata's dare and ran from it. Both morphed their way to the pool's edge, touching the water and the wriggly plants before coming to some shared decision to leave. Without a sound, without any way of communicating Svarde could see, both marred monsters shifted their glittering, gelatinous selves and moved up the tunnel, towards the surface and, eventually, Jochi's army.

"We'll need to warn them," Olgata said as the two fiends left.

"They'll be fine," Maena countered, at last chucking her useless blade into the water. "A few more hammers and instead of fiends, they'll have a fortune's worth of rubies." Maena spun, splashed once at Olgata, earning the Rana captain a glare. "Besides, how're you going to warn them? Run all the way back? Let Svarde keep going without you?"

"I'd be just—" Svarde started, only for Maena to splash him.

"Not talking to you," Maena said, throwing Svarde a

wild smile. "Olgata, I asked you a question. How? What's your plan, scout? Can't tackle your way out of this one."

Olgata, dripping, didn't answer. Instead, she swam by Maena, picked herself from the pool. Lofted the torch while Svarde and Maena joined her.

"Like the captain says," Olgata muttered as the trio stood, Kivi clutching the cave ceiling over their heads. "They'll be fine. Let's go."

You would think wandering through caves would get old. Rock, though, held endless permutations. The deeper Svarde went, the more variations he found, from dangling smooth teeth to puddles seemingly arising from nowhere, cupped in cuddly stone. The curling way would rise and fall, writhe left to right, branch and dead end to force backtracks or squeezes.

Those last dwindled now, not least because they had a clear trail to follow: the ruby scales weren't just hard skin, they chipped off plenty as the meandering mounds migrated their way through the tunnels. Every few strides would find a few red specks catching torchlight in a glimmer, leading them on.

Nobody needed to ask why they ought to follow the fiends: the monsters came from the very place Svarde wanted to be. Wherever these monsters emerged, that was the door Svarde needed to close. With his hands, his axes, or his life if need be. The others must've felt the same, as nobody objected, suggested another way.

The ruby road, as Maena joked an hour into their next march, broadened into another cavern, this one bearing a different look than the more-natural spaces they'd found before.

"Carved out," Olgata noted, and Svarde could only agree.

The walls here didn't have water's smoothing effect, but instead bore a straighter-edged cleave to them, underlying stone laid bare with a hammer, a pick-axe, something larger. The floor held itself smooth, with spare rocks missing, as though someone swept it. On the far side, several large tunnels broke off downward, with one more almost directly to Svarde's right and staying level. Smeared across the ceiling and in carved nooks along the walls sat glowing mossy clusters, their bio-light spitting a cerulean blue around the room, just bright enough to cast shadows wherever anything sat.

Those shadows spilled everywhere, because the chamber was far from empty. Kivi snorted a warning and Svarde drew his axes as they looked around. Olgata even backed up a step, letting Maena take her place beside the Foti. The reason: bodies, many. The motionless, ragged forms—Svarde could tell, even in the dim light, that this wasn't some well-equipped army facing defeat—lay still in all positions, showing the rigid aftermath of a bad battle. Between them, as if scattered favors for the dead, were ruby piles. Chunks lying in unnatural clumps, inert.

"Guess we know what happened to the other slugs," Maena muttered, stepping past Svarde and heading towards the first body. "Look at this guy. He's had his whole chest bashed in."

With Kivi sticking to her ceiling climb, an ideal ambush position, Svarde joined Maena in the gruesome inspection. The Rana captain had it right, the man—clearly a man, too—had suffered a mortal blow. Still, as Svarde looked closely, trying to find weapons or some clue beyond the faded rags as to where the man came from, he picked up other oddities.

"He took a hit, but he's looking like he never felt it,"

Svarde said, pointing an axe at the man's head. Lit in the eerie blue, the man's closed eyes and shut, straight mouth suggested an easy sleep over a sudden, painful death. "Either that or he's the most peaceful dead I've ever seen."

Maena knelt by the body, ran a hand along the man's pants-covered leg, tracing what looked like a dreadful cut. "There's only bone under here. A slice like this should've had him dead too." Maena frowned, tapped the dead man's leg twice. "Thing is, I don't recall those slugs having swords."

Olgata, behind the pair and still standing at the entrance, whistled. "This isn't a normal place. Use your noses. This many bodies should reek of death. There ought to be maggots on every one, even down here."

"Hate to say it," Maena said, standing up, "but I think the scout's right. But if these people are long dead, then who took out the slugs?"

Svarde checked two more bodies, found the same evidence. Multiple wounds that should've downed a person, none a likely consequence from fighting the slugs. More, weapons abounded on the ground, many sharp and well-cared for. Not suggesting they'd been lingering in the dark without owners. Questions upon questions, and eventually answered in the way Svarde hated the most.

Kivi's snort tipped them off, an urgent blast jerking Svarde's axes to the ready. Maena's laugh, hopeless and confused, followed. Olgata, still back at the tunnel's entrance, cursed and backed up a step. She should've run.

Because the damn dead were standing up all around them, and if the slugs were any clue, these bones wouldn't be friendly.

CHAPTER 16
NIGHT OUT

Before Noctia, Wax would've treated preparing for a wild, fancy night at some estate—not that he'd even known what an estate was back then—the same way he would've for a feast around a Kitaye fire: with not a care. Eujo dashed those dreams quick back in the Ringed City, though, taking Wax, Bliss, and Quik straight out to get clothes more suitable for the sort of civilization a Queen expected to enjoy. Those finer linens, in Wax's estimation, tended to be soft if thin, breezy but a hassle to keep clean and nice.

Much better to wear a weave and not give a damn what happened to it, because you could make another with some random vines the next day.

Nevertheless, he saw the utility in those preparations now, as their foursome walked the evening through the city up towards the estate. Torny had come flouncing back with her acquired invitation, offering Wax and Eujo something other than floundering on the boat for the evening. Deux declared he and the deckhands could use a break from entertaining, spend the time cleaning the ship, prepping satchels for the overland journey towards wherever the Whent skars were. Eujo took the sign for what it was and scooted the whole party into their rooms, demanding fine dress, and out they emerged, clad in warm furs and finery beneath.

Standing near the ramp to the dock, Wax resisted the urge to laugh at his sister in a real dress. She seemed uncomfortable enough, twisting beneath the coat Eujo chose for her, pulling at the silky fabric as if it was sticky tree sap. Torny wasn't much better off, though if the bandit thought nobody noticed the tools she'd secreted away beneath her overlarge coat, Wax would have to disappoint her.

Then again, Eujo didn't say a word, and neither did the guards outside the estate when they arrived, so perhaps Torny's secrets would stay that way.

"Once we get inside," Eujo said as they walked through the gate, heads high and faces confident per the Queen's instruction, "we'll split up. Except Bliss. Stick with Torny, so you can, um . . ."

'I get it.'

"She knows how to handle herself," Torny said as Wax readied the same words, letting them fall into an appreciative look towards the bandit.

"Right," Eujo said as they continued down a wide cobblestoned walk, its bordering bushes coated with lovely shoveled snow. Flickering torches lit the way, their flames reflecting off the white ground. "The point, we're looking for two things here. One, where the Whent skars are located and any tips on how to find them. Two, supplies, wagons for travel."

"Can't just buy all that, my Queen?" Torny asked.

"After all I've had to give up for you three, no, I can't."

Wax smiled. The two had their knives-out banter going strong. Had, well, ever since the roller back on Rana. The edges beneath had softened though. Once Torny realized Eujo hadn't always been royalty, hadn't always had life's sweet things thrown her way, the stabs stopped getting so direct.

The estate glimmered in the early night much like its own walkway. Rising up against the rock, the yellow edifice shone with its many torches, sang with soft music rising from inside, and bubbled with conversation's beat. On the various balconies, Wax picked out people mingling without coats despite the chill. Smoke rose from goblets and mouths alike, while the bodies seemed in constant motion, as if to hold a conversation for more than a moment or two was poor form.

A broad colonnade holding up a stone slab marked the estate's entry, their arrival causing a ripple among the guests standing there. Greetings rang out, led most boisterously by one Denia Sedred, their hostess who introduced herself as such in a wide, sweeping stride out to them. Gemstones—not skars, but similar in their brightness—shimmered across her, apparently accounting for her entire ensemble, no coat necessary. At a clucked tongue from Eujo, Wax closed his mouth, just in time for Denia to throw an arm across first his shoulders, then Eujo's.

"And here are our honored guests of the evening!" Denia announced, facing the estate and the assembled crowd, most of which already looked flush from the blue-white drinks in their glasses. "Renewals, and two of them! Kance and Vis, already rare enough, much less in the winter, are here. Please, welcome them, and enjoy!"

A half-hearted cheer rose, with many of the guests turning back to their conversations, their nibbles snagged from standing trays. Denia gave both Wax and Eujo a final pat on their backs before spinning off inside, as if such a greeting should've been enough to clear the way to revelry.

"What was that?" Torny asked from behind them.

"A beginning," Eujo replied. "Break off. Find conversation, get support. You know the job."

"Sure do, highness."

Before Eujo had even finished rolling her eyes, Torny, with Bliss on her heels, vanished inside the estate.

"You feel comfortable?" Eujo asked Wax, who'd been surveying the party landscape. "Ready for another one of these?"

"Wearing this?" Wax glanced down at his ridiculous coat. "Eujo, watch me work."

At her skeptical look, Wax went off. Snagged, first, a drink from the nearest stand. A sip confirmed the sweet ice wine, not all that different from the peach stuff back on Vis. Holding the glass, Wax went for a cluster to the right, a trio set about with various pipes, their output rising in circles over their heads.

A simple trick, one he'd learned with far more vicious leaves back home.

With an ask and a demonstration, Wax broke into their circle, laughing and daring the others to match his smoke rings. The inevitable failure turned to curiosity turned to stories, both from Wax and the guests in turn, as Wax made sure to break up his own breaths with questions.

He learned about the fiery giants torching the city, about the Warlord Jochi and his quest to hunt the very source of the fiends. About the academy and its more and more secretive ways these days, how more Najahn seemed to be in the city than before, though of course winter slowed all that down. One Tenet, in particular, had just made off with a prized researcher and crates of inventions.

"All under the pretext," said one of the pipers, "that she was needed for some massive project. That was weeks, weeks ago, and we've heard nothing since." The man took a long drink, a gulp, while Wax puffed out another three rings into the clear sky. "As if Noctia has the right to take our best whenever they damn well please."

"Don't they though?" asked another, a person so layered beneath furs Wax couldn't tell if they were man, woman, or hanoko. "Without them, we'd be food for the fiends."

"Oh yeah? Where were they this last time, then?"

"Probably keeping another bunch from landing on our shores."

The two kept sparring as Wax made his getaway, bouncing inside, snagging some delicious meats and cheese he could not identify. The estate's grandeur continued past the door, with crackling fireplaces set amongst lounges, stairs curling up the sides, and a three-piece band playing silver flutes and drums in the center. The revelers milled about in amorphous groups, all shifting as if the music, light and slow, demanded continual motion. Wax couldn't spot Bliss and Torny, but Eujo held court right near the music, a half-dozen peppering the queen with questions.

She spotted him and Wax raised his own glass, a toast she returned.

A second round of both drinks and conversation clued Wax into the skars, their location amid a gigantic gold vein to the north. One protected from mining by, yes, the Najahn, much to another Whent man's consternation.

"The riches they're keeping in there could save our isle," the man complained to nodding companions.

From what, Wax wasn't sure, but never press someone at a party about their points. Not worth it. He did pitch a question into the air, asking about wagons, transport, any necessary arrangements to make for the trip, and received only a laugh in reply.

"If you haven't brought your own, you're in for a sorry state," the same man said. "Jochi took everything this city had for his escapade. It'll be your boots or a long wait."

"And that'll take how long? The walk?"

"A week? More or less, depending on the cold and how much you can stand," the man said. "Whent's not a small place. And word has it there's fiends on the plains now, with Jochi pulling all our soldiers. Best keep your heads about you on the trip."

The hours spun by, the drinks dropped, and the band never seemed to stop. Wax parlayed tales into promises, eventually earning concessions from several wealthier Whents to borrow more fur, a couple shaggy pack animals, and even two bottles of stiff liquor whose owner insisted they'd need to survive the cold. All that, and he still found himself out on a balcony alone, looking over the desolate city, nursing a drink from a new round, one warm and delightful.

"You seem like you're having fun," Eujo said, the drink keeping Wax from any jump. "Your stories are spreading down there. More than mine."

The Queen joined him at the railing, her form somehow not a mix of cold and sweat like Wax's own. She glittered just as she had from the moment they'd left the ship, right in her element in every way.

"Didn't think it was a contest," Wax replied. "It's only because you're holding back, though."

"Holding back?"

"Sure. I caught some of what you said down there. You're not telling them the real stories."

Eujo glanced down at her glass, then swung her look out over the city. "You mean that I came from down there."

"Worse, if I'm picturing it right."

"Kance isn't all sky diamonds and soaring through the skies, no."

"Vis isn't all fruits and flowers either." Wax reached over, tapped his glass against Eujo's. "So long as we don't forget that, I think we'll be okay."

"At least your home's not trying to murder you." Eujo smiled as she spoke. "I bet she's so mad."

"She won't be able to touch you once you're the Aegis. Just a couple more skars and you're there."

A nod. Quiet.

"Someone else might get there first, though," Wax offered to the night. "Save us both from that stone chair."

Eujo flashed a look Wax's way. "What would you do then? Go back home?"

"Not going to think about that till it happens. Not my way. Live in the moment, you know?"

Wax drew up the cocky grin, an easy find with the wine.

Eujo matched it, laughed, "I suppose, with lives like ours, it'd be a mistake to do anything else."

A sound bounced up from below, a light sprinkling, like one of the many wind chimes in the city. Both Eujo and Wax turned, bent over the railing to sneak a look, and Wax found his hand landing on Eujo's. Neither had their gloves on for fear of fumbling drinks, and the touch, right there in that moment, stuck different than all the times they'd run, fought, swam or searched with one another. Wax found her texture, her life in that momentary grip, and in the look that followed, Eujo for once uncertain, vulnerable, real.

At least, until shouts followed, angry ones, calling out a thief.

CHAPTER 17

THE ONLY CHOICE

For all the times he'd felt sand between his toes, Quik had never enjoyed the tickling grains behind tarnished gray bars. The crashing waves out to his left, beyond the black rock arches bordering Noctia's many seaside caves, provided an echoing background, their rage synonymous with his own. Yet Quik reserved the anger for his fingers, squeezing out the sand and dumping it into small piles, just as he'd been doing for hours now.

With Sawi's last, apologizing glance, Ami and Gladdring's guards had taken hold of Quik and dragged, deposited him down here in the sandy cage. Struggle, as Ami pointed out, would be pointless. The guards had blades, as did Ami, and Quik wasn't important enough to the Najahn to be noticed if he went missing. Better, so Ami suggested, to wait and see.

Chance, possibility, all favored the living.

So far waiting and seeing hadn't brought Quik anything more than frustration. The locked cage proved sturdy enough to resist his attempts to pry open, and Quik tried every bar. Digging beneath the barrier—Ami hadn't left a guard, only a vague remark that she'd be seeing him later—revealed the sand this deep was a shallow cover, and unless Quik could flatten himself like a jungle leaf, he wouldn't be squeezing between hard rock and the metal bars. The cage ran to the overhead cave ceiling too, preventing any skilled climber from escaping.

In other words, Quik was stuck, and it sucked.

As he kneaded the sand, other thoughts made daring incursions on his budding rage. First and foremost, why, why had Sawi just left him there on the stair? She could've come up with just about any excuse, bargained for Quik's innocence—that Quik wasn't innocent didn't really matter, loyalty counted for more—but she'd just pressed on. As if Quik was a former friend, now an embarrassment.

Sure, Vis had social circles. Friendships changed over time. But those had *reasons*. This seemed to sudden, so random, so devastating.

Second, what even was this place?

Masayo and her Third Hand hadn't given Quik much of a clue when they'd cast him upon this particular mission, but if the outcome was a likely trip to a seaside prison, Quik had to believe she'd give him a warning. He was, after all, a new Najahn. A recruit in his training rotations. This couldn't be the usual way things went.

Then what was the answer? Why would a trade Tenet build a cage down here in the sand, apparently patrolled by a feisty former Guardian?

And third, perhaps most pressing as the day wound down, what would he eat?

There were small crabs and bugs crawling about the sand, though not so many came back this far away from the water. Quik might've tried to catch one of the gulls, though the prospect of eating one without fire made his stomach lurch. Fresh water, at least, had been left in a skin. Their one concession.

"Are you enjoying your new home?" Ami asked, striding from the tunnel like some warrior queen. She carried a torch, used it to light two other sconces bolted into the rock walls. A necessity given the dying light. Quik fought off a flinch as the brighter glow found Ami's face, its plated-over lower quarter. "I'll admit, it's lacking in amenities, but I'll tell you now, what we've got upstairs isn't much better."

After sliding his look away from Ami's face, he read her gear next. She had a sword—standard Najahn-issue, by his guess, though the hilt seemed larger than most—and, on her back, what looked like a thick log. The Guardian read his eyes, dipped her shoulder and let the log fall into the dirt. When she straightened, Ami held a smile that made Quik's blood run colder than any glare he'd ever seen.

"At least it's soft," Quik said.

"What's soft, the sand?" Ami pulled the cage's key from a ring attached to her waist, slotted it into the large brass lock and turned the tumblers. "Would think you'd be used to that, on Vis. Nicer sand than Noctia, if I'm remembering right."

"You are."

The cage door swung open. Quik rose onto his feet, curling forward and breaking into a dash at the opening. He made it two strides before Ami had the blade out, pointed right where Quik would skewer himself. The hunter tried to stop, threw himself to the right to smack the cage bars instead.

He'd never seen anyone draw a blade that fast. Then again, on Vis, next to nobody used swords. Perhaps Quik might have to update his expectations.

"Now, I get that you're upset," Ami said, leaving the

sword out, though she let its point drop. A potential opening Quik no longer cared to exploit. Death at her hands would come too easy without his own weapon. "I'd be angry too. I was, not all that long ago, when I found myself almost in your position." She tapped the blade against the bars, the ringing sound lost in the waves. "Then, I decided to do something useful."

"Like what?" Quik moved so that he faced Ami square, brushed the sand off his legs. They'd at least left him with his robe, though the sand caught in the linens and made them scratchy. "Give Gladdring what he wants?"

"Save the world, Quik. Save the world."

Ami's world-saving plan seemed to start with knocking the ever-loving crap out of Quik. She gave him the log, a kind gesture that soon revealed itself to be a trap. The wood had heft, could no doubt deal some damage, but Quik wasn't from Mottilan. Had no experience trying to fight someone with a big stick.

Compared to his gauntlets, using the club felt like he'd had too much peach wine.

Worse, Ami made clear their duel wasn't meant to be a fair fight. With her sword, she had Quik retreat near the cage's rocky back end. She entered, closed the door—didn't lock it—behind her. Held the sword with both hands now, twisting it so Quik could catch just why its hilt put on some size.

"I'm going to tell you something, now, that will mean your life if it ever gets out," Ami said, her tone suggesting just how unlikely that would be. "This blade, and that log, have embedded skars. Those skars, used well, can mean the difference between defeating the fiends or dying to them." Ami looked up from her sword, nodded at the log. "Can you hear it?"

Quik tried to feign surprise, failed. Of course he'd heard the skar whispering as soon as his hands touched the log. Different from the Vis skar he'd held before, a thicker and slower rumbling, but one touching his mind in much the same way. This one, rather than finding Quik's scratches and sores, seemed intent on his stance, his motion, his weight and heft. When Quik leaned back, or raised the log, the skar became excited, seeming to beg Quik to let it loose with the motion.

So far, Quik had ignored the gem. Had hoped Ami didn't know what she'd done.

"Oh," Ami said slow when Quik didn't give a clear reply. "You're not new to this game."

"New enough," Quik snapped fast. "Only—"

"Stop. You're not a skilled enough liar to make it interesting. It's good you know what a skar feels like." Ami took a step further into the cage. Five long strides split them now. "We can skip the early steps. Get right to business."

"Business?"

"Defend yourself, Vis. Use the skar."

At last, something Quik understood. As Ami broke into a charge, her booted feet sliding in the sand, Quik dropped the log into a wide swing. Slow enough that Ami's speed should've brought her right into the log's path. A crumpling knockout.

The skar buzzed, thrilled, asking for its chance. Quik denied it.

When Wax had given into the Foti skar with that Rana fiend, everything had gone up in flames. Who knew what might happen now? If he didn't need to use the skar, why bother?

The Guardian didn't arrive on time. She didn't, really, arrive at all. On her second step, right when her momentum should've been bringing her into certain doom, the Guardian kicked, jumped. In armor and gear far too heavy. Instead of pitching forward into a worthless fall, Ami soared up, clearing Quik's swing and nearly Quik himself.

Someone who'd never seen a skar before, didn't understand their possibilities, might've been killed then and there. Quik caught the impossible and reacted, dipping into his swing and turning the crossing blow into a full-on whirlwind. The log whipped by Quik's left side as Ami landed just behind the hunter, Quik letting the club's weight swing him around.

Again the skar begged. Again Quik denied.

Ami swept her sword down and right, the blade catching the log. Catching, and stopping. Not as if Quik had struck a wall, where the vibration, the force should've shattered the wood. No, more like if Quik had smacked his log into a thick honey pile. His weapon stuck on Maena's blade, the halt so complete, so total as to send Quik falling to the right into the sand.

Still, he had one hand on the club's strap, a brown leather hardy enough to handle his pull. Quik yanked with his right hand, jerked the club off the blade and back to his arms.

"And you're not a bad fighter," Ami said. "Good. That first jump? Kance. The block? The very same skar in your club, from our friends up north."

"What are you saying?" Quik asked, getting back up, sand pouring from his clothes. "You're using the skars to fight?"

"Oh, much more than that." Ami waved the blade back and forth. As she did, its edge picked up the same light as the sconces: bright and hot. "They'll change everything, Vis. Everything."

She swept the blade low through the sand. White-searing sparks, grains burning flew up through the air, flying towards Quik. He backpedaled, slipped, saw and felt those sparks land. His robes smoked and he dropped the log, rolling to try and put the small fires out. By the time he finished, he heard a singular click, the gate shutting.

Ami, the log recovered and in her possession, again stood outside.

"I'm glad you're not just a Najahn recruit," Ami said, folding her arms. "You'll help us so much more this way."

"I don't understand," Quik tried, tried to keep the desperate confusion from his voice. "Why are you doing this to me?"

"Because Gladdring's the only chance we've got to get all you morons seeing things the right way. You're not on his side." Ami started to turn away. "You should think about that. Whose side you're on. Make the right choice fast enough, maybe I won't kill you first."

CHAPTER 18

PRIVATE PAGES

A diary. Yarvick wanted a diary and Torny was going to get it, damn everything else. Well, as Torny glanced, confirmed Bliss was right on her heels as they went into the estate, maybe not everything.

But debts had to be repaid, particularly a debt like this.

The estate put its posh position into play beyond the entrance, with doors and stairs aplenty. People twisted around them all, and while Torny dodged the initial groups, ignoring some curious questions about who they were, the drinks and snacks were too tempting to pass up, too valuable to the disguise.

"Take one," Torny said, swiping a goblet off a tray and tapping Bliss's own once it found the Vis's hand. "Make sure to look like you're having fun."

'Aren't I?'

"Are you?"

Bliss crinkled her nose, scrunched her eyes. So far out of her element here that Torny would've laughed if it wouldn't attract the wrong attention. Bliss did, at least, looked like a party-goer. Eujo had that part covered, as any queen ought to. Fancy dress—Bliss chose green—and a thick coat that ought to find its way off those shoulders before sweat marred her face.

For that matter, Torny needed to toss her own coat, just not too far away.

'It's interesting?' Bliss signed between bites of some crab cakes. 'Noctia was different.'

"We weren't guests of honor there."

Not that they were here either. Wax and Eujo sucked up that energy, the two Renewals drawing more eyes than their Guardians. A couple made tentative stabs at opening a conversation with Bliss and Torny as the pair took to their drinks, and Torny shooed them off by suggesting a chat about fiend innards and their many uses.

Bliss stifled a laugh as the innocent, absurdly fancy twosome turned green and mumbled off an excuse to flee.

'Why'd you do that? Hilarious, but why?'

"Because we have work to do, Bliss."

Another tilted head, another question. Sure, Torny would reveal the mission in time, when the goal seemed secure. Now she had to keep looking. Yarvick said the diary would be a personal treasure, would probably be obvious. A battered book, brown and plain, thatched with thread on the spine. Either the library or the host's bedroom.

Not that Torny knew where to find either one.

'Who are we going to talk to, then?'

"This way," Torny said, striking off towards the estate's back, where it slammed into the rock and kept on going. Libraries, with all their books, tended to be first floor operations. Hopefully this would be the same. "I'm thinking we'll find better info in books."

'Books?' Bliss signed, keeping up with Torny's speed and whipping fingers by her face. 'What?'

"You know, things with paper. Words. Writing."

'I know what a book is. I'm just trying—'

Torny reached out, grabbed Bliss's signing arm and tugged her left, just past a waiter unable to see the approaching duo with more drink trays in his arms.

"Pay attention," Torny sniped, though cut it with a wink. "Trust me, you don't want to talk with these people."

'Why?'

"Boring, that's why." Torny slowed as they neared the estate's back, beyond the nifty drum-and-flute band. Straight ahead didn't seem to be the library but the kitchens, going by the hot air and delicious smells coming out. "Bet none of them ever fought a fiend."

'Is that required to be interesting?'

"In my book."

Glancing right, the estate wrapped around a broad open patio with doors aplenty leading to an outdoor veranda. Lounges, tables and chairs split several statues—just like Whent to have stone carvings inside and out—in a space obviously meant for parties and doing its best job now, with almost every seat taken by chattering glitterbugs.

'What else is in your book? To be interesting?'

Torny angled left next, saw stairs climbing up against the back wall. Before it and near the band on lay some small garden layout, as if to counteract the lifeless statues. A fountain fluttered, something you'd never find on water-parched Noctia. Drink and snack trays. People who preferred their conversation on the move.

Behind them waited opportunity. Midway down the left side lay a hallway, and back towards the entrance, though off to the side, an open arch to a darker room. Secrets and more.

"Don't be dull," Torny replied to Bliss's question, ditching her emptied glass and replacing it with another as they moved along the leftward half.

The hallway opportunity died as they neared, with a footman standing nearby. As Torny approached, the man, dressed in coarse brown linens, woke up like some creature emerging from its slumber, starting with a snort and finding Torny with half-dead eyes. The man muttered some excuse about family only back there, and pushed no further when Torny shrugged and kept on going.

'You don't think the library would be that way?'

Torny chuckled, "If there's one thing I know about people who live in a place like this? They like showing off. They won't hide the library if they've got one."

'Do you know much about rich people?'

"Grew up on Noctia," Torny replied, as that should answer the question well enough.

Noctia, the small, center isle, where everyone who was anyone eventually came once they realized the Najahn held all the power. They showed up, shoveled their gifts around to get their craggy homes, then, if they failed to crack the Circle's favor, wondered where it all went, disappearing in short order.

Some of their stuff, inevitably, wound up with Yarvick's band.

The dark room off to the entrance's left gave Torny what she wanted: the keen smell of musty books, literature long saved and little read. She couldn't keep her grin hidden as they neared, letting it slide only when a man entered before them, bearing a drink and a tome of his own.

'Guess you were right,' Bliss signed as they ducked

beneath an arch with Whent's hard lines carved into its sweeping overhang.

The rock god was the most boring, all his designs claiming straight sides, equal ratios, and a hard common sense. No chaos there, and no chaos in here either: Torny's first steps into the library revealed low-lit lamps, cushioned chairs, and staid shelves packed in alphabetical order, spines out. Not a single volume left on the two desks, nor straddling a chair half-read. No paper for spontaneous note-taking either. Creativity left to wither in its home.

At least the windows offered something useful: bright and large, right into the yard. No patio here, no onlookers smoking pipes and wondering what might be going on inside.

Which left the man. He, a thin and short soul, seemed to ignore the two ladies following as he took a chair, cracked his brought tome, and sighed the contented sigh of anyone finding comfort in a place without much chance of it.

Bliss didn't take as much notice of the interloper, walking right past Torny and staring at the books with a surreal wonder. Torny did a double count of the drinks they'd had—one and a half—and figured Bliss couldn't be drunk, so what accounted for the open-mouthed delight on her face?

"You okay?" Torny asked, shrugging off her fur onto a chair. Turning, she pulled Bliss's own coat off while the woman signed back at her.

'I've never seen this many books in one place before.'

Torny did a double-take. The library wasn't that large. She'd seen bigger even in modest Noctia estates. But then, maybe Vis was different?

"What, don't you have libraries at home?"

Bliss shook her head. 'Not really. Some few have books, but it's too wet. They fall apart. So we use other things. Songs, memory, etchings.'

"Well, take it in then, because we're not going to be here long."

'No?'

The small library offered another big advantage: an easy opportunity to find her target. Without an author, the diary had been packed in along the farthest end of the farthest shelf, nestled against the outer wall with a number of other journals. The twine stitching confirmed the discovery, the little threads dangling out the book's end like an overgrown vine.

Torny went over to it, confirming the man seemed sucked into his book, while Bliss scouted out some volume on the skars and their first finder. Demion or someone like that, if Torny could remember her history. Kicked off the Aegis death clock, she did. What a legacy.

Squatting, Torny eased the diary free from its neighbors. Thin enough to mean journaling wasn't a big habit of Yarvick's target—the bandit leader hadn't specified whose diary it was, only that Torny should find it and return it unread. How, though, Yarvick could prove Torny hadn't read the diary was, well, an open question.

She could, at least, flip open the front cover. See if the kind soul would reveal any secrets on the first page.

Beneath a pleasant orange glow, with the band's light beats in the background, Torny couldn't hide her grin. Ah, so that's why Yarvick wanted the diary so badly. A memento, a memory, and more inside these pages, each one written by a singular name belonging to the bandit leader's only child, a long lost son. Torny started turning more, dashing through the pages while the man read, and Bliss found a book of her own.

If Torny thought she could snag the book and dart from the party, she'd have been long gone by now. Instead, her dual role meant she'd need to kill time here, or else be noticed on the way out. A Guardian abandoning her Renewals would mean eyes she didn't want. So, instead, she read.

A story unfolded there, one of tragedy and betrayal, of morals lost and found, a lover's escape to the north with a young man growing through every entry, one who both regretted losing and understood why he had to lose his father.

"Interesting choice."

Torny looked up, saw the man, tome discarded and standing now, watching her with eyes far too wary for a casual remark. Time to drum up a lie and see if it worked.

"It looked different," Torny offered. "Thought I'd see what it was."

"Did you now?" the man took a step closer. "Have you, then, seen what it was?"

Torny flipped the diary into a single hand, waved it around like she might put it back at any moment. "Looks like a journal. Have you read it? Is it interesting?"

Behind the man, Bliss had noticed the conversation, ditched her own book back to the shelf and stood, searching for an answer in Torny's eyes. One Torny couldn't give right then, right there.

"I should hope not, at least not to you," the man said. "To me, though, it is everything."

Torny felt the sigh before it came. "You're not, are you?"

"I am, though I'm wondering at the significance?"

"Pasts, man. You can't escape'em." Torny raised the diary. "Can I borrow this for a while?"

Narrowed eyes. "What? Why?"

"Better if you don't know, buddy. Trust me."

"I don't trust you. At all."

Torny had a knife in her dress folds, more in her coat over by the chair. Pulling that would bring a swift end to the party. Then again, so would getting in a brawl with Yarvick's kid. She needed a different solution.

"Then it looks like we're stuck," Torny said. "Because I'm not leaving without this."

"And I'm not letting you leave with it," the man half-turned his head towards the library's exit, took in a breath for what was going to be a particular word Torny knew all too well.

So she punched him, with her off-hand, in the gut. The would-be call for the guards turned into a sputtering curse instead as the man doubled over.

"Time to go!" Torny snapped at Bliss, who took those words and did the most wrong thing with them.

Taking a step, Bliss picked up and hurled a chair at the window, shattering it. At once, an impressive feat of both strength and stupidity. Bliss kept right on going, slinging her heavy coat on and launching Torny's own at the thief, who caught it with her free hand as Yarvick's son recovered.

"What're you doing?" Torny said, pushing the young man into another chair and following Bliss out into the chilly night.

'You said go, so we're going,' Bliss flashed as they ran across the lawn. 'We'd never get back through the party.'

"But your brother? Eujo? They're not going to like this? You should've let me run."

Bliss didn't answer as the first shouts carried out into

the night, didn't respond as she and Torny climbed the small wall around the yard and swept into the city streets, heading back towards Eujo's boat. Only when they were well away from the estate, any pursuit a hopeless endeavor, did Bliss stop, turn, take a breath.

"Why?" Torny, catching up herself, huffed, the diary secured in her jacket. "Why're you helping a thief?"

In Sichi's rose light, Bliss flashed a single reason:

'Because you never left me.'

CHAPTER 19

BACKSTAB BETRAYED

According to Gladdring, Sawi succeeded because she didn't know how to play the game. After her first visit to the Circle, Gladdring helped Sawi find the right times, the right places to bump into other Tenets, aides, and Najahn close to Fassle and his Adept pair. With a new outfit, her robes bearing the Trade Tenet's isle-crossing sigil and some gold filigree, Sawi walked around like, if not royalty, then someone well above the usual rank. The nodding heads and opened doors put her in hallways when targets left meetings, put her in exclusive restaurants when officials settled in for a meal, now with a surprise guest. Soon, Sawi handled it on her own, finding the same parallels to a Vis sect she'd been shut out from: a hunt, a kill, the reward.

The first time, a morning coffee interruption with a secretary to the Najahn's naval Tenet, came with awkwardness, confusion about how, exactly, Sawi was supposed to probe for weaknesses in Fassle's loyalty. She stood behind the aide in the line leading to the counter, seconds to make a move dwindling in the crowded cafe.

Until the Tamas skar spoke up.

Like the other skars, its ideas came more as impressions amongst the whispers. Less discrete commands and more urges to speak in this way, poke at that thing. The aide, according to the skar, seemed nervous, glancing about as if suspicious of being watched. An opening, perhaps.

"Are you okay?" Sawi asked.

A flickered, slight smile and a nod. "Just fine."

The voice trembled. The Tamas skar pounced on what Sawi could already tell.

"You're almost shaking," Sawi said, frowning. "What's wrong?"

A quick glance left and right, a half-hearted gesture with a hand as if waving at the world. "I don't understand how everyone can be so calm. The fiends are everywhere. Attacking every day. How long till they break through here?"

And there it was, the source. Not a surprising one, but something she could use. Sawi sympathized, as she'd seen Gladdring do all too many times back on Vis, in the meetings. Make the person feel they're being listened to, that you care about them, and when you have them on your side, twist to an ask. They'd only be repaying you for the service you've already done, lending them a listening ear, a shoulder to cry on.

She made that ask minutes later, at a small table outside and masked from eavesdroppers by the morning's cart cavalcade. Noctia always rumbled, always roared, an annoyance if you wanted to sleep, a boon if you wanted privacy.

"Why doesn't Fassle do more?" the aide replied, confused. "What more could he do?"

"Plenty, but he's not."

Confusion became curiosity. The aide nodded at her medallion. "What does Gladdring know?"

"You'll find out soon. Provided you can keep an open mind."

"If Gladdring has a way to stop the fiends, he'll have more than that." The aide swirled his smoking coffee cup, steam rising into the cold gray morning. "More than my support, too. If he's got an answer to the fiend problem, half these people will jump onto his side, Fassle be damned."

Bold words. Gladdring, though, was delighted to hear them when Sawi relayed the conversation. Fassle was more vulnerable than expected, which meant they needed to move fast. No sitting around, playing it slow. Sawi would begin now. That very afternoon. No more playing with Ami and Annalyse. They had someone new to use.

Sawi didn't have to ask to know it was Quik, didn't have to ask to know he'd be safer in their skar-testing dungeon than up here, where knives were being sharpened.

"Can I talk to him?" Sawi asked when Gladdring finished relaying the plan, the people to meet. "Quik, I mean? He should know."

"He's not your concern." Gladdring at least had the grace to look apologetic, his frame bending down to put a hand on Sawi's sitting shoulder. "Do this well, and he'll escape any harm. Fail, and it won't matter anyway."

The hours and days burned after that, spinning away in targeted talks, gathering whispered support from one to another and another until Gladdring decided, nearly a week later, that the time had come to spin up the speed. Enter the final phase.

"Aren't we moving fast?" Sawi argued as they met, once again, in Gladdring's crowded tower office. "They say they support us, but—"

"And the skar agrees?" Gladdring motioned at the jewel around Sawi's neck.

"It does. So far as I understand, anyway."

"Then we don't need any more. Speed is important, Sawi, because word will spread if it hasn't already. Fassle will find out, and he will move. We must strike first, or lose everything."

Gladdring's grand plan culminated in a gathering, one Sawi arranged through passed notes and whispered times. A chance to display the skars, their potential. Sawi would do it, and after, Gladdring and Ami would arrive, ready to lead the riled up bunch in a rapid rebellion. Fassle would be ousted by dinner, Gladdring installed by dessert, and the Najahn would start their skar-supported campaign against the fiends by dawn.

Simple, effective.

Sparking a coup against Fassle wasn't something done in the open, so Gladdring posted Sawi up for the final push in a strange place down near the Najahn docks, an odd house given over to Gladdring as a result, so the Tenet said, of the owners understanding just how bad things could get crossing him. When Sawi arrived, alone, the building had nobody in it to greet her, just an unlocked door down an alley and a slew of crimson cushioned furniture inside. Wine bottles, both open and not, lay scattered around the space, goblets and glasses right along with them. Leftover food occupied plates on various end tables, as if some revel had been dispersed with no warning.

Which, knowing Gladdring, knowing Fassle's likely anger, perhaps it had.

What it felt like to be at the end of a string, dancing to whatever Gladdring demanded.

Clean it. Get it ready. You'll have an hour.

The instructions Gladdring gave in a letter handed to Sawi as she ate lunch, along with the directions to the place. Walking down the cliffside had taken most of that time, and now she scrambled, rushing the bottles and glasses into the cramped kitchen towards the building's back. Plates too, a couple breaking as she launched them into the wash basin.

Only once did she stop, question herself, why she was there and what the point of the whole thing was. Why Sawi, a Vis gatherer, was stuck in this strange place cleaning up someone else's mess.

The answer, as it so often did during these last few days, came with Gladdring's own voice:

Save our Seven Isles.

If Wax could brave endless danger by taking the Renewal's route, then Sawi could handle a little labor. Could take greeting the shifty Tenets, their aides, the ambassadors as they showed up one by one, at carefully planned intervals. Each knocked on the door, spoke the password Gladdring had decided upon, and entered.

The last one came nearly thirty minutes after the first. Cowled in black, her face grim as Sawi opened the door. One of Fassle's Adepts, the only one open to persuasion.

"With you here," Sawi said, following the lines, the steps as Gladdring had directed, "we can begin."

"Where's Gladdring?" the Adept asked, her tone parched, scared. "This *is* his doing?"

"He's busy implementing the plan," Sawi replied. "The one I'm about to reveal to all of you."

Fifteen in all, commanding hundreds, maybe thousands. All gathered on musty couches and chairs, listening and muttering as Sawi described who would go where, deliver what, threaten who. She read from notes Gladdring had given her last night, once they'd secured the likely attendance. Questions came up, and Sawi dismissed them all with a singular phrase, pushed by the Tamas skar still around her neck.

"Trust the plan," Sawi said again and again, and each time she felt the skar's whispers brighten. Whomever she addressed would sigh, nod, or simply halt their arguing and settle back into the cushion.

At its conclusion, Sawi stood, declared the session over. She read the final line, trying to find the appropriate gravity, "Go and save our Seven Isles together."

It sounded perfect. Nobody questioned it. All seemed committed, the Tamas skar again listening to Sawi's desire and projecting it upon the people, just as Gladdring said it would, just as Sawi had learned to do.

The skar, though, did nothing when the building's door broke open. When black-armored Najahn, voulges at the ready, marched into the room. When Fassle himself, in purple, black, and gold robes so spotless they seemed unreal, followed.

"And here they are," Fassle announced to the frozen crowd. "My traitors, all together. So nice of Gladdring to round you all up for me. Take them."

Sawi stepped back as the Najahn swept past her, grabbing a suddenly blubbering, protesting, pale crowd. The Adept knelt then and there, begging forgiveness, only for Fassle to hold out a hand, accept a short blade from a Najahn captain, and end the Adept's life with a single, clean stroke. The blood matched the cushions, the screams stopped only when Fassle threatened any more antics would receive the same treatment.

No Najahn came for Sawi. They blocked the exits as more came to escort the others away, one by one in a ceaseless parade of the damned. Through it all, Fassle watched with a spider's smile, satisfied and smug. Yet, when the last one left, a poor aide needing to be carried after passing out from fright, Fassle and his guard captain did not follow. Instead, Fassle appraised Sawi while the guard captain glowered beside him, voulge still drawn and at attention.

"Gladdring's apprentice," Fassle said, looking Sawi over in much the same way Gladdring often did: a master judging his tools. "He claims you carried out his orders with skill. Do you agree?"

A thousand scenarios had played out in Sawi's head during the exodus, many ending in the same bloody pool that continued seeping across the floor, though the Adept's body had been removed. None started with Fassle asking her a question, much less one like this.

"I . . . did what he asked," Sawi answered, her back against the stone wall. To her right sat a couch, in front, between her and Fassle, rested the chair she'd sat in during the speech. It all seemed too ordinary, too dull a place to die. "He wanted me to find people open to his ideas."

"And you did." Fassle nodded, then scowled. "Altogether too many, I think." He flicked his eyes to hers, matched stares. "Why? Why did they listen? Was it the skar?"

How much did Fassle know?

Regardless, Sawi felt herself on a shifting log, one misstep dooming her. This, this was all about her life now. Gladdring was probably dead. Nothing gained anymore by protecting him, what he'd been doing.

"The skar only grows. It doesn't create."

As for what that skar was doing now, the Tamas stone only gave quiet, cautionary whispers. As if it couldn't get a read on Fassle's intentions. Perfect.

"So Gladdring's argument was persuasive," Fassle mused. He drummed his right hand against his clean robes, then took a long step over the bloody pool, sat on the chair near Sawi and beckoned her onto the couch. "Give me his plan, then, Vis. I would know what is causing unrest among my people, so that I can stamp it out."

CHAPTER 20

THE DEAD KING

The corpses kept to themselves. Quiet dead. Svarde, Maena, and Kivi stayed still, watching as the forms rose up around them. Some stood erect, more sat up, while still others shifted with their faces down in the dirt. The reasons were as varied as the means by which a person could die in these Seven Isles, though Svarde noted a distinct bent here towards the physical variety: rending claws, missing limbs, bones broken in ways horrifying and utterly, by this point, ordinary. How distorted was Svarde's life that he saw all this and felt nothing more than recognition?

So many times it could've been him looking like these grubby bodies.

"What then?" Olgata called from the tunnel once the corpses ceased their motion, becoming strange obelisks amid the ruby-strewn cave floor. "I don't dare leave without warning Jochi."

Nor would Svarde want to press on with this awful force at his back. Anything fighting fiends couldn't be all bad, but fiends could fight one another too. What if these things were only taking time to wake back up, getting ready to pounce? Or tackle, grab at Svarde's ankles? All bad, all awful.

"Then go," Svarde replied, his gruff voice a hollow echo in the chamber's quiet. "Make sure Jochi's aware."

Olgata didn't wait for a second opinion, leaving nothing more than a frown for Maena before dashing off. Her footsteps made no sound and the dead didn't seem to notice.

"Getting rid of another ally?" Maena asked, her hands free and looking like they needed a weapon. "Not a smart move."

Kivi snorted up above. Not agreement, but a question.

"Pick a tunnel," Svarde answered. "We'll follow. Hope these things don't bother us."

"And if they do?"

"Take as many down as we can."

Maena laughed, "Not sure that'll work."

"Not sure we'll care either way."

Kivi clawed across the ceiling, rock dust sprinkling down amid the bodies as she moved. The corpses took the gray shower as they took everything else: without reaction.

"So who goes first?" Maena asked. "You?"

The captain's ask had a laughing tilt to it, one burying a bit of danger in the tone. A dare and a doubt together, as if she wasn't sure Svarde should, but knew she *shouldn't*. A different turn from the Maena Svarde had known, who tended to leap into deadly situations with both plans and prowess.

Svarde would make do with strength.

Hefting his axes, trying to keep his eyes everywhere, Svarde followed Kivi's line with a single step. His boots crunched on the stone, a single ruby squeezing out from his soles and skittering along. Svarde caught his breath, listened, looked.

Nothing.

Okay. Maybe these things really were just waiting for fiends. Maybe they didn't care.

Two steps, three, and Svarde neared the chamber's middle. Kivi had chosen the leftward tunnel of the choice trio, the one angling downward from the start. At the chamber's center, with few dead right around him, Svarde angled that way. Glanced to see Maena, too, had started off, matching Svarde's route.

"Copying me?" Svarde asked.

"If there's traps, you've been avoiding them so far. Only seems sensible."

Traps. One more thing to worry about, though Svarde saw little opportunity for hidden pits or darts among the rocky walls. Difficult to rig up in a place like this. Nevertheless, as he started off for the leftward tunnel, he kept his eyes scanning up and down, for threats big and small. Which, perhaps naturally, led Svarde more and more to the black, lidless eyes and gray skin, the toes, on the ones lacking boots, gnarled and yet not rotted.

As if something held these things, these people, locked in time a fraction after their death.

A curse behind him prompted a turn, Svarde seeing Maena looking at a standing husk off to the right. A full-standing man, though one lacking most of his left torso, pointed an arm. Not at the living, but instead down the rightward tunnel. His vacant eyes locked on Maena, then Svarde, a rotation so slow and determined as to be mechanical.

Svarde may have shivered, though he'd never admit it.

"Won't quite call that a riddle," Maena said. "Think we

should follow it?"

"Don't want to make his friends unhappy. You lead?"

"So you can cut me down with that axe? I don't think so."

"What?"

Maena, though, jerked her head towards the corpse. "Get going, Guardian."

Kivi's snort cracked the conversation, the ferrite scuttling above Svarde and heading right where the corpse pointed. As the ferrite passed over the body's head, the corpse moved, lining its steps towards the tunnel. Sated, apparently, with Kivi's intended direction. Which brought up a whole different question.

"Don't even think about it," Maena said as Svarde hesitated. "We're not splitting up. Not in these tunnels, unless you want the fiends to feast."

On that, at least, the captain had a fair point. Together, they followed the corpse.

The chosen tunnel split itself from the usual cave trappings quick. What would've been natural walls just a few strides in the other direction now held sconces, albeit ones made with poor craftsmanship, the iron used smelted from junk ores. Svarde's Foti blood quivered at the pitted metal, now holding glowing moss in clumps. Still, ash-marred patches behind the holders hinted at a flammable past.

The ground, too, had its worst tendencies smoothed over. Normally, rogue rocks and odd spikes made any cave walk treacherous. Not here, where a tunnel more than twice Svarde's span bore the same topographical challenges as an average Noctia street. Kivi even dropped to the ground to take advantage, as the tunnel's top had been left alone to bear its natural juts and jumbles.

"Someone's caring for all this," Maena muttered as they

paced behind the corpse. She and Svarde had kept their mouths shut, weapons ready till they'd left the room free of further pursuit: apparently the corpses had their leader, and needed nothing else. "How many years would it take to hollow out a tunnel like this?"

"Too many," Svarde replied, and meant it.

Foti mining operations, and Svarde had to believe Whent's were similar, ran long on metal and manpower, smashing rocks with pick-axes whenever ferrites couldn't be bothered to help chomp deeper beneath the surface. Actually manicuring a mine to look as nice as this would, well, it just wouldn't.

Nobody would pay for it, nobody would care.

Unless.

The realization came as the tunnel broadened into the start, and only that, of someplace massive, someplace that shouldn't exist, someplace barring them from further steps by a giant, cavern-crossing gate. Svarde couldn't keep his mouth shut, letting his jaw drop slow as he looked over the rough, ramshackle, mass before him. The base, if Svarde could really see it, seemed to be some mishmash of metal and stone, a hurried construction to make two slabs as fast as possible. A great line ran down the middle, from the jagged tooth-like points at the top to the barely-brushing bottom, where further iron spikes jutted out towards them, like some horrifying mouth. That line bisected the cavern, bisected the gate, and it expanded when the corpse reached towards it with the same arm that'd been sticking straight out this whole time.

"Are those?" Maena asked, her voice barely a whisper.

"Believe they are," Svarde said. "Think we've come to the wrong place."

"Or the perfect one."

Both watched the gate open, lingered on the white and gray shapes plastered onto its outside above and below the metal teeth. At first, Svarde hadn't been able to tell what they were, but quick enough it'd become clear: mottled, worn with time, but clearly bones, stacked and smashed against the gate. Some might've been human, but more looked alien, with swooping lines or massive jaws, talons with many claws or only one. Chopped, sliced, battered and broken, with bits of gray mortar shoved between them.

"I've seen graveyards," Maena said as the gates completed their opening, sweeping outwards and almost grazing them with the teeth, "but nothing like this."

"It won't be the worst thing we see today."

There were some things you just knew.

The corpse began its forward march again. Maena, Svarde, and Kivi followed, with Maena again keeping her steps just behind the barbarian. Her hands, thankfully, free from any knives, swords, or other implements of random murder.

Those dark thoughts were hard to dismiss as they followed the corpse into what may have been a city once, but seemed closer to a mausoleum now. The cavern broadened beyond any Svarde had seen thus far, though buildings filled the space: strict, brutal shapes bearing carved stone's hard lines with a lacquered edge, as though the makers wanted every corner, every side to shine with the silver-blue light coming from the ever-present moss. Dark holes offered windows, though only one way.

Did eyes follow Svarde as he walked, the buildings growing and shrinking alongside him in a ramble reminiscent of a city growing too fast for itself? Were the standing hairs on his neck, the dryness in his throat imagination or a real threat?

The corpse, for its part, explained nothing. Maena and Kivi kept to themselves, the latter even forgoing her snorts.

They passed open squares, storefronts with signs long lost to dust. Fountains running dry. Empty stairs, deserted stone tables. Yet nowhere did mosses grow save in controlled lots, nowhere did water or weeds run free. As if the city designed its desiccation.

At last, though whether Svarde had walked for an hour or a day he couldn't be sure, they reached wide, yet shallow steps. Twenty or so leading up to a building, no, not a building, a . . .

"What is that?" Svarde asked as the corpse kept going up the planks.

Unlike the stone city, their apparent destination lacked the strict lines, the block structure. Instead, its ends curled on either side, brushing up against the stone. Sigils ran the dusty gray length, black lines on an otherwise slate surface. The lacquer found its marks around a sharp arrowhead door, the point rising well above Svarde's head. At the building's top, a couple cylinders, possibly smokestacks, rose the distance at an angle to the cavern's roof and vanished into the rock.

"I know better than to guess about anything here," Maena said, her voice still quiet. "Feel like we're being watched, and heard."

"You're not the only one."

"Follow the thing?"

Svarde nodded. "We've come this far."

Hardly a courageous Foti battle-cry, but Svarde couldn't muster up much else. They crested the steps in quiet, caught up to the corpse at the arrow door. The battered body stepped to one side there and gestured through.

"No further, eh buddy?" Maena said to the corpse,

whose mouth, a sallow thing that may not have opened for more years than Svarde had ever lived, didn't budge. "Guess not."

Svarde, his hands ever on his axe hilts, led the way through. Immediately, on either side, he noticed nothing. No benches, no chairs, no tables or flags. Those sigils, dancing unnatural lines, continued on the inside, though, and across the floor. No columns broke the space, no walls, only a broad emptiness leading to a single light shaft piercing down from above.

That light, silver, as if Sichi had lost her color, splashed on a solitary, sitting soul. The man sat at rest, both arms holding the hilt of a massive, yet ugly sword. With frayed ends sticking out from its black-metal body, the sword looked less like a craftsman's work than a wild fury embodied in . . . Svarde couldn't tell, from strides away, what metal forged the blade.

The man's armor, covering him in head to toe, was easier to read. An old make, ancient now. Stiff and heavy, for when humans had to tangle with fiends as a matter of daily life. A fact Svarde knew because it was Foti that made the armor, Foti that preserved its knowledge around the Grand Forge, in case such moving bastions were needed again.

"Hey there," Maena said, and Svarde snapped a glare her way, waved a hand to get her to shut up. If the man was sleeping, no need to wake him. An effort Maena ignored. "Neat place you've got here. Mind telling us what it is?"

The man creaked, his head, masked by a helmet graced, like the gate, with small columns made from stolen, mortared bones, rising to stare its nothingness at them.

"Welcome," the man said, his voice a chill wind, a harsh whisper. "Welcome to the unending nightmare."

CHAPTER 21

GOD PLAY

A Guardian and a thief. The role's latter half, part of Torny's past but not, unfortunately, staying there came to the fore quick as Wax and Eujo left the balcony and returned to a party in chaos. Some young man killed the band's drumming with loud calls about an assault, a smashed window, and a burglary. Revelers found sobriety quick, couples and groups searching out each other, confirming belongings and bodies intact.

Wax even reached for, found his skars in place on the necklace, an unnecessary check given their whispers floated in his mind's periphery.

"We should leave," Eujo whispered as their hostess began wrangling the party together, overriding the caustic yells with a controlled call to come to the ground floor's middle. "If that's Torny we saw, then they'll turn on us."

Wax snorted, "Turn on us? If that was Torny and Bliss, why would they—"

"Because your Guardians are the same as you, Wax. Don't you know that?"

"On Vis, you're not responsible if your brother does something stupid."

Eujo took a deep breath, the kind she seemed to take a lot around Wax, the kind that usually meant a lecture would be forthcoming. Wax could guess what it was, too: something about his position giving him responsibility, how he'd need to make things right, so on and so forth. Eujo seemed to love giving him these lectures, as if Wax wouldn't know the first thing about civilized society without them.

Not that this party would be civilized much longer.

Eujo started towards the curling stairs down as the young man, invited by the Denia went in on the scene. Two young women patrolling the library, looking for books to steal and finding an old family diary. One that must, so the young man surmised, starting to play to the interested audience, contain some secret worth knowing. When he tried to stop them, the foul thieves knocked him aside. Rather than prolonging the fight, scared, no doubt, of the man once he recovered his wits, the pair shattered the window and ran.

"Then we must chase them!" one listener shouted, only to realize what he said and amend it a moment later. "The guards should, anyway. Where are they?"

"The good ones left with Jochi," someone else, drink sloshing in an angry wave, said. "The warlord's made us vulnerable, given us up to the vultures!"

A din broke out at the words, screaming back and forth as cocktails and worse found their hold on the crowd. Wax noticed Eujo had stopped her descent, instead sidling back to him. The noise, the tension, pushed Wax to reconsider her remark: leaving now did appear to be the better play.

Reason had left the building.

"Don't think I want to wander into that," Eujo said. "Is there another way?"

"The balcony? It's a jump, but makeable. Or is that too far for royalty?"

"Before I ever wore a dress like this, I could make my way across any sky island. Let's go."

What a sky island was, Wax didn't know, didn't have time to ask. Instead, with Eujo pulling his arm, they retreated back through to the balcony and the cold night beyond. The railing invited a leap, the snowy ground below gave them a good place to land. Wax took stock of himself, the nice clothes Eujo had put on—that Wax found those clothes uncomfortable seemed unimportant—and asked if she cared they'd be ruined.

"There's a hundred more of these," Eujo replied. "I'll go first."

"Lead on," Wax said, and Eujo didn't wait.

Despite her dress, the Queen took two even strides, then lifted up, kicked off the rail and launched into the torchlit air. She didn't plummet, duck into a roll, or fall in helpless abandon like Wax expected. Instead, Eujo glided into a gentle landing. The snow puffed up in a pleasant welcome at her touch, and Wax only killed his shock when he remembered just what Eujo had in her possession: the Kance skar, again proving its worth.

"Cheater," Wax muttered, then squared his approach.

Only to stop when a heavy hand landed on his shoulder.

"An unusual way to leave a party, wouldn't you say?" asked a gruff voice, an older one.

Wax shrugged off the arm, looked back to see the man in a guard's thick, gray coat. Beyond the open hand, the guard had a second on a fat blade's hilt resting against his substantial waist. Dark fire glowed in the man's eyes, a flush on his face. A vanished life coming back.

For a moment, anyway.

"Looked a bit exciting downstairs," Wax replied, backing up to the railing. He tensed his legs, a little hop to the railing and off and he'd be clear. "Figured we'd get going early."

"Don't think you'll be doing that. Everyone's gathering below. There's going to be questions." The guard shifted, showed a second man behind him, equally old and equally thrilled at the chance to do something more than watch their employers eat, drink, and dance. "Colby's a good shot with his crossbow. You won't make the jump."

"You'd shoot a Renewal for nothing?"

"This is Whent in the winter, boy. What happens is what we say. Shame if you were to break your neck in a bad fall." The guard shifted again, now against the balcony's side, but still within reach of Wax's arm. His friend, Colby, had a clear view and, indeed, had a crossbow ready. "You can either give up your Guardian and her thieving friend, or you can pay their price."

"Some justice here. Who says—"

"We do," the guard cut him off. "Step away, now, or he shoots you in the leg. See how far you can run then."

Okay. Words wouldn't be cutting it here. Wax figured he could make a backflip—though the landing would hurt —but the crossbow might make the move fatal. Going back down into the party wouldn't be much better. Even if they didn't knock him dead right away, there'd be no leaving without turning in Torny.

Wax fought off a scowl, instead bathed in another smoky, cold breath. That thief would have a lot to explain once he caught up to her.

The heated thought sparked a new whisper, one sharp and vicious. Meaningless muttering urging Wax to act, to give into his frustration and let the skar handle things.

"C'mon. Three seconds more, and you're a wounded man at best," the guard said.

Maybe the skar had it right. A little flash, some surprise, and Wax could jump off the railing. Easy, just like before. Colby and his crossbow wouldn't stand a chance.

"You're not taking me anywhere." Wax gave into the skar as he spoke, the hot stone resting against his chest.

The Renewal's body killed the cold, filled with a searing heat. Like being on the Foti lava river, or maybe inside it. Wax's vision blurred, the Foti skar's whispers became a raging shout, hurling slamming syllables Wax couldn't understand at nothing, at everything. The air shimmered, the guard starting asking a question, when the floor, the walls, the two guards around Wax lit up.

One moment, a pleasant balcony illuminated by twin torches. The next, a roiling inferno, one casting back away from Wax into the massive estate. The fire reeled and writhed like a thing alive, flames jumping along an unnatural wind to grab artwork, furniture, the crowd coming to see a Renewal held to task. Colby and his crossbow vanished behind a frothing blue and orange blaze, someone's scream reaching Wax through the skar's mind-melting rage.

He jumped. No, fell. His hands, in sheer panic, gripping the railing behind him and pulling Wax over into a stiff plummet. Instinct saved him at the end, turning Wax into a roll, saving his shoulder from a dead strike, his head from a worse one. The landing sizzled, snow breaking his fall before bursting into steam. Wax at once froze at the chill wet and burned with the skar's whipping anger, its desire to cast yet more fire upon everyone, everything that might threaten Wax now or ever.

No. No. Desperately no.

Wax tried to focus, push away the skar. He found a source in his fingers, plunging into the frozen ground beneath the melted snow. The sturdy earth served as a center, his fire-blinded eyes finding comfort the dark brown.

"Get up," Eujo's fervent words. "We have to leave, now."

She pulled Wax to his feet, a stumbling move made worse with her sucking curses at his hot skin, his coat's singed edges. As he found his balance, Wax looked back, followed the screams, the calls for water, for help of any kind.

The reason was impossible to miss: the estate, not just the balcony, burned. The beautiful corridors, their arched openings the cause of so many quiet, wonderful nights crackled with orange death. Ash met drifting snow already. Other bodies copied Wax's move, leaping from balconies to land in dead thuds on snowbanks. Still more fled the estate's main doors, dragging their partners, their instruments, or their last, necessary drinks with them.

"Wax," Eujo said, icy as ever, "you've done this, and they'll come looking for you. Our time is up."

Not yet. Wax fought off terror, guilt, confusion and looked to the other whisper in his mind, the Rana skar's bubbling curiosity. If the Foti skar could create fire, then Rana should be able to make water, put out the fire.

So do it.

Wax pushed the command at the stone. Wished, ordered, demanded the Rana skar pull water from the sky, from the snow, from anywhere and quench the flames. Yet the stone didn't respond, its whispers the same muttering as before.

"It's not working," Wax said as Eujo pulled him back another step, the Queen tugging on his arm. "The Rana skar's not listening."

"They're not tools," Eujo replied. "They're pieces of the gods, Wax. They'll do what they want."

"I didn't want it to burn the whole building!"

"What *they* want, Wax. We open the door, we give them a chance, what happens then is up to them."

The words, the reasoning snapped Wax's hope, doused it in Eujo's cold logic. The estate burned. He'd lit it on fire, and he couldn't put it out. To stay any longer would mean death, prison, or something worse. Their only hope, the Renewal's only hope, was to run.

And at last he did, following Eujo beyond the abandoned gates into the city, while behind them the building burned bright.

CHAPTER 22

THE SCIENTIST'S SKAR

They shared breakfast on the small dock spearing the ocean off the Tenet's secret cave hideaway. The fourth day in a row Annalyse had come down a little after the sun made its start on the horizon, unlocked Quik's cage, and led him near the sea, plying him with fresh oat cakes and eggs. At first she'd done so with a knife by her side, a weapon Annalyse later said she could barely use. She'd dropped it after that, trusting Quik's word that he wouldn't try to overpower her, try to run.

Not that Quik wasn't thinking it, not that he didn't spend most seconds with those oat cakes tracking the distance from the dock around a black-rock mass curling into the ocean. Swimming around there would take him right to the Najahn docks, where workers would help effect his rescue. The timing, though, would have to be perfect.

Otherwise, with how much Ami destroyed his body, Quik would drown after a few strokes.

"She's working you hard?" Annalyse asked on the first day, an obvious question made to break what'd been a nervous silence.

The scientist—her own title for herself—seemed to have a hard time with casual conversation, a trait Quik noticed whenever he tried to turn their chats to Annalyse's life, her past, her interests and hobbies. Rather than answer, she had a habit of looking away, mumbling something noncommittal and returning to skewering Quik with one direct question after another.

"She's not lazy," Quik replied.

"I hope not. We're doing important work."

Work. Annalyse used that word a lot too, as if smashing small fiends with skars or dancing duels on the dunes was the sort of stuff that'd bring the Isles to peace and prosperity. Ami, at least, didn't distract herself with those ridiculous notions, setting every day's objective and pressing Quik until it was through, a process that tended to leave him bloodied, bruised, and exhausted.

At least now he knew he'd wake up to something pleasant.

"What's the end?" Quik asked. "Do you have enough skars for the Najahn to just win? Will you train them all?"

A good question. Quik could tell because Annalyse picked up a sparkle every time he hit on something right. Her hands would fidget, as if wanting to grab some invisible toy and demonstrate it. A dichotomy: Quik in his battered linens eating with a hunter's control, while Annalyse wore something Quik could only describe as pockets and belts, all tying into various pouches. Sometimes Annalyse would reach into one, pull out some odd brass or silver device, and describe how it could, someday, work with a skar to make something incredible.

A lot of possibilities, not a lot of actual, so far.

"If we do this right, they won't have to," Annalyse said.

"We'll make weapons so simple, so easy anyone can use them. Anyone can keep themselves safe."

She spoke with such blind belief Quik almost hated to push back.

"On Vis, we don't let anyone hold the spears," Quik said, dipping fingers caked in breakfast into the water. "You need to be old enough, responsible enough. It's an honor."

"What happens when danger comes after someone who doesn't have one?"

"The rest of us protect them."

"If you're not there?"

Quik shook his head, "Then they've made the wrong choice."

Annalyse stuck up a single finger, "See, that's what I'm saying. This way, with these, they won't need to worry. They won't need your spear."

"What about the Rana? Won't they use these in their raids? Couldn't they hurt so many more?"

"That's what the Najahn are for, Quik. Anyone abusing these, they get tossed in a cell."

Quik snorted. "Or to the ocean's floor."

Annalyse looked away, let the sea breeze spray out her snarled hair. The conversation killer, that look. Whenever things became too real, too beyond the invention, the possibilities, she did this.

Guess that's what being locked in a Tenet's tower could do to you.

Time for a different tactic.

"Why are you doing this?" Quik asked, and not for the first time. "Almost a week you've been coming down here every morning with food."

"You don't like it?"

"I do, but," Quik nodded back towards the caves, "I've been used a lot. I want to know why."

An honest smile. "Because there's not many people to talk to. Gladdring doesn't let me leave the tower, he thinks I might get in trouble. The other Tenets don't know I'm here, what we're doing. It's all secret, so I have the guards, I have Ami," Annalyse chuckled. "Ami, you know, the world's best conversationalist. Sawi was okay, but she always seemed to want to be somewhere else. And now you."

Quik had tried the Sawi route before, found that a dead end time and time again. Annalyse would only say Sawi and Gladdring had their own things going on, things she didn't know. Which left Quik himself, and his potential escape.

"So I'm fun to talk to?" Quik asked.

A sly smile, "Look at your competition."

He had to laugh at that, one that died as he noticed a ship coming in on the horizon, looping up from the east. Probably a Foti galleon.

"How much longer will you keep me here?" Quik asked. "Until I'm dead?"

"Or we get far enough along to reveal everything. Then it'll all be over."

"Cold comfort, Annalyse."

"You say that like I'm not a prisoner too. It's what dreams do to you, Quik. They take and take and take until you have nothing else."

Ami broke up the meal minutes later, coming down and declaring she had a new fiend, some new skars to test. Annalyse took the interruption without enthusiasm, wincing and mouthing a silent 'sorry' Quik's way. That gesture stuck with Quik down the dock, across the sand, beneath the caves, to a second, smaller cage newly stocked with a scrabbling critter.

Looking a bit like a furry beetle, the fiend fluttered from bar to bar, its child-sized self seeming incapable of landing anywhere for more than a second or two.

"It's fast," Ami said, handing Quik a knotted club, albeit one with a familiar metal hilt along its lower handle. Fitted with several skars, the hilt buzzed when Quik took hold, whispers alighting in his mind. "The goal isn't to kill it, but to slow it down. Stop it if you can."

They'd moved past sheer slaughter to more refined skills now. Annalyse called it finesse, a way to expand the gems' utility. The scientist stood behind Quik and Ami now, her ever present paper and charcoal pencil ready to scribe the observations.

The whispers told Quik which skars the club had: Foti, already snarling away to get going, get bashing. Rana, a mild bubbling murmur only picking up excitement if Quik looked towards the ocean. And the intended for today's test: a Kance skar, skittering about in his head as if Quik had downed too much coffee.

"Do it without going in the cage if you can," Ami continued. The Guardian, as ever, dressed for battle. As if her every day was a war, and she'd never be caught surprised. "I want to see range."

Quik nodded, focused on the Kance skar. However much he obsessed with escape, with getting free from his own prison, these tests always forced his attention. Ami had shown right away anything less would earn a slap, a slice, a battered punishment. So he looked at the flitting beetle fiend, sent his impression, what he wanted, for the monster to stop its flight and crash to the ground, right to the whispering Kance skar.

The club seemed to warm in his hands, the air around Quik picking up an electric tinge, as if a lightning storm neared. The Kance skar's whispers lost definition, became a fuzzy, excited static. The beetle leapt again, the spotted brown fur splitting to show iridescent wings in another fruitless journey across its cage.

Midway, only a couple beats later, Quik felt the skar snap. Like a fast exhale, a rush left Quik's body and found the beetle, knocking the bug into a sideways spiral. The fiend hit the sand, bounced, righted itself as Quik tried to hold his focus, eyes blurring with as the Kance skar swirled the air around him in a rapid, targeted funnel towards the fiend.

"Keep going," Ami ordered.

The skar listened when Quik urged it on, the gusts wrapping the beetle, shoving it down into the dirt. Pressing the struggling fiend to the sand. Quik found himself getting lightheaded, realized he was trying to breathe and failing as the Kance skar shoved all the air around him at the monster.

"Don't stop," Ami continued. "Crush it, now."

Another command, another skar strike, even as Quik fell forward, legs no longer able to keep him up. Ami caught him with one hand, continuing to urge him on.

"Stop it, Ami," Annalyse shouted, sudden and with more anger than Quik, in the dim fragments of his air-starved consciousness, had ever heard. "We have what we need. Let him go."

"We need to know the line, Annalyse." But Ami released Quik, let him fall to the dirt. When the hunter lost sight of the beetle, the skar relaxed, returned to its skittering. He breathed, tasted the sweet salt air again. Felt Ami's disgusted spit strike the sand near him. "If we don't know when a skar, whether a skar, will kill the person using it, we don't know the limits."

"Maybe we don't need to." Annalyse put her hands on Quik's back, slung an arm over her shoulder and helped him stand as the hunter heaved in one breath after another. "The whole point of this is to save lives, not spend them."

"One for a thousand, Annalyse. One for a million," Ami replied, then sighed. "It's fine. Gladdring wants to see us anyway. Something's in the works. Let the Vis rest."

Annalyse did just that, guiding Quik back to his cage, setting him in. Quik lay on the sand, letting his tired lungs put themselves back together. Heard Annalyse return, say he'd left part of his breakfast uneaten. There it was, waiting. She locked the door, walked away with a soft goodbye.

When Quik sat up, he saw the plate, the remaining cakes. Nestled in among them, wrapped in folded paper, was a turquoise gem, a Vis skar. On the paper, scrawled in quick letters, was a note:

Stay healthy, stay alive.

- Annalyse

Yet, as Quik took the skar into his hand, heard its comforting whispers, he had a different idea.

CHAPTER 23

FLEEING NORTH

Amazing how different it was to run with someone else than alone. Picking through unfamiliar streets, down random alleys, jumping obstacles and confusing pursuit were all things Torny knew how to do as well as she knew how to breathe, skills Yarvick hammered into her over and over before letting her take on her first jobs. Skills that faltered quick when she had to keep track of the particular person on her heels.

Bliss slipped and slid along the icy roads beyond the estate. Her boots kept what balance they could, but the Vis had no experience on the ice and it showed. Every time Torny twisted around a corner, every time she told Bliss to jump, to squeeze through a slim opening in a fence, the thief had to stop, turn, and catch the Vis before she splayed out on the ground.

The sloppy flight didn't do much to keep them quiet either. The city wasn't exactly what Torny would call populated—having a good part torched by the recent fiend attack must've dampened the mood—but enough were out in the late evening tending to repairs, scrounging for food, or just staring up at the snowy, clouded dark to ensure the pair never went without shouted questions or curious looks.

All in all, a crappy time for thievery.

The diary, though, kept its weight in her coat pocket. Success salved many things, and Torny, in those brief stable moments dashing along an avenue or behind a building, flashed to the approval, the compliments, the kindness Yarvick would finally show when she returned the book to him. A sweetness she'd gone far too long without, quiet in its impossibility but now tantalizing in opportunity.

Perhaps a problem to consider some time when she wasn't dodging around a wagon, ducking an ox's chuffed look, or picking a new route on unfamiliar roads.

'Where are we going?' Bliss signed when Torny slowed, coming to a broad circular square. In its center burned a bonfire, a beacon in the night and the repository for things too damaged to save. 'Or are we running at random?'

Several ash-flaked people who'd given up their fur coats in the fire's heat tossed scrapes on the blaze while carts filtered in here and there to add to the piles. Nobody paid the pair any mind, and without a guard's chorus on their tails, Torny figured they could take a beat.

"I wanted to get to the *Storm's Edge*," Torny said. "Turns out, it's hard to navigate this town in the dark."

Not totally true, but an easier explanation than detailing how going right to the most obvious destination was a mistake. The people at the estate would figure out quick, if they hadn't already, who Torny and Bliss were. They'd swarm to the *Storm's Edge* first in a frantic search, then slowly scatter out when they didn't find anyone. That's when there'd be gaps in the patrol, a way to slip past, get to the ship, and—

'Wax will understand,' Bliss signed, apparently reading the worry in Torny's face as they stayed standing on the square's edge, watching embers spark up with every toss. 'He trusts you.'

"After this? I doubt that."

'You have your reasons.'

"Doesn't mean he'll understand them. Doesn't mean I'm right, either. It's a choice I made, Bliss. I'm not going to run from it."

Bliss took Torny's arm, a grip too tight for affection, more one to keep a captive from running away.

'You're not going to give all this up for a book, are you?'

"What would you give up for a chance at getting your life back?"

'I don't understand?'

"This book is my ticket. It pays a debt." Torny again felt for, found the diary. Right where it was supposed to be. "When I bring it back, I'll be forgiven."

'And what about us? My brother? Your oath?'

Juggling debts. Nothing new there.

"I'll find a way to pay him back too. Square everything."

'You believe that.'

Not a question. Torny appreciated that. Bliss wasn't some rube waiting to get scammed, though maybe she had been back on Foti. Not anymore. Something, at least, Torny had done for the Vis. Now, she could do Bliss one more favor and let her escape without something worse.

"Let's go," Torny said. "Circle down to the water. They'll be getting to the ship soon."

This time, they walked. Bliss kept her footing, Torny kept their pace controlled, and the people they passed lost their curiosity. Just another pair lost in the ruin.

The beach didn't provide many answers. More frigid

than the town, the sand speckled with flashing sparkles. A mystery answered when both Torny and Bliss approached a mound brighter than all the rest, finding a strange obsidian stone at its head and a glassy sheen beneath. Bliss touched it, proclaimed the glass a bumpy version of what they could find on the *Storm's Edge*.

"Fiends are getting worse and worse," Torny said. "Now they can do this?"

'This isn't so bad. It's almost pretty.'

Torny laughed. "Bliss, how do you do that? Turn every situation into something better and brighter than it should be?"

At first, Torny would've called it innocence, a lack of knowledge about how grim the isles were. Bliss didn't have that excuse anymore, and yet she still persisted, determined both to succeed and not to lose her soul in doing so. Admirable, and almost irritating.

'Because I'm a Vis, Torny. I'm a lucky one. I will not lose that.'

"Even looking at this?" Torny pointed at the glass, the obsidian. "What's going to happen when these things are everywhere?"

Bliss shrugged, the furred shoulders barely moving beneath the thick coat. 'They killed this one. How bad could it be?'

Torny flicked her head back to the ruined town. "Think that's your answer."

'They'll rebuild. Just like we did.'

Another argument started to form in Torny's mouth only to die away. There wouldn't be any changing her, not this way. And was it so bad, having some hope for once?

"C'mon," Torny said, "let's head back. Slow and quiet. We'll see if they're gone yet."

The guards had never arrived at all. On the way towards the ship, Bliss pointed out the orange glow against the cliff walls towards the city's back end, right where the estate had been. A massive blaze, and one Torny credited with saving their skins. Whatever good fortune had made it, Torny thanked them.

Though that thanks died fast when they found their friends aboard the *Storm's Edge*, Eujo and Deux packing up satchels while Wax stood on the ship's bow, glassy eyed and stunned. Bliss went to his side, started signing up a furious series, while Eujo cornered Torny and demanded an explanation.

The Queen threw up her regal poise, but Torny picked out a soft crack in Eujo's stern jaw, eyes, mouth. A bond, there, of one thief to another.

"You understand," Torny started, the two in Torny's cabin while the thief threw her vital things, the tools and knives necessary to survive wherever they were going. "You know what it's like to owe a debt."

"The one I owe Kance is larger than any you possibly could have," Eujo said, blocking the slim door out. She'd changed from the party's finery to thicker pants, shirt, boots made for a hike. A hint Torny should do the same. "I'm sacrificing everything to repay that debt. You nearly threw that effort away tonight."

Torny shook her head, "They wouldn't have hurt two Renewals. You're safe."

"Two *competing* Renewals? You're as cynical as I am, Torny. Betting on their kindness is a poor choice."

The satchel packed, Torny stood, squared up to Eujo. Set up a sardonic smile, folded her arms. "The bet paid off." And now for the play's second act, slipping that smile into a serious, straight face. "You want me gone, I'll go. But this was my one job. I'll never risk you or Wax again."

"A fine thing to say now that you've turned an entire isle against us."

Torny snorted. "It's winter. By the time word travels anywhere, we'll be done here." Torny nodded down at the boots. "Guessing that means we're walking?"

"Deux says the ice is going to be too thick to sail around the isle's north side. So we're hiking."

"Long and cold."

Now Eujo put on the grin. "Too cold for a thief?"

"Never said that."

"Then finish getting ready. We're leaving tonight, before the people you royally pissed off decide to come looking for us."

"So I'm still your Guardian?"

As if copying Torny, Eujo let the grin fall into a glare. "Until I find someone better. Don't screw up again, thief, or I'll turn you over to those rockbiters myself."

According to Deux, their departure began a little after midnight and well before the estate escape's energy ran dry. Wax kept quiet, his eyes often moving to the still burning mansion in the distance, but at least he walked. Torny led the way, again marching the quartet, now burdened by packs, across the beach to the town's western end before cutting north. The streets were finally deserted, leaving nobody to accost their travels, much less any guards hunting thieves.

As getaways went, Torny ranked this one among her smoothest, though she found pride hard to claim. After Eujo mentioned Wax's skar and its ensuing blaze, Torny couldn't quite give herself credit. Neither, yet, did she fall into muted discomfort like Bliss and her brother. Eujo, at least, seemed to understand she couldn't control everything: move on with the quest, don't get caught up in disasters.

Just like a good thief, or someone who needed to maximize every opportunity, slim as they were to find.

At its northern end, the city dwindled as it ran up a slope breaking, at last, onto Whent's vast plain. The cloudy dark meant nothing save a windy, swirling snow lay beyond. The road, at least, had sturdy stone poles jammed into the earth every few strides to keep travelers on track in the blizzard. A trail, so said the lone watchman at the gates, a sleepy man too somnolent to register shock at their odd departure time, that would take them all across the isle if they chose.

"And the skars?" Eujo asked. "Will it take us there?"

"The Golden Gash?" the man replied. "Go straight, don't turn once, and you'll make it. Or, I should say, you might."

"Might?"

"There's fiends out there sure, but worse still if you're not traveling with a bigger crew." The man peeked out from his guard house, nestled near great wooden gates and a torch forest. "Not big enough, and on foot too? You're liable to freeze or starve before you make the Najahn."

"We'll be fine," Eujo countered. "Open the gate."

Before she'd stolen the diary, Torny might've argued there. Suggested they find a cart, some ox or something to pull them along. Now, as the man shook his head and opened the doors wide, revealing the blustery tundra, Torny kept quiet.

Every job had its price.

CHAPTER 24
ASSASSIN'S ASK

What did loyalty get you?

Sawi kept repeating the question to herself within her new confines. Stone, small, barred. High up in a tower Sawi hadn't seen from the outside —Fassle's appointed guards moved her through tunnels and cramped stairs, back ways designed to keep curious eyes away. A bench with a stale mat, a dirty pot beneath for her body's needs and not much else. The window somehow shrank on her old one, now little more than a dinner plate in size.

No glass either, giving winter's chill free rein to bluster about her suddenly thin clothes.

Fassle took those too: no Najahn robes for a prisoner, no Tamas skar either. Only what must've been a grain sack in a prior life and the thinnest, rattiest sandals ever forced upon feet. Nothing more, everything less. She'd been tossed in the cell and told to wait, then left there.

Hours ground away with Sawi, her regrets, and little else. She'd had two meals already, if you can call stale bread, moldering fruit, and melted snow as a meal. Any attempts to voice displeasure were met with silence. Not even a shrug.

At least, Sawi supposed, the guards don't seem to relish it. They didn't beat her, didn't mock her, just said nothing beyond any instructions and left her alone.

For a time Sawi tried to put herself back on Vis, argue that staying home would've meant constant regret, wondering why she hadn't taken the new chance when it'd come her way. She put herself back among those trees, climbing high and almost touching the sky, the birds.

Wax had a Renewal's cloak. No way they'd imprison him, not when, as Fassle put it, Noctia and the Najahn safe-guarded the world. Sawi had no such leverage, had no such—

"So the Vis has made a mess."

The voice had an alien familiarity, as if someone were trying to match a Vis accent, what Sawi's family sounded like, but didn't quite get there. It belonged to a lanky man not in Najahn robes, but clean clothes, gray and blue. Several silver chains gathered about his neck and looped his ears, a make-up Sawi recognized as Kance. No purple and black anywhere. Not a Najahn, then?

"Who are you?" Sawi asked.

"Someone who sees trouble and looks to trade on it. My name is Livier, and I'm looking for my queen."

"What?"

Livier, rather than answering Sawi's question, nodded as if she'd answered his. He reached out a hand, a bandage tight across its palm, and ran it along the bars. "Fassle thinks you aren't party to the Vis Renewal's actions. I hoped otherwise, but alas."

"Again, what?"

Livier wrapped his fingers around the bar. A loose hold,

then tight, as if gripping some chicken's neck. "The Vis Renewal and our Queen are, to their vast misfortune, traveling together. A mistake brought by several people who failed in a most miserable way."

"You keep talking in riddles."

"And perhaps the Vis are exactly as simple as the rest of the isles believe."

Sawi stood, hit the bars fast enough to reach, grab Livier's hand and pin his wrist against the metal.

"I push on this, I'll break it," Sawi growled. "My day's been, how'd you put it, messy, and I'm not feeling you. Say what you want, what I'll get out of it, and then we can be done with this dance."

Livier whistled. Not a frightened sound, nor did his gaze waver. He left his hand in Sawi's grip, relaxed.

"At least you're willing to take initiative," Livier said. "And I believe you have time to waste. Seasons upon seasons, according to Fassle. The Najahn aren't big fans of traitors once they're caught."

"Still not saying anything I care about."

Sawi fought hard, though, to keep Livier's words off her face, her ice nerves intact. Seasons spent in this cell? She'd wither up. Lose her mind. Join the occasional mad screaming from elsewhere in the tower, sounds that only shut up when the guards grew bored enough to make them.

Not a death, a life, meant for a Vis.

"Then how about this," Livier said. "Confirm my intuition. You know the Vis Renewal, yes?"

"Why do you want to know?"

"Because my Queen assumes your Renewal can keep her safe. He cannot. Not from what's coming."

Sawi blinked. Dropped Livier's hand and took a step back inside her cell.

"What's coming?"

LIvier nodded, a slow move, as if he'd decided now to rest Sawi with some formal respect.

"Kance has two Queens. Their rule is always uneasy by design. No power gets too comfortable. However, one Queen has decided the other no longer needs to live. Assassins are in play, more dangerous than any fiend. If the Vis Renewal travels with their target, his life might well be forfeit."

Any kid on Vis grew up learning not to trust a single source. While that lesson tended to come with lies about fresh fruit, a good vine route, or the size of the fish caught for dinner, caution with wild claims had Sawi narrowing her eyes, tapping a finger on her thigh as she stood in the cell's center.

"So, what, in the middle of a Renewal your Queens decide to kill each other?"

"Chaos often makes for opportunity."

"Then you're, what, the other queen's buddy? Trying to warn her?"

"Protect." Livier fell into a stern mask at the word. "It's a step too far to do this now, with so much danger. And if Kance claims the Aegis, then my Queen's problem is resolved anyway. She's giving into aggression."

"She's going to get Wax killed?"

Livier tilted his head, "Wax? Is that the Renewal's name?"

Damn. Sawi bit at her lip, brushed away the mistake. The Tamas skar had been keeping her fed these last weeks, whispering emotions and intent in her ears. Without it, she felt lost, without any way to navigate Livier's conversational fog.

Retreat, then. See if she could reset.

"So you want to find the queen, your queen. You want me to help with that?" Sawi asked. "Because I don't know where they're going. I'm not a Guardian."

"I can see that. We have their destination. With a little luck, the storms will thin the ice enough for us to catch up. No, what I'm here for, what I want to know, is what your Renewal cares about. His loves, his fears. Can you tell me that?"

Astounding how fast curiosity could turn to loathing. Sawi would've called for the guards right then if she thought they'd come.

"Even if I could, why would I?"

"A very simple reason, Sawi. When we find our Queen, your Renewal seems like he will try to get in the way. When he does, we'll need something to convince him to leave us alone. Let us do our jobs and protect her. That thing, that rope, that will save his life . . . I think you can give it to me."

So Livier wasn't just walking up here on a hunch. He had information, and Sawi saw it now in Livier's stance. Not a man fishing for answers, but who had most of them and needed just a little bit more. Worse, the loose arms, the slightest curled smile, suggested he was someone who'd do what he thought necessary to get it.

"You're not trying to hurt Wax?" Sawi asked, doubting she could trust him, but needing to ask it anyway.

"Why?" Livier, for once, gave genuine affront. "I live in this world. Kance does too. We need an Aegis, and Wax could be the next one. Not everyone, though, has those scruples."

A manipulative response? Yes. One she could argue with? No. What could Sawi do anyway? Get tortured or twisted for nothing? Maybe the guy would take what she said and really do what he proposed, use it to keep Wax safe.

Either way, Sawi would still be here in the cell. At least this way she wouldn't get hurt.

"His sister is a Guardian," Sawi said. "She's mute and fierce. If you get her on your side, Wax will do what you want."

Livier nodded. "Anything else? For his safety, you understand."

Sawi hesitated. A glimmer. A sick warmth spread through her gut at the thought, at knowing the thought was about to become action, but she couldn't stop the words. The cell was too small, the stone too cold. She couldn't stay here, not one moment longer than necessary.

"Me. Tell him what's happening to me, and he'll forget about your queen," Sawi said. "We . . . "

"Say no more," Livier gave another nod, this one more formal, a bargain struck. "I'm sure Fassle will see his way to mercy should the Vis Renewal ask for it. I'll offer the same before we sail." A full smile, genuine as the snort before. "Thank you, Sawi. You might have saved many lives today."

Yet no comfort came with the cold after Livier left. Only the screaming, only the wind, only her thoughts growing ever darker.

CHAPTER 25

THE FIRST GUARDIAN

In a ravaged world, there were two. Amid desperation, destruction, and violence, there were two who left behind the ashes and the blood in hopes of something better. They stole and strove, fought and fled across the Seven Isles, then a savage ruin amid the chaos of dying gods and wild fiends. Sword and dagger, rope and axe, Demion and her Guardian crossed the mountains, the plains, and the rivers as four long years burned by.

Their goal arose by accident, a chance discovery amid the high Kance mountains. A glistening silver stone and its whispers, fragments of what the gods had once spoken when they lived, when all the people were merely gnats upon greatness. Demion, then just a scrabbler, a survivor, guessed what those soft fragments meant.

The last musings of dead divinity.

The skars, as they came to be called, held power. Random, yes, but enough to shift the balance between the people and a hostile world. Demion enlisted her friend, a man more accustomed to hollowing out rock for cavern shelters than wielding those same tools against monsters.

When hope has little to hold onto, it grabs what it can.

Six skars, and the last brought them to Noctia, to the crater's center, the Wound's mighty gash. The pair, battle-scarred and bruised, descended, aided now by followers, as legends often are. Demion's hope proved infectious, doubly so when she followed speeches with skar-powered slaughter, driving fiends away or destroying them outright.

Long ropes brought the pair down, ladders into the deep. Clinging to rock, Demion and her Guardian retied their ropes and descended further, further into the dark. Their followers, from soldiers to smiths, weavers to woodsmen, put their feet on the knots behind them. Songs rang out, mixed here and there with a clash of blade on flesh as rising fiends met their end. Through it all, Demion used the skars, their fire, wind, and rock to clear their path.

"Until we came here," the Dead King said, as Svarde and Maena rested, with Kivi munching on fallen rock nearby. "Only a cavern then, and not a large one. Demion and I followed the caves to the end. There, we found Noctia's last light, her skar, and with it, the source of the fiends. She took the skar, told me to hold to the end, build a redoubt while she secured the surface. Then, with all humanity behind her, we would march together and end the monsters."

"Didn't work, did it?" Maena said, crunching through a dried apple.

"As I said, it's easy to find hope. Harder to realize it." The Dead King, still sitting on the rough dais holding the sword, helmet and armor on, stared back. "We had supplies coming down, people too, ferrying them. The Wound became our road as we hollowed out this place, built it into, if not a city, then a home." The man's left fist, unburdened by the blade's hilt, gave a gentle pound on his thigh. "I still remember it. The shock when the ropes fell.

One after another they thudded into our dust, cut from above."

"Demion abandoned you?" Svarde asked.

"Did she? I don't know. You're the first one from the surface I've met since that day. We've sent emissaries, groups, chances, and all failed to return." The Dead King sighed, a hollow sound. "Hope dies quick down here. Life isn't made to last in the dark. When it became clear, after seasons and years, that Demion wouldn't come back, that our lives were being spent to block the fiends, we tried. Those of us that were left, we tried to make an end."

The man shifted his grip on the jagged sword, lifted its massive bulk a fraction off the floor.

"We found this. I found this. A shard of Vis's dagger, and within it, a power over death and life together."

That phrase prompted a thousand questions, but Svarde held them back. Focused on his water skin instead. Something in the man's tone said he'd not had a chance to tell this story for a long time, that interrupting now would be a grievous offense.

Not a chance to take with someone claiming mastery over the bodies littering the caverns beyond.

"At first, a blessing. Then, a curse. Every friend I made, their children and their children's children became less than memories. Fiends, disease, simple accidents turned my family, for that's what we became, into tools. Bodies to throw at the unceasing stream. I wield them like you might twitch your fingers, a command acted on without resistance, with blind force, until all that remains is torn apart."

"Okay." Maena held up a finger, tilted her head. "You've got this blade, it can take the dead and make 'em do what you want. Why don't you wake up all these fiends you're killing and march them against their own?"

The Dead King turned to the blade. "Like fingers, I said. Perhaps someone else could find a way, but I can't cross the gap. A dead fiend is as blank to me as it is to you, but bring me near enough a human's body, and I feel it waiting."

"So you've been sitting here, dithering, all this time?" Maena asked, her apple finished and replaced with an angry confusion. "Building up your bone gate, with the fiends right there?"

"We tried. More than once, we carved our way to the source, and more than once we tried to destroy them with what we had. Axes, rocks, blades, we found our methods ineffective. So I turned again to Demion's last words, to hold this place, and did as she asked."

"Not very well."

"Hey," Svarde started, only for the man's jangling, clanking rise to cut him off.

"A dead man makes for a poor fighter," the old warrior said. "A broken body less so. We've faced the fiends as best we can, but our numbers are dwindling. They make it past often now, and soon there will be nothing left to stand in their way." Svarde picked up an almost happy note in the man's voice. "I'm going myself, now, to stand at the gate and wait for my deserved end."

"So you're giving up?" Maena spat off to the side. "Coward."

The Dead King didn't bother replying, walking past Maena with his slow steps. The thick metal boots rang through the dwelling with every footfall. At the room's exit, as Svarde packed up his own meal, the man stopped, the heavy blade now balanced on his shoulder.

"Do you want to see why?" the old warrior asked. "Do you want to see the source of it all?"

"We're here to end it, so yeah, let's go," Maena replied.

"She's right," Svarde added. "We have friends on the way. Together, we'll—"

"You'll find what we found," the Dead King cut him off. "One last look at our unrelenting horror."

He continued out the arched door, down the steps and away.

"Not an uplifting guy, is he?" Maena asked, following Svarde's example and making ready to walk. "You'd think he'd be happy to see us."

"Demion was hundreds of years ago." Svarde slotted his axes at his waist. Brushed off the exhaustion, the continual aches and pains following his every move. "He's been down here so long. Does he even remember what it's like to be happy? To enjoy anything?"

"Nothing to lose, then. Might as well go for it."

Svarde glanced Maena's way as they started after the Dead King. "You're not sounding or acting like yourself, Maena. What's wrong?"

The Rana captain snickered, a sound that made Kivi snort in surprise. "You're not going to believe this Svarde, but being just about killed a few dozen times in the space of a season changes a person. Getting your soul sucked out by a fiend might shift your outlook, your mind. Makes things a bit scrambled." She gave a wild wave after the King. "But I'm still here where it counts. When those fiends come, I'll get all stabby stabby with the best of them."

"I don't understand?"

Maena, though, only laughed, and followed.

An ancient warrior with a fragmented mind, bent on his own final rest in the dark, an unstable Rana captain liable to do anything at any time. Those were his allies here at the last step. Svarde found Kivi, reached down to give the loyal ferrite a pat on her stone head.

"You and me are going to have to stick close," Svarde muttered to the lizard. "Don't do anything stupid, and you might get out of this alive."

As for himself, as Svarde trailed the other two back through the dead city, what did it matter. The only thing that would bring him a little smile, a little happiness, was Jochi's army, and knowing it might bring word back to Catya about their grand end, and the deliverance Svarde would finally bring to her.

CHAPTER 26
SNOW MARCH

Strange how excitement, anger, and will to live could die in a few hours, curdling into a menacing exhaustion as Wax stepped one booted foot after another on the hard ground treading north into Whent's vast tundra. Gale-blown snow whipped across a road bordered only by poles jammed deep into the earth. In a way, the wind kept the drifts from growing too deep to cross. In another, the air felt like knives digging into his skin.

Eujo and Torny seemed less affected, their warmer blood waging a better stand against Winter's chill. Wax, his furred hood ruffling into his eyes, shot glances at the pair every few steps, both in envy of their apparent resilience and to confirm he hadn't wandered off into the white. The night's misadventures left Wax's legs heavy too, a burden clinging ice did nothing to alleviate.

The skars, though, made their benefits known.

First came Vis, its turquoise brilliance serving as a continual rejuvenation, healing up Wax's frozen limbs, parched skin, and blistered feet. Both he and Eujo passed their Vis skars around to their Guardians, spreading the benefits to keep their foursome moving. Sharing the trip, too, were the Foti skars and their endless warmth, little fiery pockets Wax held in his hand, rested against his chest, or even dropped in a boot just to nurture some life into a dragging foot.

"We should've taken a dozen of the things," Torny said as morning stretched to noon, not that any of them could really tell: the day's blinding snowstorm made time an impossibility. "Nobody would've stopped us."

"Until the next Renewal came along and found themselves without a chance," Eujo replied. Both had to shout over the wind's snapping noise, a prospect making Wax's throat itch. "That wouldn't be fair, right, or good for the Isles."

"I hate how what's good for the Isles never seems to be what's good for me."

"That estate burned for you," Wax said, "because it was good for the isles we survived."

"Bliss and I were gone by then."

Wax shot the bandit a glare, one Torny answered with a shrug. The bandit's acerbic tongue always seemed to target other people, a trait Wax hadn't noticed till right then, till Torny played off what'd happened last night as a random act, a poor choice, and not her fault.

At least the rising anger served to push away the cold, give his footsteps more heft.

"We wouldn't be out here like this if you'd kept your hands clean," Wax said.

"You don't know that," Torny shot back. "Didn't see any wagons for sale. No beasts to pull'em either. That warlord took'em all underground. We'd be marching either way."

"With better supplies and friends behind, instead of enemies."

"If those people are your friends, Wax, you ought to find better ones."

"We could've used them, Torny," Eujo entered the fray, her royal tone adding an iron logic. "They would've helped for their own gain. Not friends like you and Bliss, but friends we would have liked."

"Sure, until they stabbed you in the back."

"Only one stabbing back there was you," Wax muttered.

"What's that, Renewal? You saying something?"

Bliss lurched to her left, grabbing the bandit's arm and forcing Torny to look her way. Fingers flashed, the snow making it too hard for Wax to catch. Not that it mattered, he could get the gist: calm down Torny, stop making an ass of yourself, so on and so forth.

The same conversation she'd had with Wax time and time again, when he'd had too much peach wine or fallen in love with his own ego.

A level-headed woman, Bliss. Without her, this whole adventure would've fallen apart a long time ago. He would've given up, been back on Vis, enjoying some nice morning sun. Failure's sweet consolation prize.

Evening brought respite, the snowstorm slowing down enough to show off some rocks clustered just off the road. A sign hung there with grim distances plastered on its lacquered board, ones claiming they'd made less than half a day's progress at their awful pace. A week to their goal now looked more like two, far longer than the rations they'd packed.

"Turn back?" Torny answered Wax's question as they huddled beneath the stones, the jutting slabs looking like granite flower petals launching to the sky. "They'll kill us."

"Better than freezing to death out here," Wax said.

"Besides, maybe if you give them back the diary, they'll, well, probably still kill you."

"Exactly."

"There's no going back." Eujo nodded at Bliss, who'd been scrounging around the stones' bases to find grasses, shrubs, and dried weeds. She'd stacked them up, with some help from the others, and now had a small fire on the way. "Bliss has it right. We're here, we're Renewals, and this journey won't end till one of us sits on the Wound's throne."

"Or we're all frozen statues," Torny said. "Guess they could take the diary then. Pry it from my icy fingers."

"There's a thought," Wax mused.

"A better one would be sleep. Food. Getting what rest you can, because we'll need to walk faster tomorrow," Eujo said, then waved a hand into the air, as if surfing it on the breeze. "The wind's dying down. It'll be an easier journey."

"Hope so, because my legs are about to fall off," Torny said. "Bliss, give me a nudge when something's cooked." The bandit started to roll over, her satchel on some snow as a makeshift pillow. "Someone wake me for my turn at the watch."

Wax snorted, "You think anyone's out looking to steal something tonight?"

"Not a thief," Torny said into her satchel, sleep already snatching at her words.

"Whent has more threats than snow and ice," Eujo added, staring into the growing flames as Bliss spurred them to life. "Torny's right. We'll set a watch."

"Then I'll take the first shift," Wax said. "Not tired anyway."

After some light nibbling—the cold seemed to steal appetites as well as warmth—Eujo and Torny gave in to their dreams. Bliss came over, sat next to Wax with the fire glowing against their backs. The tundra sprawled before them, an endless dark beneath a clouded sky. No stars, no sights, and little sound save the wind's slowing rustle.

'I know you're upset with Torny,' Bliss signed, tucking her hand back into her pockets between flashes. 'She had a reason, Wax.'

'I'll bet.' Wax adopted the hand signals, saving his voice from breathing in any more cutting air. 'I'll bet, too, it's nothing compared to the Aegis.'

'To her, it is.'

'Then she needs to adjust her priorities.'

Bliss frowned, an expression hard to see in the shadows. She turned, bored a sullen hole into the ground with her eyes. Wax kept his to the distance, tried to imagine a jungle there, vines to swing on. Sawi in the summer sun.

'She's not just a Guardian,' Bliss signed after several minutes.

'I know. She's a thief.'

'That's not what I mean. You know that's not what I mean.'

Did he? Wax read his sister's face, her clear eyes and bright stare. Not a person scared, a person cowed, a person wondering who and what they were. No, Bliss seemed to be right where she wanted to be. He drifted his look to the bandit's sleeping form, replayed Bliss's signs.

They did spend time together, Bliss and Torny. Everywhere the group stopped, those two tended to spirit off. Well after Wax and Eujo might call it quits on the ale, Torny would have Bliss downing flagons, signing sloppier and sloppier signals. They'd come back from another Noctia night talking about rooftops scaled, sights seen not meant for normal eyes. A certain kind of adventure Wax knew well.

'You think you know what you're talking about,' Wax signed and drew a scowl. 'Trust me. I've been there. It feels real, like the best thing you'll ever know.'

'It is the best thing I've ever known.'

'Right, but Bliss, you're young. You've never had something like this before.'

'Oh, because you're some sort of expert?'

'Well, Sawi—'

Bliss had her head shaking before Wax finished signing the name. 'You left her. That's not what Torny and I have.'

'We grew up, Bliss. Just like you will. Torny's fine, but she's going to get herself hurt or killed with her tricks. I don't want you winding up the same way.'

'Says the brother who asked her sister to come on this thing.' Bliss stood up. 'I'm sorry that you can't be happy for me, that you're being sour, because if there's one thing I've learned over these last weeks, it's that anything can end at any time. I'm going to find my fun, no matter what anyone says.'

Bliss turned, walked over near Torny and settled onto the ground, threw her hood up over her head, and offered nothing more to Wax. A cold goodbye, one salved not in the least by the skars whispering in his head. The stones, those castoffs of the gods, offered no advice, leaving Wax to banter with himself, argue with visions against the dark.

He'd made his choices, Bliss could make hers. Back on Vis, Wax hadn't ever judged Bliss, Quik, or anyone else for their romances, their flings. Why start now?

Because his life, their lives depended on sober minds and stout hearts?

The tundra gave no answers.

CHAPTER 27
TRAITOR'S TURNABOUT

His hands bled, the fingernails torn. His arms bore scratches, some bleeding and others scabbing over. His back bore gouges where the cage's bars made their marks, his hole not quite deep enough for a seamless escape.

Yet Quik stood beyond the bars a free man, albeit one in enemy territory. He wasn't alone: the Vis skar kept up its whispering comfort, a sound Quik knew well, had trusted in during the frantic hours after unwrapping Annalyse's note. The skar's healing kept Quik invigorated as the afternoon wore on, kept him digging well after Ami or Annalyse should have returned. That they hadn't was a question in itself, one Quik resolved to answer after he'd done the important thing and left the Tenet's terrible tower.

The cave network near the sea wasn't large, with its several chambers drawing back from a single surfside opening. Those chambers all ended in cages like Quik, the other two holding fiends waiting for their chance to dance with the skars. In the network's center rested a stone stair, one that'd take Quik back up into the tower and Najahn life. The only other option would be to take a dive and hope the waves didn't dash him against the cliff rocks, a foolish move for a man who knew he wasn't the Isles' strongest swimmer.

On Vis, one didn't need to live in the water.

The stairs, then. A tricky path to climb in quiet, with little cover. Nevertheless, the hunter approached with as much stealth as he could muster, clinging to shadows beneath the dark rock as the sea echoed its usual grumbles. Quik's hair, skin bore saltwater's dryness, a starchy discomfort shoved aside, at last with purpose. Those steps called, and with no shapes, no sounds up above, Quik took the first.

Stepping on something other than sand for the first time in days had Quik wobble, had him reaching and gripping the narrow railing with his left hand, his right occupied with the skar. The stone chilled his bare feet, but held, a marvelous feeling after so long uncertain on shifting sand. Another step, up and around the tight spiral, climbing up the drill into the tower's base.

The lowest level marked Annalyse's lab. Or was it Gladdring's? Quik shook off the question, emerged into the torchlight circular room through the entry, the spiral loosening into a languid curve ending with a flat platform. There, sprawled throughout, waited the chests, the artifacts, the wonders. Quik caught himself staring, having never seen the room before save a brief glance as they tore him down, captive, that first day.

Then, he'd been occupied with more immediate pressures.

Quik crawled his eyes over the skars, the devices, marking each and how many. A few days ago so many of these metal constructs, the weapons and tools with carved insets would've been mysteries. Now he cataloged their spots, their functions, the skars set alongside for their use. More Vis and Foti skars than most. Rana and Kance seemed fewest. That fit what Quik surmised: the wind isle kept the Najahn as far away as they could, while Rana was a fiend-disrupted disaster.

He listened and heard no voices, felt no tremors from quiet steps on the stone-and-wood floor. Quik stayed in a crouch, feeling his way along the room's perimeter, his eyes always looking up, watching for any surprise arrivals.

That attention earned him a chance to duck behind a skar shelf when the door above, connected by another sloping stair, banged open and two familiar voices cascaded into the room.

"We'll get as many as we can and leave," Ami said, her voice stretched with suppressed panic. "Gladdring can hold them long enough."

Steps, loud. More than one person.

"Hold them with what?" Annalyse, the second voice. "He's a talker, not a fighter."

"Then he'll blather their ears off."

The pair landed hard in the central floor, Annalyse with two satchels over her shoulders. Ami in leathers, a blade over her shoulder. The scientist, hands twitching and face pale, froze for a long moment, until Ami reached, pulled a satchel off Annalyse's shoulder and started stuffing it at random.

"No, we can't just take anything," Annalyse said, batting the first device, what looked like a hammer with a skar inset in the handle, from Ami's hands. "Only the stones themselves. Those'll make the biggest difference."

"Then get to it."

The door above rattled. Someone shouted. Ami cursed.

"So much for Gladdring's tongue," Annalyse muttered, loading the satchels with more skars than things, the small gems making for easy transport. "Get those. The Foti ones are the farthest along."

Ami took up the other satchel, stepped towards the Foti skars, and stopped when Quik rose. Revealed himself. The choice came easy, a stalker's analysis finding he'd be discovered soon anyway, and better to not get Ami's sword in the gut as a result. Even so, even with his hands wide and clear—save the Vis skar still clutched in his right—Ami had her gritty iron short sword drawn and pointed before Quik could even get a word.

He gulped instead.

"How'd you escape?" Ami asked, Annalyse giving Quik a similar, sharp stare but not stopping her packing.

All about the priorities, that one.

"Dug," Quik answered. "What's happening?"

Ami scowled, the souring prospect of questions she knew she'd leave unanswered. Quik had been there a time or two himself, though his sympathies were rather low at the moment.

"Fassle's found out what Gladdring's doing and he's cleaning house," Ami said. "Choose, Vis. With us or against us?"

Quik flicked his eyes at Annalyse. Ami noticed. The door shook again. Something hard striking it.

"They catch us, they kill us," Ami said, then found a smirk, an idea. "They'll probably kill you too, just for knowing what was going on down here."

"Masayo sent me to do just that," Quik countered.

"Of course she did," Ami shoved the sword against Quik's stomach, the point pressing into his skin. "She's not here now. Choose."

Now Annalyse stopped, her glassed stare finding the hunter's. He found, as he always did, no calculation in the look, none of the conniving, the hatred, the fear. Only desperate desire to save a valued work. Work Quik knew, *knew* could make the difference against the fiends.

He'd seen enough to be sure of that.

"Give me the satchel," Quik said.

Ami replaced the sword with the bag as fast as she'd drawn on him, and Quik filled the satchel with skars in sweeping strokes. First the Foti, then the Rana, snagging devices as Annalyse called them out. Ami, meanwhile, scampered back up the stairs to the door, splintering now as axes hacked away at the wood. The Guardian targeted a blow, stuck the sword through a new hole and withdrew it.

The scream came through clear. Annalyse sucked in her breath. Quik kept shoveling skars.

"Almost done?" Ami called down. "This door's going to collapse."

"We've enough," Annalyse said, meeting Quik near the stairs down and demanding a look inside his satchel. "But, Ami, how're we getting away?"

"You're the genius, think of something!"

Annalyse glanced at Quik.

"Down," the hunter said. "Gets us more time."

Ami agreed, leaping from the stair as the door shattered. Najahn soldiers howled for surrender, received nothing save retreating footsteps in reply as the trio ran down the spiral stair. Without any doors, any defenses, the run down the steps didn't get them as much time as Quik might've hoped, but the sand offered options.

"Split up," Quik said as they hit the bottom, a second idea forming as he spoke. "They'll have to pick tracks to follow."

"Only to corner us," Ami replied. "We can hold them better as a group, you and me in a line, Annalyse behind."

"We'll do neither," Annalyse spoke before Quik could run his mouth again. "Follow me. We'll use the skars."

The scientist spun on her heel and dashed through the sand, towards the sea. Quik turned to follow, felt Ami's blade cross his chest again.

"Keep her and those skars safe," Ami said, Quik tilting his head. "She's the best chance these Isles have, and you know it."

"What are—"

Ami pulled the sword back, hit Quik with the flat of the blade. "I'm no damn swimmer. Go. I'll hold them here."

Quik nodded, his legs already breaking into motion. A brave sacrifice or a stupid one, Ami could do as she wanted.

Annalyse ran right on down the beach to the pier, one hand digging through the satchel. As Quik caught up with her, Annalyse pulled three sapphires from her satchel, flicked one to the hunter, who caught it with his left, adding the watery whispers to the Vis skar's continued mutterings.

The pier creaked as Annalyse talked up her plan, waves lapping around them. Gray overhead, a chilly wind promising icy waters. No ships in the distance, no rescue if currents pulled them out to sea.

"Where's Ami?" Annalyse asked, stopping her explanation to look around Quik's broad shoulders. "She didn't follow?"

"She—" Quik started, then trailed off as clashing steel echoed out from the rock.

"No." Annalyse tried to step around Quik only for the hunter to grab her shoulder. "Get off me, Quik. I'm not letting her die for us."

"You're not. She's choosing to." Quik ran the scenario, found the reason. "Think, Annalyse. If those soldiers see us jump into the sea, they'll know where we're going. We won't have a chance. She's giving us one."

Annalyse relaxed her press, rocked back on her heels. With a swipe, she tore her glasses off, stuffed them in her satchel. "Then let's go. Follow me."

How fast she could turn. Quik hadn't quite wrapped himself around Ami's choice, the Guardian again performing her role, and here Annalyse was, accepting the new situation and jumping off the pier into the waves. The scientist cursed as she leaped, a quiet yelp swallowed up by the icy sea.

For a too-long second, Quik watched the lapping waves for a sign, wondering if the current, if the satchel's weight or Annalyse's own linens had dragged her under. A hand broke the surface first, followed by her head, hair spreading out like some octopus against the dark water. Feet kicked off her boots, breaking into a fast stroke to the south and west.

Back towards the stair, into those caves, Quik heard more ringing metal, heard Ami's voice calling out challenge after challenge. She'd make those Najahn work for it.

He could turn back, right now. Carry this satchel and wait in the shadows for Ami to fall, or strike her from behind. Be heralded a hero by Fassle, secure Najahn support for his brother.

"C'mon!" Annalyse called, bobbing in the waves already so far away. A strong swimmer, or a strong skar. "Quik?"

Ami had it right. Annalyse's inventions worked miracles, could swing power from the fiends to the people. She ought to survive, ought to thrive, and she wouldn't have much chance of either wanted and alone.

But if someone asked Quik why he dove into the sea at that moment, why he embraced the Rana skar's sudden excitement to push his every stroke forward and shoot him across the water, the answer would be a simple one:

A friend in need.

CHAPTER 28

MIDNIGHT MOTES

Keeping watch, to put it frankly, sucked. Every second Torny sat, her back to the small fire, her eyes staring off into the middle, black distance carried with it possibility's baggage: things Torny could've been doing instead, like reading the diary and learning whether Yarvick was as crappy a father as he was a bandit leader. Sharpening her weapons or messing with her thieving tools would make too much noise, demand too much concentration to be a good guard.

Or so Sledge had told Torny, several times, in their journeys through Foti's awful wastes.

At least Whent offered a better temp. Torny would take a chill wind and a thick coat over Foti's blistering days and suffocating nights. Frosted tundra and snow drifts, while annoying, offered softer steps than hard lava rock, not to mention the lava itself and its tendency to melt anyone who wasn't careful.

Otherwise, the deep Whent night was about as crap as Foti's, with little save Torny's fidgets to keep her awake.

That and the knowledge that Wax, and even Bliss,

might excise her from the group should she fall asleep. Coupled with the thievery and its attendant disaster back in the city, Torny figured her Guardian scale was tilting too far in the wrong direction.

So when an odd, green-tinted light rose up on the horizon, like a star that'd lost its spot in the cloudy sky overhead, Torny saw it, and thanked Noctia for something interesting. The light grew slow, like a candle finding its wick and emerging into full brilliance. Growth meant the light might be coming closer, and Torny saw, now, its reflection on the snowy ground a ways off into the distance. Beyond bowshot, beyond being able to pick anything out, but close enough to warrant a response.

The bandit stood and the light stopped. Flickered there, a wisp in the night, but it came no closer. Torny ransacked her memory for anything about Whent, about what might be waiting in its cold wastes, but found nothing. Not that she expected any revelations there: Whent hadn't been a stop in her travels before, no reason to brush up on its wildlife.

Because that's what she stared at now, right? Wildlife? Torny drifted a hand to one of the dagger pair on her waist, huddled beneath her coat's ankle-length fur. The light could belong to a fiend, but Torny figured a monster would just come charging into camp. The green mote's hesitation suggested caution, nature's mediating instinct.

Torny cocked her head, lifted her off hand and gave a slight wave at the light.

Wax and Eujo hadn't discussed the rules of the watch, no parameters or particulars over what was worth waking up the soundly-sleeping crew. They'd hiked hard all day, with little rest the night before, so Torny wasn't surprised the other three snoozed so hard. She'd been the same before a near-delirious Wax shook her awake for her shift. With another hard day coming, breaking serenity for a harmless glow seemed a poor choice.

At her wave, the light bobbed. A sway, really, back and forth before settling into its standstill spot.

"Okay, now you're messing with me," Torny muttered.

She wouldn't be able to sit down, relax, or think about anything else while the light hovered there, making the choice an easy one: get closer, resolve the mystery, and either wake the rest for reinforcements or return mollified and ready to wait out her shift.

Still, Torny drew the daggers.

The firelight died quick as Torny moved away from camp, Sichi's pink doing little to pierce the clouds. Someone less suited to working in dim light might've stumbled, felt the night pressing in, but Torny accepted the gray slate, the shadows upon shadows as she walked with careful purpose.

A thief, so Yarvick said, needed to make friends with the night, as they'd be seeing each other often.

The light bounced as Torny approached, the green glow bobbing up and down, side to side, as if a small child held it and wouldn't sit still. No noise save the slow breeze—a calm change from the prior day's storm—and no scent on the nose. As silent a night as Torny had ever heard. Enough so that the green light held her focus, all of it.

It shrank as Torny neared, the blurry aura around the green core dwindling till it seemed little more than a hand's breadth across when Torny approached a couple strides away. Beneath it, the tundra sat undisturbed under a snow drift blanket. No tracks, though any made would vanish quick enough with the moving flakes.

"What are you?" Torny asked the emerald light. "Some trick? Am I dreaming right now?"

The light answered. It bobbed towards her. Torny lifted her thumb from the dagger's hilt, reached out towards the glow. A touch, at least, might tell her what made up the light. Fire, some magical glow, another—

The mote flashed. Bright, harsh, enough to make Torny squint and stumble back a step. Her eyes caught a silhouette behind the glow, black and large, sculpted and wide. She blinked, only for the glow to flash again.

This time, she heard the snow shuffle. Something surged towards her.

Torny cursed, moved to fling a dagger and thought better of it: abandoning a weapon out here with no sure replacement seemed a bad idea. Instead she turned, the twist coming easy in the snow, back towards camp, towards reinforcements.

And saw the dwindling orange fire had two friends, a pink and blue dot on either side, closing quick with the slumbering trio.

"Get up, idiots!" Torny screamed as she ran, the green glow flashing again behind her.

Her first shout prompted some squirms. Her second had Bliss sitting up.

Torny didn't get a third.

Something snaked out and caught her right ankle, sending Torny sprawling forward. Her face hit soft snow, slid while the bandit twisted, pushing down with her dagger-holding wrists into a roll-over. With frozen cheeks Torny looked up at the green glow above her face. It swung down in a curl, brightening again to show a descending maw, razor teeth rows behind chapped, black lips. Mottled skin rose away from the mouth, a poxed, pitted medley showcased in shadow.

Ripe, at least, for a stab.

Torny jutted up both daggers to meet the teeth, their points digging into the lip before the monster could commence its bite. The creature slurped at the impact, a wet cough coming with hot blood as Torny's daggers found gristle. As it reared back, Torny at last had her answer: a sloping tendril connected the green glow to its host.

"Pretty light for an ugly beast," Torny said, kicking her heels into the snow, planting her left hand to get back to her feet.

Only to catch a flat blow along her left side. Torny rolled and sprawled, snow clogging her nose, mouth, ears. Instinct and a killer's grip kept the daggers in her hands, Torny already pressing again to the ground for a chance to get up.

Torny's curses found partners now from the camp, Wax and Eujo adding their own invectives to what'd become an absolute crap night. That Torny might've succeeded in stealing the diary only to get devoured by some nightmare tundra lizard seemed so unfair, that two Renewals might meet the same fate after all they'd gone through, well, Torny didn't have time to measure that on her cosmic justice scales.

The monster was on her again, its green light giving Torny clues to its swipes and snaps. She backed up, a slow, slippery evasion accompanied by wide dagger slashes. The beast shied back whenever a knife came close, a caution Torny figured she could use.

Her feet hit a shallower snowdrift, the boots catching actual footing amid frozen grasses and rocks. The monster pursued, the dancing green and the teeth behind it at

Torny's height and coming in fast for a lunge. The bandit had danced back before, no doubt she would again.

Ah, simple enemies. How nice they were.

Torny bounced her weight from retreat to resist, bending her knees. She broke ahead and right as the beast drove the green glow in. With her left hand, Torny swept a dagger down and away. The monster flinched, the green glow sliding to Torny's left, the teeth away from danger. Torny, though, hadn't taken herself out of the play this time, instead brushing up right into the beast's left side. In the emerald shadows, Torny took in the three legs, each ending in a broad, lily-pad like foot. Several times her size, sure, but awkward and made for surfing the snow.

The monster twitched its foremost left leg her way.

An attack that might've worked if Torny had some distance, but she brushed shoulder to slick, wet skin and the left leg overshot its mark, leaving Torny with a wide open double dagger draw. The knives did their damage, sliding into what Torny hoped was the monster's gut. Again a wet cough, a gibbering slide away, the snow now bearing darker stains than nature intended.

Any good bandit would follow up an attack like that with a killing blow, and Torny tried. The snow foiled her move, aggression meeting a slippery surface, throwing off Torny's momentum as the monster scrabbled away. If the thing had tried a quick counter, its teeth might've found Torny's head an easy snack. Instead, the bandit steadied herself to find the green glow fleeing fast.

"That's right, run," the thief said, before breaking towards the camp.

The time on Foti and Rana must've done the trio good, as all three had themselves up with weapons in hand. Bliss and Eujo had their enemy encircled, trading strikes and dodging sloppy counters. The monsters apparently had their hopes in sneak attacks, as even Wax seemed stable enough in his one on one dual, the Vis man's scrap blade holding the flitting blue light at bay.

A few seconds had Torny jumping on Wax's beast's back, the shadow easier to find with the fire in the foreground. Again she used her knives like claws, driving them in and out in a scrambling, slicing run over the hapless creature. Much like her own enemy, the new beast coughed, turned, and ran, leaving Torny rolling off before Wax.

She managed, this time, to land on her feet, dropping into a flourish.

"Very nice," Wax said, glancing to see Bliss and Eujo finishing off their own creature. "Next time, how about you give us a bit more warning?"

"Think of it, instead, as me giving you the most sleep you could get."

Torny's crack might've gone over well if Eujo hadn't pointed her rapier out to the dark. The sword drew their eyes to where solid night should've been, to where several dozen lights bobbed in all colors.

"They travel in packs," Eujo said, as serious as ever, scooping up her satchel. "We need to move."

"Oh really?" Torny asked, slinging her own over her shoulder. "You don't want to fight them all?"

"Not the wake up I had in mind."

"Then we run," Wax said. "Yell when you need a skar. We go until we can't anymore."

Torny fell into line with the others, sprinting through dark snow, leaving the fire and the rocks behind. Unhurt, cold, and already feeling her muscles burn, Torny nonetheless found breath to curse the night, the watch, and the whole damn Isle.

CHAPTER 29
BREAKOUT BANTER

Bloodied, cursing, and bereft of everything Sawi had ever known Ami to wear save that golden faceplate. That's how the Guardian showed up on Sawi's floor, getting shoved past the Vis's cell towards a neighboring one. Sawi, scooping her midday gruel with a thin wooden spoon, stared as Ami went by, listened as the Guardian tore her captors down with one vicious line after another—cowards, blind sycophants, motherless dogs, and more—until the Najahn trio hauling her along locked the bars and strode away, chuckling to themselves.

Ami went quiet quick. Sawi finished her meal, washed down the fatty rice with stale water before nestling up to her front bars, shoulder near the corner. She heard Ami muttering. Quiet curses, sure, but more too: talk of strategy, plans and probabilities.

The Najahn, confident in their own cells and the tower's apparent invulnerability, took occasional laps but spent their time near the stairwell. With tables, chairs, and playing cards, the guards could burn their shifts in relative comfort. Their laughs and jabs echoed up here and there, a good hand drawing a shout, a pound on the table.

Nobody eavesdropping on a couple doomed prisoners.

"What happened?" Sawi asked first, loud enough to carry around the cell.

Ami's mutterings died at the sound. A hesitant silence.

"Sawi? That you?"

"You didn't notice on your way in?"

"Was a bit busy. And they busted up my right eye."

Sawi winced in sympathy. At least her capture had come without violence. The wince faded to a hard frown. Twice captured now. First by the Mottilan bruisers on Vis, and now here. A dangerous habit, one she'd have to correct.

Ami asked and Sawi relayed her story, Gladdring's set meeting and Fassle's ambush. There'd been nothing to hide: Fassle had all the information he needed already, it was a loyalty test, a chance to see whether Sawi would turn at a tempting offer. She'd spoke up for Gladdring's ideals, at least the ones she thought he stood for—skars saving the isles—and dodged a knife waiting for her neck.

For the moment, anyway. Fassle spared her life to stick Sawi in a cell awaiting a trial.

"A show, nothing more."

"Show?" Sawi asked

"Fassle wants to squeeze every benefit from you. They'll haul us up before the Najahn, proclaim us traitors, and kill us slow," Ami said. "The Najahn like to claim they're civilized, but when the going gets gritty, they're as brutal as any of us."

"We'd never do something like that on Vis."

"Oh, no. You just cast your criminals out into the jungle where they meet disease or a cat's claws. So much better."

Sawi wanted to say that at least Vis let a person have a

chance, but they didn't, not really. Exile was permanent, and surviving in the jungle alone, with no tools, no shelter . . . Svarde managed it on a cliff side with a ferrite, but the Foti barbarian stood among few others.

"You don't sound depressed," Sawi said, a little hope lighting in Ami's casual tones and sticking to it. "Do you think there's another way?"

"Always another way."

"And that is?"

"Just wait."

Sawi heard it then, as Ami wrapped her words. Exertion. Hard breathing.

"What're you doing?"

Ami didn't answer. Sawi stopped talking, listened closer. A sawing sound, quiet and sharp. Metal on metal. Minutes simmered as Ami worked, the guards played. Errant snowflakes drifted through the window, Noctia falling victim to another winter storm. Sawi bunched up, pulled the thin blanket over from her cot and curled into the corner, waiting for a chance.

"Get up," Ami whispered, her voice close, too close.

Sawi jerked awake, eyes snapping to Ami's, a shadow with a lit lantern glimmering behind her. The look almost had Sawi screaming, a disaster prevented when Ami clamped a hand over Sawi's mouth. The Guardian wore a devious grin, as if she knew just what Sawi was staring at, because what else could it be?

Ami's face looked split in two, the piece to her right where her faceplate normally rested exposed as a white and red snarling, pulsing nest of scars, veins, and ridged tissue. Framed in the Guardian's tangled flame hair and glaring eyes, the sight was enough to blast away Sawi's sleep and get her to her feet.

Only then did Sawi understand Ami stood outside her cell, right there in the hallway.

"Sawed through," Ami whispered, answering the obvious question. "The faceplate just looks like gold, but it'll stop a spear's strike."

Sawi saw the glittering mask in Ami's right hand. Its edge held burrs, jagged hairs that'd no doubt leave a scratch on any wayward finger. Ami's left hand clenched into a tight fist, loosened as she let Sawi in on the secret.

"They let me keep this when I said I'd die without it," Ami said. "Morons."

"You will, though, right? Die?"

Ami set the faceplate against her skin. Pushed with a grimace, eyes closed. Pain. Red rivulets opened, ran down her cheek as those burrs found purchase. So too did the metal, slotting into points Sawi neither saw nor wanted to think about.

The fiends made monsters of them all.

"What's this, then?" came a voice, the same one that'd brought Sawi her lunch. The Najahn didn't hold a voulge—quarters too tight—but had a short sword in one hand and a lantern in the other. "Thinking you should be in your cell, Guardian."

Ami, fist holding that skar tight, rose with a shudder. Her back to the guard, only Sawi saw the woman set her shoulders, her legs. In nothing more than a ragged tunic and trousers, Ami looked very much like a person ready to slaughter hundreds, like a hanoko who'd found its prey.

"I'd run if I were you," Sawi offered to the guard, who only grinned.

"My friends are coming around the other way," the guard said to Ami's back. "You've nowhere to go, and all you're earning now is a good beating. The Circle won't care if you look good for the killing, so save yourself the pain."

"Don't think I will," Ami muttered, the words almost a growl.

"Your choice."

The guard adjusted his grip, came in with a hilt-first swing at Ami's head. The man's lantern swung low and back, a target as Ami ducked and swiveled in a single motion. She reached with her right hand as the guard's strike whizzed by overhead, grabbing the burning lantern's handle and forcing it, along with the guard's left hand, up. The lantern looped on its simple hinge, smashing against the guard's arm and bursting into hot, burning glass.

A curse killed the guard's coming counter, one cut off as Ami, close in with the man, delivered a knee shot with her left leg to the man's stomach. The sword clattered to the stones, a sound matched with a hard thud as Ami grabbed the doubled-over guard and drove his head into the stones. The man collapsed, and Ami kicked the lantern's burning fragments away as she bent down, swiped the cell keys off the man's belt and tossed them through the bars at Sawi.

Someone who hadn't been sparring with Ami for weeks might've been stunned at the speed, might've stared in disbelief at the keys as they jumbled to a stop near Sawi's foot. The Vis only whistled, picked up the ring and went for the bars. Several keys, with only one long enough to fit in the cell's lock made it an easy choice.

Less clear was Ami's response when the guard's buddies came rushing up from the left, blades drawn and barking challenges. By now, some other prisoners on the level had found their voices too, calling out to be freed or sending jeers at their distraught captors.

Ami scooped a ragged sandal beneath the first guard's

fallen blade and flipped it up, catching it with her right hand. At the same time, she pressed her left against her faceplate, withdrawing it to reveal the Vis skar back in its set spot. The two guards, side-by-side in the narrow hallway, watched both moves with drawn, gulping looks.

"Ready?" Ami asked the pair, settling into a blade-forward stance, standing over the unconscious guard.

The two guards looked at one another. One took a step back. The other set his lantern on the ground, gripped the short sword with both hands.

"Return to your cell," he said, the trembling in his tone undercutting any message, "and we'll not tell Fassle about this."

"How about you go in my cell, and you don't get to see your guts tonight?"

The lock popped clean, Sawi swung the cell door open. Both guards slid their eyes her way, and in that moment, Ami took advantage. She rushed the forward guard, planting her left foot and lunging into a skewer. The guard used his two-handed grip to frantically deflect the strike, a move Sawi appreciated till she saw Ami's follow-through: the Guardian let the deflected blow cross over the guard's left shoulder, right in at the second soldier. Ami herself followed the thrust with a shoulder charge, knocking the first guard's chin back even as her blade struck home into the second soldier's chest.

Ami dropped the stabbing sword, releasing the weapon as the first guard tried to recover. Even as he brought the blade back, Ami punched the man in the throat, right between his leathers and the knocked chin. He coughed, eyes going wide, blade falling as hands went to try and get his breath back. Ami completed the takedown with a snap kick to the man's left ankle, dropping him, choking, to the stone ground.

"Okay," Sawi said, looking over the devastation. The stabbed soldier had a hand on the sword in his chest, tugging at the hilt. "Guess you weren't trying all that hard with me."

"I didn't want you dead," Ami replied, bending down and scooping up another fallen sword. "Let's go."

"What about the other prisoners?" Sawi jangled the keys, nodded at the calls for rescue. "We could—"

"Some people belong here." Ami crouched, began pulling off boots, leathers from the bodies. "We only know ourselves."

"Then, shouldn't we leave?"

"Take some gear, Sawi. As much as you can. There's no alarm yet, but there'll be one soon. We need to be gone by then."

The words pierced a frenzied veil, Sawi realizing in that second a true prison break was underway. This wasn't some fun brawl, but an escape. A thing Sawi knew nothing about, save that they'd be hunted, wanted, pursued.

"Where are we going to go?" Sawi asked, quelling the sudden confusion by doing as Ami asked, giving up on the too-large boots but snagging a knife, the unconscious soldier's leather.

"The Ringed City doesn't cover all of Noctia," Ami said, keeping her stolen sword visible in case either guard wanted to make a show. Neither did, both groaning, cursing, crying on the ground. "There's places the Najahn ignore."

Couldn't be that many of those on the home isle. None, too, the Najahn would overlook chasing two prisoners like her and Ami.

"They'll find us."

"We'll have some time to think," Ami replied, then cursed. "Sawi, you want to stay here, do so. I'm leaving."

When Ami swept by, wearing a Najahn guard mish-mash, Sawi didn't hesitate. There were questions, there were problems, but where Ami was going, there wouldn't be bars and stone. Fresh air and a chance would be enough.

CHAPTER 30

THE GATES

S even swirls, like stars pulled down and spun together with blood. They whirled in the deep, far below and yet so much closer than Svarde could have hoped. The Dead King had guided them from the forlorn city, past his standing ranks, down the middle tunnel, its sharp sides decorated with fiend bones, all the way to a jutting precipice overlooking a vast, dark pool. As large as a sea, the far ends vanishing beyond sight beneath a toothy ceiling. Glowing mosses speckled the edges, a dim outline bright enough to illustrate the straggling forms swimming free or, by the ripples on the surface, moving below.

"Fiends," the Dead King said, planting his blade in the rock at their feet.

On the precipice's sides, a hard slope made more level with skulls and ragged, rotted skin, told a siege's story, a defense long held now given up. Svarde didn't need to ask why: too many of those bones belonged to humans.

"Wait," Maena said, stepping up next to the king and pointing. "The fiends come from those?"

"Arise, spawn, travel. Pick your choice, but yes. Those are their birthing places, and they are all different."

"Look the same to me," Svarde, forming a line with the King and Maena, said.

"Then look closer."

The Foti Guardian did as asked, crouching and trying to pierce the water's veil. Study those depths and . . . Oh. What had seemed to be seven red circles were different now, the colors not the same, though close. This one here had a purple tint to the edges, while another bore a darker, blacker stripe running through white starlight specks.

"Their colors aren't the same," Svarde voiced the conclusion, and heard Kivi snort her agreement.

"Why, we can only guess," the Dead King said. "Demion and I haven't found a reason, and no fiend has sought to explain it. Yet, there are seven. That we have seven isles, seven gods, seems too perfect to be coincidence." With one gauntleted hand, the king pointed to a far slope on the right, where several lanky fiends climbed the rock. "They emerge, and those that don't drown eventually find their way here. We destroy them, or they get past to Demion's net."

"The little ones do, anyway," Maena said. "There's a lot worse fiends in the waves."

The King clanked through a slow nod. "There are large holes beneath. Scratched through to the ocean by, I believe, fiends desperate to be free."

"Oh yeah, you go down there yourself? Take a swim?"

Svarde threw Maena a frown, but the captain wasn't paying attention to him. She'd continued to be so flippant, so carefree, so unpredictable.

"I sent someone long dead down to be my eyes," the King answered, unperturbed.

"Guess that works." Maena joined Svarde in a crouch. "So, what's the plan? Doesn't seem like we can shoot an arrow at the swirl, or can we?"

"We've tried arrows. Rocks. Bodies. Nothing holds. The gates are unaffected."

"Gates? So you've given them names?" Svarde asked.

The three lanky fiends had reached the same height as the precipice, were now making their way along towards Svarde, Kivi, and the rest. He reached back, found his axes. Ready to draw when the monsters closed.

"Gates, portals, doors," the King said. He hadn't shifted once as the fiends closed. "What does it matter? They can't be closed, and the fiends continue to come. Faster and faster. Your quest is an impossible one, Guardian. Better to fortify and defend. Hope your friends up above can devise enough weapons, hold enough skars to keep the fiends at bay."

"That's grim," Maena muttered.

"But accurate," Svarde said, standing, drawing his axes. "Jochi has the engineers, the expertise. We can rebuild the city, hold it. Then find a way to plug the tunnels. If we can't deliver victory, we can at least prevent defeat."

"You're all talking like losers." Maena picked up a stone, walked to the precipice's edge, cocked her arm and launched the fist-sized rock. The missile flew, smacked the leading fiend in its lumpy head. The six-limbed creature faltered, slipped on an old rib cage, and rolled down to a satisfying splash. "We've come all this way. Let's make it count."

Svarde was about to answer the Rana captain, about to say they could get themselves established and try new things, try using Jochi's army and its expertise to attack those gates with something different. He had the growling speech ready to go only to let it stall out as the pool below them bubbled, hissed, clouded.

"They're coming again," the Dead King rumbled. "Every time there are more. They use the water and the land." He took a long step back, pulling his blade free. "They've fought past us before, all the way to the Wound."

"Who's 'they'?" Maena asked, not following the Dead King's retreat to keep looking over the edge.

Svarde, though, figured he knew, that she knew too. The two remaining fiends on the slope stopped their advance at the noise, looking down at the sea. Kivi let her vents loose, a worried hiss. Metal sprang forth, black, burned, and defiant. The construct, an edged, wheeled thing as wide as the tunnel Svarde had just walked, burst free from the sea and onto the bones, crushing them with its grinding progress. Rounded tanks along its sides sent hot geysers forth, releasing searing air that burned Svarde's skin all the way up.

The two fiends howled. Svarde moved back a step.

"Oh, it's these guys again," Maena said, wincing as she joined the retreat. "They're not great."

The two fiends reacted much the same way as the humans, breaking into a fast run towards the precipice. Their rapid advance lasted three short seconds until the metal construct made a clanking sound, like a blacksmith's hammer hitting forged iron. One massive black bolt lanced forth, spearing the first fiend like Svarde might jab an ant with a knife's point. A second followed, finishing the lanky fiends and marking their fall against the rock slope with those metal pillars.

"Not good," Svarde said, but slowed his retreat as they reached the precipice's end. "But if we're going to hold them, this slope hands us an advantage. We shouldn't give it up."

The Dead King raised his great sword, held it in both hands, but continued walking back, up and away. "They will only destroy us from below. The tunnel's turns will serve us better."

"I'm with metal head," Maena said. "Tight quarters have to be tough for that thing. Let's go."

The Dead King turned as he reached the tunnel's entry, picked up his pace and vanished towards his undead army. Maena followed. Svarde hesitated. The metal grinding had slowed. Maybe the vehicle wasn't able to scale the slope. Maybe they could hold here after all and give Jochi's army time to arrive, build defenses further back in the tunnel.

This was a military campaign now, not some expedition.

The Foti Guardian dropped to his knees, used his elbows to crawl forward the rock. Kivi snorted behind him, asking a question.

"Intelligence," Svarde replied. "We have to know what's coming, if they can reach us."

The metal machine wasn't alone anymore. Looking over the edge, Svarde heard and counted two more of the things rising free from the deeps to beach upon the skulls and bones. The water still bubbled, and the reason came clear as smaller pods broke between the massive machines, pods like those that'd crashed onto the beach near the Whent city.

The iron tops bubbled and popped, clanked and spun. They opened one by one, and as they did, things Svarde never needed, wanted to see again emerged. Obsidian heads, blue-burning bodies. Only these didn't wield the long flails Svarde saw before, but instead held hammers and wore scalded black bags along their bodies, the solid sides sparking every time they touched the burning skin.

"Now, what're those for?" Svarde muttered, only his eyes, his rough hair peering over.

The answer came when another door opened, a hatch at the middle, the first machine's top. From it rose the largest one of those burning giants Svarde had seen, its obsidian gilded with a silver lining. Its head swirled and flashed, sparks and embers tracing lines that all the others, nearly a dozen now, turned to watch. When it finished, its audience flashed back in turn, a show that would've been dazzling if it didn't fill Svarde with a dire dread.

The creatures turned, opened those bags, and began pulling out thin bars. Hard beams, of the kind Svarde might see in a Foti forge. Their purpose became clear quick as the monsters hammered them into the bones, breaking apart the aged remnants to drive the bars into the rock beneath. With every placement, the fiends took another step up, then repeated the swinging.

"Treads," Svarde said to Kivi, the ferrite crawling low up near him. "They're building a ladder for their damned machines."

He glanced back towards the tunnel. A hard charge now, while the fiends were distracted, might break them. Might give them an opportunity. But the cowards had run.

"Do what we can, right?" He asked the ferrite.

Kivi snorted.

Svarde rose, stood tall on the precipice. As he did, the lead fiend, still watching from its machine, turned that great obsidian face his way. The other fiends followed the look, stopping their hammers. Behind, the sea bubbled, frothed.

"Go back, you damned things," Svarde shouted. "This world doesn't belong to you."

The lead fiend flashed something back, an unintelligible spark spatter.

"You heard me," Svarde yelled again. "You're far from home, and the road ahead's going to be paved with your bodies."

The yell flushed his face, rose the anger, the energy Svarde always nursed to its forefront. This was the sort of thing he was meant for, not skulking through tunnels or wasting away on a cliff side. Fighting the enemy to save his friends, his Isles.

Kivi's stumpy tail hit Svarde's ankle, knocked him back as the barbarian prepped a third threat. Over the precipice, right where Svarde had been standing, came another dark iron bolt. It lodged into the stone above, scattering rock around them. Svarde sat up, shaking the dust from his hair.

The ferrite snorted, looked back towards the tunnel.

"Yeah, maybe you're right. The tunnels it is."

And Svarde, Foti Guardian, champion of the Whent Pits, turned and ran.

CHAPTER 31

A REFUGE AND A REASON

The ice frogs, as Torny coined them, followed through the snow, their dancing globes and ever-present line in the dark behind the quartet. Wax and Eujo led, if he could call it that, through the dark snow drifts, every footfall pushed by panic. The skars again changed hands when breathing grew shallow, when paces began to slow, but even with the Foti and Vis stones doing what they could to stave off exhaustion, Wax found himself stumbling every few steps.

Eujo and Torny, though, were even worse. Neither one, with lives burned in cities, had little experience navigating tricky natural terrain. They had no torches, only what scant pink light from Sochi pierced the clouds—and that lack made it hard to gauge bumps, rocks, or deeper snow pits.

Without the metal poles along the roadside, Wax figured they'd be long lost, destined to freeze or starve in Whent's forlorn fields.

"What's the point?" Torny huffed some unknowable time into their flight. "We can't keep walking forever. They're just waiting us out now."

"And do what?" Eujo countered. "Fight them?"

"Was thinking we could lay down real nice, give them a meal for all the hard work they've done."

Wax laughed, lunged through another knee-high drift.

"You think that's funny, Wax?" Eujo asked.

"Tonight, I'll take it."

Wax couldn't really make out Eujo's face, could barely see the snow puffs as she trudged alongside him, but he felt the glare, the disappointment readily enough. Demanding some leadership or something, some strong speech about pressing on in the face of danger and defeat.

Well, Eujo could give it as well as Wax could. Better probably.

Besides, his boots were soaked, his feet blistered, and defeat seemed pretty damn likely.

Bliss, of them all, had energy to burn. Wax's sister loped ahead, taking on a scout's role without being asked. She'd wait for them every now and again, report the only thing farther ahead was more featureless snow. Nothing to hold, to defend, to help against the chasing frogs.

Those things, at least, did seem content to let their prey lie down and die.

"It's not about being funny," Torny said. "It's not because I like where we are, what's happening. It's about trying to distract and delight."

"Delight?" Eujo countered. "You're wasting breath on smart cracks when you should be using it to walk faster."

"It's my breath, I'll use it how I want."

Another scowl Wax could feel, couldn't see. Time, it appeared, for the mediator.

"You both can do what you want, so long as you keep moving forward," Wax said. "Guardian, Renewal, bandit, Queen, I don't care what you are and neither do those things chasing us. So save your spears for what really counts."

"Spears?" Torny asked. "Who's got a spear?"

"A question I also have," Eujo added.

"It's a phrase."

"A weird one," Torny, to Wax's left, muttered.

"Senseless," Eujo agreed.

Wax sighed, smiled, even as his legs burned and sweat froze along his back. They might die from a thousand things out here, but at least they wouldn't die angry with each other.

Like a frosted phantom, Bliss faded into view, standing with one arm pointing ahead and to the west. As the trio caught up, Bliss tried making signs, a difficult series to parse without much light. Nevertheless, Wax picked up the gist, spoke for the others to know, "Bliss says there's a roadside inn not far ahead. Deserted, but it's shelter."

"Then what're we stopped here for?" Eujo asked. "Let's move. If we're fast enough, we can get it ready for those frogs."

Wax was ready to ask why a random inn would be out here in the middle of nowhere, but then he recalled the Jarl's Tooth back on Foti. A tiny spot rising right where a day's journey out from the city would put you. Travelers would need rest, someone wouldn't mind profiting.

But why was it deserted?

"Because nobody travels across Whent in the winter, duh," Torny said when Wax broached the question, the group tromping hard through the snow after Bliss. "Board up the place, go have fun when the snows fall, come back and have your summer party."

"Summer party?" Wax asked.

"Sure, the time when you get all the goodies from everyone else."

"You're a strange one, Torny."

"Look who's talking."

Bliss's directions held true, the inn arising right where she'd pointed. A deeper shadow than the ones surrounding it, Wax made out the several story building, a small snow-covered wall, and a few nearby structures as they stumbled into them. The pursuing frogs slacked their pace, though the lights began to circle to the east and west.

"Trapping us," Eujo said as they sloughed through a gate Bliss opened by scrambling over the wall, lifting a crossbar. "They're not letting us go."

"Better than fighting in the open." Wax clutched the Vis skar tight as they crossed a speckled yard broken up by a well, animal pens, and places to park the carts and carriages he'd seen back in the city. "I'd like to see one of those fit inside the inn's door."

Bliss led the way to that particular construct, putting her shoulder into the frosted wood slab. One push proved it locked, an unsurprising turn given the abandoned look. Torny didn't even bother taking out her gadgets, instead marching off to the inn's right side. In the dim night's glow, broad glass windows reflected winter's frosted stain and, as she moved, the thief's shadow. Wax asked what she was doing, and Torny said to follow.

"That door's barred," Torny said. "Only way in's going to be through the window or the secret."

"The secret?" Eujo asked, glancing at Wax and Bliss as if they knew the thief's mind.

Bliss shrugged, smiling wide. A bold expression for the half-frozen and hunted group, but Wax admired her confidence in the bandit. The two had become so close, it almost had Wax thinking back to Vis, to Sawi, and . . .

"See?" Torny said as they circled around the inn's rock-and-mortar base to the western side. "This is what I'm talking about."

A snow-covered rise lay at an angle along the ground, going up about as high as Wax's knee. They stared at the unblemished snow while Torny bent over, swept her hand across the surface. The shoveling revealed only more snow and a snide comment from the queen, but Torny ignored the words, brushed at it again.

"A door," Wax said. "How? Why?"

"Don't have cellars on Vis, do you?" Torny asked.

'What?' Bliss signed and Wax echoed.

"Places under the ground. Lets you store stuff when it's cold and miserable outside," Torny continued her sweeping, now with the others bending over and helping out. They all kept looking back between swipes, confirming those deadly lights weren't coming closer. "Also a great way to get out if you want to keep it quiet."

"Why would someone this far out care?" Wax asked.

"Either we'll find out inside, or we'll just have to guess."

The cellar door had a lock too, but this one came with a conventional metal latch around two small handles. Torny, requesting a Foti skar to warm up her fingers, worked her tools on the thing's keyhole, pressing in at the right angle to make the bolts pop off. She snorted as the lock slid off the door into the snow.

"Cheap lock too," Torny said, putting away her tools. "Probably figured anyone who found this door and wanted in would manage it."

Wax pulled the doors open, their creaking spread giving way to a musty, yet clean odor. A step ladder waited on the other side, though its bottom rungs vanished into a lightless dark.

"Let me," Torny said, not bothering to wait for approval before she slipped down into the gloom.

Seconds ticked by, Whent's wind starting to pick up again as the night tilted towards morning. Those lights had the group encircled, and Wax thought they were moving closer. Hop by frigid hop.

"It's not just me, right?" the Vis asked. "Those things are coming in?"

"I'd rather risk the dark than—" Eujo's words slid away as light erupted behind them.

Bliss clapped once, then swung herself into the cellar. Wax and Eujo followed, squinting at the lantern's golden glow, as snow drifted in behind them. Torny held the lamp aloft in the cellar's middle, whistling at bags, barrels, and thick wood chests.

"Looks like this place was stocked," Torny said, then swung the lamp back towards the cellar door. "Mind closing that, unless you want our friends to come inside?"

The inn had stocks and security. Wax and the others explored its rooms up and down, confirming the place seemed ready for an active winter. One probably murdered by that warlord's call to pull an army off the surface and send it underground. Not a soul waited here, though the beds, the mugs, and the wood were all ready to use. Bliss and Eujo would've been up for watches, but Wax let them escape, claiming he had too much energy after the rush to collapse right then.

A lie, but a gentle one.

Instead he lit a fire in the inn's common room, a task made easy with Torny's lantern and its ready wick. The wood burned merrily amid its stone fireplace confines, melting away the tension, the fear, if not the frustration, stalking Wax's mood.

"Here," Torny said, coming back from behind the bar with some dried meats, nuts, and two small glasses. "It's not quite a Foti skar, but it'll warm you up all the same."

Wax clinked his glass with Torny's, another custom he'd picked up since leaving Vis, and the two shared a sip. Wax puckered his lips, blinked, and found himself gasping an agreement to Torny's assessment. The bandit, though, didn't laugh, didn't do much except stare into the crackling flames.

"There's a reason you're not going to sleep, isn't there?" Torny asked.

Wax nodded.

"Has something to do with me, doesn't it?"

Another nod.

"If you kick me out now, Wax, I'm—"

"I don't want you to leave, Torny. Trust me, I don't. But," Wax slowed, threw a look upstairs, or rather to the wood boards marking the ceiling, "this is already hard enough. Eujo, Bliss, and I have given up everything for this. Absolutely everything."

"It's a crap world."

"That's the thing, Torny. It's not. Not all of it. I didn't really see that till I had to leave Vis, but it's not. It's worth saving, even if it means throwing myself on that stone chair." Wax dropped his voice to a whisper, put up a sly grin. "Though I won't be mad if Eujo gets that prize."

"You bastard." Torny's eyes, though, sparkled.

"Never argued otherwise. But I can't, Torny, can't lose because you won't commit like we did. So I want you to choose. Give it all up, put it all on hold, or whatever you have to tell yourself, because that diary almost killed us. We can't risk that again."

Torny, at least, gave Wax a nod at that. Stood up from her chair before the fire, wandered past Wax towards the windows.

"They made this glass thick," Torny said, tapping the window before her. "Keeps it warm. Keeps the dangerous things out." She flicked a look Wax's way, as hard a stare as Wax had ever seen from her. "You asked me to come with you, Wax. You got me, and all that comes with me. If that's not worth it, then I'll be out that door before it's light out."

CHAPTER 32

TO STAY, TO LEAVE

If Quik could have a Rana skar in hand every time he took the water, he'd be fine living as a fish. The little stone turned the waves into helping hands, the crashing white tops folding around the Vis hunter and funneling him towards Annalyse. Together, the pair skimmed through the rough waters like dolphins at play, every stroke an effortless delight. Even the ocean's bone-numbing chill stayed at a distant remove, like how Bliss described the fiend's slime coating her after the fight off the coast.

Despite what was happening behind them, Ami's likely capture and death, Quik couldn't fight off a wild grin. He'd never been a huge fan of the Guardian anyway, with Ami more likely to deliver a slap to the skull or a kick to the shins than a compliment, no matter how well Quik used the skar's strength. Annalyse didn't match that enthusiasm when he neared the treading scientist, but he could've sworn he saw upturned lips as they slithered through the surf.

Their destination was an obvious one: the Najahn docks

split from the Ringed City's commercial ports by an intimidating sea wall. The private Najahn piers never quite bustled, though ships tended to come and go at odd hours, and mostly small ones at that. Now, the afternoon getting well along and winter in full grasp of the seas, the four piers lay empty with nothing save a foul gray overhead. The usual barrels and crates were missing, a sign the Najahn kept their docks in order. No bars offered music, no sailors threw curses to the winds.

The absence would've been eerie had the circumstances been different.

"C'mon," Quik said as they came close to the first pier, a stone dock jutting out like a blunt board into the sea, "let's use it."

"Where is everyone?"

"Busy with something else. Not us."

Quik wasn't an expert on information and the passage of it, but if Fassle wanted to destroy Gladdring, crowing about it beforehand seemed a poor choice. Particularly if he wanted all those skars. A secret raid, a subtle cleansing made more sense.

At least, that's what Quik told the scientist as he scrabbled onto the barnacled stone ledge. Reaching down, Quik gripped Annalyse's hand and helped her up. Almost at once, as the swimming's effort receded, the day's icy grip took a terrible hold. Quik's teeth began smattering against themselves, while Annalyse's lips morphed into an unhealthy shade of blue.

"We need a fire and some new clothes," she chattered, joining Quik in a look up and down the dock.

Several warehouses greeted them, all looking dark and lonely. Behind those great blocks waited alleys with uncertain endings. Any could bring them to Najahn guards and unpleasant questions. For a moment, Quik considered jumping back into the waters, swimming around to the port proper, and emerging that way, an idea floated and quashed by Annalyse.

"There's always eyes at the main port. Najahn collectors, guards. They'll see us and wonder. Let's try that one."

Annalyse pointed to a squat house to the warehouses' left, what appeared to be a quartering spot for any guards and officials holding down the port. Dark windows and a smokeless chimney suggested as quiet an existence as everywhere else here, a confirmation achieved when Annalyse gave the salty wood door a brisk knock. Quik stood behind her, arms looped around himself in a mindless shiver.

"No answer," Annalyse glanced back at Quik. "Going in, okay?"

"H-h-how?"

"The same way we've been doing everything."

Quik didn't know what that meant till Annalyse reached back into the sopping pouch tied around her waist. The scientist withdrew a small ruby, clenched it in her left hand, and pressed her right against the door's locked handle. The iron loop began sizzling, burning off the sea spray, before melting away. The malformed handle hit the ground with a dull thud, a thin metal river flowing from its socket down the door, tracing the wood's patterns in black.

"Melted the lock itself," Annalyse mused. "You really can get these things precise."

"You were trying to do that?" Quik forced his teeth to stop bouncing for a moment, but only just.

"It wanted to blow the whole place apart." Annalyse pushed with her free hand, the door swinging in clean. "I told it to control itself."

Inside, the guardhouse gave them options. Several narrow cots, a coal-fired furnace, table, and chests filled with cured meats, cheeses, fresh water, and, best of all, clothes. Fresh purple and black robes. Any modesty flew away fast as both Quik and Annalyse tore off their ruined, soaked outfits and tossed on fresh and dry options. None fit perfectly, but robes were robes: the fabric twisted and flopped in the best of times.

With some nameless, salty jerky in his mouth, Quik moved to the guardhouse's window and watched outside while Annalyse finished her own changing. Still quiet out there, and getting late in the day for any ship to come in.

"We might've made it," Quik said. "Somehow."

"Not somehow," Annalyse replied. "We acted, we did it right. And we were lucky Fassle chose a day without dockings to make his raid."

"So you admit luck played a part."

Quik glanced Annalyse's way, ready with a cocky smile, only to see her finishing pulling the new robe up over her back. On Vis, in hot weather, bare skin was a common appearance. Since coming to the colder, more fashion-forward Noctia, Quik had lost that familiarity. Though, seeing one as barraged with marks as Annalyse's would've given him pause anyway.

"What happened to you?" Quik asked, rising before he could stop himself. "Your back?"

Annalyse didn't turn her head around, shrugging her shoulders into the robe and pulling it up around her neck. "You have your scars, Vis."

Frowning, Quik reached towards Annalyse's robe, only remembering himself when his fingers touched fabric. He jerked his hand back, settled on a cot instead, waiting for Annalyse to turn towards him. She did, folding her arms in the process, skar pouch already retied around her waist, determination evident on a face for once cleared of goggles, ink stains, and the general grit they all gathered in the skar experiments.

"My scars are nothing like those," Quik countered. "They come from learning weapons, from testing myself against hanoko. Yours didn't seem so random."

"Progress is painful. How do you think I learned to work with the skars? To build all those things we used? For every success I had to fight through a hundred, a thousand failures."

"Alone?"

A soft snort, a quick head shake. "I worked with the smartest people on Whent. Some earned worse wounds than I did. A couple didn't survive. Their sacrifice brought me here."

"How?"

"Gladdring said the right rumors reached his ears. He's the Trade Tenet, he learns when an isle starts offering something new. So he came, found me, and bought me."

"Bought you?"

"My time and talents." Annalyse jerked her head towards the door. "Any ideas on where we should go next?"

"Drink some water. Eat something first. We don't know when we'll have it again."

The scientist softened. "Now there's a suggestion I can take." She went by Quik, dug out her own helping from the chests, and collapsed on the cot next to him. "Not exactly my favorite meal, but if it has to be my last ... "

Quik sat silent, eating his own jerky but barely tasting it. He'd seen Annalyse as one thing up till now, his captor and an odd one at that, obsessed with the skars and their potential to, as she put it, save the isles. Now a life spread itself, one not all that different from his own, with dreams and disappointments, sudden ups and downs. Death often close, even if for Annalyse it might come with an exploding skar rather than a predator's jaws. Wax or Bliss might've made the connection earlier, but Quik . . . Vis wasn't so complicated. You had your role, you performed it, you drank the fruit wine beneath the stars with a smile.

"You thinking real hard over there?" Annalyse asked. "Because I'm waiting for ideas. We're squarely in your territory now, Vis."

"I've never escaped from something before."

Annalyse laughed, a bright sound for once not tied to some experiment. More pure, somehow. "Not true, Quik. You escaped our cage just this morning."

"Sure, but . . . " Quik stopped, grinned. "You're right. I guess I did."

"So then, what's the plan? You're no novice anymore."

Whether Annalyse was right about that was up for interpretation, but Quik figured she did have one point. After busting from their cage, Quik had adopted a stealthy stance, sure, but the important part was the clear objective: knowing where he needed, wanted to go gave his every action a direction, and he gave that plan to Annalyse now.

"We need to decide where we're going," Quik said. "What do you want to do?"

"I have a couple pouches filled with skars and a couple trinkets to trade. Winter's closed the shipping routes back home," Annalyse winced, "not that I'd want to go to Whent anyway. If Fassle's trying to get me, he'll aim there first."

Leave the Ringed City, leave Noctia. Of course Annalyse would have to do that. Always another vine to swing.

"Vis," Quik said. "That's where you should go. Nobody's going to look there, and they'll accept you."

"Vis? No offense, Quik, but I'm not sure your isle's the right place for someone like me."

A dozen possible responses to the rude remark, but Quik brushed it off. Panic made fools of us all.

"Have you been there?"

Annalyse glanced down at her hands, seemed to understand she'd said something stupid. "No, I have not."

"Unless you want to go to the smelly Foti forges or join in Kance's murderous games," Quik started, the latter suggestion drawing a curious look from the scientist, " I'd say our isle's the nicest one. You'll have a home there too. We'll find my parents, they'll help us."

"You'd do that for the person who stuck you in a cage?"

"My brother's risking his life for the isles. What you're doing can help him. Can help us all. I'm not so stupid I can't see that."

Another laugh. Light. Quik smiled with it.

"You're not stupid, Quik," Annalyse said, standing up, holding out her hand. When he took it, she tugged him to his feet. "Maybe a little gruff, but you're kind where it counts."

"Thanks?"

With their goal figured, getting to the main port without suspicion proved easier than expected. The Najahn docks and the climbing pathway up remained almost deserted, an explanation coming from a couple harried scholars Quik and Annalyse passed on the way up: the Tenets had canceled most work for the day, with Fassle planning a big announcement that evening in the main square, and not a happy one.

"Everyone's preoccupied with themselves," Annalyse said after the robed man dashed off, claiming he had jobs to do. "Making sure they're not the targets, that their initiatives are safe."

"Safe? I don't think—"

"If the Circle decides your work isn't worth doing, they'll pull support. Assign you to something else," Annalyse said as they neared the last Najahn gate, distracted guards waving the few people through. "Gladdring protected us from all that nonsense."

"Power and politics."

"Always."

The guards glimpsed their purple and black robes, gave them no trouble, giving credence to Annalyse's idea about Fassle's secret raid. Once they'd moved beyond the Najahn borders, Quik found himself feeling oddly free. No more eyes watching his move, no sword ready to stab out from the shadows, no ranks or rituals. Annalyse, too, kept his attention, peppering him with questions about Vis, ones he answered with relish.

Talking about home felt a bit like returning there, warm and comforting. A feeling that lasted till they hit the docks, till they found a Foti merchant's sloop ready to leave that very night. Aiming to beat a coming storm and hit Kitaye's inlet before any floes, any rough waters could disturb its Noctia luxury cargo.

"Luck again," Annalyse said as they stood on the pier, the boat's ramp only a few strides away. "Hard to say how this could've gone any better. Ready?"

Quik started to say yes, found himself stopping. All the talk of Vis had done one wrong thing, had reminded the hunter of why he'd left the isle in the first place, of why he'd stayed on Noctia while his brother had sailed on.

"I, I might not be," Quik said.

At Annalyse's questioning look, the hunter explained

the debt, the reason, the need to get the Najahn to help his brother face the fiends. Leaving would pin him with the scientist, would curse Wax in the Najahn's eyes. A betrayal Wax couldn't afford, and one that only occurred to Quik as he talked it through, right there beneath the setting sun, the calls to board, and the crying gulls.

"You're leaving me, then?" Annalyse asked.

"I swore an oath. I can't break it. Not now."

Quik wasn't sure what to expect, but a pressed hand to his heart wasn't it. Annalyse's palm, though, brought a hard warmth with it, one Quik found to be more than just her skin when he took hold of her hand. Two skars rested within, a Vis and a Foti stone.

"Keep these, use them if you need them," Annalyse whispered, bringing her head close to his. "Stay alive Quik, and when you get that power you're looking for, bring me back."

"I will."

"Good." Annalyse took a long step back. Wagged a single, slow finger. "Because if you don't, I'm going to give all your hunters my new toys. Then Vis'll never be the same."

CHAPTER 33
CAGED POSSIBILITIES

How far did bravado get her?

Over a lifetime on Noctia's fringes, Torny found an insult could cut as sharp as any knife, head off a fight or open a door otherwise closed to the meek and mild. Massaging interests to match her own worked too, particularly with the gullible minds all too used to getting what they wanted. Like, say, most of the Najahn.

Wax and Bliss weren't like that. Torny stood with the fact, running a finger along the inn's thick inner windows while her ale rested in her off hand. Neither one seemed willing to go along, ignore her and focus on their desires. In other words, the thief kept getting called out for being what, who she was.

And now Wax had done it again, here in these snowy wastes with predators waiting just outside. Hardly a fair situation: join us or get eaten by some horrible ice frog. Wouldn't it be easy to forfeit your past and roll with a new present?

Save the world, Torny!

She sniffed. Looked back towards the fire. Wax stared into the hot flames, his own ale barely touched. The Renewal seemed as likely to pass out as sit there all night in some deep thought. Was that what it looked like, to have fate weighing upon you?

As if. Above them both lay the real winner, the one they all expected to take Noctia's cursed throne. Eujo had the demeanor too, haughty and cold. Like she'd forgotten all about the gutter she grew up in. Perfect to get stuck alone in an ugly crater, waiting to die a few decades too early.

Wax had nothing to worry about. He was, like Torny, an accessory.

She walked towards the inn's barred door, a sturdy iron length cutting across the thick wood. An axe and a lot of effort might be able to hack through, but otherwise nobody would be getting that open without some help from the inside. The thick glass too meant those frogs would have a hard time pressing their advantage. Though they might just wait, camping out and wondering when their food would make a move.

That, at least, could happen whenever Wax and Eujo wanted. The inn had food aplenty. Firewood and blankets. They could ride out the winter here if they decided to give up the Renewal game entirely.

Though Torny might find herself slipping a dagger beneath Eujo's ribs stuck this close for so long.

The inn didn't provide much else for distraction either. The only artwork, if you could call it that, came by way of animal bones hung here and there on the walls. No books, no lutes lounging around begging to be plucked. Bare essentials.

With Wax zoned out, Torny continued her tour, wandering by the stairs leading up and forgoing those cold steps. Well, maybe not. Bliss lay up there. She, at least, understood Torny, but the Vis had disappeared quick, exhausted after her exploring efforts. Better to let her rest.

The main level had a kitchen, a bar, the tables in the broad main room and a single, lonely straw bed in the very back, a room better used as a closet. Where the owner might sleep during those scant moments an inn might be quiet. Until their short stay in Rana, Torny hadn't ever worked a real gig, slaving over dishes and slopped soup for hours.

She never would again, dammit. That was a torture reserved for more resilient people than her.

Torny's descent to the basement was a silent affair, feet brushing steps without sound. A second nature skill at this point, one honed in by Yarvick years ago. He'd stand behind her, stick ready for a whacking if Torny made the slightest creak. They'd find quiet houses, rob them, then train thieves until someone chased them away, and every new target gave new tests.

The inn's solid construction made the silent walk easy, solid boards into the cellar supporting her weight without a crack or a quack. Overhead, a few brave spiders spun webs to catch mites and centipedes sneaking through the ground. The cellar floor was little more than pounded dirt, kept in submission by those barrels, sacks, and boxes. Shelves slammed into stone shone as Torny ran her lantern —snagged in her run around the main level, jars promising pickled delights to whomever pried them open.

Those were all ordinary things. Less so was the flat, square wood piece lying on the floor near the slanted double doors they'd used to get in. Sprinkled with blown snow, Torny hadn't noticed it till now, a forgivable lapse given the rush they'd all been in.

Torny smiled to herself. Yarvick wouldn't forgive her the slip: Never miss an opportunity, no matter the moment.

The bandit bent down, set the lantern on the floor and traced the wood square. A dark iron loop came up about to her wrist on one end, begging to be pulled. A curious thing, a trap door within a cellar. What would be worth digging so deep?

Torny took another long look around the basement, double counted the food, the jars, and came upon an idea. While the ale and a some harder things waited up behind the bar, there hadn't been any wine. Tamas was close enough to Whent, and Torny thought the rockbiters crafted some of their own, that there should've been a few bottles in a place like this.

Maybe they kept the good stuff way down here.

Yet, as Torny reached for that loop, her head fogged, her arm wavered. Exhaustion. The late night walk, the little sleep coming back now that they'd gone from risking their lives to living them again.

Go back upstairs, take a snooze, let Wax's ultimatum play out in her dreams?

Not yet.

Torny pinched herself. Another trick, this one learned before Yarvick, a way to keep awake and snag the food right when the Noctia restaurants finally threw it out. Fall asleep on the sly and there wouldn't even be scraps when she woke up.

A tug on the loop opened the door without resistance. The door swung up, struck the cellar wall with a dusty thud. A small ladder lay inside, resting against ramshackle dirt, with old roots and gnarled remnants poking out. The smell coming with it reminded Torny of the Noctia trader's ship, the old treasures waiting to be sold in its hold.

"What secrets do you have?" Torny muttered, leaning over and holding the lantern into the pit.

The glints gave the first clue. Sharp and irregular, like the Ringed City at sunrise. Not something nature made, and not something Torny had seen before. Something begging a closer look.

The thief swung her legs onto the ladder, tested the rungs. The narrow wood passed the test like everything else in this well-made inn and soon enough Torny hit the lower level's floor, this one not so flat. Between the dirt walls, wood beams buttressed the space, giving Torny plenty of height, width to work with. Good thing too, because what waited down there didn't make sense.

Cages. Four, spread along the room's boarders with a narrow walk between them. Big enough to hold a person—Torny, having been in a cell not long ago, would know—yet small enough to ensure they'd never be comfortable. Each one had a bench and nothing else. A single dead lantern hung from the ceiling. To the ladder's left, pounded into the wall, waited a small board with four keys looped on stubs.

The thief gulped.

An inn, sure, but who belonged down here? People who couldn't pay?

Torny turned to hit the ladder again, get out of there. A certain level of creepiness lay well within a thief's realm. This? Nah.

A sound stopped her first step. A shuffling, a sigh, deeper, beyond her lantern's reach. Torny snapped back, the lantern swinging. She'd left her ale mug up a floor in the cellar, and replaced it now with a drawn knife. Shadows only waited, silent. Torny forced her breathing slow, told herself her lantern exposed enough that anything back there would have to be small.

Still.

"Hello?" Torny asked the air.

With the lantern held high, she couldn't exactly hide. Might as well see if something would show itself.

Another sigh, another shuffle. Some dust rose, caught by the lantern's light. Torny kept her grip tight on the knife's hilt. Told herself these were cages. They'd hold anything inside. Nothing was coming to get her.

She took a single step forward. Repeated her call.

This time, a huff greeted her. The air moved. Something shifting places in that back left cage.

Don't be a coward, Torny. See what it is.

Or go back. Get Wax, and—

Wax. The guy who didn't think Torny was committed enough? Not a chance.

The thief shook her head, narrowed her eyes, and took another step forward. Raised the lantern, blotted out all the shadows, and cursed.

CHAPTER 34
JUMP

The problem with towers was that they had more than one floor. A Kitaye treehouse would let you go down a rope or a ladder and be free, on the ground and open in a moment. Instead, as Ami and Sawi broke past the break room, they found themselves on the same twisting stair they'd both walked to get up here. Stone steps and torches. Voices above and below in idle chatter.

At least their escape remained a secret.

"Which way?" Sawi asked as Ami hesitated.

"Down's more obvious, but they'll have more guards," Ami muttered, more to herself than her Vis tagalong. "No guarantee there's a way out up top . . ."

"A small chance over none?"

Ami blinked, shook her head. "Not how it works, Sawi. Up we go."

"But?"

Ami brushed by the Vis, holding the stolen sword steady as she rose with determined steps. Sawi followed, their Najahn robes close enough to swish into one another as the coming storm sent its blusters whirling through the tower. Another marker of its status: few windows sealed with glass. Gladdring's tower came off cozy. This one, the prisoners could suffer.

The thought almost made Sawi pause mid-stride, did make her stumble and draw a glare from Ami.

Before she'd been a prisoner, Sawi hadn't ever once thought of what happened to people hauled into places like this. Part of that could be excused away, as they did things different on Vis, but she'd been on Noctia long enough now to notice the guards hauling away everyone from street thieves to would-be deserters to merchants with loose morals. They'd disappear from sight and that'd be that.

Except now she knew they'd be strung out on plain cots, freezing, till the Najahn gave them a clean exile or a cleaner cut.

"Focus," Ami whispered as they hit the next level, another cell set. The door through to the guards' area was shut, muffled laughter beyond. "If they open it, you need to strike first."

Sawi mouthed a prayer to Vis that, in the interest of all their lives, the door would stay closed and indeed it did, the god doing his part to keep the guards interested in their cards or their dinner.

The next level didn't grant them the same luck, though words and creaking hinges gave the sneaking pair a warning.

Ami bolted up as the landing came into view, a guard holding a dinner basket walking out. The man's eyes went the wrong way, back to his buddies, and with both hands occupied, the man never stood a chance. Sawi thought Ami would go for some brutal stab, a gutting, but the Guardian flipped her grip, instead mashing the sword's hilt into the guard's face and crumpling him into the doorway.

"Run!" Ami called back, her mauling not unnoticed by the two other guards waiting inside.

Sawi gave them a brief glance as she sped by, wide eyes and fumbling feet their primary traits. Ami's victim sprawled in moaning uselessness, the basket and its dirty dishwater scattered all across the floor.

Better than blood.

The next landing put their strategy to the test, the stairs ending with the stone floor and several doors. All three looked the same: solid caramel wood, the black iron handles favored by the Najahn. Ami almost spun in place, trying to decide, only for Sawi to brush past her and pick the rightward one.

An easy choice, as the others likely led seaward. Maybe Ami couldn't hold her directions straight in the spin, but keeping track of herself amid heavy cover was something any Vis had to learn, or else the swinging vines would leave you lost.

Beyond the door waited a deserted room stuffed with trunks, heavy ones labeled with numbers. The room's only light—a lantern near the door hung dead—came from a broad, arced window at its back. Unlike the narrow slits in the tower's stairs, this one had glass, its glint matching the falling snow in the dimming day outside.

"No exit," Ami said, looking around Sawi into the room. "We have to—"

A crossbow's quarrel slammed into the wood over Ami's head, quivering in the splintered board. Ami cursed, pulled herself inside as Sawi went deeper amid the trunks. Ami slammed the door, turned and started tugging a trunk over.

"Help me," the Guardian snarled, and Sawi did, the pair working quick move one trunk before the door and stack another on top.

"What are these?" Sawi asked as they moved, the simple question doing its part to edge off the fact that some Najahn had just tried to shoot them.

Shoot them. As in, not trying to take the pair alive.

If Sawi ever found Gladdring again, the man would wish she'd left him to rot in Mottilan.

"No idea," Ami said, stepping back from their makeshift barrier, sword ready, as if that'd do anything against a crossbow. "Try one. Might be something we can use, because we could damn sure use something."

Sawi picked one at random, flipped it open to see assorted clothes. Decent garb, not Najahn, but nothing that'd help them. The contents, though, clicked with the numbers outside.

"It's prisoner's stuff. What they had on them," Sawi said, shutting the trunk. "Not, uh, great."

"Unless one'of them had a big sword," Ami swore. "Think, Vis. You're supposed to be clever, aren't you?"

Was she?

Sawi glanced around the room, but the trunks were the only things there. A thud bounced against the door. Someone jostled the handle. Ami cursed—she was always cursing, but their barrier held. For now.

The window came next, and when Sawi pressed her head to the glass, she almost screamed. The tower had height, sure, but they'd built it into the Noctia cliffs. Outside, a leap away, lay rugged rock and open slope. A gap between the window and that freedom, sure, but nothing a good Vis couldn't manage.

Sawi didn't hesitate, taking her own stolen sword and

smashing its hilt into the glass. The blow punched through a crack, a second one—Sawi had never broken glass before, but she'd seen a drunk Ami cut herself on a shattered wine bottle, so treated those shards with caution—splintered the window the rest of the way.

"What're you doing?" Ami called as the door rattled again. The Guardian had her back pressed up against the stacked trunks, pushing with her legs. Sweat ran down Ami's face despite the chill now racing into the room. "I didn't come all this way to jump."

"Hope you like getting shot, then."

The tricky thing with the window was that it didn't hit the floor, and its height meant the leap would be a face-forward, diving affair. Get a good lift, arc your body, and plan on a roll as you hit the ground. Harder than a fern's frond, but the same idea. Sawi took a deep breath, the fresh icy wind going in and filling her with ecstatic life.

Something cracked the door. Sawi glanced, caught a big ax's silver edge as the weapon withdrew.

"C'mon," Sawi said. "We're out of time!"

"If you think I'm jumping out some window, you're insane."

Sawi was about to make a standard Vis coward crack when she caught Ami's tone, the sensible fear sitting in the words. A Foti Guardian, that's what Ami was. She'd never gone swinging through the jungle, probably saw every jump as a risk to her ankles, not a chance to fly free. Leaping out a window, much less one into space, wouldn't be a first, second, or fiftieth choice.

"You have to, Ami," Sawi said as that ax struck again, withdrawing fast to let a guard's blinking eye peek through the hole. "Either that or they'll kill you, skar or no."

"Yeah, figured that was a possibility." Ami grinned,

gripped her sword in both hands as she stood up from the crates. "Better this than letting Fassle get his fancy execution."

Sawi felt her mouth hang open as Ami assumed a fighter's stance a stride away from the trunks. She wasn't going to jump? Was just going to swing that blade till the guards tore her apart?

"Don't throw your life away," Sawi said.

"We're proving a point, Sawi," Ami replied, shaking herself loose. The axe struck again, tore a whole board free. Someone stuck a crossbow into the opening, so Ami flipped the top trunk's lid up, caught the quarrel as it fired.

"What point? That you're a moron?"

Flipping her short sword to her off hand, Ami snagged something from the trunk. A guard in the room pushed, sending the trunk lid falling forward. The Guardian chucked the object, some heirloom, through the broken board, laughed as someone in the other room cursed.

The ax struck again, pulling at a second board.

"I'm a Guardian," Ami replied, flipping up the trunk again. "Dying for my Aegis, Sawi. That's what I swore an oath to do." She laughed again, pulled another object free. "This guy's shoes are the stiffest things."

The trunk lid slammed down, Ami chucked the second shoe.

And Sawi jumped.

The wind swam through her robes, the window's edges brushed her own, but Sawi took flight into the dim air. For a long moment Sawi felt her stomach lift, felt the god's hold on her relax. As the beat died, Sawi curled her arms over her head, swung her face towards her stomach, and hit the frigid cliff side in a roll. Pain and panic played a pattern at first, Sawi's momentum carrying her quick on the icy rocks as scrapes and bruises broke through the Najahn robes. Her fingers, legs, feet struck out wide, aiming for purchase and finding it in pieces, every grab, every kick slowing her speed until Sawi came to a sprawled stop. On her back, bleeding, with a shoulder telling her it might not be in the right place anymore, Sawi stared across a curling, wide crater wall running away from the Ringed City's Najahn end.

Free. Sawi smiled, ignoring a bit lip and its leaking blood.

"Where'd you go?" Ami's call came through the window, stressed and confused. "Don't tell me you decided to end it without a fight?"

Sawi flipped herself over, scrambled up the rocks. "I'm out here. You can make the jump!"

Could Ami?

Better that she try, at least.

"You're crazy," Ami's reply, the Guardian unseen through the window, but closer.

A loud crack hinted the door's last moments were fast approaching.

"You're saying a Vis can do something you can't?" Sawi asked. "Am I better than you, Guardian?"

Ami didn't reply. The sharp clang of metal on metal rang through, followed by a scream. Sawi stood, was about to turn and beat a survivor's run, when the Guardian's form appeared in the window, not just measuring the distance but flying at full speed. Ami had strength, didn't have accuracy, and her jump through the window scraped the stone's side, throwing her leap into a warped spin.

Sawi cursed, kicked herself to the edge and reached out, aiming for Ami's hand and getting the Guardian's boot instead as the spinning, falling Foti smacked into the steeper cliff Sawi herself had cleared. The hit sounded like it crunched bone, and Sawi's arms burned as she doubled up her grip on Ami's boot, trying to shimmy back on her knees.

"C'mon, Ami," Sawi said, freezing teeth chattering. "Don't be dead. Don't be dead."

Ami's ankle cleared the slope as Sawi tugged, then the Guardian's thigh, the Najahn robes falling all over. The progress, though, gave Sawi hope: she'd get Ami over the edge, and with the Vis skar, she'd be—

A click. Sawi glanced up, saw the crossbowman taking aim through the window. Right at her.

"Sorry Ami," Sawi said, doing the only thing she could.

Letting go and rolling, down the frozen rocks into the dark.

CHAPTER 35

ENDLESS EFFORT

The bodies could move.

Svarde and Kivi scrambled into the cavern where the Dead King's band had been scattered about, standing in eerie silence. The pair pulled up, Svarde dripping out a Foti prayer as he watched the forms shamble. Some walked as well as any man while others, missing a foot, a leg, or both, tugged themselves across the stone and dirt floor. Like a disturbed ants nest, the bodies seemed to move at random. Though, as Svarde watched, patterns and reason emerged.

Some vanished down the side tunnel towards the deserted city. Others piled stones around Svarde's entry, the beginnings of a barricade. Still more set about to sharpening what weapons remained, or breaking rocks to make new, crude versions. If this was a normal force, Svarde would've declared no time for such things, that instead they needed to rush back to the city, close the gates, and pray the fiends passed them by.

Instead, he saw those bodies work without fatigue, without needs, without hesitation or distraction. Taking out their physical imperfections, the dead were the most efficient force Svarde had ever seen.

Which prompted a question, one Svarde tossed Kivi's way.

"If he's had all these around for so long, how come this whole place isn't sealed up?"

Collapse the tunnels, fill anything you couldn't block with spikes, traps, and fiend-flaying material. Easy enough with years upon years at your disposal, so why hadn't it been done?

Svarde sighted the Dead King in the chamber's middle. He stood with that blade of his stamped into the stone like some carved statue. Maena circled at his side, muttering to herself as she often did these days.

"C'mon, Kivi," Svarde said. "Let's see how we can help."

The ferrite snorted. A question as they edged around the forming barricade.

"Because Jochi's army's coming to us," Svarde answered. "They'll meet us here, and together we'll destroy the fiends. Simple."

Another snort. Hard enough it drew a questioning look from the Foti.

"Yeah, I know it's dumb to stay here, but somebody has to. As the guy with the sword said, the fiends can go anywhere once they get past this room. You saw the damage three of those monsters could do to a big, defended city. Set one or two on a normal town, and . . ."

Svarde trailed off as they reached the Dead King, his approach interrupted when Maena planted herself before him, a scheming question in her eyes.

"You see anything interesting?" Maena asked.

Svarde took in the Rana captain, her capering glint a far cry from the soldier she'd been back in the *Rat's Fang*. A desperate madness, perhaps, overtaking her after so long in these endless tunnels. She didn't have Svarde's bulwark, the decayed love for a dying woman so far beyond his reach and its purifying fire.

Though a madness like this . . .

"Going to answer my question, or use those?" Maena asked, nodding at Svarde's hands. He hadn't realized they'd slipped to his axe hilts. "Thinking of taking my friend's sword for yourself?"

The reference pulled Svarde to the Dead King and his solemn stand, the man silent beneath his armor as he directed the bodies in defense. If he'd heard Maena's quip, the man didn't show it. Whether he'd notice if Svarde *did* try to tear the blade away or stick an axe through his armor, who knew.

Svarde wasn't going to try and find out.

"It's you," Svarde said. The burning fiends hadn't yet made any incursions. A moment to find whether his friend could still be trusted seemed a valuable thing. "You've changed."

"Lot's happened since we first set sail, Svarde. Are you the same as you were?"

"Same goal."

"As do I. Carve these fiends into gristle and then see if we can't use their bones to plug the portals. That's my plan. What's yours?"

Kivi snorted soft at Svarde's foot. A bit grim indeed.

"If it were that easy—"

"Isn't it?" Maena back-stepped, reached down and scooped a stone off the floor, the chipped rock making an easy toss from hand to hand. "This stone, your axes, his sword and these mangy corpses are what we've got, Svarde. We'll throw them all at those bastards you saw coming out of the water down there and try, try, and try till we're either immolated or crushed beneath their metal husks. Simple enough."

"Is that how you planned your raids for Rana? A blind charge onto a Whent vessel, come what may?"

"That was then. This is now." Maena, still tossing the rock back and forth, moved aside and opened Svarde's path towards the Dead King. "You want to strategize, be my guest. You'll find our friend's not the most talkative sort."

"You're calling this conversation here? You're not giving me any answers."

Maena sniffed, spat out to the side. "You don't deserve any, Guardian. Who I am is my concern, and mine alone. Keep your mind on your own problems."

Svarde was about to argue that's not what friends did, particularly ones about to march into battle. Something in Maena's stiff look, though, pushed away the crack and killed the talk. The Rana captain had drained away as they spoke, going from pithy and playing to brittle and bristling.

At least, seeing as she had no real weapon, Svarde didn't have to consider her a threat.

The Dead King gave a different conversation, namely one beginning and ending with Svarde's greeting. The plated man didn't respond, save the soft in and out of his breathing. When Svarde tried again, the silence persisted, though the work continued around them. The Dead King seemed a rock until his work was done, so Svarde set about doing what he could to get himself ready.

Hours passed as the bodies worked at their stone bulwarks. Carts rolled in from the old city's tunnel, fractured wheels scraping against the floor shoved with tireless effort by their rotted pilots. Inside lay the very thing Svarde didn't want Maena to have: weapons.

Crude swords, spears, shields and knives. Hammered out and sharpened with pitiful skill, their edges held more pits than Svarde's battle-scarred skin. The spear hafts weren't sturdy wood but old bones, fashioned together with tar and spit. Many didn't have hilts at all, wielded by jamming a single end into the soft, barely-there flesh hanging from the Dead King's soldiers.

Svarde muttered one curse after another watching the display, as the entire chamber filled with its fetid ranks, the ones not working to bolster the makeshift wall lining up in battle formations.

"You asked me a question," the Dead King said, his voice quieter than before, drained and yet, immovable. Undying like its subjects.

"I wanted to know your strategy. Whether you'd consider taking the fight to them while we have the high ground. Force them back into the sea."

"For your friend's force, viable. For mine, the dead don't swim, and the water eats their flesh to nothing, till they are nothing but a bone pile. Better we fight in here, where every one of ours struck down has a chance to rise again." The Dead King unfolded as he spoke, rising from his kneel to his taller-than-Svarde height. Amid the chamber's mosses, the Dead King glimmered in blues and greens, a blooming shadow. "They can charge, as they will, but they will find every step earned will stab their backs, their legs, their feet until they are as dead as their enemies."

Svarde started.

"Can you take them? Where are the others?" Svarde swept an arm around the chamber, and for once Maena seemed to be on his side, echoing the question. "Shouldn't you have fiends everywhere around here, ready to defend us?"

"It isn't so easy." The Dead King nodded towards the barricade. "Are you ready?"

"Hold. One more. You say you've been down here for so long. Why aren't the fiends walled off? Why not have thicker walls, stronger swords?"

"Demion tasked me with protecting the isles. Walling off one way would simply send the terrors in another direction, down farther tunnels I cannot protect. At least here, in this crucible, we can stop some of them." If the Dead King had more to say, something sapped his words. The black iron helm and the head within it turned towards the barricaded tunnel. "The fiends approach."

The Dead King didn't need some skilled scout to make that call: a low rumble had started some minutes ago, the vibrations peppering Svarde's feet. Now a distant golden glow shaded in the tunnel's far end, like a creeping, chaotic dawn.

Maena, carrying two misshapen scimitars, those curved weapons favored by Tamas soldiers, what few of those fanciful folks there were, tested out her range with a dance. Kivi, with Svarde's blessing, gave up the ground for a spot on the ceiling, an ambush waiting for its moment. The dead shuffled, spear-bearers rising to the front, while those few with limbs able to wield rock-throwing slings brought themselves space.

The Foti barbarian took one last pull from his water skin, drew his axes, and picked his chosen bellow.

"When they arrive, wait," the Dead King said, his mighty sword still planted point down into the dirt. "Let them tire themselves against my old friends first."

"Don't want our bodies added to your collection?" Maena asked.

"You will be," the Dead King replied. "Better to make the most of your life before you hand it over."

"Not much for inspiration, are you?"

The Dead King turned her way, his helmet grinding on the plate. "This is our purpose, dancer. We fight here to save the world. What more inspiration do you need?"

"Well, when you put it that way . . ."

Svarde whistled. Drew their attention back to the barricade, where gold had become yellow had become orange. Heat rushed into the chamber, drawing the first sweat Svarde had felt in days among the cool underground. The ramshackle stone wall blocked their sight, but not the sound: not just the rumbling floor, now, but machinery's steady grind, those vehicles pressing against the loose stone. With it came the jangle, the clinking as chains rubbed on the ground or crunched against the pressing cave walls.

At some silent command, the dead slingers commenced a barrage, stones arcing up and over the barricade with more violence than Svarde expected. Tireless force, all-out effort given to every spin and throw. Bangs and breaks rippled. Sparks flew up, rising in their hot glitter over the dark wall. Another volley and a third, an unbroken assault maintained as other dead gathered, dropped further ammunition.

A vague hope found its purchase.

For as the fourth volley flew into the air, a rumbling crunch, a bright gout enveloped the wall, and its simple stones melted away. The roaring glow didn't fade, didn't calm as the barricade died. It advanced, the only break in the inferno coming from those obsidian triangles, marching forward in burning silence.

CHAPTER 36
A LITTLE LIFT

A broken leg and a battered beast. Torny's discovery erased Wax's exhaustion and replaced it with possibility: he'd seen those large creatures on Foti and knew what a good hauling animal could do. As to why it'd been left in the cage with large straw piles strewn around within reach, the answer came with its limping, huffing form as the great ox regarded the two beyond its bars.

"But wait," Wax said, sense gradually filtering through his muffled mind. "How'd it even get down here? We used a ladder?"

"One way trip," Torny muttered, glancing back at the wide door. "Bet they knocked the poor boy out and shoved him down here."

"One way?"

"Not every place has as much food as Vis, Wax. Big boy like this guy here could feed a family most of the winter. Bet they hated leaving him behind and tried to buy time with the straw."

Why they left seemed obvious enough: before Wax had blown up the party, all the talk surrounded the mad warlord and his conscription frenzy. If Wax dared suggest another topic, the chattering guests turned towards the fiend assault on the town, the gathered defense pulled in beforehand. Anybody left in the area would've been yanked along, handed a crossbow or a sword and told to defend home and country.

More Isles needed a force like the Lira, ready to jump in.

"We're not going to use it for food, though," Wax said, tapping a finger against the empty cage to his left.

"No? Wax, think. Between this ox and the drinks upstairs, we could wait out those frogs, make a nice spring time walk to the Gash."

"Torny, if I have to spend months locked up in here with you, my sister, and Eujo, I'm going to lose it."

The bandit frowned, "Not a nice thing to say about your Guardians, buddy."

"I'm a realist." Wax nodded at the ox. "No, we're going to get our friend back upstairs, because I've got a plan."

"Why does that make me more nervous?"

"No idea, Torny. No idea."

Wax's ox excavation hopes died a swift death when confronted with reality, like how the two of them were going to get the massive beast from its cage and up a ladder. While ropes and random tools clogged the inn's basement, none seemed a viable option to bring an animal all the way up, much less with only two people to work them.

But if you couldn't do step one, move on to step two. Wax took a rag, bundled up his Vis skar inside it, then returned to the ox. The creature, either so docile or despairing, didn't bother moving more than its eyes as Wax came in, wrapped the skar around the ox's injured leg. He gave the beast a gentle pat, whispered a prayer to his god, one asking for health, happiness, and hope, and left to spin plots with the thief.

Wax's bright idea, there in the early morning dark, continued to earn Torny's skepticism, but the bandit played along as Wax described the plan, one commencing in earnest . . . after a nap. Even the ox seemed to agree, resting its head on straw and closing those big brown eyes.

The inn held a different, savory smell when Wax woke up, having traded beds with Eujo. The Queen and, later, Bliss had put their earlier wakings to use, pilfering the inn's supplies to make an oatcake breakfast. Snow, melted over the fire, provided fresh water, while chopped potatoes and carrots continued Wax's acclimation to foods common in the other isles but found nowhere in Vis's hotter, swampier jungle.

The foursome gathered in the late morning, the frogs maintaining their idle distance as snow flurries whipped around outside. The inn's many tables and chairs felt a bit empty, but cozy in their fashion, and Wax found a meal without a boat's rocking a pleasant change. The fire's merry crackle, a thing also avoided on the *Storm's Edge*, added to the scene, letting him ease into the day.

"And wait until you try this," Torny said, carrying a boiling pot over to the table and setting it down. A loamy, bitter odor rose, one Wax recognized. "Coffee. Can you believe it? They actually have real coffee here. Know what that is?"

Wax and Bliss glanced at each other, the Renewal giving his sister the nod to break the terrible truth to the bandit.

'We grow it all the time,' Bliss signed as Torny started

pouring the steaming drink into several thick gray mugs. 'Kitaye trades it to everyone.'

Torny blinked at the signals while Eujo chuckled. "Okay, well, nobody talks about where it comes from. And I've never seen you two drink any."

'Because we don't need it.'

Now Torny and Eujo shared a look, one accompanied by the first, gentle sips. Bliss held a growing smile at the other two's disbelief, a joke Wax decided to spoil so they could get the conversation onto what really mattered; the creature in the basement.

"We chew the beans," Wax said. "It's far less work, and way less hot than boiling the coffee. But we didn't bring any when we left. Maybe a mistake."

"You can just eat the beans?" Torny asked.

"Try it."

The bandit did just that a few minutes later, after they'd finished the cakes and carrots. Her face scrunched up and Wax swore he saw a tear form in one eye at the bitterness, but the bandit kept it down and even reached for a second. Whether she ate that one or simply palmed it, showing off for the watching trio, Wax wasn't sure.

"You want to give it a shot, Eujo?" Wax asked as they used more snowmelt to clean their own dishes. Even Torny had been on board with the idea, seeing as they'd used the inn for free and were about to, well, steal its old ox. "Coffee bean?"

"I'll keep it the way I know, thanks."

With breakfast conquered, Wax unveiled the plan: use the skars with the ox, have the thing, powered by Vis and Foti, propel them away from the inn all the way to the Gash.

"On what?" Eujo asked. "Or are you thinking we'll just ride the beast the whole way?"

"To that, I say, who wants to go for a walk?"

Bliss volunteered, while Torny and Eujo continued the clean-up and packing more supplies for the journey. That nobody shot Wax's idea down with harsh sarcasm or doubt put some verve in the Vis's steps, enough that, with his thick coat, Wax shrugged off the blistering cold and hiked into the snow with a grin. Bliss followed, matching her boots to his steps as they went west, away from the inn and towards the barn off that way.

The frogs, invisible during the day, made no forays. Maybe, Wax dared to hope, they'd decided to hop after easier prey.

The hunch bringing Wax into the snow, supported by Torny's casual Isles knowledge, said this barn would hold livestock during the harvest, but might also store gear the inn didn't have room for. Like, say, some sort of sledge. The big double doors on the barn's near end rose more than twice Wax's height, the whole building as tall as the inn it supported, but no lock laid on the handles. The Vis, with a shrug at his sister, gripped the iron loop and pulled.

The doors went nowhere. They shivered at his effort, but moved not at all, a confusing stalemate until Bliss pointed out the obvious issue: the snow, all the snow, clustered up against the door's base.

"Don't look at me like I'm an idiot," Wax said as they bent down, scooping the fluff away with their gloves. "I've never seen snow like this before, much less tried to open a door covered in it."

Bliss replied by throwing the flakes in his face, a full on scoop that left Wax's skin cold and glittering in the sun.

An attack that could not go unanswered.

The siblings cleared the barn door in the best way: launching snowy handfuls at each other, with Wax shouting and cursing every time Bliss landed a chilly bunch down his neck or inside his coat sleeves. Bliss lost her hair to the flakes, her head soon coated in fluff before both realized they were reaching beyond the door's edges for their ammunition. Together, almost as one, they turned back to one another with empty hands, red-faced and grinning.

"Can almost see why people would live in all this," Wax muttered when Bliss nodded at the door.

This time, the tugged wood gave a groan, scuffed along the thin white still on the ground. An earthy scent greeted the pair as they stepped inside, seeing a bottom floor arrayed into stalls beneath an upper deck coated in hay bales, the latter a term Wax had only just learned since arriving on Whent, seeing them stacked here and there in the city.

Without the wind, the pair's snowy fight had them warming up quick as they moved through the barn, confirming empty stalls all around. Towards the far end, four large sections with locking gates seemed too open for animals, a suspicion confirmed when they hit the last one, near the barn's rear doors.

Wax couldn't help it, the whoop came easy. Bliss did one better, hopping on the small, ramshackle sledge and raising her hands in two-fisted triumph. The sledge had two long, thick skids, room for their packs, and while only a single bench sat forward—perhaps the reason it wouldn't serve an evacuating family—they traveled light enough Wax could see them cramming in.

The find pushed the plan into the next phase, rescuing the ox from the basement. Wax had an idea there too, one Eujo came around to with the cautious reluctance of someone pushed by circumstance. Namely, that walking any further towards the Golden Gash would end in their frozen, frog-devoured deaths.

The wrapped Vis skar hadn't magically restored the ox to full health, but the creature managed a shaky stand. Eujo added her own Vis stone to Wax's wrapped one, the ox remaining its gentle self, though confused snorts broke out when Eujo revealed the white Kance skar. With Torny leading the ox from the cage, the Kance Queen grabbed the beast's fur and pulled herself into a hugging ride.

"Careful now," Wax said, calling down from the basement. "Don't spook her."

"You ever ride an ox before?" Eujo replied, her voice a whispered shout. "No? Then I don't want to hear a word."

Not that Wax had to say another thing: Torny guided the ox to the trap door's base, the beast looking at her as if to declare in no way was it climbing the ladder.

"Okay, Eujo, now's your time," Torny said.

"I'm trying."

From above, the Queen looked like she was trying to give the ox as tight an embrace as possible, gripping the animal around its shoulders, her left hand pinning the skar between them. Her eyes shut. Wax thought he caught a shiver.

Eujo's thick coat bubbled, its edges rising up as a wind, seemingly from nowhere, flowed up from the cellar into the basement. The shelves rattled. A jar of pickled something hit the floor and shattered. Wax started to back away; any wind strong enough to lift an ox through that door would tear this whole place apart.

Except the air died. The wind vanishing as suddenly as it started, only to be replaced with a panicked snort. Wax returned to the door's edge, only to fall back again as the big beast's head rose through, the ox's eyes whirling and wild. Eujo, eyes open and telling the ox to stay calm, followed with the ox's body, the whole creature, its hooves hitting the ladder, the floor, pulling through into the basement as though lifted by a gentle hand.

"Well, look at that," Torny quipped from below. "Thought I'd seen everything, but guess I was wrong."

CHAPTER 37
TENET'S TASK

A disturbed hornet's nest, and one Quik had to wade through. The Najahn scurried, shouted, hid their faces and murmured to one another as evening descended and the knives came out. Quik himself earned little notice, his unadorned robes giving nobody a reason to look closer, not when their own lives could be at risk.

An innocent ask to a nervous guard gave Quik the update he needed: Gladdring and the entire Trade Tenet's tower was being rounded up, interrogated, with their loyalty under question. Fassle would take every incorrect answer, every shifty glance as a reason to throw you in a prison tower. Some few, the guard whispered, had been killed that very night.

The Najahn streets seemed alive with the tension, the torches burning brighter, the stones shivering under steps, a coming storm whisking snow between the towers. Sichi offered a pale violet light, casting it upon the cliffs where the clouds didn't cover, scars on the rocks.

Quik watched those more and more as he closed with his target, his supposed home with the Third Hand. A place he'd spent scant little time after Masayo's order and subsequent imprisonment in Annalyse's beachside cage. Nevertheless, he remembered the words to get in, and the watchers standing outside bore the chaos as little more than a curiosity.

Masayo would never let such a thing bother the Third Hand, or so Quik assumed.

His room appeared as he'd left it, with the remnants of his Vis things, the gear off the *Storm's Edge* stored untouched in his trunk. Nobody had assumed he'd died, despite days and days disappeared. His bed made up, the pillow waiting for an exhausted head, one Quik wanted to plant right on the soft fabric.

Wanted to, wouldn't.

Because someone stood in his door, shrouded and waiting.

"You're back," Masayo said, her voice strong and scratched with vigorous age.

The two words invited an explanation, and Quik gave it. No sense wondering how Masayo knew he'd returned, whether she knew if he'd helped Annalyse escape the isle. Both wouldn't change the situation, which, at the moment, was that Quik lived and Masayo didn't seem about to kill him.

"The skars as an answer?" Masayo snorted. "That they've power has been known for a long time, that they're too hard to control has been known too. Every Renewal someone gets excited and blows themselves up, flies too high and lands on their head." The Third Hand Tenet hadn't moved from Quik's doorway, though she did take up a small pipe, strike a spark into its bowl. The puffs between sentences had a languor, a loamy scent different than anything Quik remembered from Vis. "Gladdring thinks he's onto something new, but that's only because he hasn't looked hard enough at the past."

"You think Fassle knows?"

Masayo nodded. "My little Najahn, Fassle and the Circle know more than any one Tenet. He's putting an end to Gladdring's work before it endangers the isle, before it endangers us."

"Us?"

"Give the people an unreasonable hope and they'll slaughter themselves trying to claim it. The Najahn control the skars because of this very reason, even if our soldiers don't know it. Can you imagine a horde of scared people grabbing Foti skars and burning up whole villages?"

Quik frowned, "They wouldn't."

Masayo pointed a bony finger at him. "That's your naivety speaking. Disaster is everyone with a weapon, instead of the few who know how to use them. We protect the isles, Quik, both from the fiends, and from themselves. If the Najahn fall, then the isles descend into chaos."

So far apart from Annalyse, her words and ideas aiming for strength, for safety given to everybody. The distance between them, the day's exhaustion, put Quik into a spin and he sat on his own bed.

"You're tired?" Masayo asked, then answered herself as Quik sighed. "Of course you would be. Escaping Ami's clutches must have taken extreme effort." The pipe puffed. "You have two hours. Then you're up and we're moving."

"Why?"

"Because your old Vis friend has escaped, and Ami with her, though the insipid prison guards insist they've left them both wounded."

Amazing how a friend's peril could push away any exhaustion. Quik parsed Masayo for details and received them, though every sentence came soaked in condescension for the Najahn who'd let the pair escape. Masayo felt the whole lot should be slaughtered with Gladdring's crew, incompetence being as fatal to any organization as treason.

"But where are they going to go?" Quik asked, pulling Masayo back to the point, to Sawi's life.

"The crater's ring isn't uninhabited. There are small places, where small people live. They grow their mosses and their mushrooms, catch their fish, and wait for a fiend, a storm, or time's grind to render them to dust," Masayo said, ending in a husky laugh. "Sawi and Ami, if they are alive, will find one. They will stay there, just long enough for us to catch up."

"Why?"

"Because it is Winter. There will be no ships. Their only option will be the caves, and it will take days for them to realize they have no other choice."

Another laugh. Grating. Quik looked past it, beyond the pipe and its smoke, Masayo's hooded form. Why was she still here, telling Quik all this? What was the point? There had to be a reason . . .

"You want me to go with you," Quik said, his hunter's instincts sleuthing the truth. "You want me to track them down."

"I always thought Vis were smarter than the rumors suggested," Masayo replied. "Yes. They'll have some head start, but there's no other Vis here. I trust you'll know how your friend thinks. You'll help me find them."

"You want me to kill my friend?"

"Find them, Quik. That's all. The knife work comes later."

Quik glanced at the pillow, the bed, the purple and black robes he wore. The unsaid stakes were obvious. Do what Masayo said or he'd find a knife in his own back, a traitor to the Najahn cause. No help for Wax, no rescue at the head of an armored force for good. But, kill Sawi? Or get close enough as to make no difference?

"She's been a friend her entire life," Quik said. "I can't."

"You can and you will, or do you think we didn't notice your little escape? The scientist will be followed, of course. Whether she lives, now, is up to you. A life for a life."

Quik found his feet before he knew what he was doing, a hazed red over his thoughts. He took a step towards Masayo only to see a dagger, long and sharp, out and pointed at his gut.

"You're monsters," Quik snarled.

"Did you listen at all to what I said? Your friends, whether they know it or not, will destroy everything if left alone. We are the only ones who can stop them. Your brother is on your same path, faced with the same choices, and he continues to put the isles above his own feelings. Can you?"

How Masayo would know what Wax thought, what he chose and why . . . That was a play, but it made Quik wobble nonetheless. He'd seen the skars, their power, and could envision a town, a city burning as people did what Wax had done time and again with that Foti skar. Give them swords, spears, or Annalyse's stranger devices, and what more harm might be done?

"I'm too tired for this," Quik said, rocking back on his feet. "I don't know."

"You don't have to. Not yet. We find the Vis, the Guardian. Go from there." Masayo pulled the dagger away, ready to discard the threats and give Quik a way out. "Take your nap. I'll have bags packed and readied."

As the Third Hand Tenet turned away, Quik found his voice, a question to ask with it:

"Why?"

"Searching for reason is a fool's errand, my young friend," Masayo replied, continuing to walk away. "Best do as the birds, and fly as the wind blows."

Whatever that meant.

Quik sat back on the cot, put his head on the pillow, sure he wouldn't sleep more than a moment. Instead, the dreams came fast and troubled. By the time Masayo's rough hand shook Quik awake, he felt no rested than before and said as much.

"Nevertheless," Masayo said, the pipe again glowing as it hung from her parched lips, "we go. Get dressed, Vis. The hunt begins tonight."

CHAPTER 38
SLEDGE SIPPIN'

Nestled back between satchels and provisions pilfered from the inn's crowded stores, Torny adopted a new perspective on winter travel: namely, that when you had nothing to do save nurse a stiff, burning potato vodka while the frozen land bounced by, it wasn't so bad.

The only thing she'd change would be the company: Wax and Bliss sat up front, they being the pair with any wildlife experience. The closest Torny had come to dealing with a creature had been the occasional Foti ferrite, and Eujo, lurking beneath her coat across from the bandit, hadn't found time to train any beasts in Kance's streets or while coasting through the Palace of the Winds.

"That's really the name, then?" Torny asked, passing the bottle, one of many she'd shoved into the sledge over Wax's increasingly raised eyebrows. "Palace of the Winds? Pretentious, much?"

"Pretension and royalty go well together." Eujo took a drink, didn't cough once at what must've been a tasty, harsh ride down her throat.

The Queen earned an iota of Torny's respect.

"But that's not really you, is it? Royalty?" Torny held out her hand for the bottle's return, shivered as the sledge caught air and her stomach floated for a moment.

The ox, it's stamina boosted by the twin Vis skars and its hooves lightened by Eujo's Kance gem, zipped north with a frantic, delighted fervor that was doing as much as the boredom to make Torny, and, she suspected, Eujo dip into the bottle despite the day barely passing into the afternoon. From the back, the two couldn't see where the sledge was headed, and better to absorb the unknown's shock with a solid booze buffer.

"Depends on the day." Eujo's banter, like an untangling knot, had started as stiff as ever, but the liquor was doing its work. "Sometimes I would wake up beneath sheets more valuable than the entire street I scrounged on and want to run down the hall, leap from the windows, and see if I could steal a biscuit for breakfast. Others, I'd have some ceremony, some reason to be in front of people who had to place hope in me simply through accident. Then, then I try to be what they need."

"Awful kind of you."

Eujo had a faraway look, the sort Torny suspected had the Queen lost in a place far warmer and friendlier than this one.

"People are depending on me," Eujo said. "They didn't get to choose me, but I'm what they've got. I don't want to disappoint them."

"How's that on you, though? Not your fault you're in this."

"I could have refused, Torny. Or let one of the other Queen's assassins take me out, exile me from the isle."

Torny sniffed. Drank some more. At this rate, both the

bandit and the Queen would be good and toasted by the time they made the Golden Gash. A good first impression on whatever fools found themselves stuck there too. Torny, after handing the bottle back to Eujo, patted the pocket beneath the furs, felt the diary still there. So long as she had that, who cared what some morons in an outpost thought?

"So do you even want the Aegis?" Torny asked. "Is that what you're going for, what your people want? You owe them enough to burn out a short life sitting on that stone chair?"

"I owe them a reprieve from the fiends as fast as I can give it." Eujo gulped down a larger share than Torny managed. Went for it again. "I had my time getting the best we had. Now it's time I gave back."

"Damn, you really are noble."

Eujo shook her head. "Just fair."

"What were your guards, then? The ones that wanted you dead? They didn't seem to like you much."

Eujo frowned, her hands gripped the coat as if wanting to strangle something.

"They were traitors."

"They thought they were doing the right thing."

Not what Torny would've said if she'd been stone sober, but better get the truth out there than sit suffering Eujo's saintly proclamations any longer.

"You read the letters," Eujo said, leveling it as a fact and nothing more.

"Absolutely. There's a lotta rules to being a thief, but one of the big ones is not letting free information get away."

"Doesn't change that they were traitors, even if they had their reasons."

"So what're you going to do? Ignore it?"

"I'm not sure." A glance towards the gray clouds overhead, the snow always falling. "Either I hide it. Claim they died from some fiend. Or I call it out, pin the blame on the other Queen. Rift my isle in two."

"Chaos is profitable."

"For some."

Torny laughed, "For your old friends, I'd bet. For mine too."

A sly smile swapped the Queen's frown. Despite the sledge's rush, the snow continued to gather around them, on their hooded heads as a silver wreath.

"The Nimble Fingers," Eujo said, handing the bottle back. "We hated you."

"Because we were the best. Are the best."

"I . . ." Eujo laughed. "You're right. I can't even argue. Your thieves would sneak onto our isles and take our marks, lift our targets before we'd even have a chance."

"Because your hearts weren't in it," Torny said. "Easy. All you Kance have these higher ideals, even the gutter hounds think they're on some noble quest. We'd try to take in some of your better ones but it'd be a struggle every time to get them to nab a tomato. They'd mutter the whole way about whether this vegetable would pave the way for a happier world or some crap like that."

"As if that's a bad thing."

"You want to be a bandit, it is." Torny washed another swallow down, lounged in the warmth. The sledge hit another bump, caught air. Wax whooped his Vis call.

"So that's not you. No greater good bones in your body?"

"Just the next move, that's all."

A curious, iron stare. "Then why are you still here? You took your goal, that diary. Surely you could've slipped away." Eujo hesitated, threw a glance towards the front. "Or did Bliss tail you too close?"

"I could've lost her, if I wanted to."

"But?"

Torny held up the bottle. Decided against another drink and went for her water skin instead. Being a bit loopy was one thing, being unconscious on arrival was something quite different. Besides, she had enough courage, now, to open this particular door.

"There's rules when you're working with a group," Torny said, and Eujo nodded. "Some are loose, like who gets to take the credit for a job gone right. Some aren't, like what you do if you get caught."

Eujo stayed quiet. Smart one, the Queen.

"That was me. Took on a gig that went wrong. Bad luck. Guy came back with buddies hours before he should've, all because he forgot his Najahn voulge. I tried to get out the kitchen window, one grabbed my leg, pulled me in and put a blade to my neck." Now Torny took that drink. The story, the memory demanded it. "They pulled me along to Masayo that same night, and she made me an offer. Three thieves for one."

"You didn't."

"I'm here, aren't I?" Torny snapped back. "Maybe you're made of steel stuff, Eujo, but I prefer to keep my neck unbroken. I gave'em another job, and they caught their culprits. Word came around, and Yarvick kicked me off the isle."

"He should've killed you."

"Probably would've, if I hadn't jumped on the next boat out. Self exile."

"Sounds like self preservation."

Torny tossed the bottle at Eujo, light enough to catch,

hard enough to deliver a good thwack, but the Queen snatched it fine.

"Judge me all you want, I don't care," Torny said. "But now you know why. The diary's paying down a debt I'll never clear. The Guardian thing, that's it too. People died because of me, and I'm living with that."

"You always will. That's not a weight that ever leaves."

Torny's turn to get curious. "You have a story there?"

Another pull. Eujo looked like she wanted to say more, but Wax gave another whoop, said the Gash was in sight, they were moving so fast. The Queen stashed the bottle away, gave Torny a single, sad look, then climbed from her makeshift nest to take a look. Torny followed, peering over the stacked satchels.

The Golden Gash stretched not like the jagged Foti mountains, but rose instead in a smooth ripple up from the earth, rising soft over the horizon before sloping off into the distance. Despite the gray day, the Gash earned its name with a vast stripe running along its upper edge, as if someone had painted sparkles all along the curve. They caught the light like a million stars, almost blinding in their golden twinkles.

At its feet, visible as a smudge with wispy smoke, lay their goal, another Najahn outpost. With it would come instructions, a test, and another skar. Another line on a debt Torny would never repay.

CHAPTER 39
ON THE ROCKS

Noctia wasn't comfortable. A cliffside fall on Vis and Sawi might find herself nuzzling sand amid a quiet cay, ready to slip away into a blissful sleep for hours, days healing away the traumas. She would've liked that, would've embraced it without issue, except dreams weren't reality, hadn't been for so long.

Her eyes snapped open, the rough rock pressing into her side, her cheek. She'd caught on a narrow ledge, a slope all the way down and down until a pebble-strewn beach bled into smashing icy waves. Far out against the horizon, looking north, Sawi could make out pearly smudges, ice floes on the move. Matching, if only in color, the flakes drifting down from the sky. Evening, late. Cold and dark would be coming soon, and Sawi wore little more than a prisoner's rags.

Nobody ever died freezing on Vis, but that didn't mean Sawi hadn't heard tales of near misses in the mountains, hunters getting caught too far out, breaking an ankle and having to pull themselves back down. Here, she had nowhere to stumble to: everywhere would be the same chill, the same biting death.

Ami, though, might have a solution. Might know where the two fugitives could go.

The idea had Sawi sitting up from her impromptu fall, a desperate dodge away from crossbow bolts while holding onto Ami's leg. She'd lost that handle somewhere in the roll, a second or two before collapsing onto the stones and laying there, eyes closed, bruises boiling up, waiting for the killing shot that never came.

Not that it wouldn't eventually.

Sawi shook her head, an act of mild defiance that nonetheless sparked a desperate life. She'd fought this far. She'd not stop now. Not now.

A careful stand—the Najahn boots worked well enough to keep traction on the stones—let Sawi look behind her, up blessedly deserted cliffs. Beyond the sloping stones, she caught the prison tower's very top. No window, no sight lines to let pursuit know where the pair had wound up. A few minutes free, then.

To run, to rescue.

Ami's body lay crumpled further down and to the left, a more sheer dive to a roiling pool filling with icicles as abandoned drops froze. Ami's form dotted black and gray rock, chilled mud green corals clustered in the crevasses. Sawi picked her way down, hands and feet trading off turns and uneven grips.

The task helped wake the Vis, its simple, determined nature leveling Sawi out. The steps to get near Ami's body played in a line, one Sawi extended as she reached Ami's side, knelt on the narrow band over the crashing waves.

Get the Guardian up, run away from the Ringed City.

Scavenge, forage, survive. Build a small shelter with stones. Use the skars to stay alive.

Ami already had hold on that last. As Sawi turned the Guardian's body, a light hand on the shoulder and a twist, Ami's golden half-face came into view. The scratches that should've littered her body already looked like soft pink smudges, receding as the two green skars nestled in her faceplate did their jobs. Feeling her own aches, Sawi reached towards one then stopped.

What you couldn't see from a fall like this could be far worse than what you could.

"Gladdring would leave you," Sawi muttered, plotting a course along the rocks. "He'd make some sour claim about it being a pity and wouldn't lift a finger."

Then again, Gladdring was probably dead already. That, or getting dressed up for a public execution. To her own surprise, Sawi found herself muttering a prayer to Vis for the man's soul. He'd been awful, yes, but he'd also saved her life, given Sawi something more than gathering fruit to fill her days.

Broadened, if she could call it that, her horizons.

The Tenet's whirlwind impacts on Sawi's life played out in flitting memories as the Vis pulled Ami onto her shoulders, then made a halting hike away from those waves and out onto the cliff side proper. Far from the stark drops on Vis, Noctia's natural world seemed built, this far down, from pebbles. As if some playful trickster stacked so many stones atop one another that they formed the isle. The truth, as Sawi knew it, was something grimmer: those stones were all part of Noctia herself, the goddess, split from her in the same strike that formed the Wound, the crater.

A war between gods, for reasons unknown. People,

creatures, Sawi wasn't sure what to call them, but for all their power they had enough faults to get them all killed. Humans, fiends, animals, all left over after the divine squabble to populate a shattered world.

Big thoughts for a gatherer. Sawi smirked at herself, winced as the cold tugged at her own lips. The elders in Kitaye would give her sidelong looks if they knew what she was thinking, wondering at. What use, they would say, in trying to understand the gods? Better to mutter a prayer and move on.

Then why pray to dead gods, Sawi might ask.

"Because you never know."

Ami's voice came as a whisper, but one with a backbone. Sawi wouldn't have heard it save Ami's head rested near her own as they trudged, each step a weighted lurch, along the stones. The uneven footing had them bouncing with every move, slow progress forced by the surf's spray, the slick round surfaces. Sawi must've been focused so much that she'd been talking aloud.

"You're alive," Sawi said. "I thought—"

"No damn Najahn's going to kill me. How far have we gone?"

"A few steps."

"Too slow."

Sawi rolled her shoulder, dumped Ami off against the rocks. The Guardian sprawled with a grunt, but she gave Sawi a smile flush with menace. Those eyes focused. Her hair, like Sawi's own, remained a gnarled mess and both of them wore clothes better suited, now, to a fire than their skin, yet they lived, and the moment pushed Sawi into a half-crazed chuckle.

"They'll follow." Ami said, after she joined Sawi for a

gleeful second. "And not those boneheaded guards either. It'll be real soldiers, or worse."

"Worse?"

"I'll tell you later, when it'll give you proper nightmares," Ami said, pushing up to her feet, a wobbly stance stabilizing only when Sawi offered her shoulder.

To lean on, not to carry. Not again.

"You'll tell me now, because I don't trust you to stick around."

"Where else am I going to go?"

The pair began their shuffling again, following the waterline east. The dimming daylight promised a treacherous path, one the clouds ensured would stay hidden after Sichi rose. A concern Sawi dismissed for herself: nighttime jungle swings offered as much risk. The deadlier enemy here, by far, would be the cold.

"If Gladdring's trading maps are right," Ami said, "there's a small village not far ahead. A half day's hike at most."

"It's almost night."

"Then we'll walk in the dark."

"Might die in the dark too."

Ami didn't stop moving, but Sawi felt her head turn. "You're not worried, for all you're saying."

There were people to bluff, situations to hide, this wasn't one of them.

"We're here, Ami. Worrying's not going to change anything."

"First smart thing you've said."

Another insult, but Sawi let it slide. Ami, all thorns. Gladdring had hinted it hadn't always been this way, that the Aegis's favorite friend used to be a warming presence all around the isles. The years, though, had ground away the jokes and the smiles, a vibrancy murdered at last by the burning fiend and her scarred face.

For all Sawi had been through, Ami had seen worse.

At Sawi's advice, the pair hiked down almost to the surf, where the pebbles shrank to fine gravel, giving them surface filled only with crab holes. At least the stumbles there only came to their knees, to shallow, albeit icy, water. A twisted ankle beat a shattered skull, particularly when the Vis skars were around.

As darkness claimed the evening, reducing the world to dimmest pink where Sichi could sneak through, Ami turfed off one skar to Sawi. The stone's warmth, its whispers knitting her sore muscles, massaged her bruises back to health. While Sawi's stomach still groaned and her throat scratched, the gatherer kept Noctia's cold grasp at bay.

"When we reach the town, what're we going to do?" Sawi asked. "Build a boat?"

"Find a way to leave it." Ami still leaned on Sawi, though the Vis sensed it was more about keeping her footing in the dark. "The Najahn will know where we're going, but we don't have another option."

"Leave it how?"

Ami laughed, one of her snippy, dire chuckles that served as both insult and relief. "No boat's going to these towns in the winter. No, we ask, and of the options they give us, we pick the worst one."

"So the Najahn go the other way."

"Sawi, we're being hunted now. Every second, every minute, every hour we gain on the Najahn is one we get to live. So we lie, misdirect, and scramble as much as we can."

The words crashed along with the waves, the wind. Sawi let them swirl. Wondered at the force behind them, where Ami found her strength.

"Until what, Ami? What's the end?"

The Guardian took her time in answering, the soft stones grinding beneath their boots.

"I thought I had one once. Had a friend with one too. An end, a goal, a dream."

Ami's voice, like Sawi's, had grown raspy with water's lack. In the chill gloom, the Guardian seemed less a person, more a spirit, an ethereal beast. As Wax would say, Sawi was letting her imagination get the best of her, but out here, what did it matter?

"And now?"

"I'm picking a new one," Ami replied, the rasp changing, picking up a familiar edge. "We're going to find a way to get back at Fassle, those Najahn monsters, and save my friend in the bargain."

"And how are we going to do that?"

Ami tightened her grip on Sawi's right shoulder, made the Vis turn her way. The woman's gold plate took what light it could, glimmered almost like bloody glass as the rest disappeared into shadow.

But Sawi could see easily enough when Ami tapped the stone near her left eye, the Vis skar.

"With these, Sawi. With these we'll break their world."

CHAPTER 40
OPENING FLAME

Against the burning fiends, the Dead King's soldiers had little chance. The barricade broke apart and with it came a sweltering heat wave, the orange-yellow glow washing into the assembled rotted ranks. Sweat blanketed Svarde's skin in a second, the cavern's normal chill vanishing as his vision swam, his breath dried, and his eyes itched. A breaking dawn underground, the world seared in glorious flame.

The Dead King's ramshackle army, only shadows against the aura, made their charge and died anew for it. What rags remained sparked aflame as fiend and friend neared. Those lucky warriors with spears and slings struck the enemy from slight distance, marring those burning idols with white and black patches.

The rest vanished, their ashen remnants blowing back towards Svarde, Maena, and the Dead King like Foti's own blizzard.

Behind and beside the fiends themselves, those flail-wielding, obsidian crowned monsters, came their machinations. Belching noise and fire in equal measure, the constructs rumbled over the barricade's remnants and crunched through the Dead King's shambles, turning numbers into fodder for their treaded wheels.

"This isn't even a battle," Maena shouted as the Dead King raised his heavy sword, pointing it towards the fiends. "We've got to run and wait for Jochi while we still can!"

Svarde had to agree and said as much, but the Dead King didn't appear to listen. Instead, the armored soul, his black seal coated now with his side's drifting remains, strode forward with indomitable purpose, a clanking counter to the fiends Svarde would've respected if it wasn't so stupid.

Courage in the face of impossible odds wasn't bravery, just suicide by another name.

"He's going to get himself killed," Maena said, moving up beside Svarde. "I say we beat it back. Wait for Jochi. This guy's done."

"What about the sword? If they can use it, then—"

"It'll probably melt."

Svarde was about to argue, amid the cavern's growing heat, that these fiends probably couldn't match a forge's fires, but found his words faltering as the Dead King merged with his soldiers and entered the morass.

The man had said he'd been Demion's Guardian when the isles were dark, after the gods died and nothing save chaos had a hold on the world. Svarde hadn't considered it till this moment, but the journey across the isles then must've been treacherous, filled with desperate souls and creatures unleashed by the Wound. To survive all that, to survive so many years down here with nothing but death to keep you company . . .

The Dead King dodged the first flail to streak his way, slanting his step to the side so the weapon's clawed head streaked past. Letting his left hand take the heavy sword, the Dead King snapped out with his gauntleted right and gripped the flail's heavy chain. With a strength that had Maena cursing, the Dead King yanked the link, and the fiend holding its end, forward. As he did, the Dead King lunged with the blade in his left hand, delivering a strike right to the stumbling fiend's chest.

Embers shot in all directions as the sword dove in, black and white spreading over the fiend as its obsidian triangle flashed wild designs. The flail's handle hit the stone floor, followed by the fiend's darkening body. Still holding the flail's chain in his right hand, the Dead King withdrew the strike, raised the blade and slipped his grip, angling the point low as he kept moving forward.

A single downward thrust put an end to the monster, the cavern's glow flickering as one fire went out.

The Dead King couldn't have attracted more attention than if he'd jumped up and down while shouting his own name. Svarde saw almost every fiend turn those black gazes towards the armored man, saw them shade away, keeping those flails headed towards easier targets. Instead, one of the three grinding machines, each several times larger than the tall monsters, rotated towards the Dead King and pressed forward. The snout-like nozzle at the machine's front steamed, found its energy, and poured forth a burning liquid.

Swinging his left shoulder forward, the Dead King took the splatter on his armor. The Dead King swept his captured flail, his right hand moving up the chain to grab the handle near its owners body. The swing brought the clawed head along and over the ground, knocking more than a few dead soldiers away. The flail cleared the fallen fiend, and as the fiery shot died down—the Dead King's left shoulder glowed with heat, but the man seemed otherwise unaffected—the flail's head sang through space to bash into the machine's nozzle, clawing, breaking the piece clean off. Like some pipe left unfinished, the construct's next blast poured forth over itself, smoldering into its own ruin.

"He's buying us time," Maena said after another impressed curse. "We've got to run, Svarde."

"Then go." Svarde hefted his axes, caught Kivi's eye as the ferrite held her position on the ceiling. "Get Jochi and bring him here. We'll hold the line."

"You'll die."

Svarde laughed as the Dead King found another fiend, found another victim for his giant blade.

"We all die, Maena. Better to do it for something than nothing at all."

As good as it felt to say the words, the familiar Foti rush Svarde expected as he took his opening strides, axes high, died as fast as his battle cry in the cavern's swelter. The heat sapped his drive, yet restored his senses, leading Svarde to head left, around the Dead King's corpse battalion towards the cavern's edge. Above, Kivi tracked the barbarian.

Behind, Maena slipped away.

The burning fiends seemed to realize the true threat lay with the Dead King and not his dwindling dead horde. Svarde didn't have to see the fiends themselves to notice the changing tactics, as the orange-gold light shifted to match their movements, the auras focusing in on the Dead King. The old Guardian took hits from all angles now, shrugging some off with his armor, batting and blocking others with his hands and that blade. Defense, for a man so bulky, with strikes coming at a flail's range, didn't lead to offense.

Only opportunity. At least for Svarde.

Two fiends held down the left flank, reigning over a swath of simmering corpses. One flared at Svarde while the other spent its energy swiping at the Dead King. A dozen spear-wielding bodies remained upright, their numbers falling fast as flail sweeps took off legs, tore apart withered torsos. Getting close, his eyes almost shut with the heat, Svarde threw his axes. The weapons needed him too near to survive, and their battered edges did better work from a distance.

Both whirling counter-weighted weapons hit their target, lodging into the fiend's blue-orange body and showering sparks. Black and white patches grew where they struck. The fiend's obsidian shimmered, its flail raised. A strike meant for Svarde, and one he planned to counter with a scooped-up spear.

The fiend's massive mid-arm, one of four, went back, the flail rattling along behind it. Its other limbs swept away the pestering spears and swords of lesser bodies like they were so many insects. Svarde bent his knees, readied his dodge. Evade and strike, then—

Kivi dropped, the ferrite landing her stone self on the fiend's flail arm, bending it towards the ground. The ferrite's claws bit in, its jaws clamped down, and the obsidian skull flashed brighter than before, a dazzling blue and gold sparkle.

And giving Svarde his signal.

The Foti charged two long strides, hefting his spear and launching it as his left foot hit the floor. The missile flew, unseen and unblocked, towards a straight-on strike at the fiend's chest, burrowing itself in above Svarde's molten axes. A true shot, a devastating shot, and one who's success

Svarde couldn't celebrate, as the fiend's friends had noticed.

The fiend's left-side ally twisted, drawn by some communication Svarde couldn't parse—did the heat the fiends gave off change? Could the others see their friend's flickering obsidian sparks?—and grabbed Kivi off its friend's arm. The snatching fiend threw the ferrite, sending Kivi crashing into the cavern wall deep behind the fiend lines, where the glow only shown brighter.

"You'll pay for that," Svarde muttered, picking up a second spear from an owner who wouldn't need it, or anything, ever again.

The fiend Svarde had struck collapsed, its burning body cooling to hard black rock. The axes, the spear haft fell free as Svarde, along with a corpse trio, faced the second fiend. Behind the monster, the Dead King continued his doomed effort, though freeing up one side seemed to give the Guardian some life: while his armor bore dents, while it shone with hot strikes, the Dead King drove forward now against another of the constructs, blade leading in a gnashing cross-cut to splinter the machine's front plating.

Living, Svarde understood, depended on keeping the Dead King standing. Dying would be all too easy.

His own fiend swung its flail low, a leg sweeping shot Svarde leapt by climbing the corpse next to him. The body's legs shattered, but the claw and its chain passed by the time Svarde rolled to the ground. From his crouch, Svarde hefted, threw the spear. Right on target, and right on time to get snatched by the fiend's smaller, shoulder-height arm. The fiend began sweeping the flail back, shifting the spear around as it did so, aiming to skewer Svarde should the barbarian make another move.

To jump back meant getting smacked by the flail. To go up meant a spear to the chest. To go forward, well, that was what a Foti ought to do. Svarde lunged ahead, breaking into a dive as the flail's heavy chain came back across, the claw scraping the floor behind him. Svarde stretched out his hands, felt pain flare along his back as the thrown spear cut too close, and his fingers closed on the chain links. Any triumph at the grab died quick as the flail kept sweeping right, dragging Svarde across the rough floor, tearing at his leathers.

But, for all the pain, the motion gave Svarde momentum. As the fiend slowed the swing, Svarde let go, rolled off the chain and bounced amid ruined bodies near the Dead King's back.

Not exactly a safe place to be. Svarde pressed his palms to the ground, stood as the Dead King's familiar clanks suggested the man settling into a guard stance. The reason shown around them: several more fiends and the second construct lay dead and cool. Behind them waited more, their flails ready, their arms moving to deflect the few stones slung by those few bodies still slinging them.

Svarde coughed, pushed away the gritty aches, and stood next to their only chance. He looked for some sign Kivi survived and saw nothing save fire back towards the tunnel.

"You live?" The Dead King rumbled into the baking quiet.

"For now," Svarde replied. "I'm going after my ferrite."

"A foolish move."

"This whole thing's a foolish move." Svarde bent down, picked up some metal shard of some sort. "Better make it worth it."

"We can't win."

"Nah, but we can make the bastards bleed. That's good enough for me."

The Dead King, in the burning cavern, gave a slow nod. As if in reply, deep in the tunnel down where the portals waited, came a rolling crackle, an inferno finding its thunder, heading their way.

CHAPTER 41

BONE SOUP

If the skars were but a small piece of the gods, their power put the gods' own into perspective. Wax and Bliss spent the hours behind the ox speeding across the Whent landscape—no sign of the frogs—talking about Vis, about their journey, about the two passengers getting steadily drunk behind them, but Wax kept returning to the stones and the deities that made them.

In a way, the skars confirmed humans like him were just cosmic playthings, tiny motes in a big and dangerous universe. Wax's own injuries, the persistent nightmares visiting his sleep, the frequent trailing off and staring into nothing all found a home in the relation: Wax was nothing, his traumas were nothing, he was just a random speck in a random whirl.

"And that's why I'm still going," Wax said as the ox closed in, night making its descent, on the Golden Gash and the outpost at its base.

'What?' Bliss flashed with one hand, the other holding the reins as the sledge burst through one snowdrift after another.

"I'm saying we're nothing, Bliss, so there's no pressure."

'To do what?'

"Get these skars, become the Aegis. Save the isles. The gods obviously didn't care, or they would've stopped all this." Wax held up the necklace, a thumb rubbing the ruby Foti skar, its murmurings an ever-present companion in his mind. "We're struggling so hard all because the people who made these couldn't keep their heads. They made a mistake, and they had all the responsibility."

'I haven't had enough ale to follow you.'

"I'm saying, Bliss, that if we make it, great. If we don't, it's not our fault." Wax leaned back against the sledge seat's headboard, a rough frozen surface whose cold didn't penetrate the Vis's thick coat. "Whatever happens, let's just have fun."

Bliss didn't reply save to slide a squinting frown at her brother. Which, fine, she could have her opinions. Bliss, and Quik, always tended towards the more serious tack, trying to parlay this or that into a bigger meaning, some broader lesson. Well, Wax was doing that now, and if she didn't like his conclusions, that was her problem.

He rather enjoyed feeling insignificant.

The Najahn outpost, however, didn't share Wax's opinion. Unlike the Vis and Foti counterparts, which operated in relative calm, the Whent fort had high palisades with pointed tops, more than one bearing blood's faded red stain. Purple-black flags whipped, their rippling shadows glinting over the dozen guards standing outside the main gate to greet them. Voulges and chakram stood ready, and a watchtower overseeing the affair held two more crossbow men with quarrels set and targeted.

As they neared, Bliss pulled back on the reins, the ox starting to slow. What should've been a calm approach faltered as the ox found its grip on the snow slip. The Kance skar, always eager to float and fly, didn't take the ox's response well, and the great creature lost its footing, falling and skidding as the sledge whipped around. Torny, Eujo, and Wax lofted curses, going for handholds. Bliss tried to pull the reins tighter, a panicked move that served only to pick her up off the sledge's seat as the whole thing caught the snow sideways and flipped.

How fast fates could change.

Wax caught air, diving free from the sledge and hitting the snow at speed, sending up a cold spray as he tumbled through the drifts. Satchels and supplies rained every-where, accompanied by cracking, snapping wood as the sledge spilt apart. Somewhere in there the ox snorted, moan its own confusion, rolling end-over-end to stop at the palisade with a heavy thud. Wax himself wound up sitting, brushing snow from his face, only to find a voulge's speared end lowered toward him.

"Hey there," Wax offered to the helmeted glare staring his way behind the setting sun. His heart thudded, his shoulders felt a tad sore, but no serious injury made itself known. "We're two Renewals, and we'd love some hot dinner."

BONEMEAL SOUP DID, indeed, come in hot once the foursome had their supplies gathered up, their tired bodies escorted to the outpost's boarding house, and the skars retrieved from the very confused, very exhausted ox. Served with, as ever on Whent, soft potatoes and carrots, the meal none-theless carried a different buzz: namely, the sounds of other voices ignoring them.

Not since Noctia had Wax been so bereft of attention,

and even there Eujo's presence brought them enough probing eyes to keep the Vis squirming in his seat. Here, though, they had stiffer competition: first, the Foti Renewal had beat the pair to the spot, but hurt his leg in the journey. Wax offered the man, a burly joker with forge dust seemingly stuck forever in his skin, a Vis skar to speed the healing only for him to turn it down. A wink, a crack that getting stuck here meant a guarantee not to get locked into the Aegis's chair, and Wax had his offer waved away. The man's entourage held more enthusiasm for the northern ale than anything to do with the Renewal anyway, and their laughter echoed among the immense wood rafters.

Second, and more serious, came through the weaponry on display. The loud strategy discussions, the postings detailing shifts and scouting reports. Whent, on the northern end, was apparently a dangerous isle. Fiend incursions were increasing, explaining the bloody palisades, and fights happened every few days. The Najahn responded in kind, bolstering the force here to several hundred, far more than Wax had ever seen or heard of at the Vis outpost.

The military effect put on a different mood, with those joining the Foti crew in celebrating doing so less out of boredom or fun and more their own survival, their hope of a quiet tomorrow. The bonemeal soup reflected slim rations, buttressed less now with the Whent Warlord pulling so many of the Isle's traders into his suicidal campaign beneath the ground.

The outpost's leader, a stocky woman decked in purple-black leathers, joined them at their long table. Utna bore her duty with fortitude, as if command's burdens floated above her shoulders, "At least Jochi's taking the fiends with him. We've been able to range farther, sweep some of the damn monsters from the Gash."

Torny and Eujo had begged off quick after downing their soup, the crash and the booze before it sapping their already short sleep. Bliss looked about ready to join them, her eyes heavy-lidded. Wax, though, embraced the communal coziness around him, the roaring fires, laughter, and smells of civilization. Much like Cassignol's Foti casino, the Najahn boarding house thrummed on Wax's frequency.

"You're saying there's fiends in the Gash?" Wax asked, Utna nodding like she expected the question.

"It's a slice right out of the ground," Utna said. "Made when Whent tried to stop Vis from killing Noctia. Could've been another Wound, but we get gold instead."

"Why?"

Utna shook her head, drank the hot tea given someone with too much responsibility for stiffer stuff. "That's a question for the scholars. All I know is there's caves in there for fiends to climb."

"Think we'll find some?"

"You want to go up tomorrow?" Utna asked.

"Don't think the Isles want us to wait around." Wax flicked his eyes towards the Foti crew and Utna sighed.

"A stain on the Renewals, that one," the Najahn commander muttered. "We'll send a detachment with you. They'll cover you to the skar section. That part you have to do on your own."

"Why? Why do we have to do it? Couldn't you have all the skars just sitting in a room in Noctia, ready for us to take?"

Utna blinked. Her hand drifted beneath the table, and for a moment Wax wondered if she was going to go for some knife. Beside him, Bliss sparked awake. While her own weapon waited back at the room, Wax's sister seemed ready to jump on the table, deliver a kick. The Foti skar, back in Wax's necklace, thrummed with a desire to immolate the captain and everyone around them.

"Tradition," Utna answered, after too long a beat. "Tradition, and understanding. The Aegis is an honor, it's also a sacrifice. Only the one who's earned it, deserves it."

'Sounds like a line,' Bliss flicked with her fingers, a dance Utna noted.

"You don't believe that," Wax said. He didn't need to push Utna, but it'd been a long day, their journey had been so dangerous, that its necessity suddenly seemed pointless. "Why risk so much?"

Utna somehow tightened her mouth even further. She pushed back her chair from the table, stood up.

"You want an answer to that question, you ask it when you get back to the Ringed City. Maybe the Circle will tell you as they set you on the Wound's chair, when it'll be too late to matter."

"What's that mean?" Wax asked, but the words faded against the Najahn leader's back as she stomped off to another table.

'Means I'm liking all this less and less,' Bliss signed, frowning at Utna.

"Seconded." Wax gulped down his ale, a caramel, hard flavor that played well with the cold outside. "Guess it means we'll have to make it all the way back to find out."

'Maybe.'

Bliss, though, didn't elaborate on the way up to their rooms, saying instead she needed to do some thinking.

Always dangerous, getting his sister stuck on something.

. . .

UTNA WAS, at least, true to her word: a full twenty Najahn waited for Wax, Torny, Eujo, and Bliss the next morning. Their satchels had been stuffed, their stomachs filled with a potato cake breakfast, and their boots replaced with spiked versions better able to grip the icy terrain up the Great Vein's sloping side. The morning greeted them with crisp sunlight, no clouds mucking up the blue sky. The outpost's rear gate opened, their steaming breath lead the whole bunch out, and Wax pushed last night's puzzling conversation aside.

Looking up at the Great Vein this close brought adventure's familiar rush back. The skars leapt to join in, their murmurs rising to rapid chitters as Wax took his first steps. The Najahn broke into a marching song, one Wax didn't recognize, but caught onto quick enough. Feet pounded, snow parted, and their force climbed.

On his right, as they walked, Eujo looked at a tool given each of them that morning by Utna herself. A diamond chisel, its edges glimmering brighter than the snow. Necessary, so the Najahn captain said, to get deep enough to find the skars. Necessary too, she added, to get out.

"The Golden Gash holds Whent's power, and his vengeance," Utna declared as the gates had swung open.

This time, when Eujo asked the commander for more, Utna cracked a smile. Met not the Queen's, but Wax's eyes.

"That's for you Renewals to find out, not for me to say. Good luck, and don't give this damn god another soul to keep."

CHAPTER 42
ALWAYS A VIS

Swinging through the Vis jungle, grabbing vines and trunks, watching the ground sweep by beneath his feet, made the slow journey across Noctia's rocky northern cliffs an exercise in tedium. Quik suffered the slips, the scratches on hard stone, the growing numbness in his fingertips in silence as he trailed Masayo. The Tenet embraced nighttime travel with practiced ease, never once stumbling so far as Quik saw. Her wrapped multitudes, cloth flowing around itself in a robe medley Quik couldn't track, caught Sichi's scattered light when the wind kicked up, a silver-pink shade in the black.

Quik himself eschewed the robes for more traditional tracking garb, suiting up in Najahn leathers—he had neither earned the heavy mail nor wanted it for this trek— and hiking in a thick furred coat kept Quik warm enough. His gauntlets, abandoned in his room when he left on his first spying expedition, rested against Quik's thighs, a comforting presence amid the frigid rocks. Like old friends, those wood claws, and ones he wouldn't soon leave behind again.

Their target, so Masayo said, was a hamlet a half day's strong march along the coast. They'd lost some time confirming neither Sawi nor Ami's bodies lay in the stones beyond the prison tower, finding nothing save some spattered blood and torn fabric. Masayo claimed the evidence suggested the pair lived, were walking away to freedom. Quik, watching the gray waves crash, wanted to say they'd rolled into the waters and drowned.

His own hunter's instinct said that was false, but better a lie than having to watch, having to rend his old friend.

That thought more than anything claimed responsibility for Quik's wandering feet, his slower-than-expected walking in the dark. Masayo hadn't pointed it out, but Quik figured she held the question, and possibly the answer, in her mind: why would an experienced Vis hunter like himself have so much trouble stalking through the night?

Because every step didn't bring Quik closer to his quarry, to something he desired.

They stopped in the early, pre-dawn morning for a meal. Masayo and Quik each had their own satchel provisioned by Najahn cooks. Rolls and dried fruits, long gone cold. Water skins full and chilling. They ate in silence, Masayo puffing on her pipe, only breaking the mood once they'd both repacked their gear.

"We're getting close," Masayo said. "Shortly after dawn, I expect, we'll see the town. Then we see who you are."

"What?"

"You're not dumb, Quik, so don't play that way now. The Third Hand, my Tenet, and one that existed well before me, that will remain long after, doesn't tolerate other loyalties, other feelings."

"Not even to the Circle?"

Masayo smiled, a shadowed orange behind her pipe's

smoke. "We're not some Tamas puppet-master, we don't pull the strings, if that's what you're insinuating. But we do, if the Isles need it, if our survival depends on it, take matters into our own knives."

"I gathered."

The Lira, back on Vis, operated in the shadows just like Masayo's cult did here. A society willing to act to save the Isles, a force of some comfort to folks who'd rather not worry about such things. To people who didn't dig a little deeper, wonder who among the Lira decided the Isles were at risk. A thought Quik himself didn't have till he sat right there watching Masayo calculate.

If she could make the call on who lived, who died among the Najahn, then why not across all the isles? A dagger stuck between ribs on Kance could be a poisoned dart in Kitaye, a falling rock on Foti. All that mattered was Masayo thinking someone, something was a threat.

"You don't approve," Masayo said, nodding, though Quik had tried to keep his expression as straight as possible. "Not that you would understand. It's too early. Your skills are valuable, your potential great. Your heart and mind are the only problems now."

"Or my only hope."

"Oh please. I'm as prone to dramatic speech as anyone, Quik, but we're on a cold cliff tracking two traitors. Let's dispense with the lofty words and get right to it." Masayo jabbed her pipe at him. "I brought you hoping you might help me track these two, an insurance I didn't need because you Vis leave as obvious a trail as anyone. Now you're a risk, one I won't tolerate."

With her left hand, Masayo reached beneath her robes, pulled out from some pocket or hidden pouch a wrapped wire tangle.

"This is a Kance bind. You'll tie your feet, then your hands with it. Do it, now." Masayo tossed Quik the bundle. He caught it, felt smooth fibers with none of a rope's weakness. "When you're done, I'll check. If it's right, if it will hold you well, I won't kill you now."

The first time Quik heard a threat thrown his way had been on Foti, after more than twenty years on the Isles. His life till that marked point when Sledge, bow in hand, dared Quik to move and die, had been built on cooperation, on light scuffles and heavy hunts. His size deterred anything more serious. Kitaye's own society, with anyone making a nuisance of themselves getting shuffled to the edges, kept things safe enough.

Back on Foti, Quik had to decide right then what to risk. Continuing to face off against the bandits meant his brother, the Renewal, might take an arrow through the heart. An easy equation, even for someone with little care for math—despite what Annalyse had tried to teach Quik during their few days together.

Here, he sat alone. Nobody to protect, at least nobody Masayo could kill then and there. No witnesses either. If the Third Hand Tenet disappeared among the rocks, Quik could blame it on Ami, on bad weather and a misstep in the dark.

"What are you waiting for?" Masayo said, though the small smile as she puffed away seemed to say she understood, that she dared him.

Well, maybe she'd dared the wrong man.

Quik flicked the wire at Masayo as she took another drag. He kicked back as he threw the tangle, pressing down with his hands on the cold stones to rise up to his feet. As Quik's legs straightened, he shoved his hands down into his gauntlets, sliding his palms along their taut straps, fingers finding homes in those smooth claws.

Masayo let the wire glance off her robes, patter to the rocks. She took another puff, watched Quik get himself ready.

"So that's your choice, then?" Masayo asked. "Your loyalty to those traitors is greater than to the Najahn and all they can bring your brother?"

"I don't hurt my friends."

"Pity they didn't feel the same way," Masayo said, rising at last. She left the pipe, smoking and orange, on the stones. "They hurt you, Quik. Locked you up in a cage and battered you near to death. Why protect them?"

"Sawi did nothing to me."

Holes there, if Quik wanted to dig, but not here. Not now. Introspection and interrogation could happen after this, when he went on and found Sawi, Ami in the town. Then they could hash it out, find a way forward.

Masayo wouldn't twist his mind anymore.

"If that's the way you see it." Masayo sighed. "Come on then. Show me what you've got, Vis."

Again, Foti played about Quik as he bent his knees, mapped out the short distance between him and Masayo. That rocky, lava-plagued isle had been his first real fight against another human, and he'd learned one damn thing: humans fought by no rules.

Masayo's hands disappeared beneath her robes. Waiting to draw some knife, some stone, some needle laced with poison. Quik made two assumptions: one, that Masayo didn't want him dead. And two, that he needed to run more than he needed to win. A team up with Sawi and Ami would more than even the odds.

So he scooped his right gauntlet low, letting the claws scrape and pick up several stones. With a hard under-handed toss, Quik sent the rocks, a couple pebbles and one with real heft, flying at Masayo. The Tenet turned her shoulder, took the missiles like Quik might brace himself against a breeze. An easy shrug-off, but that was the point.

Masayo's turn put her arms out of position, one Quik exploited by kicking off with his left foot as he flung the rocks. He bounced to his right, landing on his bent right leg and launching into an overhand swing at the Tenet's turned shoulder. The shadowed robes shifted in the dark, and Quik felt his claws bite into cloth, saw Masayo turn further, letting Quik's swing carry past her in a harmless tangle with her robes.

All according to plan. She'd foiled one gauntlet, but Quik's left came in high and hot, striking straight over his right and in line for Masayo's hooded head. Fast, lethal.

Except the Tenet crouched with her turn, Quik's swing collecting more cloth as Masayo's body went low, as her left hand completed its whirl to deliver an unprotected jab to Quik's stomach. The hit came with an icy pierce, no blunt punch or slicing gash.

Quik tried to pull back, found his gauntlets caught up in the robes. Masayo stayed close, worked into the seams as Quik tried, failed to free himself. Everywhere seemed to be the flowing cloth, as if he was in a battle with a blanket. Those sharp jabs continued, small stabs walking up and down his stomach, legs, chest.

Enough.

Quik broke his arms wide, tearing the robes off with his gauntlets, the sweep forcing Masayo back a step. The robes fell away to the rocks, revealing Masayo in taut leathers studded over with bracers, belts, and there, lining a necklace Quik had never seen, several familiar stones.

Masayo's shade flickered and Quik felt another piercing, up near his shoulder. He flicked an eye down, noticed a familiar dart. Slim wood, tiny feathers laced into its back end. Mottilan-made.

"Coward," Quik said, his tongue growing stiff in his mouth, legs and arms shaking. "You have skars."

"Fighting without knowing your opponent is a terrible mistake," Masayo said, approaching, though her hands stayed ready.

Not that Quik couldn't managed a swipe, not anymore. His knees hit the stones hard, and his head would've followed save for Masayo's reach, catching him and lowering Quik to the ground.

"There's more to the Isles than Renewals and fiends," Masayo muttered. "Games are played, power changes hands. Some want to control, others want to survive. Some few, Quik, some few can do both."

The Tenet found the wire bundle, and while Quik struggled to stay awake, to thwart the dark dancing through his mind, he felt the tight lines wrap around his wrists, his ankles.

"I can help your brother live, I can help you thrive, so long as you help me," Masayo continued. "But no more games. When this is over, I'll come back for you, and give you one more chance to make your choice. Think hard, Vis."

The pipe's orange glow, picked up and puffed, receded into the night. The waves far below crashed against the cliffs, a steady rhythm carrying Quik into a sleep he didn't want, didn't deserve, and couldn't avoid.

CHAPTER 43
THE GOLDEN GASH

mazing what good sunshine and slicing wind could do to a hangover. Torny's headache, persistent despite the long night's rest, finally succumbed to nature's icy kiss as the group hiked up the path to the Golden Gash. Being surrounded by armed authority should've made Torny nervous, but after the hunting frogs, all that armor and metal felt a little like a strong blanket.

She and the other three wore that Najahn shroud all the way up, passing the couple hours with their usual cracks, quiet conversation, and silent, steaming breath. The Gash filled in the quiet on its own, with rumbles, snaps, and whispers as snow and ice formed, fell, and found new homes.

'I like it,' Bliss signed, walking beside Torny and responding to the bandit's question, asking whether the Vis found all the noise eerie. 'The jungle back home sings too. A different song, but it feels the same.'

"So long as it doesn't crush me," Torny replied.

Bliss grinned, 'Nervous?'

"After the lava, the river, and the ocean, yeah, I'm nervous. About had enough of nature."

Not that Noctia's Ringed City didn't have its own music, whether free-flowing song from a concert, street corner, bar, or the hiss and shouts from ships and the sailors. It's just Torny knew all those, understood how they aligned in her world, but out here every crack could be something deadly. As it had been on Rana and Foti.

"Then you'll like Tamas," Eujo broke in, leaving Wax a stride ahead near the Najahn front. "The isle's overrun with people and their playthings."

"And good spirits, or so I've heard."

"The best. You'll have a hard time going back to the Noctia swill."

"You're over-estimating my tastes."

"No doubt."

The Golden Gash grew as they closed in on the entry, covering their view in boulders and snowy cliffs. A few ragged pine braved the altitude, their tops shivering as the breeze whistled through stone ridges. A cave's looming mouth, buttressed with shaped rock columns, offered shelter and the adventure's true start. The Najahn anticipated the moment, with a camp site in miniature spread around the opening: stumps and smoothed stones serving as chairs, two fire pits, and chests stocked with provisions.

All frozen, those, but as the Najahn sparked up fires with carried flint, the thawing method became apparent. Other soldiers dropped packs carrying wood cords, sleeping mats, and tools to shine up, sharpen gear.

"We'll stay here the day," the Najahn guard captain told Wax, Eujo, and their Guardians as the camp assembled. "When dusk nears, we'll march back to the outpost, then return tomorrow near dawn. Don't try a descent in the dark. There's food and shelter here."

"Think it'll take that long?" Wax asked as Torny eyed the frumpy mats. Nothing compared to the boarding house's beds. "Is it that far?"

The Guard Captain looked towards the opening, curled a lip, "Far, no. Distance isn't what you need to worry about. Keep your heads right, don't panic, and you'll be fine. The same with any skar."

"Never big on helpful advice, are you?" Torny asked as Wax nodded. "All you Najahn, everywhere we go, talk in these vague phrases. Do you want us to die? Is that it? Keep that chair empty so the fiends get more playtime?"

"I'm following orders." The man's face went hard, the frown a cutting scowl at Torny. "The Aegis can't be weak. You have to earn the right."

"Sure, buddy. You tell that to the towns getting torched right now. Bet they're real concerned about 'weakness'."

"Torny," Eujo said, "leave it. Let's go."

Wax agreed, the two Renewals starting off down the cave. Torny figured she had time to deliver another barb or two at the Najahn, and would've let'em loose had not Bliss grabbed her arm, pulled the bandit after her supposed charges.

'They're not the enemy,' Bliss signed as Torny struggled free. 'They're protecting us.'

"C'mon. You don't really believe that, right?" Torny asked. "The Circle probably has a thousand skars in the Ringed City, they just don't want to give any up."

'You really think so?'

Torny was about to reply that she didn't think it, she *knew* it. The Nimble Fingers, and anyone who really paid attention, understood the Najahn 'protected' the skar troves on the isles less for the Renewal and more for their own benefit. What that benefit was had been a mystery for Torny until this trip, until she'd seen what the skars could do.

Now the question changed: if the Najahn had all that power sitting in the Ringed City, why didn't they use it?

The glittering cave, a break from Foti's black stone and ash, didn't answer Torny, but did distract her with its prismatic shimmers. Ice and snow coated everything for the first leg, a stiff breeze following the quartet inside and snapping through hanging icicles, hard snow drifts, and a scuffed path with frozen boot prints. The sunlight died quick enough for Bliss and Wax to crack torches, the flames dancing with a thousand reflections of themselves.

"At least it's beautiful," Eujo said. "The Whirlpool was dark and wet. Foti, sweltering. Vis had all those bugs in the webs."

"But the view," Wax added as they ducked beneath a toothy icicle array. "At the top, you had to enjoy that, right?"

"With Silvrin and her sword breathing down my neck every second."

Torny let the conversation play out, instead drawing her chisel and spinning the diamond instrument around her fingers. About as long as the knives Torny worked with, the chisel had a good edge. If it could really cut through ice like this, then it might make a good tool to crack a chest or a stubborn door.

Utna wouldn't notice if one went missing, would she?

"Anyone else think this is getting smaller?" Wax asked, pushing Torny away from chisel thievery. "The ice is closing in."

'And getting golden.'

Bliss's signs cast shadows through the torchlight, and when her hands dropped Torny saw what Bliss meant: the snow and ice no longer held just blue and white, but honey-like drops scattered throughout. They grew thicker as the group walked, the confines indeed tightening until Wax stopped hard, facing an ice wall as gold as it was silver-white.

"Guess this is where the chisels come in," Torny said. "Get to it, Wax."

"Why me?"

"Because you're in front."

Wax laughed, took out the chisel and stared at it for a long second. Then put the instrument up against the ice. A light tap. Another, with the tiniest ice flakes falling to the ground. He didn't get a third.

"Allow me," Eujo declared, swiping the chisel from Wax's hand and adding her own, swiveling the grip around to the chisel's heavier, blunt end. "Don't use these on Vis?"

"Never."

"Then watch."

Pressing the sharp end against the ice wall, while using the blunt back of the other, Eujo hammered along the top. Torny, taking Bliss's chisel to copy the move, started working on the right side. She'd not chiseled much, but working with small tools came naturally enough to the bandit, and together the pair and those diamond edges pried apart half the wall. A strong shoulder shove—Wax and Bliss helped—cracked the barrier, sending it crumbling before them.

Beyond, the cave floor fell away, disappearing into a chasm covered in golden veins no thicker than a rope. The straight spider-web-like lines criss-crossed the chamber, forming a strange maze wherein a misstep would send you plummeting who knew how far. As if to emphasize the point, Wax kicked an ice fragment over the edge, the group watching, listening far too long before its cracking demise echoed up to their ears.

"Well, this is delightful," Torny said. "Any takers?"

The destination, at least, wasn't hard to parse: crossing the chasm, its far edge visible at the torchlight's end, hinted at the cave continuing.

"I'll go," Wax said, grinning. "At last, a challenge I can get behind."

The Vis didn't wait, didn't hand off his torch either. With a single tap, he tested a gold ice rope. Finding it sturdy, Wax stepped out over the dark, his free hand finding other cords to balance on as the Vis stepped heel-to-toe along the line, switching to others with impeccable poise.

Yarvick would've loved having Wax on his crew.

"Definitely goes on over here," Wax called as he reached the far side without difficulty. "C'mon, Guardians. Let's move."

Bliss followed her brother at the invitation, crossing, without a torch, faster than Wax had. Torny joined Eujo at the chasm's edge, looking down into that dark. Her stomach twinged. The Vis pair, and Eujo with Kance's tall peaks, probably saw enough heights to avoid getting lurched by the downward distance, but . . .

"Can you go last?" Eujo asked. "This . . . isn't my speed."

Torny flicked a skeptical eyebrow at the Queen, "I thought Kance was all about nifty footwork."

"With both hands in the open air. Not on ice with bulky coats." The Queen held the torch out Torny's way. "Please."

The bandit was about to counter, say she didn't vibe much with this crossing either, but the worry in Eujo's otherwise steely face silenced the comeback. Brought up a softer, newer sheen instead: a Guardian's job, Bliss and everyone kept pointing out, was to help get the Renewal to the skars. Eujo needed Torny to take the torch, and Torny was her damn Guardian.

She might've stolen the diary, but, as Wax had put it to her, Torny was still here. She had a responsibility.

"I've got you," Torny said, taking the warm torch and its oil-soaked wrap. "One step at a time, right?"

"Right."

The Queen followed the path chosen by Wax and Bliss, taking one tentative foot and setting it on the ice rope. It slid at her touch, Eujo yanking the foot back. A deep breath. A gulp. Confidence on the brink. Eujo rubbed her wrists, one holding a particular bracelet with particular stones.

A chance Torny didn't miss.

"Hey," Torny said, "you'll be fine. You've got that Kance skar, remember? It'll save you if you fall."

As if the bandit had taken a load off Eujo's shoulders, the Queen straightened, grinned. "Know what, I think you're right."

This time, Eujo stepped with strength, conviction. Her planted foot didn't move, her hands found the same help Wax and Bliss had before. One before the other, strong strides taking Eujo across the chasm and into Wax's outstretched hand. A lift, and there they were, a trio ready to go.

"C'mon, Torny," Wax called. "Easy."

If only. Torny didn't have any magical skars ready to save her life. That thought echoed with her heartbeat, the torch's nearby crackle as she took the first step. The rope held, as did the one Torny grappled with her left hand, moving out into space. Old instincts took over, guiding her silent steps one by one, just like she'd done countless times on thin Noctia rooftop railings. Her mind ran silent, her muscles working smooth, the chasm rolling along beneath her, a black pit not worth noticing.

Bliss waited, arm and hand ready to grab as Torny neared the end, a last rope tangle.

"See?" Torny said as she angled onto the last set, the torch merry near her head. "Just as good as you vine crawlers."

Two more steps. Torny reached, grabbed a crosswise golden rope, ducked beneath it to make the next move with her right leg. Felt something drip on her shoulder. She glanced, saw the wet mark, saw another drop hit it.

A look up. The torch. Its flame melting through a rope already thinned by Wax's earlier passage. Torny's heart froze as the flame burned a hole, as the line cracked, swung down, collided with the same one the bandit stood on like death's own pendulum.

Her rope cracked, Torny's foot slipped, and without even a worthy curse, the bandit fell.

CHAPTER 44
SEASIDE CHARMS

Stumble into a Vis village and you'd find help given freely. The isle had so few agendas, so few schemes, that a stranger in need wouldn't be a pawn, a suspect, a future victim.

At least at first.

When Sawi and Ami stumbled, wrapped in grim morning dawn, into the stone hut collection climbing the crater's northern side, Sawi didn't expect the same. Enough time on Noctia led her to believe the first eyes seeing them would be suspicious ones, the hands reaching their way holding knives instead of bread.

Expectations weren't met.

A fisherman, body laden with gear, saw them first. He'd cracked open his hut's warped wood door, shuffled out in a thick coat onto the smoothed, stone-strewn paths marking the town's avenues, and stopped short at the sight of the pair, both leaning on one another as they hiked forward. He watched for a long moment, perhaps considering if he was seeing a phantom, until Ami croaked a tired, dry rasp for help.

Action, then, as Sawi had never seen it broke out.

The fisherman stuck two fingers to his lips and blew, a shrill whistle cutting above the waves smashing below. He set his pole, his pack, down, and came, with as sure a knowledge of the rocks as Sawi would have of the forest vines, scampering down to their side. He asked few questions, a tacit acceptance echoed by the other townspeople coming out quick to assist. A fire, one fueled less by wood and more by mosses, shrubs, and oils, struck up in the town's centerpiece structure, still a hut but one whose stacked stone walls doubled the others in size.

Sawi and Ami found themselves settled on a squat stone bench, some thin, warm soup thrust into their hands. People moved about, trying to tend to wounds only to find the pair, despite their exhaustion, seemed largely unscathed. Sawi almost said why—Ami's faceplate held the skars now anyway—but kept quiet at the Guardian's head shake, nodded instead when Ami said they'd been ship-wrecked, were near-starved and lost.

At first, the town seemed to buy the lie. Breakfast, the morning passed by in peace as the town turned itself back to the day's normal order. Wrapped in a blanket, the thin fire crackling, Sawi almost allowed herself to relax. To think maybe they'd made it, escaped the Najahn's iron axe.

"Not for one second," Ami said, keeping her voice low, when Sawi closed her eyes. "They're kind to us now, but that'll change when the Najahn show up."

"You think they will?"

"I'm a former Guardian. You're Gladdring's Vis chosen. The Circle won't let us go so easily, especially when they know we're still on the isle."

Ami had her second soup bowl now, was attacking it as she had the first, rivulets running off her chin and dripping onto the crusted stone floor. Those thin stains added to a salty morass coating most everything, a damp sea skin worn about the spare stone inside. Like some Foti forge, everything in here seemed made of rock, though lacking that isle's skill. Bowls and mugs bore chips, handled with rough sides. Moldering thatching covered what couldn't be handled by smashing rocks, like a narrow gap in the roof for the fire's smoke to escape. A town living on little, but Sawi found few unhappy.

A life chosen, just like those in the Vis outer villages. Quiet struggle, yes, but in that quiet a dignity, an independence.

She smiled. Wax would've lost his it a place like this. Too little action, too little drama.

Would she?

"If we're lucky, we'll have today," Ami continued after her latest mouthful. "We'll need to take what we can from here and move on."

"To where?"

Ami's eyes winced, flicked towards the door and its view of the slate sea beyond. "That's the real question. We can try to circle the isle, see how far we can get before they catch us."

"There's a plan."

"A bad one, I agree. There's another way, but I like that even less."

"Do tell."

"Make our way up the crater wall and down the other side. Evade detection as long as we can. Get to the Aegis and plead for her protection."

Ami returned to her soup, fished out another spoonful. Sawi had eschewed the utensils, drank from the bowl itself like everyone on Vis. Those free hands now found more warmth beneath the blanket's folds, where nobody could see her fingers kneading.

"The Aegis doesn't know who I am," Sawi said. "It won't—"

"I know it won't work. They'd kill us. The Aegis doesn't have power anymore. None that really matters anyway."

"So what, did we do all this just to get an extra day tacked onto our lives?"

"Wouldn't that be worth it?"

Sawi shrugged, "Guess I was hoping for more."

Her own death remained a concept Sawi refused to consider. She'd come too close in that Najahn tower, and now that she'd found a slip of hope, going back to that terrifying miasma was a trip she would never, ever take again. Better to find her final destiny believing she'd stay alive. Better that.

"There's one other," Ami said. "One as likely to kill us as anything else, though maybe not by a Najahn blade."

"You keep hinting at these things, Ami. Spit it out."

"It's because I don't like the idea, and I'm trying to find another one." Ami set the soup aside, remained hunched near the fire. "The mosses and supplies these towns survive on don't just come from the ocean. I know, because I've lived on this isle for too long. I've walked it enough times."

"Again, you're talking around the point."

Ami shot Sawi a glare, "Is everyone on Vis so rude?"

"We've got things to do."

"There's caves, then. One just up the slope from here. They'll have barricades put up stall fiends, but we can go past them. Escape into the tunnels."

Sawi laughed. A dire chuckle. "You must have the worst ideas of anyone I've ever known, Ami. Every single one's going to get us killed."

"Not for certain." Ami shook her head. "The more I think about it, the caves make the most sense. We know they sprawl beneath the isles, the tunnels connect them all. It's how the fiends get around. We could get to Tamas, Kance, or even Vis. After a few hours down there, the Najahn would never find us."

The Dark Below. A whisper relegated to higher powers whenever Sawi heard it back home. Fiends lived there, strange things unseen and unheard. The domain of the Najahn, the Aegis, and the foolhardy. The one time Sawi had come close to the total darkness had been in that pool, that last innocent moment with Wax before the monster, before Svarde, before all this.

Could she face it again?

"There's no ships?" Sawi asked. "What about running across the ocean ice? I've heard—"

"You've heard about games and dares from people who die trying. Besides, it's still early Winter. If enough ice forms between Noctia and Tamas to try it, we'd have to wait another month. That won't happen." Ami stood, brushed off her ragged clothes, the blanket. Waved at the sole townsperson, an older woman, keeping watch. "The more I think about it, Sawi, there's no other option. I'm heading for the caves. I'd suggest you come with."

"We have nothing, Ami. Nothing. How're we—"

Ami fished in her faceplate, popped out the light red Foti ruby. "This."

An hour's demonstrating the skar pulled half the town over in wonder, procured in trade fresh satchels, dry (as much as anything here could be) clothes, and provisions. Ami chose a vicious, serrated harpoon while Sawi, without much confidence, took a large knife meant for filleting massive fish. Fresh water poured from rain barrels and melted snow topped off new water skins. New coats, new boots, all made with animal skins thick and warm completed the ensemble, a heavy selection that had Sawi questioning how they'd manage to march anywhere for long.

"You'll get used to it," Ami countered, and because Sawi saw no alternative, she didn't push back.

All that for a single skar, the ability to start a fire, heat a home, melt a stone with a little thought and focused effort. Both Ami and Sawi demonstrated the stone's ability, focusing it as best they could on small actions for the townspeople, like heating soup or melting away an icy patch on a path. In its whispers, the Foti skar seemed less enthused about these mundane uses, but the stone was a stone, it would serve.

"Don't get excited with it," Ami said as a final warning after a lunch-time break. "You could hurt someone, yourself, or destroy a home. Work with it slowly, let it teach you, and don't be stupid."

"Helpful, Ami," Sawi muttered, adjusting her satchel yet again.

How people went on long journeys with such heavy loads . . . On Vis, you could forage enough to not need so many supplies. You could never swing the vines with a pack like this.

"They're making the trade," Ami replied, nodding as one townsperson, eyes closed and holding out the skar in a clenched fist like the stone was some deadly device, made the air shimmer with sudden heat. The watching townspeople cheered, whistled, clapped the man on the back. "Just trying to keep them alive."

Whether Ami's rapid education would suffice, Sawi wouldn't know. They started up the rocky cliff in the afternoon, leaving behind the buzzing town and the sea's salty spray. Their new clothes kept the cold at distant remove, Sawi even starting to sweat with the climbing effort. Ami led, her harpoon's butt end serving as a pocked metal walking stick. Silence settled, punctuated only by seabird cries and the scattered noises back towards the town.

Yet, far from the quiet the previous night, when death seemed so close, Sawi did find that hope. One skar, one trade, and they'd gone from ruined to having a chance. As for the caves, the jittering edge the idea brought to her nerves, Sawi would confront that when they stepped inside those awful tunnels.

She would face her fear, and—

"Stop," Ami said, just before Sawi would've walked right into her. "Something's off."

"Everything's off, Ami."

"No." The Guardian looked left, right. Hesitated. "The cave's just ahead, but something's not right."

"Some mystical Guardian sense telling you this?"

"Ever feel like you're being watched?"

Sawi started to answer, to say that something was always watching you in the jungle, only for Ami to snake an arm back and pull the Vis to the hard ground. With the pack, Sawi hit hard, a curse bubbling up and dying down as a black dart whistled by overhead.

"What was that?" Sawi said as Ami shirked off her pack in a smooth motion, the Guardian swinging the satchels before her like some makeshift wall.

"Death's opening move," Ami replied. "Draw your knife, Vis. We've been found."

CHAPTER 45

A FIGHT IN FIRE

Svarde and the Dead King made the impossible charge. Flanked by flimsy corpses, the pair barreled like a spear's point towards the tunnel and the crackling flame. For Svarde, the reasoning lay simple: Kivi was back there, and dying beside his ferrite was worth more than a lingering decay without her. The Dead King's motives were a mystery, but perhaps he was tired of his time in the endless dark.

Regardless, the massive lord and his equally massive blade made the first contact against the fiends, a wide crosscut slicing through a spinning flail and drawing a line across the fiend chest behind. Svarde, searing warmth on all sides, broke for a third construct, metal wheels and gears sliding its turret their way. He jumped, digging his axes, recovered from their first victim, like claws into the burned black armor plating on the thing's front. The barbarian's own leathers sizzled at the touch, an unwelcome sensation Svarde ignored in an end-over-end climb up the rolling thing's front.

The turret sat before him, nearly Svarde's height and

ready to box him over with its smoking nozzle. Svarde ducked the rotating cannon, hacked at it once with an axe and found his weapons lacking. The rebound, the sparks, brought on a wince, a second's splash of the world around him as Svarde tried to find a next move.

The fight embroiled seven fiends around the twin machine carcasses murdered in the initial assault. Those fiends whipped their flails, swung their four-armed fists, or kicked at the smaller, withering corpses. Yet those same bodies, when they could, picked themselves back up, found broken spears, stones, or shattered chain links and charged back in to poke, stab, or simply dive on the fiends. Distracting, at times deadly, the Dead King's shamblers spared the pair's lives.

At least for the moment. Even as Svarde broke for the turret's link, where the cannon connected to the bulky round top, the cavern brightened with new flame. The glow's source, caught in Svarde's view by chance as he charged the turret, seemed the same as the other fiends, only larger and clad in what appeared to be flowing rubies, a crimson garb melting and re-forming itself. The monster filled the tunnel's width, bore twin, shorter flails in its two larger arms, and, with the dazzling display crossing its obsidian crown, seemed to be directing the assault.

"There's our goal," Svarde muttered, ducking again beneath the nozzle as the construct swung it back. A desperate defense, better against, say, those larger fiends than the smaller human. Not that Svarde was complaining.

The turret's home offered a plated door across the top, nearly blocked by hardened ash. Svarde saw no way to open the thing, figured his own assault was lost, until a scurrying, stone form snorting her way up the construct's rear birthed a grin.

"Kivi!" Svarde shouted to nobody, to everybody, a familiar wellspring of the sort that'd come up every time he, Ami, or Catya beat the odds rising up in his scalded heart. "Have any appetite left?"

The ferrite, claws doing a better job than Svarde's axes, joined the barbarian on the construct's top. The machine, deciding the pair couldn't be whacked by its gun, refocused its efforts on the Dead King, who was busy putting the final stab in yet another fiend. The nozzle began to glow its pre-pouring orange, only for Kivi to dash around Svarde to the cannon's joint with the machine's body. The ferrite opened its stone jaw, bit down, and gouged out the metal.

And drew the wrong attention.

A fiend, just into the larger cavern and sweeping itself free of clinging corpses, turned, whipping its flail in a clearing swipe towards the ferrite. Svarde, bellowing a Foti curse, leapt at the strike, swinging both axes to catch the chain with body and edge. The barbarian's weight, his blow's force, bent the blow into a skittering bounce off the machine's front plate, the flail's metal head wedging itself against the turret, trapping Svarde against the construct.

Ribs may have broken, bruises and burns came through his melting leathers, but Svarde had passed beyond pain.

The machine trembled, what air Svarde could see shimmered. Kivi took another massive bite, the metal shards flaking around them.

An obsidian skull, ablaze with glittering stars, leered into Svarde's view. The monster tugged at his flail, prompting a gasp from the trapped barbarian as the metal bit into his waist. Svarde tried to work his axes at the links, found them of little use with his arms stuck. He settled instead for another rasped curse, a sweaty glare at a fiend who no doubt didn't care, didn't understand.

Kivi bit again.

The construct fired.

Orange, red, black exploded in an arcing spray, one without direction, without intent. It splattered before Svarde, caught the reaching fiend in its obsidian face and sent the monster backward into a heavy fall. Glowing bits laced the tunnel's ceiling, burning through hanging rocks to send them plummeting towards the ground. Some caught the Dead King and his current target, driving both into a stalemate as they assessed their newest injuries.

And Svarde, watching all this, found himself spared as the cannon lay to his left, the rivulets from its failed fire going far overhead or dribbling straight down into a ruined stream.

The barbarian laughed. A harsh cackle. A success, a minor victory in what seemed to be a lost war, but one he would claim nonetheless. The laughter turned genuine when Kivi, that invincible lizard, rolled down near him, steaming and covered in the glowing orange, her sapphire eyes as bright as ever.

She bit into the chain once, twice, three times. Snapped the links. Svarde pushed them away, tried to stand, and found he could not. Burns criss-crossed his waist, and anything beneath that lay numb, in pain so far beyond his comprehending that his mind shut it off. He seemed to be blocking more than that too, as Svarde found himself unable to pick up his dropped axes, hands no longer able to move well enough to form a grip.

As sure a death sentence as anything.

"Run, Kivi," Svarde gasped, only to see the ferrite, stumbling now as the cannon's gout melted further into her stone shell, knock her head against Svarde's side.

He rolled against his own will, pushed by the ferrite

along the machine's front plate. The cave thundered, crackled again as the monstrous fiend and its ruby raiment found the fight against the Dead King. A battle the old Guardian would have to fight alone.

"I'm not going to—" Svarde started as the ferrite shoved him again, his voice cutting off as a newer, smaller form cut into view.

"Quit talking," Maena snapped. "For once, you've got a good excuse to stay quiet." The Rana captain, balancing as clean as ever on the dead construct's sloping front, slipped her shoulder down for Svarde to ride on. "My worse half wouldn't let me leave without saving your dumb self, so let's not disappoint her."

Worse half?

Svarde had questions, couldn't voice the answers as their bedraggled trio shambled off the construct's front and broke to the cavern's far side, heading deeper into the large chamber and away from the losing war.

The Dead King's remnants were now truly that, battling a lost cause with their battered dozen against half that many fiends, with more burning bastards coming up the tunnel behind their apparent leader. The Dead King seemed to be standing yet, playing a desperate defense against the larger demon's twin flails, those flowing strikes bashing the great blade like a devil's drum. Screeching metal, sparks, and the endless furnace searing the air sizzled in Svarde's cooked ears.

"Here's the plan, Foti," Maena said, continuing to keep them on the cavern's outside wall. "We get back to that city, hole up behind that gate, and pray Jochi gets here in time to save our skins." She looked at him, Svarde meeting her eyes with his crusty face, and she swore. "You look like shit, Svarde."

He tried to smile, found his lips too crusted to move beyond a shiver. Kivi snorted, weak and desperate.

"Don't tell me we're not going to make it," Maena said, beginning the desperate heave across the cavern's center, over bodies burned and broken through uncounted decades. "I didn't come back just to die here."

The Dead King didn't hear her, but they heard him. A wrenching yell, one both surprised and, Svarde thought, relieved. Their eyes turned his way as the great fiend broke the Lost King's guard, slipping through with a flail's strike to smash the old Guardian's sword arm to the side. A second, wild swing cracked the Dead King's thick helmet with enough force to throw the soldier back into the cavern. The helmet shattered as the Dead King struck the rocky floor, his hand flying behind, the great blade whistling through the air to slide along the stones.

"Well, if that isn't the worst luck," Maena muttered, continuing to pull.

As the Dead King lay there, the cavern seemed to quiver, a sensation Svarde didn't understand until he noticed the bodies, those that yet stood, those that crawled along the ground, and those that tried and couldn't, crumpling into that final stillness. Leaving only the fiends at the tunnel's entrance, their brutal burning figures, watching, as if suspecting a trap.

"C'mon," Maena cursed again, "can you not help me at all?"

Stride by stride, with Kivi lifting Svarde's feet in a gentle bite, they made their way across the cavern. Svarde himself found his breath coming short, his eyes growing spotty, the pain dwindling away into an icy end. He wanted to tell Maena to drop him, to let him go, but he couldn't say a damn thing, could only stare in blurred silence as they passed by the Dead King's body.

The shattered helmet showed a face so pale with time, skin pallid and beyond death, already shriveling with decay's dam broken. The man's eyes closed, wrinkled, shrunken. A long barred peace?

No. An ill rest, one Svarde figured would be better brought with fire's finality than waiting here in this broken cavern. That, at least, these fiends could deliver.

"Ah, damn it," Maena said, drawing Svarde's fading glance up. The fiends flared, their leader breaking into new sparkles across its obsidian skull. Burning feet strode forward, fanning into the cavern, with the ruby-coated leader angling straight for their trio. "Sorry, Svarde. Tried, but I don't think we're going to make it."

The Rana captain tugged Svarde another lunge, then dropped the man on the rocky floor. Maena took a step ahead of him, drawing out a rusty scimitar and holding it in two hands. A weak weapon for a massive foe, but Maena snarled out a Rana challenge anyway. Brave, insane, and likely as dead as he was.

But, perhaps, not stupid. As the massive fiend approached, Svarde caught a dark glimmer in its fiery reflection, one near the barbarian's own head. A jagged line worn by time, by conflict, but held together with a power beyond any simple forge. A possibility, a hope, and Svarde put all his aching effort towards it, a nod, a nudge, the slightest finger twitch.

A clue that amazing ferrite, itself battered and nearly broken, saw. With stone jaws, as Maena ducked the flail's first swing, Kivi brought the Dead King's blade to Svarde's hand.

CHAPTER 46
WHISPER WARDS

The gold frozen ropes snapped, Torny faltered, and Eujo jumped. The Kance Queen didn't ponder, didn't second guess, even as Wax did the utterly useless thing and shouted Torny's name, the Queen disappeared over the edge. Bliss and her brother went to that same icy cliff, the lone torch doing its best to show where their friends had gone, and saw nothing save shadows.

"Alive!" came the shout, Torny's voice, just before dread and doubt crept in. Not so far down as the dropped rock either. "Alive, somehow."

"How?" Wax called, confusion and elation bleeding together. Bliss dropped to her chest, head going low into the chasm, as if by leaning a little further she could make them out. "What—"

"The Kance skar," Eujo this time, as confident as ever. Wax found a smile at her sound. Two down, two up. "We're on a ledge, but there's another opening here. We'll find you."

"You have no light?" Wax asked, feeling a bit odd to be shouting into nothing.

"You're talking to a pair of guttersnipes, Wax," Torny, again. "We're used to stalking in the dark. Get going."

Torny had that invincible tint to her now, the laughing delight that comes with dodging death. Wax had it too, and so did Bliss in her wild grin as his sister popped up. Another fatal mistake made well by the skars. At some point, Wax would find himself sitting in the Aegis's chair just because he owed the gods that much.

First, though, he'd have to make it that far.

"Shall we, sister?" Wax said, turning to the ongoing tunnel. "Like old times?"

'Not that old.'

True, and those not-so-distant memories bobbed their steps down the cold rock tunnel, the Golden Gash losing its icy coating as they went deeper inside the mountain. Their torch caught the glitters aplenty, making Wax squint as the sheer amber, yellow sparkles overwhelmed. A mystical, magical sight, walking on a treasure that would've had all of Noctia jealous.

"The Najahn control this place, right?" Wax asked as they walked, the tunnel staying just wide enough for the two of them to go in single-file, Wax having to duck here and there to dodge low swoops. "Why aren't they digging all this out?"

Bliss tapped his shoulder. 'Because they don't want to offend the gods?'

An earlier, younger Wax might've agreed with that, but spending those nights among Noctia's business captains, its merchant marauders, told him otherwise. The Najahn, the powerful and wealthy didn't care about the gods, not in any sacred way. No, if the Najahn weren't digging up in here with the Whent, there had to be a different reason.

No answer presented itself by the time the tunnel

widened, ended in a curling chamber whose broad base led to a chimney-like rise at its back, the climb vanishing behind a golden roof. Not only gold here, though: as if Whent, the dead god, decided one precious metal wasn't enough, gemstone strings looped and swirled throughout the room, dazzling ruby spirals and sapphire circles. The gold and gems also rose here and there as strange mounds, odd misshapen lumps of all sizes, though none much taller than Wax. As if the room had once bubbled up, only to be frozen in time. As he looked, Wax started forward, nearly stepping on an emerald star just inside the entry, Wax almost stepping on it till Bliss caught him, held him back.

'Careful,' Bliss signed. 'All these skar chambers have tricks.'

Good point. Wax knelt, holding the torch before him. That this was the skar chamber was no question: the skars themselves sat on a central mound, rising up like a natural growth and dotted with the small stones. The torchlight seemed guided to it, reflecting off the gems, the glittering walls, to shower the center in an orange-gold halo. Beautiful, if you preferred treasure to more natural things.

The difference between the tunnel at Wax's feet and the skar chamber proved minimal: the gold suffused stone continued, now free of ice. The gemstone shapes scattered everywhere inside seemed to be the only difference, and perhaps the marker of a trap. Avoid them, or make only for them?

'Let me go first,' Bliss signed.

"Why?"

'Because I'm faster than you.'

"Hey—"

She squeezed past Wax before her brother could lay out all the examples, the admittedly few, when he'd bested his sister in a race across the jungle. Bliss made for the golden floor, stepping along the rock, avoiding the gemstone patterns, and crossed to the middle mound without a single fiend, collapsing wall, or other horror arriving to separate her head from her body, or some other gruesome end.

'Looks like that'll work,' Bliss signed.

"Easy, then."

Wax took a step, following her. His foot hit the golden floor and a rush ran through his mind, the three skars on his necklace waking up at once and chiming in with fast, unintelligible whispers. Wax hesitated, tried to sort out the urges, what those dumb stones were saying, only to see Bliss frantically flashing her fingers up ahead.

'Your foot!'

The gold stone wasn't content to lie there. The glitter rock no longer felt sturdy. Instead, it swarmed up his planted foot, climbing him like a rampant moss on Vis. Wax tried to raise his boot, found it immovable. Not even a wiggle. His left foot, too, seemed jammed. By this point, Wax had found instinct and reaction a better guide to survival than deliberation, and he didn't stop to think what losing a boot might mean in a frozen mountain, instead jerking his socked right foot free and stumbling forward.

That same instinct aimed his step, the torch in Wax's hand giving enough light to spot that emerald spiral. Wax landed on the smooth stones, dragged his left foot free to match it, his wriggling toes and their cloth wraps at once catching cold, but otherwise remaining unshared amid the green gems. Wax wobbled, watched, but the emeralds didn't rise up to devour him. Behind, both boots vanished in the gold stone, swallowed up into small mounds.

The mounds.

Those shapeless lumps took on a new meaning as Wax

swept a look across the chamber. Not just pointless features, then, but things snared by the strange ground. As Bliss said, every skar chamber had a trap. Now they needed to figure out how this one worked.

'Why aren't I getting attacked?' Bliss signed, standing by the center mound with the golden skars. 'What's the difference?'

"It likes you more?"

'Who wouldn't? But let's get serious, Wax.'

"Just because I'm cracking jokes doesn't mean I'm not thinking."

A ruby line lay to Wax's left, leading towards the room's middle, while a brown stone cross glowed to Wax's right. Gold lay between both, though Wax felt a good jump could get him over. Still, better to confirm he needed acrobatics. Who knew, maybe the room just hated boots?

The Renewal knelt, shifted a single toe off its emerald home onto the gold stone. The rock quivered, like still water starting a ripple, and Wax scooted his foot back. Okay, definitely not the boots.

"I'll have to jump," Wax said.

'Obviously.'

"Don't see you helping!"

Bliss frowned, then walked back across the chamber, near Wax. 'I can boost your jumps, maybe?'

"Which way, you think?"

They looked at both options, ruby against topaz, and both wound up facing the Foti-colored line.

"Tell me why and I'll say whether I agree," Wax asked his sister.

'The emerald isn't eating you, and you have a Vis skar. Maybe the ruby won't, because you have a Foti one too?'

"But you don't have any skars, and you're not getting attacked?"

Another shrug. Still, Bliss's idea aligned with Wax's own, and any chance was better than none. With a nod, a measuring look, Wax jumped. Bliss followed, reaching out and steadying Wax on the narrow landing. His eyes went to his toes, found them uneaten, and the easy, cocky grin came back.

"Another god conquered," Wax said, the skars in his mind seeming equally pleased. "Look at us, Bliss. Professional Renewals."

'Sure, Wax. Professional.'

The gemstone shape route to the middle required some haphazard choices, circling them around the room and more than a few mounds, ones Wax refused to think about. When he landed on a sapphire splatter near the center skars, Wax didn't hesitate, reaching out to pluck one of the golden stones free. The skar left its home without argument, a new, low whisper joining the ones burbling in his mind. Wax slotted it into the necklace, nodded at Bliss's question.

"It's the skar. Now we just have to find Torny and Eujo."

'There wasn't another tunnel.'

"Then they might be back at the chasm," Wax said. "Head that way?"

Before Bliss could say yes or no, Wax popped his foot off the sapphires, right onto the gold. The Whent skar's whisper sped up, and no mound formed. Safe, easy walking. He flashed a smile at his sister.

"Professionals," he repeated.

"What're you yammering about?" Torny asked, striding into the room with Eujo on her heels through the same tunnel Wax and Bliss had used. "You found them? Good. Because I'm tired after—"

"Stop!" Wax shouted as Eujo set foot on the golden floor. Torny, left alone, only looked confused. Eujo kept on going, her feet getting just past Wax's mounded boots before getting stuck fast. "Get out of your boots, Eujo!"

"What?" The Queen replied, yanking at her leg, then looking down. The gold stone climbed, swooping into her smaller boot as she bent to untie the strings. Torny whirled, gawked, as Bliss and Wax started across the chamber. "I can't—"

Eujo broke off in a curse, the golden rock flowing over her fingers as they tried to push the laces free. She tried to pull her hand away, found it fastened tight as more curses streamed from her mouth. Torny, armed with her chisel, tried delivering a whack to the rock, only chipping away the barest bit. As Wax reached Eujo, the gold rock consumed her hand, climbing towards her wrist, while her left leg had a mound covering her ankle, growing fast.

"Get your chisels," Torny snapped, whacking at the rock again. "Maybe we can—"

'It's not enough.' Bliss signed, though she did as the bandit asked, delivering her own pointless hack.

Wax, though, met Eujo's look as she pulled, her eyes wide, face red with effort. A deep fear found her, the same Wax had seen in Sawi as they scrambled away from the fiend. The sure knowledge death wasn't far away. A couple months ago, Wax might've believed that look, might've given in to the fear, that they were far beyond their abilities, their place in the isles.

With the skars thundering in his mind, Wax entertained no such thought. Instead, he listened to the whispers and unleashed their desires.

CHAPTER 47
THE HUNTER

Deshiva, Kitaye's lead hunter and commander, if such a word could be used, of the city's weapon-wielders, stood in the circle's center. A grove carved out in the wilderness, beset with animal bones, hanoko among them, won by the year's successful hunts, by the very recruits now circling her. The twenty or so souls graduating into the city's hunter ranks that year had their fresh tattoos glowing in the few sunbeams making it to the jungle's floor, all with tooth necklaces made from their own kills, silence earned with their own honor.

Words poured from Deshiva's lips in a steady cadence Quik barely heard, didn't recall. His ears felt mushy, his eyes red from a night spent staring at the sky in his hammock, overwhelmed and awed with himself. With the weeks spent stalking creatures at one hunter's side or another, at his first solo victory over a hanoko three days prior. He'd stalked the cat back to its den without being detected, took a whisker off its face while the creature slept and returned with the trophy, a better marker of skill than a pointless kill.

Those hunts, the ones necessary for sustenance or protection, would come later, though Quik dreamt of them now.

Deshiva picked up her spear, adorned with myriad feathers, and began the anointing, inviting every hunter she touched with its glistening point to declare their names, their family, and their weapon. Many chose spears as Deshiva wound through the circle, few picked swords, and only a couple decided on the cowardly bow and arrow, a utility at best should a hunter's true skill fail.

The hanoko he'd tracked was a graceful creature, purple, gray, and dashed with the scars of a long life among the vines. Quik had watched the cat take its lunch, its dinner from critters roaming the forest floor, its claws every time adapting to the need, whether a quick climb or a chase through tight quarters.

Deadly utility.

His choice earned Quik an appraising look, earned Deshiva's curiosity, if not quite her respect. That couldn't be gained in the circle, that could only be gained with time, with success, with—

A yellowed beak pecked at him, biting and tugging at Quik's cheek. He jerked his head and the bird squawked, took to the dawn light and fled. A blink or three chased the dream away, the Mottilan dart's after effects keeping his muscles sluggish, his mind more so. Replaying the reasons he lay on hard rock in the cold felt like recovering from a night with too much wine, too little water.

Until Quik came to the reason why.

The hunter curled up. Looked around, saw his satchel, his gauntlets piled a stride away. Masayo, then, assuming her task would be done well before Quik could find her and strike again. Maybe she thought killing Sawi would make Quik change his mind. Maybe she thought he would give in.

Maybe she didn't realize how patient, how determined a Vis hunter had to be.

Quik left the satchel behind, slipped on the gauntlets, and broke into a loping run to the east. Frigid wet had formed overnight, coating the ragged cliff in death's own ice. At first the hunter stumbled, slid, fell, every mistake molding into mastery. He picked out the drier tops, where gray sun made dried spots. He reached for shrubs to balance, planted feet even to keep from sliding. The gauntlets left his waist and found hits wrists, their hard claws good to spring out, catch himself.

He moved. He chased.

Though there was no trail.

The jungle left many signs. Noctia's barren stones gave few, save for the odd overturned rock or a smudged dirt stretch. At first Quik tried to play the hunter's game, eye Masayo's path, before giving it up for the broader goal: Sawi and Ami were heading towards a town. Masayo would be too. He wouldn't miss that.

And though the day had burned on too far by the time he caught the smoke, the buildings beneath him, the townspeople clustering in the small village's square, Quik still felt that same satisfied burst: a correct hunch, the hunt continued.

He would've descended to the village, would've tried talking to the townspeople to see if they'd seen his wayward targets, but Vis made things simpler for him: Ami's Foti curses carried clean on the winter wind and drew Quik further east, around a jutting slate stone outcropping.

The sight traded the hunt's pleasure for panic. Ami and Sawi were hunkered down behind their bags while Masayo watched from above. The Third Hand leader wasn't speaking, issuing demands, but instead seemed to be working her hands beneath those devastating robes. As to what, that answer came quick, with a flickering spark whistling from Masayo's fingers to the satchel, where the speck burst into flame, charring the satchel's leather and grabbing at the satchel's easier stitching.

A hard move, one countered when Ami pressed her legs to the stone, shoved up the satchel barricade, and charged forward up the slope. The Guardian used her left arm for the lifting, her right leveling some odd metal stick like a short spear. Sawi, abandoned, broke alongside the stones.

Split and force Masayo to make a choice. Smart.

Quik himself began a low shuffle, his chest almost on the rocks, cutting above Masayo. A wild charge might work, but the hunter's instincts said a secret strike held a better chance. Even as he crawled, the gauntlets walking their claws along the pebbles, Quik kept his palms feeling, searching for a throwing stone.

The Tenet didn't wait for Ami to arrive, instead cutting to the right and flicking something at Sawi. Another dart? Quik couldn't tell, though Sawi yelped and fell. Tripped or out, unclear, and not something he could change.

Masayo's move gave Ami the time she needed to reach the Tenet, and the Guardian refused to consider anything other than full-on assault. She barreled into Masayo from the Tenet's left, up and under with a throwing push at the last bit to get the hot satchel into the air, smacking into Masayo like—

No, Quik's mouth dropped as Masayo ducked, weaved around the thrown bag, seeming to fold around its sides like water rippled along a thrown stone. Masayo came around the far side, a small knife somehow in her right hand, and struck at Ami.

The Guardian, though, wasn't some wayward Vis, some Najahn recruit or hapless noble marked for death. Ami had her weapon crossing her body after the toss, apparently anticipating Masayo's move in a brawler's instinct Quik could only admire. Masayo found her strike batted wide, Ami's cocked left fist striking the Tenet's face in a hard jab.

For once, Masayo lost her footing, stumbled back a step. Ami brought her weapon in a backhand, the hooked end screaming towards Masayo's face only for the Tenet to fall, plant her back on the rocks as Ami's strike missed overhead. Masayo kicked out her left foot, cracking into Ami's knee, sending the Guardian to a cursing kneel, her head right where Masayo's kick could take it.

Ami rolled with the blow, rocks scattering everywhere. She kept hold of her weapon, stopped her slide, rose just in time to catch Masayo's follow-up, another lunging stab, in an arm block, punching the pierce up and over her shoulder. The victory left Ami open for defeat, a second Masayo kick to Ami's chin, pushing the Guardian up and over, onto her back. Masayo had the knife flipped in an instant, ready for a gutting end.

Except she'd taken too long. Quik had his position, had his chosen stone, and he flung it fast. The rock, near palm size, took Masayo where her hood wasn't, crashing her forehead and toppling the Tenet. Her gray robes whirled as she fell along the slope, Quik springing to his feet and following.

"You?" he heard Ami ask, groggy, as the hunter went past.

A question to answer another time.

Masayo snapped free from the roll, angling off to Quik's left, where another outcropping offered gravel ground and some stability. She stood, the knife in her left hand now, as Quik closed. Blood ran, splitting around her left eye. No smile now, no cocky bent, only a killer's focus, the same as a cornered hanoko.

"I gave you a second chance," Masayo said as Quik drew to a stop across from her. "I thought you were smarter."

"I'm only a Vis."

"Pity."

Masayo's wrist twitched. A movement Quik didn't really process till he noticed the knife she'd held wasn't in her hand any longer, till a red flare confirmed the blade now stuck from his thigh, where his thick coats left a part in the wind. As he noticed, Masayo moved again, both hands returning to her robes and coming out with more knives. She settled into an even crouch, waiting.

And telling Quik what he needed to know. He swiped at the blade, knocked the knife free, though the burn remained.

"Such useful things, knives," Masayo said, holding her crouch while Quik brought his gauntlets to bear. "Coat them with poison, conceal for close work or throw for a silent end, no crossbow required. The gods' finest invention."

Quik didn't dignify the words with a response. He forced that burning leg to launch him ahead, a dust-scattering overhand swing just like he'd done before, back on the slopes. Masayo went forward to meet it, darting ahead and down, ready to get inside, stab up and take Quik with a single stroke.

Only Quik wasn't going for the overhead blow, instead scooping his left hand and its gauntlet in an underhanded swipe. The move forced Masayo into a desperate sidestep, Quik's gauntlet catching, shredding her robes. The hunter's momentum carried him past Masayo's counter, the knives too small to do anything more than nick his coat. Quik planted his right leg, the burn spreading below his knee, up to his waist, and pivoted to, this time, an overhead swipe.

Masayo hadn't turned around yet, the counter attempt leaving her arms, legs leaning forward and not to the side. She flung her left arm, the knife up to meet the coming gauntlet, but the small blade wasn't built for blocking. Quik shoved it to the ground and carried on, pressing into Masayo and cutting through her already-torn robes, into her side. As the slight resistance slowed the strike, Quik again brought his left hand in an upward swing, only to feel a new needle's bite into his forearm.

Masayo's knife tore his leathers, snarled his skin. It should've stopped the swing, should've ended Quik's move right there, but Deshiva trained her hunters well: when you can make the kill, you stop for nothing, no pain, no wound, no threat.

Quik drove the left gauntlet to meet its sibling, accepting the deep stab to catch Masayo in the middle, the sharp wood talons going deep, drawing a gasp, a spasm, and silence. Quik caught the Tenet's fading eyes, their faces only a breath apart, and in them saw nothing, no answers, no secrets, no promises.

Like any other quarry, in death Masayo was quiet.

In life, the burn spread, Quik's blood ran, and he pitched forward on his victory, toppling them both to the rocks as the day's first snow began to fall.

CHAPTER 48
MOUNTAIN'S MIGHT

Being a thief, skulking about in secret, prepped Torny for all kinds of nefarious things. Backstabs and betrayals, traps and tricks. It did not, it manifestly *did not* prepare her for the damn skars. She'd seen Wax blow up monsters and ships with the Foti stone, she'd felt the Vis rock knit her cuts back together, and Torny had ridden the sledge just fine while Eujo's Kance skar let the ox glide over the snow. All terrifying, wondrous, and out of step with the rational world she'd grown up in.

So when Wax put his hand on Eujo's rapidly petrifying body, Torny backed up. Fast. Faster when the chamber started shaking, when golden chunks broke off and crashed, hammering onto gemstone designs—who made those, anyway?—and shattering. Fighting the urge to snag some of those precious stones, and she might've bagged an emerald or two that broke off in the crackles, Torny hunched down behind the large central skar mound and watched.

Eujo, who'd been half golden stone when Wax stuck his hand against her, stepped free from her prison as the rock peeled off. Cracks ran along the casing, cracks that didn't end when they ran to the chamber's floor, instead spreading along, up, and around. When the snapping, snatching lines struck a hanging stone, it fell. When they struck nothing, the cracks just kept right on going.

"Stop it!" Eujo said, stumbling out as the room shook. "I'm free, Wax!"

But she wasn't free. As she spoke the words, the floor at her feet grabbed at her boots again, even as the chamber kept shaking. Wax said as much, the Vis Renewal trying to trace Eujo's progress with his skar magic and falling over after a violent rattle. Bliss grabbed her brother, dragged him away as another rock chunk smashed the ground where he'd been.

Worse, beyond them, the room's only exit looked lost behind some hefty stones.

"Torny!" Wax shouted, the bandit peeking around the mound to see him sitting up. "Throw Eujo a skar!"

Hey, that she could do. Torny grabbed a golden skar, shoved off the growling whispers in her mind, and launched it across the room. Eujo, again encased up to her thighs, caught the skar. Slotted it into her bracelet. Her prison, as if triggered with a switch, stopped. Eujo's eyes closed, the Queen looking as royal as Torny had ever seen in the glittering chamber, still lit by Bliss's torch. The gold stones holding her in peeled away, rushing off like flowing water.

The chamber shook harder. Enough to force Torny onto her toes, dancing with the shifting ground. A massive crack split the ceiling, Wax's warning shout getting Torny to back up. The boulder hammered down between the bandit and her friends, cutting them off, mashing the skar mound, and sending Torny's half into a rattling dark.

Well, save for those skars.

Those golden motes stood out amid the rumbling, the falling, the shifting. Torny made for them, a desperate mind seizing on something, anything, that might get her out of the dark before another plummeting rock turned her to so much mush. She scrabbled on smooth gems, on jagged stone, picking up cuts on her way to the motes.

What she'd do with them, who knew, but in the dark, amid panic that should've paralyzed her but that now, after too many bouts with this particular nerve-shooting shock, merely rendered into focus, Torny saw in those motes an opportunity.

The first skar she grabbed, body on the floor, scrunched up save for her reaching arms to minimize the chance a wayward stone would break her leg, gave her an idea. Not in words, no, but in vague, strong rushes through Torny's mind, like a spastic dream lingering after waking, calling her to let the skar loose.

Torny held on. Didn't give in. Not yet.

She saw what Wax and Eujo had done with one, but melting away a little gold dust wasn't going to do it. Not here, not now. Instead, Torny reached out with her left, grabbed a second skar. Fought against its whispers, added to the first. She passed the stone to her right hand, grabbed a third, a fourth.

The rumbling continued. Some muffled shouts came from the large stone's other side. Where Torny needed to be.

The skars took that thought and ran with it, the quartet a barreling force pushing Torny to her feet and towards the barricading boulder. She couldn't see, and struck the stone with her shoulder, a hard rush that should've bounced Torny back, knocked her down, bruised both her bones and her ego. Instead, the impact felt like hitting a soft straw mattress. Glowing white-gold lines spread from the point, what Torny thought was magic before they winked out, revealing themselves as sparks fired as the boulder split apart.

Not yet to the other side, the skars kept up their pushing, kicking Torny's feet along the ground, through the battered, blasted boulder and into Bliss's torch glow, the Renewal trio back near the chamber's exit, trying to melt away the rocks blocking their path. They all turned amid the crumbling rubble, variations of shock and joy playing about their faces as Torny tumbled into the room.

Again, the skars caught the bandit, hearing her desire to leave the chamber and biting at it, seizing it. The rock-riddled floor caught Torny's fall and lifted her back up, rolling her feet forward as the bandit cursed, told the other three to get out of the way. The gems, the golden stone rolled up behind her, a stone cape following Torny and wrapping around her as she collided with the tunnel-blocking debris.

Like with the boulder, bright lines sizzled through at the impact, blowing the blockage down the tunnel. The skars, presented with an opening, whispered an indistinct question, one Torny knew how to answer: get her and her friends free.

The skars obliged, Wax and Eujo adding their shrieks to Torny's own as the skars carried the group down the tunnel, rippling the earth to move them in a rolling cascade. Where the tunnel proved too narrow, where a swift strike against hard rock presented itself, the skars would roar in Torny's mind and shove the problem away, melt it, remake it into a smooth scallop shooting the group along their path.

The stars took the chasm as a minor hiccup, lurching the tunnel's end forward, the rock itself growing like a weed into a spanning bridge. A spectacular move, and one Torny borrowed Wax's habit to whoop through as they flew to the other side. Their rampage pulled the remaining golden ropes down in a shimmering rain, one joined by more stones from above, large and small.

The tiniest doubt scratched as Torny flew into the tunnel on the chasm's other side. The mountain rumbled still, shook and rattled. Cracks followed their rush. Those rock fangs above kept falling.

How much could the Gash take and keep on standing?

But the mountain didn't fall on them. The skars spat the foursome out the tunnel's exit onto the path they'd walked up hours before. Running before them, farther down towards the outpost, were the guards that'd been their escort. Fleeing a shaking mountain seemed prudent, but Torny couldn't resist a grin as the rocks let her down at the mountain's entry.

"How about that?" Torny said, snapping that same grin at her friends, all three looking a bit queasy, a lot confused. "Never say I can't get us out of any fix."

"How?" Eujo croaked as she knelt on the ground, breathing hard. "What did you do?"

"Ever realize these babies can work together?" Torny held up the skars, now divided in pairs between her right and left hands. Their whispers almost made her wince, but she could handle it. Like any conversation she wanted to ignore. "Don't know why you didn't grab a handful at every spot. We'd be—"

"The Najahn'll kill you," Eujo said, shaking her head. "You're not with them, and you're not a Renewal. That's the law."

"Well, sure. If we tell them."

Torny expected help from Wax and Bliss, but both Vis just looked at her with nervous doubt.

"Oh, c'mon." Torny wiggled her hands. The power was obvious. "Don't you see how much easier this would all be? Look at what we just did!"

The skars jumped at her words. Their whisper rush, showering Torny with an urge to show off their power, their energy, what Whent's fragments could do. The bandit tried to push back, tried to tell the stones to stay quiet, but like the boulder rolling down a hill, the skars couldn't slow down.

The mountain, still rumbling, shook harder. The snow at Torny's feet shuffled. The ice cracked. The bandit gulped.

"What's going on?" Eujo asked, turning with the others to look up at the Golden Gash, at the ice and snow tumbling off its top, rocks not far behind.

'Time to go,' Bliss signed.

"Agreed." Wax put his words to action, pulling Bliss's hand and breaking down the path.

Eujo followed, made it a step before noticing Torny wasn't following.

"You coming, thief?" Eujo asked.

The skars . . . they wouldn't let her. They'd show Torny, if she waited right here, all the power they had. Four stars, together, working in concert, they could bring down this mountainside, bury everything, and coast Torny free. Unstoppable, incredible, all Whent's might at her fingertips.

Dead quiet. Torny started, her own thoughts alone in her head. Looked at her hands, found her fingers free. Eujo, before her, gripping Torny's wrists. Anger, understanding in the Queen's eyes.

"They're not tools," Eujo said. "They're not meant for you. Go, now."

For the briefest second, Torny looked for the skars, buried instantly beneath the snowdrifts. Then Eujo pushed her, and the bandit, feet working the same old regular magic they always did, found their steps on the icy path. The two ran, and behind them, the mountain shook. The snow thundered.

"Okay, maybe you're right," Torny said as she and Eujo grabbed at each other on the way down, shoves and pulls keeping each other moving, standing. "But we were dead if I didn't get those skars."

"You're not wrong!" Eujo shouted above the quaking rumble, one only growing. "But we might be dead anyway!"

Torny would've looked behind her, but she didn't need to. The shaking ground gave one awful answer, and the terror on Wax's own face, just ahead, confirmed it: the skars were right, the stones could bring down a mountain.

And now they had no way to escape it.

CHAPTER 49

TO THE TUNNELS

Sawi watched, feeling creeping its way back into her limbs, as Ami and Quik folded up Masayo's small form in the Tenet's robes. Quik lifted a necklace from Masayo's body, the several skars twinkling, and stuffed it inside his satchel. Proof, he said, that she'd died. Ami and Quik descended to the village, to the grand fire those townspeople started with their Foti skar, and dropped the body inside. What agreements were made, what promises whispered down there, Sawi didn't know.

And didn't care.

For the second time in too few months she'd been shot with a poisoned dart. She'd been on death's edge, had spent more days wondering whether the person next to her might slip a knife between her ribs, than Sawi had ever imagined possible. Adventure, what Gladdring promised, instead proved to be constant anxiety, suspicion, threat. Maybe Wax had it different, on his isle-spanning journey, but from here, from here all Sawi saw were reasons to go back home and forget any of this ever happened.

Picking fruit in the sun sounded pretty perfect right

then, as she sat surrounded by satchels, salt-speckled hair stringing in the wind.

Quik and Ami returned in dour shape. Both held injuries, apparently not serious. Both held ideas about what to do next, aligned in awful fashion.

"You're not coming with?" Sawi asked as the trio stood before a jagged cave mouth, one, so the townspeople said, would lead into the endless tunnels beneath the isles. "Why?"

Quik, for his part, looked as drained as Sawi felt. His normal strong gait, tall shoulders, and proud face curdled beneath battered Najahn leathers. The gauntlets, blood-spattered, hung from his waist like a beast's killing claws. Quik's hands stayed stuffed in folds, as if he didn't know what to do with them. A man caught between dreams.

Like Pan. All those times pressed to be something more than a forager.

"I made a promise to Wax," Quik said, hardly fortified by the oath. "The Isles are dangerous, and he needs help."

"And you think the Najahn, these Najahn, will give him any?"

Ami, busy stuffing their satchels with a few things taken off Masayo's own pack, snorted. Sawi nodded her way.

"There's no other alternative," Quik continued. "They need a Renewal to succeed. We need one too. And we need it to be Wax."

"Why? Why can't he just give it up and come home?"

"He won't, Sawi. There was a moment when I thought he might, after Rana. The Kance Queen convinced him."

The details Sawi had heard secondhand, passed back to her from Ami and Annalyse during the days they held Quik in the cage, in the sand, while Sawi pressed Gladdring's little rebellion forward. Wax's harrowing journey, his near-death at sea and in the Whirlpool. He should've folded back at the Ringed City. Caught a ship back to Vis. Like Annalyse.

An escape Sawi would've taken, given the chance.

"I should've gone with him," Sawi said, looking away as she did, as if the waves might assuage both the guilt at the words and the unsaid truth that, now, she wanted anything but.

"Don't look back." Quik nodded at the cave. "You'll need all your focus on that."

"He's right," Ami interjected, stepping into the conversation, her pack and satchels on, holding Sawi's out towards her. The Guardian's faceplate once again holding Vis skars. "It's time to move, so we can make some progress before nightfall."

Sawi frowned, "What's night matter in there? It'll be dark all the time."

"Exhaustion, then. The sooner we get away from this isle, the better."

"She's right," Quik added. "It's time. I'll take a couple days getting back. After that, I don't know what the Najahn will do."

"From one danger into another. Say goodbye, Sawi. Let's move."

The Guardian gave them space, moving to the cave's mouth and striking up a makeshift torch. Torn cloth from Masayo's robe soaked in fish oils down at the town, wrapped around a wood rod. It'd last them the first bit, after which, so Ami said, they'd find mosses, or wander by touch alone.

"Don't die down there," Quik said first. "Wouldn't be nice to waste all my effort."

"All your effort?"

Quik grinned, "Didn't see you doing anything. Just lying there."

"I was—" Sawi sighed, scowled, but let it fade to a smile. "I'm sorry, Quik. Sorry about not doing anything when I saw you. I was surprised, and Gladdring told me to keep away."

"Sounds like I should have a talk with this Gladdring." Quik jangled his gauntlets.

"Fassle's going to hang him, if he hasn't already." Sawi shouldered her satchel. "We were on the right path, Quik. You know that? The skars are our only chance."

"Not something you need to worry about. Get home alive." Quik started to step away, then stopped, tilted his head. "You believe that, really, that the skars mean everything?"

"Don't you?"

Quik nodded, his eyes seeming unfocused. Ideas churning.

"Then, when you get back to Vis, find Annalyse. Help her. She'll need it."

Picking fruit. Watching the sun rise over her much-loved jungle. Swinging on vines. Hopes muddied in the moment, as Sawi felt adventure's strings again snaring her, pulling her back in.

"Never ends, does it?" Sawi said, soft, against the distant crashing waves.

"Not anymore, not for us."

The torch did indeed hold up for the first two hours, though the last bit was less a bright flame and more a sputtering glow. In that time, their cave went from well-traveled and picked over, to warped and wandering, the ground veering between dusty stone and soaked, slick slopes with rivulets running nearby. Sawi and Ami passed by large chambers, picked paths at almost random, with both the Guardian and the Vis pooling instincts to aim in one particular direction: south.

Vis became their goal, though Sawi didn't ask Ami her reasons for choosing the jungle isle and the Guardian didn't state them. Silence, save at those intersections, became the defining trait of their march, and Sawi didn't try to break it. She had thoughts aplenty, replaying the last few weeks, with what focus remained tilted hard on keeping her feet planted one after another. They found mosses, some in bright blues and purples. The satchels became carriers for the plants, and their boots too, Sawi wondering if they'd eventually cover themselves with the stuff.

Dried fish and skimpy root vegetables made their meals, supplemented by what few mushrooms they found amid the rocks. The fungi could be poisonous, but Ami gave Sawi a Vis skar to hold after eating the things, and its whispers calmed whatever ills befell their stomachs.

They walked, and walked, and walked, until they reached, with the moss's gentle aura guiding them, a small offshoot. A single entry to the rounded room, just large enough for the pair and their gear. Clawed marks and scattered bones said some fiend or other creature had made its home there, but dust and spiderwebs suggested that home had long since been abandoned.

"We'll stop here for the night," Ami announced, a unilateral decision, like so many were with her.

A responsibility Sawi was happy to abdicate, for now.

"How far do you think we've come?" Sawi asked once they'd shed their burdens, had another small meal split between them, the chewy fish as appealing as dirt but, at least, taking the edge off her appetite.

"Sawi, the isles take days to sail between them. At our

rate, we'll be lucky if we're under Vis within a week. And that's only if we go in the right direction the whole time."

"Wait, our food won't last that long?"

In the moss's purple light, Ami's golden plate took on an ethereal cast, Sichi's pink glow striking Kitaye's inlet. A better look than the Guardian's snarled smile.

"We'll find more," Ami said. "And what we can't forage, we'll hunt."

"Hunt? You mean fiends?"

Ami tapped the harpoon lightly on the stone next to her, "The monsters are made of meat, same as you and I. If we're going to make it through this, Sawi, we'll have to be worse than they are. We'll make the fiends afraid of our footsteps, of our weapons, of our scent. They think this is their home. We'll make it ours."

A younger Sawi, one more accustomed to sitting on Sanas and watching sunsets, might've felt a chill at Ami's words. Might've curled up or looked away, spouted a denial or even laughed. Instead, the Vis took in the Guardian's gaze and returned it, dirty, tired, and, to those creatures lurking in the Dark Below, deadly.

CHAPTER 50
LIFE UNENDING

From the first, any child of the Isles realized their home was not a normal one. That is, things didn't always make sense. Most days, rocks would roll down the hills like they should, but every so often, someone would come by and those stones would climb back up. Birds might fly and ferrites might walk, but every so often a fiend no lighter than those lizards would take to the sky. Svarde's mother always used to blame the gods for these breaks in the norm.

"Divine mistake," she would mutter.

Svarde heard her voice as he touched the great sword's massive hilt, the length reaching down the barbarian's entire forearm. Her mother's words followed a sudden spread, as if Svarde had fingertips running all around the chamber, poking up here and there, waiting for his twitching command. One he was only able to give because death had yet to claim him.

Noctia's grasp stopped. Not the blood flowing from his wounds, the aches in his bones, or the rattle in his lungs as Svarde sat up, dragging the sword along the stones. All the pain remained, but it seemed unable to halt him, to keep Svarde from moving, from acting, from fighting.

The blade's wonders were spoiled by the great fiend before him, heat roiling off its massive form as it battered Maena's manic defense aside. The rotted scimitar held no danger for the monster, whose flails bashed the Rana captain's blades away and forced her into a retreating scramble. She glanced at Svarde, worry and curiosity mingling in golden heat-light. Kivi, the loyal rock lizard, shambled into Maena's place, less a threat to the fiend and more a mote to be snuffed out.

"Back," Svarde said, his voice hardly his own, a ragged, shredded thing better heard from an old man than the one now standing, gripping the Dead King's sword with both hands. "Move aside, Kivi."

The ferrite, flicking her sapphire eyes back in question, only obeyed when she saw the barbarian standing as he had so many times before. Face hard, body beaten but upright, a quiet fury in every corded muscle. A man who, going by the bloody puddle at his feet and the red lines coursing his skin, ought to be dead, but one who looked too alive to falter, to fail.

And yet, despite his challenge, Svarde did not march to the great fiend. Instead, he chased those fingertips, those tiny blips on his consciousness. Some faded even as Svarde found them, those pinpricks nearest the other fiends, and as he made the leap, he found the cause: those walking dead, the undying fighters, that's what he felt, and that's who he could command.

At least, the ones remaining.

A retreat. Svarde ordered it without words, only an impression, even as he spoke the same to Maena and Kivi.

Run back to the city. Close the gates. Wait for rein-forcements.

"You sure, Svarde?" Maena called back, though her shout said she'd already started running.

"Just go."

The fiend, four arms, the lower two gripping those flails, closed the distance to Svarde with a single stride. There was no bow, no spark, no words. Just a strike, flying in from the left, the chain whistling through the chamber's sweltering dark. Svarde shifted the great sword, braced feet willing to stand against a mountain's weight, and caught the blow. The flail wrapped around the metal, the clawed head firing embers as it clashed with the ancient blade. The force moved Svarde to the right, his feet sliding, but sticking.

So he braced, and swung.

The blade, pulling the trapped flail with it, crossed Svarde's body, bringing the weapon's chain into line with the fiend's second blow. One flail struck another, clashing into and severing the hard metal links. The monster's fire flared bright blue and white, hot waves roiling, and the fiend yanked its weapons back, one returning whole, the other only half a chain.

Svarde swiped the great blade low, letting the flail slide off. Around him, giving the conflict a wide berth, went the remaining bodies, shambling along down the side chamber. Pursuing them in slow walks, flails making occasional swats at slower victims, came the other fiends. All ignored the duel on the chamber's right side, all gave them space.

Because, Svarde assumed, they all guessed the outcome.

The barbarian didn't fight with swords. They were Kance and Rana weapons. Foti fighters preferred axes and hammers, unless, like Ami, some fate gave you a blade too good to ignore. For him, the great sword seemed shifty in his grip, too heavy for a stab, too cumbersome to bring overhead for a killing chop.

His first wondrous moments clouded to a confused present as the great fiend set its remaining flail spinning, plotting another strike. How did the Dead King use this thing?

Until Svarde found his weight, he'd settle for staying . . . alive?

Whole. He'd settle for whole.

The fiend launched another strike. Svarde tried to cut forward, underneath the blow, and found his step slowing at the intense heat as he approached the fiend. Immortal or not, the fire still hurt, and the hesitation cost Svarde, the flail slamming into the barbarian's shoulder and driving him to the ground. The claws bit into his ash clothes, to the skin beneath, and tore out when the fiend pulled his weapon back.

Pain that should've left Svarde unconscious, dead, unable to think. His right arm, likely dangling by broken bones and shredded muscle, nevertheless kept its grip, moved when Svarde told it. Planting the great blade's hilt in the dirt, Svarde pressed with both hands, rose to steady feet. Those black skars along the blade shimmered, drawing in the fiend's sweltering light.

Noctia's gift, keeping Svarde alive. Letting him fight for her isle.

Well, he'd best get to the fighting then.

Bellowing out a Foti challenge, Svarde brought the blade up to his ruined shoulder, above it as he charged the great fiend, whose obsidian skull sparked with confused fire. The monster's flail jerked, a belated defense as a foe destroyed again advanced. Svarde swung the blade, beat the fiend's slow response, and gashed the monster's left leg. Hard white scales formed along the strike, a watery contact without the bone and gristle Svarde would've expected. He overbalanced, the swing carrying Svarde to his right, almost to the chamber wall, as the fiend sank to one knee.

The monster seemed to realize its predicament as Svarde steadied himself, found the strength to hold the blade like a spear. Svarde charged, the fiend cracked its remaining flail like a whip, sent the clawed hand barreling towards its enemy. Svarde cut right, bringing him behind the fiend's arm, the flail breezing by without contact. A straight line run, now, to a fatal blow.

Through the blazing heat, the chamber filling with fiends, more wheeled constructs. His friends gone, but one victory yet possible. Svarde would see it done.

The point came close, Svarde's burning feet kicking off the ground, until something struck his back heel, sent the warrior sprawling, Svarde switching his focus only to keeping hold of that blade, his only chance.

The flail. Svarde saw it as he struck ground, rolled over once. The fiend had snapped it back, its clawed end getting a grazing hit. Enough. The monster, limping, at a crouch, drew back its weapon and leaned over Svarde. Embers burned along the obsidian skull, everything else a roaring orange and gold. The fire overwhelmed, consumed.

All save one of those pinpricks, one fingertip, close. Strong. Unmoving. Svarde reached to it, asking, screaming, begging for help, for some hope before the end.

A twitch.

The fiend's lower right arm bent down, put its blazing hand on Svarde's own, the ones holding tight to the blade. Another move, another act that should've put Svarde far into Noctia's realm, and one yet again kept distant. The obsidian skull descended, tilted as it neared Svarde's own broken body.

What was it saying? Was it a victorious gloat, in those sparks? A respectful end to a well-fought battle? Or simply a question shouted through sapphire lights?

Svarde didn't get an answer, because the fiend's tracings exploded, their patterns disintegrating as the great monster fell away. The fiend's press on his hands relaxed, the giant fire combing over into white and gray ash. Falling to the side, revealing the broken flail's clawed end jammed into the back of its cooling head. The killer, the twitch, standing behind it, clad in gashed iron armor.

Vengeance, albeit from beyond the grave.

The Dead King bent, extracted the flail's clawed head as the chamber's fiends realized something had gone amiss. The collective turned, almost as one, towards the dark space on the chamber's right, where the air sweltered not quite so much, where the fire's light didn't flare so bright. They saw one man who should've been dead a hundred times over, standing with a blade held tight in both hands. And a second, one they'd watched get struck down, taking the weapons off their leader's ashen corpse.

If those realities broke their spirits, the fiends didn't show it. White-gold sparks ran across their obsidian skulls, the constructs turned their nozzles, and Svarde wondered how much damage he could take before even the sword couldn't save him. A test he'd rather not fail.

"To the tunnel," Svarde said, or perhaps imagined. Difficult to tell.

The Dead King, though, acted on the command, whipping the broken flail head at the fiend standing in their path. At the same time, the ancient knight swung up the great fiend's intact flail, starting a spinning advance. His target caught the thrown claw on its smaller, upper arm and smacked it aside. Readied its own flail in response.

Only for a horn's blow to ring out through the chamber. Loud, bright, a winter's yowl. In the instant following its announcement, the several fiends at the chamber's far side, opposite the fiend's entry, jerked aside. One fell, several large iron bolts protruding from its back. Crossbow twangs filled the air, quarrels buzzing in. White patches appeared where the missiles struck targets, the fiends whirling, stumbling, sparking.

Svarde and the Dead King took advantage. They carved into the constructs, leaving the more vulnerable fiends to Jochi's too-many archers. The nigh-invincible pair cleaved through one after another. The battle turned, the fiends abandoning their machines and running back to the sloping tunnel, down its dark, and leaving, all too soon, a charred chamber in quiet.

"You ought to be dead," Jochi said after, the warlord standing, sweating in his furs before Svarde and the Dead King. "Don't know who this is, but he looks like he ought to be dead too."

"A long story," Svarde replied. "But with you here, I think we'll have time to tell it."

"Those fiends. They'll be back, won't they?"

"If we give them time."

Jochi nodded. "They'll have a bit. Olgata came back, and we ran. The rest of my force is well behind, too far to make a push now. And if our hunch is right, this is just one batch of the bastards. We fortify, then we advance. Together, Svarde, we'll end this. All of it."

With the blade's weight in his hands, Svarde believed it.

CHAPTER 51

POWER'S PRICE

Bliss had to hit Wax, a panicked slap, to break the Vis from his open-mouthed stare at the mountain crashing towards them. Whent's Golden Gash emptied, its stone and snow barreling along the slope at their little party like a billowing wave. The glittering plume erupted high into the afternoon sun, meshing with the yellow sky while darker, roiling masses descended.

"We can't run," Wax muttered, taking backward steps as Bliss pulled him along.

A few strides up the mountain, Eujo and Torny half ran, half fell after the two Vis. Their arms flung wide, their legs sloppy, missing the stone stairs in a stumbling slant. They wouldn't outrun the avalanche—was that the word Torny cried? None of them would.

The skars knew it too. They whispered suggestions in Wax's ears, wordless urges to melt the world from the Foti stone. The Rana skar seemed confused, trying to decide whether it could use the snow for something. The Vis skar did its thing, humming along about Wax's various scrapes and scratches beneath his heavy coat.

Only the Whent skar offered an idea, one that had Wax returning Bliss's pull, tugging her down into a kneel next to him.

"Catch them," Wax said, planting a gloved hand on the stone stair before him.

Bliss, smart as ever, sprang out, snagged Torny's arm as the bandit went past. Tugged the lithe thief in beside them. Eujo slipped at the swing, falling to the side and bouncing off the hard path. Wax yanked his attention away from his friends: they'd handle themselves. He had to handle disaster.

Like a ripple's touch when sticking a hand into a stream, the Whent skar let Wax feel the cold rock beneath his palm. A rush, yes, but one he could direct with a little nudge, a little push against the rock's current. It trembled beneath him, the roar screaming in. Torny screaming too, yelling at Bliss, at Eujo, at Wax.

Ignore her.

Wax flicked his eyes up. The gray mass thundering down. No flight, only fortitude. And that, the Whent skar could provide. Wax pressed with his fingertips, then arched his palm, as if to scoop the stone like a snowball or a muddy sand glop. The rock shivered before him, stones cracking at the edge of the skar's influence. Wax, as the skar roared in his mind, pulled up farther. This time the granite, the hard black-gray rock, responded with a lurch. Wax's knees bounced as, before him, the path burst upward in a thick, pointed wedge angling towards the oncoming avalanche.

The Renewal guided the rock, trusting the skar and the rippling sensation. A swim left extended the wedge that way, a jagged ripple thrusting up along the icy slope. To the right found the same, snow breaking into chunks as its stable home broke for the sky. A sudden, makeshift shelter, and one Wax found himself crowded into as his three friends crunched in close.

Nobody said a word, not even Torny, as the avalanche obliterated all other noise. The world shook. The sky vanished as a gray-silver torrent broke over their wall. The shorter sides of the wedge disappeared, snapped off and joined the cavalcade. Wax's boots, a hair lower than his body up against the barrier, sank into more snow than the Vis had ever seen. But he could breathe, he could see, and the avalanche wasn't interested in sticking around.

Seconds slipped by and the sky reappeared, the noise settled, and the chaos continued on below, leaving a flattened ice, stone, and snow medley in its wake. A speckled plain, leading all the way down towards the outpost.

"It's going to get crushed," Eujo said as they waited, watched, caught their breath.

"Maybe not," Torny offered. "Those big palisades, you know, they can—"

The bandit's excuses withered as she spoke them, but she offered them nonetheless. Trying to evade the demons waiting for her, the ones Wax saw every time he reached for the skars, their unbound power.

"It's okay," Wax said as Torny broke into shocked silence, the Najahn town shuddering, small dots running, as the avalanche ran into its spread. "You didn't know. It's not your fault."

Torny dropped her head, stared at the ground. Over her back, Eujo met Wax's eyes, the Queen's frigid look as thawed as Wax had ever seen it. Not days ago, Eujo might've burned Torny's actions as reckless, deadly, even monstrous. Now she put an arm around the bandit's shoulders, pulled Torny into a hug.

"You saved us," Eujo offered. "You saved our lives, Torny. One of us will be the Aegis, because of you."

"But—"

"When you accept a Queen's responsibility," Eujo went on, trampling the bandit's words, "you come to understand there's scales for everything. You weigh one life against another, no matter how awful that sounds, because you have no choice. The Isles against one outpost. You made the right call."

"And you didn't even know," Wax added, throwing his arm on too. "Not your fault. I'll say it again and again."

A crunch ahead. Bliss, rising up from their shelter and taking the first steps along the snow. She glanced back at the foursome, nodded towards the disaster.

'Come on. There might be survivors.'

Bliss, always with the right approach.

They found life. What could've been a horror turned out only awful, the dead numbering less than a dozen as the avalanche petered out near the valley's bottom. The buildings were shunted aside, the walls destroyed, but the Najahn had time to run, to prepare. Torny started to say that she'd help bury every person lost, only for Eujo to pull her aside, give her a more careful way to assuage her guilt.

Avalanches on Whent, in the mountains, were terrible, natural things. The bandit didn't cause it. Random tremors did.

Wax didn't hear that talk—he'd been busy digging out supplies, looking for any more souls trapped beneath the snow, but Bliss repeated it to him later. They huddled around a fire, one of several inside hasty lean-tos erected from viable wood. As she signed, Bliss frowned further, his sister's brave lines sinking into serious thought. Wax, now eating some frosted potatoes, mulled the words.

"Smart," he said, finally. "We don't know what people would do."

'They're confused,' Bliss signed back. 'You hear them. The Golden Gash doesn't do this. The avalanches don't come this way. They'll never know why their friends died.'

Eujo and Torny had stomped off to gather much-needed ale—the barrels, safely tucked away in cellars, survived—but Wax flipped to the signs anyway, as several Najahn took up other spots around the fire.

'If Torny admitted to using all those skars, what would happen?' Wax signed. 'They'd call her a murderer and kill her right now.'

'You don't know that.'

'We should. How did they treat the bandits on Foti?'

With arrows and voulges. No trials, no considered debate.

Bliss looked back at the fire, the smoking edges as the heat waged its war with the snow. Her left hand signed, slow.

'I'm worried we're losing ourselves, Wax. We're becoming killers, and excusing it.'

'We have to keep going. Someone needs to become the next Aegis.'

'You?'

'Eujo.' Though as he signed the Queen's name, Wax winced. 'Or me. Someone.'

'Then promise me, Wax. Promise me we won't keep doing this. If we have to fight fiends, so be it. But I came with you because we were going to help the isles. Not destroy them.'

The yes came easy, because Wax had no other choice. He couldn't lose Bliss. He needed her staff, her skills. Just like, no matter how much chaos she caused, they needed Torny too. Guardians to see them through to the end.

Eujo had taught Wax that much: the Aegis was all that mattered. They would succeed, no matter the cost. What that price would mean to him, Wax would deal with later.

The skars, their whispers always in his mind, their urges dancing in his bones, seemed to agree.

CHAPTER 52

THE NEW WAR

Power abhors a vacuum. An idea Quik hadn't considered, ever, until he returned to the Najahn quarter with news of Masayo's death. He said nothing to the gate guards, nothing to the scholars in the streets, leaving the words only for several Third Hand leaders Quik himself didn't know, but who grabbed him three steps inside the Tenet's cliff-side building and began an interrogation.

Their eyes, greedy and glinted, showed they took Quik's lies with calculated glee. Masayo, to hear their muttered asides tell it, had been leading the Tenet for too long. Here, at last, was an excuse to do away with her knives and replace them with someone, perhaps several someones, new.

"That, though, is not your concern," said one, cowled like the other two in purple robes, as if in mourning for their lost leader. "You'll leave this room, say not another word about this, and continue on through your training."

"My training?" Quik asked between fresh water, fruit, reveling in the warmth of the room's crackling fire. Once the risk of a knife to his neck had gone, civilization's benefits bled through his diminished caution. Quik had made the right choice, otherwise he'd be in the cold Dark Below, wandering lost with Ami and Sawi. "What training?"

"Your rotations. Masayo's notes say you showed promise, but this was only your first assignment," the leader's voice was bright, a teacher delivering a common-sense next step. "After today, you can head to the next."

"What happens today?" Quik also wanted to ask where, what Tenet came next, but those were details he could figure out later.

"The Circle's addressing us all, and soon. Get yourself some fresh robes, maybe take a bath to wash the grime off, then follow everyone else." Glances passed between the trio before settling on Quik again. "It promises to be interesting."

Quik did as they suggested—the bath, especially, was necessary after nights on the rocks, amid saltwater and bird droppings. He took a shaving knife and cut away the scruff around his cheeks and neck, tied his hair back. Without the robes, his Vis tattoos showed through, out of place in the otherwise ornate Najahn world. He'd have to look at them more, remind Quik of why he was here, and where he'd come from.

But the wind outside was cold, the dress was expected, and so he covered up his body with the same purple and black as everyone else.

The Third Hand leaders at least had one thing right: everyone was in the main square, a cobblestoned swath before the Circle's main tower. A statue of Demion stood in the middle, tall and fierce in the gray morning light. A dark wood stage stood near the Circle's tower, erected with a podium planted for speaking. Chairs lined either side, two scholars tasked with brushing blowing snow off their seats.

Quik's attention, along with the crowd, swerved to the gallows. A simple set, higher and to the stage's right, held four nooses. Today's subjects already waited, hooded and kneeling. Behind them stood three Najahn in gleaming armor, two with voulges at the ready and the third, wearing an all-black helmet showing no face, gloved hands. Quik hadn't seen a hanging before, only even knew what it was thanks to the whispers flying around him.

Who, though, were they executing? Was Gladdring kneeling there?

Without any friends to ask, not trusting the crowd around him, Quik kept quiet and watched. Told himself to play the hunter's game and study the people who might be his next enemies, or Wax's much-needed allies.

The Najahn weren't much for music, at least on official business, but the guards on duty around the square began stamping their voulges against the stones when some signal Quik didn't catch went around. The doors into the Circle's tower swung open, snow swirling in their wake, revealing more guards. Behind them, walking to the stage, came the Circle: Fassle at its head, behind him the two adepts, and after that the Tenets. They approached the stage, took the chairs, and the one Quik expected to be empty was already filled, a face from a couple hours ago already sitting in it.

More whispers, curious, at the sight. A few touching on the more important, the stranger thing, the sight that had Quik forcing his mouth shut, mind racing with questions.

Next to Fassle, with an Adept's gold raiments around him, sat Gladdring. Impassive, imperious, silent, but alive.

How? Sawi had said Fassle murdered one Adept, had declared death to the potential traitors. Yet Gladdring . . .

The Circle's leader stepped up to the podium, drawing a hush. Even the snow seemed to still its bluster, the wind calming as if to let Fassle's voice echo hard and clear through the square. Traitors, the man said, had plotted to steal the Isle's most sacred weapons, the skars. Had plotted to destroy the Najahn and give the world over to chaos. Those traitors, Fassle continued, had been caught. Some had already paid the price, and more would now.

"The Guardian, Ami, and the rogue Whent scientist Annalyse, along with their two closest collaborators," Fassle announced, "go now to Noctia, where they will suffer in the eternal darkness for their crimes."

The man made a cutting gesture towards the gallows, where the executioner grabbed his kneeling prisoners, one by one slipping their heads through the nooses. For being doomed, the people didn't struggle, didn't protest. Silent, almost limp, they accepted their fates. No last words, no speeches, no fiery anger like the real Ami would've delivered.

Only a snap, a fall, an end.

The sight tore something in Quik, a muscle the man didn't know he had till that moment. Right and wrong were malleable. Only a child believed otherwise. But this? Who had been chosen to die instead of the real Ami, the real Annalyse? And why?

"These dissidents, however treasonous, did not leave us without value," Fassle continued once the victims finished their struggles. "They showed us that skars can no longer be left alone, cannot be trusted to their isles. Instead, we, the true guardians, must take up the charge." Fassle swept his pinched look across the crowd, nodding the whole time.

"The Renewals are finished. The Aegis is over. We will stamp out the fiends, we will set the world at peace. We, the Najahn, will rise and our enemies will fall."

The cheer came first from the guards. From various corners throughout the crowd. It rose into a roar, a clapping, stomping, shouting promise to protect, to fight, to dominate.

"Look to your Tenets for direction," Fassle continued at length, after the noise died down. His grin stretched from end to end. "The new Najahn, with the skars in *our* hands, begins now."

More cheers, more shouts, and amid it all, Quik stood confused. At least until a guard caught the Vis's eyes, frowning. The hunter, then, opened his mouth, joined the chants, his hands moved to clap.

The Renewal was over. The Najahn would take control. Wax and Bliss, then, could go home. Be safe.

Wasn't that worth celebrating?

CHAPTER 53

CRIMINALS

Death, destruction, loss, all things Torny had dealt with before. Not, though, at her own hands. A stolen trinket, sure, but Yarvick didn't play the murder game, so it wasn't until Torny found herself with Eggrad and Sledge that bodies began appearing underfoot. Those bandits earned their name, backing up threats with violence. Even so, Torny stayed back, only drew her knives in defense. Never played the executioner. The bodies weren't hers.

She didn't sleep the first night in the snow-swamped Najahn outpost. Burned her every moment working with Unta and the others to dig the base out. Never once did Torny mention the skars she'd stolen, the ones scattered now along the mountainside. Never once did Torny say she kept seeing the roiling snow burying its victims alive. At least, with the Kance guards drowning in the ocean off Rana's coast, Torny didn't watch. Didn't have to remember.

She collapsed in the late morning of the second day, with Bliss helping her to a makeshift bed in a scrappy shelter. Torny slept among the wounded and the sick till night-

375

fall, rising again to continue the work. For several days more she salved the guilt with effort, alongside old friends and new, bonds forged in labor. Runners returned from other Whent towns with emergency supplies, sledges carting materials to raise new shelters, even as blizzards and freezing cold interrupted life.

Burials marked the passing time, one in the morning and one in the afternoon for a week. Each given their proper due by Unta. Torny attended them all. A penance. Yet, not an absolution: she still saw the avalanche, and she still held the diary, secreted away in pockets. Compartmentalize. A term Yarvick did teach his thieves, a way of sealing away guilt so you could focus on the next job. Not as easy as it sounded, but the gradual labor did its work, and by the week's end, Torny was sipping ale again, talking with Wax and Eujo about their next moves.

Getting to Tamas wouldn't be possible by ship this deep into the Winter, so Eujo said and Unta backed up. However, crossing the narrow eastern sea on ice floes, temporary bridges, could be done if one was desperate enough. Otherwise, waiting several months till warmer weather made for safer sailing was the only option.

"Well, that's not happening," Wax said after Unta voiced the delay as the five of them sat around an evening fire. The outpost continued to dig out around them, some buildings standing up again, those palisades a spiked ring against the dim twilight. "The fiends aren't waiting. Neither are the other Renewals. We have to move."

'We don't know how to cross the ice,' Bliss signed.

"We'll learn." Wax reached up, tapped the necklace around his neck with the skars. Torny noticed every time he did that, if Eujo noticed, she'd touch her bracelet with the same stones. Skar holders stick together, or something.

"We've got the skars too. With Eujo's Kance one, we could probably float most of the way there."

"Sure," Torny said, "until it decided to do something different and throw us all into the ocean. Guess how long it'd take for us to freeze?"

Wax shrugged, "Aren't you cold enough here as it is? Tamas is at least a little south."

The bandit raised a finger, "Now there's an argument I could get behind."

Bliss signed her agreement, exaggerating a shiver while springing a wide grin. Unta huffed a laugh, cutting it off when a Najahn came up, tapped her on the shoulder. She begged off, leaving the Guardians and their Renewals to keep up the planning.

"Deux said he'd wait for us on the eastern edge," Eujo said. "I say we go, see if he made the town. If he's not there, then we try the floes. Otherwise, the *Storm's Edge* is a good ship. Deux's a good captain. He might have a way."

"And what about your friends?" Torny asked. "The ones that chased you two off Noctia? What if they're waiting for us?"

Eujo narrowed her eyes, looked right at the fire. "They might be. They'll find us again, and they'll keep coming until I take the Aegis's throne. There's nothing to do but stay ready."

'Why won't they stop?'

"Because she's scared. She's scared of me. Of the fiends. She thinks a few skars would give her security."

"The other Queen knows what the skars can do?" Wax asked. "How does everyone seem to know except us?"

"Not everyone," Eujo replied. "Not me, until I held one. And even if you did, the Najahn keep the skars protected. I didn't understand it till Rana, but the Renewal was an opening for her to get some real power."

"Well, when we get to Kance, we can show her just what she's missing."

Torny was about to agree, was about to add that after what they'd dealt with, a few crummy assassins and a confused ruler wasn't all that bad, when she noticed the shadows shifting. Bliss signed something to Wax, the Vis laughed, repeated the joke, and Torny caught none of it. The sounds around the camp, the digging, the chopping, the conversations all dwindled.

The Najahn were moving.

And not to get in line for a late dinner.

"Guys," Torny said, dropping her voice. "Something's up."

"Something is," Unta said, striding back near the fire, a voulge in her hands. She'd found some Najahn armor, still snowy but fitting nonetheless. "The Circle's made a declaration. The circumstances have changed."

"To what?" Eujo asked.

"There's no Renewal anymore." Unta barreled on, not letting that truth set in. "The Najahn will lead the fight against the fiends. All the isles will support us, with soldiers and skars alike." She pointed the voulge at Wax, then drifted the point at Eujo. "That includes the ones you've already collected."

"Wait, what?" Wax asked, standing, taking a step back off the battered log he'd been using as a seat. "What happens to the Aegis?"

"It's done. No more." Unta settled into a hard stare. A professional's look, duty-bound. "I don't know why, but I know the Circle wouldn't do this without reason. We're going on the offensive, Wax. Like the Whent warlord here."

Torny glanced between the two as Wax, and Eujo, continued peppering Unta with questions she didn't answer. She asked for the skars once, twice, and a third time. All through the dialogue, the other Najahn kept moving, encircling the group. Some harsh mutters drifted by, not everyone buying into the new mission.

Even so. In a moment, the Renewals—Torny wouldn't give up that name so easy, because if they weren't Renewals, then she wasn't a Guardian, and screw that—would be surrounded.

'Choose,' Torny signed, clear enough for Wax and Bliss to catch, while Eujo made yet another pointless ask of the Najahn captain. 'We run now, or they'll take us.'

'Then we run,' Wax signed back, settling an icy fire in Torny's gut. The same that'd gripped her when she took the diary. A dire move, one with no retreat.

"Okay," Wax said, loud, interrupting Eujo and drawing the Queen's eyes his way, where she could catch Bliss signing the sentiment. Torny's hands drifted to her knives. Could she fight off a Najahn guard? A dozen? "We'll do it, Unta. Where do you want them?"

The commander wasn't an easy mark. She didn't relax, didn't put up her voulge. Instead, she held out her hand.

"Give them to me. We're to send them away tonight, back to Noctia. You four can stay here till the thaw, then we'll barter your trips home."

"Sounds fair," Wax replied, reaching for the necklace, catching Eujo's eye as he did so. As always, Eujo went for her bracelet.

Being a thief, skulking through the night in places you weren't supposed to be, trained Torny to be ready for surprises, to control her flinches, make determined moves even when the unexpected happened. Like, say, when the campfire blew up.

The merry flames puffed out in a bright flash, heat splashing Torny as she winced, rising and breaking into a run. As she made the first step, not fully up from her seat on her own log, the snow slashed into a near-blinding whirl. Curses and calls came up, metal striking metal as haphazard voulges and chakrams exited sheathes and holsters. Through it, Torny kept her feet, broke towards the only place that made any sense: the makeshift stables, where those carriages were kept.

The stable loomed in the sinking daylight near the palisade's only opening. A boarded roof and four tall logs salvaged from the avalanche. In it, Torny guessed, would be five or six sledges and carriages nestled near the oxen who brought them. After their awful walk across the Whent tundra, any attempt to run now meant stealing a ride.

Shame that theft would mean getting by three Najahn soldiers, their voulge-wielding arms up near their faces, keeping hard snow from their eyes. Still, three soldiers against one thief made for poor odds. Better to avoid a fight than pick a bad one.

"They're crazy!" Torny cried as the fire burst again behind her. Wax and Eujo laying into the skars to keep themselves alive, to keep the soldiers back. How long that'd work, who knew? "Help me!"

The panic Torny put into her own voice made her proud, and it befuddled the already nervous Najahn. A few minutes ago they'd been prepping for a night's work, or an ale and a hard sleep. Now a sudden snowstorm, strange magic, and an order to apprehend the very people meant to be saving their lives must've been giving them whiplash. Either way, they hesitated, their looks going past Torny towards the fire, and the bandit ran right on by.

Only one, after Torny made it halfway to the stable, turned and started after her, calling for Torny to stop. With her way clear, Torny risked a look back, saw the stumbling Najahn, and behind him a net closing tight around her friends. Bliss, always ready with a snapped stick serving as her staff, stood strong as Wax and Eujo glowed beside her. The two Renewals alternately had their eyes closed, their hands waving, looking like odd puppets as they gave into the skars.

Or rather, as the skars took them. Like the Whent gems did back in the mountain, Torny could imagine the rushing words, the wild urges drawing unknown power and casting it about.

Some, she didn't have to imagine. The ground trembled in sharp bursts, jutting stone up from the ground and throwing Najahn guards into the snow. That same snow slicked over, froze in instants to thick ice to trap its victims. The blizzard whirled, intensifying whenever a Najahan came close, battering them with hard flakes. Unta attracted all the fire's focus, the flames lashing out like angry whips to strike the Najahn captain, forcing her into a backward retreat.

An awesome display, a terrifying one, and Torny might've stared longer if her feet hadn't kept their own focus. The oxen clued Torny into her arrival, their lows anxious and confused as they lurched to their hooves. The Najahn guard came too, seeming to realize Torny's destination might not be all accident. The voulge found his hands, leveled its pointed end her way.

Torny dashed left, cutting around an ox and then breaking right, looking at the cargo carriages and trying to find one still set up to leave. Not the first, and not the one she ran alongside now, the reins lying off in the snow. Torny had neither the time nor knowledge to set up a ride, a lack she might've bemoaned if the situation wasn't so absurd.

At what point in her life could Torny have expected this, a flight in a distant outpost in Winter's dead grasp?

She rounded the second carriage's end, noticed the fourth. Its ox pair stood above the third, a small sledge, and bore effort's sheen. The carriage itself still held supplies, the reins attached. Gilded purple and black, the light coming in off the lanterns hung here and there, the carriage looked so ready to leave it threw Torny, till she remembered Unta's words.

The skars were to leave tonight. No fiddling about with the gems, no leaving them in other's hands. Just like the Circle. No time for trust.

"Stop, dammit." The guard put himself in the narrow lane between the third and fourth carriage, voulge leveled at Torny. "I gave you an order."

Breathing hard, Torny cocked her head, "Ever hear of panic? Makes it real hard to listen."

The guard, eyes hard to see beneath the Najahn helmet, didn't budge. "Then listen now. Come over here, keep your hands clear, and no harm will come to you."

As he spoke, the earth jumped again. A scream carried on the wind, a pained one. The guard twitched. Torny took a step. Buried her hands in her coat. Measured the distance.

"Hands out," the guard said again.

"It's cold."

Another step. Halfway along the carriage now. If he wanted, the guard could lunge and stick her with that curled spear.

"I don't care if you're about to freeze to death," the guard snarled. "Hands. Out."

"Fine, jerk." Torny stepped along the voulge's edge as she drew out her hands, both holding small knives. With her left, Torny slapped the finger-length blade against the voulge, pushing it just wide enough for her to dash in. Her stab glanced off the guard's armor, the man turning to get his plate right where it needed to be.

On sturdy ground, Torny would've been dead. The guard could've corrected his swing, clocked Torny in the head. On slick snow, matted down into ice with carriage wheels and ox breath, the man's boots didn't hold when Torny's shoulder, following her bounced stab, struck the guard's chest. He stepped back with the hit, slid, and fell forward, dropping the voulge to catch himself on the snow.

Which put the guard's head at perfect kicking height.

"Sorry," Torny said, delivering the snap to the man's unprotected chin.

He crumpled, moaning, and Torny turned on her heel. Cut the rope tying the carriage to the stable's side post, and hopped on the driver's bench.

"Hope you're not too tired," Torny muttered, grabbing the reins and snapping them once. The ox pair huffed, stared at her. "You heard me, move!"

With a second snap, the pair made a grudging lurch forward, giving Torny another look at the battle among the fire. The Najahn net grew tighter, with Bliss actively swinging now, trying to keep away the points, as Wax and Eujo leaned on each other. The fire's whips were spastic, the earth's tremors quiet, and the snow only ruffled.

"Go!" Torny shouted, snapping the reins again. "Bliss!"

The call, the name, echoed over the frosted outpost. The words found their target, the Guardian found her Renewals.

Hope spurred a revival, and while the oxen shied away from the fire, they couldn't evade the ground, the rising ice and mud surrounding Wax, Eujo, and Bliss as they half ran, half stumbled through Najahn blown aside by sudden gusts. Bliss threw her brother and Eujo into the carriage's back half, among satchels and straw, before joining Torny as the bandit tried directing the oxen back to the exit.

"How do you do this?" Torny asked as Bliss took the reins, steered the creatures towards freedom.

Behind, more shouts, more curses, some stomping boots, but the Najahn didn't launch their chakrams, didn't call for hard pursuit.

'Easy,' Bliss signed with one hand as they passed by the palisade's last lanterns. 'You point them away from danger, and tell them to run.'

On the run from assassins and worse, Wax and his friends cross the ice to a strange and deadly land.

Continue Wax and Eujo's adventures in *The Dance of Gods* by scanning the code below or clicking here!

A̴FTER A DISASTER ON THE M̴OON, Mox's search for strength brings him to a dangerous scientist and a choice between the life Mox knows and the vengeance he desires.

Jump into a new science fiction adventure with *The Metal Man*, available free when you sign up for my author newsletter by clicking the link or scanning the code below:

Acknowledgments

There's this idea that writing is a solitary act, but that couldn't be further from the truth. Every writer depends on friends, family, and, yes, the readers to keep spinning their stories.

Specifically, I'd like to thank my wife, Nicole, who's endless love and encouragement make every day brighter. My brothers, Jonathan, Justin, and Matthew, and parents, Bob and Mary, who help keep a smile on my face.

And, of course, all of you readers that make this life possible.

Thank you.

About the Author

A.R. Knight writes sci-fi and fantasy in the frozen north of Wisconsin. With a pair of cats keeping him company, he enjoys delving into adventures that are as much about the villain as the hero.

After getting a degree in journalism and touring the country installing healthcare software, A.R. Knight thought it would be good to get back to what he loved. So now he's got a small office and early mornings to spin whatever tales come into his imagination.

When he's not writing, A.R. Knight tends to travel anywhere he can, whether that's islands off the coast of Ecuador, the rainforest, snowboarding in the Rocky Mountains, or sipping scotch in Edinburgh. That's the nice thing about the writing life, you can take it anywhere.

To contact or see what he's up to, visit www.blackkeybooks.com

arknight@blackkeybooks.com

For Blythe and Clint

* 9 7 9 8 8 8 8 5 8 0 6 6 0 *